OF FIRE AND BLOOD

E.S. PORTMAN

First Edition published by E.S. Portman 2024

Copyright © 2024 by E.S. Portman

All rights reserved. No part of this publication may be reproduced, stored or transmitted in any form or by any means, electronic, mechanical, photocopying, recording, scanning, or otherwise without written permission from the publisher. It is illegal to copy this book, post it to a website, or distribute it by any other means without permission.

This novel is entirely a work of fiction. The names, characters and incidents portrayed in it are the work of the author's imagination. Any resemblance to actual persons, living or dead, events or localities is entirely coincidental.

E.S. Portman asserts the moral right to be identified as the author of this work.

First Edition

Cover design by Estratosphera Designs

This book contains elements that may be unsettling to some readers such as graphic language, violence and torture/murder with descriptions of wounds, brief mentions of violence against children/young adults, mentions of previous domestic abuse, anxious thoughts/panic attacks, explicit sexual scenes, mentions of abandonment & neglect, descriptions of mental health conditions, descriptions of animal death in mostly humane scenarios (hunting), and mentions of parental figures with addictions/alcoholism.

For the ones who love true love.

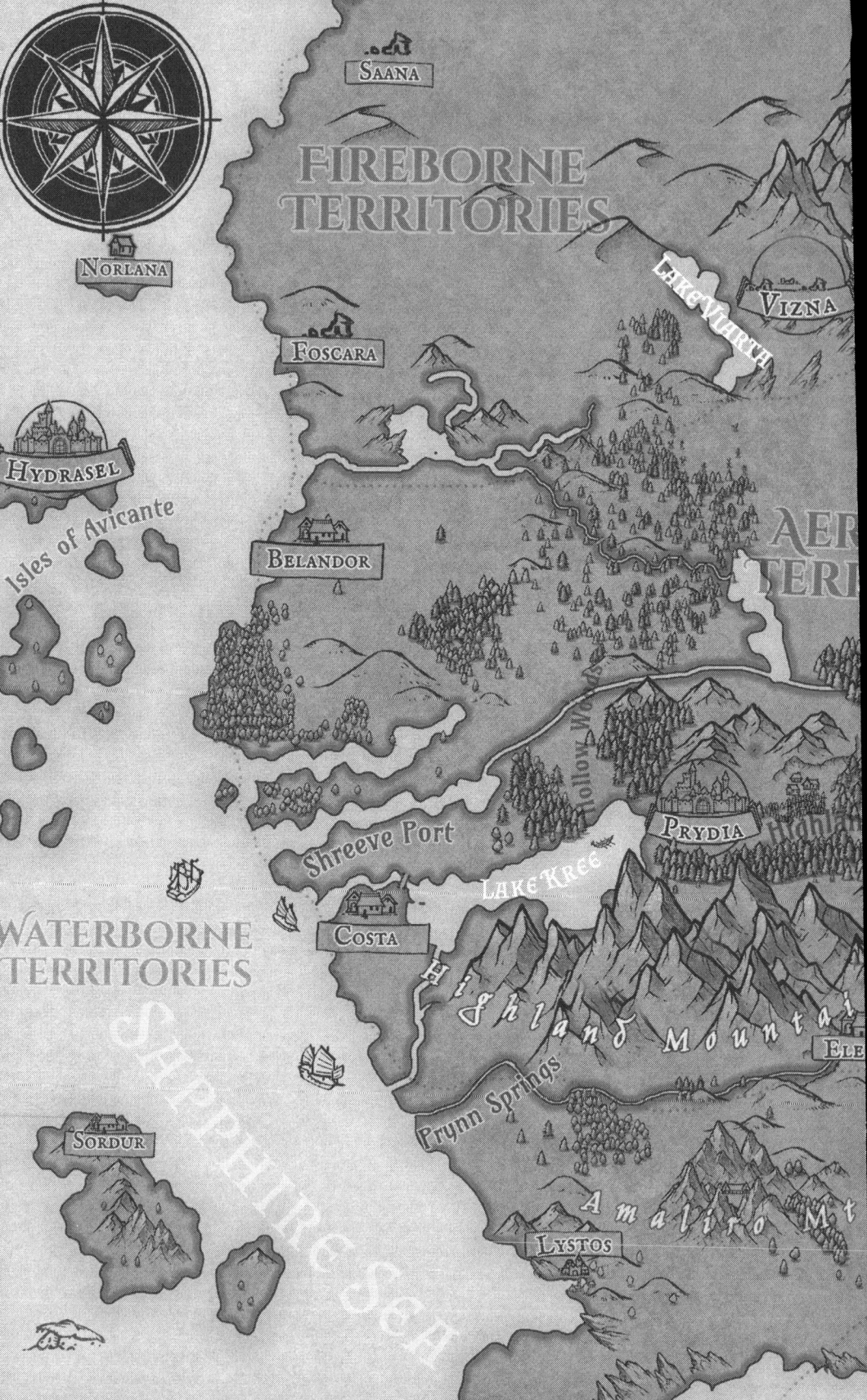

PROLOGUE

"Rennick?" Her soft voice faded in through his sleep. He stirred, moving his bare arm up the smoothness of her partially exposed stomach, and drew idle circles around her navel. His eyes hadn't quite peeled open, yet he knew if he could see her face, he'd be met with plush lips, blushed cheeks, and a faint smile. One he knew was reserved for him. One he could paint in his mind with his eyes closed.

"My love?" He buried wanting lips into the crook of her neck, breathing in her light ashen and vanilla scent and kissing up to the edge of her delicate jaw, her cheek, her ear.

"He will wake..." she whispered low. Breathy. The way she always did before she came undone in his hands.

"He is with Karla, an entire wall divides us." His hand stroked lower, moving to the edge of her sleep shorts. She let out a moan that turned into a sigh as her hand trailed down to meet his before raising his arm to lie across her ribs.

She patted his hand, a warning to not move further although that is all he could think of when he held his wife in his hands. She was the most exquisite woman he ever laid eyes on, and they were finally alone after what felt like decades of running—the only surety of time progression from—

A gurgled cry broke through the boards of wood beside their head, and Savaria let loose a laugh. "Told you."

His cries lasted mere seconds before Karla's song lifted through the air and Aeden began to sooth again. He was getting so big so fast, crawling and babbling and looking back at them with the same eyes as his mother.

"*I* will go to him. My wife should stay here, catch up on all the sleep she missed from last night." She swatted at his hand as he made a move to leave and he chuckled at the gesture. The hand-fasting ceremony had led to a night he would never forget—the way she shone against the fading sunlight in her lacy white dress, barely covering the marks through the sheer fabric. The marks that made them the prey in a world full of eager hunters.

But they had been safe in this carved out hollow of woods. And he knew the intentions of the dwarves they rest their very lives on were true. It was his gift, after all. The one that had finally bore the greatest service to his Lady, his love, his wife, and the little life they had created.

"You are supposed to be in your cottage." A spindly small finger jutted out to Rennick as he approached the babe hanging in Karla's arms.

Another smile filled his features, the soft part of his chest he created for his son and Savaria alone sending heat through his body like a simmering, ever-burning flame.

Rennick knelt down, his knuckles caressing over the chubby, baby-soft cheeks of his son. His finger flicked up to move the dark-brown lock of hair pressed to the side of his son's face by sweat.

"I will ask Savaria to cool the room down." Karla only nodded in response, her focus never abandoning the task she set herself to. "You look well-rested, Karla. I don't know how you manage with this one." His grin betrayed him and she rolled her orange eyes, where she did indeed have dark circles beneath the creases of them. But anytime he demanded she rest, she demanded with equal ferocity that he not tell her what to do.

He was used to being ordered about by women—his sister had ground that facet into him at an early age before she left their home in Vizna, and his wife... his wife was the one to bring him to his knees in more ways than a guard should.

Karla snapped her fingers in front of his face, making his brows draw down. "Did you hear me, Ren?"

"Hmm? No, Karla, I apologize. I was...trapped in my thoughts."

She only nodded, then moved to place the now sleeping babe back in his crib. The one Rennick had made from twining branches that cradled his son's body, furs lining the inside to comfort him. The dwarves at the nearby village offered one of their own cribs, but at only just past sixteen months of age, his son was already showing signs that he was not dwarven. His body was fae—tall and built and advanced. The boy was nearly the same size as Karla, yet she cradled him as if he were more fragile and smaller than he truly was. It still amazed Savaria each time Karla hauled him around as if he were her own. And he was so strong. He could throw a toy violently too hard and far across the room in his childlike anger—anger Aeden seemed to have inherited from his father, if Ren were to be completely honest with himself.

Rennick had fought alongside Karla for years. There was no one better than her as his second, and she had proven her worth time and time again. Had saved his life far more times than he could count on both of his hands. And there was no one he trusted more than her to protect his son in the night. So when she forced both of them out last night to their own thatched cottage beside hers, he didn't bother to fight with her on it.

Her song continued as Rennick moved to sit on one of the small stools in the corner, his tall, brawny body close to snapping the flimsy thing. "You are too kind to us, Karla."

"Nonsense, Ren. I swore an oath to both of you years ago. It is my duty—"

"You do not operate under the same oath, now that most of the wards have fallen and the kingdom is gone." His words were firm although the beating within his chest threatened to crack through his ribs.

"No matter the state of the kingdom, my oath was always to Savaria first, and now that you are hers, it extends to you." She smiled distantly, her hand brushing through the ends of her short white hair. She had pledged her oath to him as her second, yet that meant nothing in the eyes of any kingdom if the kingdom was no longer standing. But their allegiance to each other, the way they had formed a family of their own, would never falter. He knew it, as did she.

Ren's eyes slid between her and his resting child. "You were always my favorite, you know."

She nodded again, then moved to sit beside him. The wooden seat did not groan under her weight, not like it had every time he shifted within his own. "You are far too large for this cottage, Ren. Do you not want to go back to your wife?"

He did. But he also enjoyed the security of the sight before him—his best friend and his child. Safe. They were both safe.

"I'm sure she is asleep after the night we had." Karla burst into laughter, slapping her knee as her shoulders shook with it. A sound so rare these days, so clouded with the noises of the woods that shifted with the wind and led to eerie silence, that he had forgotten to let loose enough for the roaring laughter to take over him as well. His ears were tuned in, not only to listen as Aurors did for the intentions of others even from a mile away, but for the sounds of metal, of crunching leaves and hushed voices. If any one of them had a gift to negate his, he had to be ready to hear their bodies—their movements.

It could be any day now. Any day they'd be discovered within their small cottages and sliced down the way the Lord of the Aerborne line would prefer it.

How the Stars ever found that man suitable for a kingdom, he'd never be sure. Nothing made him question the Stars more than seeing Gedeon on the throne. Than seeing that man cut down their home before their very eyes.

"What has you so troubled this time, Rennick? You see your child is safe here with me. You know your wife is well in your bed. Do you sense something?" Did he sense something? He wasn't sure. He knew the winds stilled too much that morning as he made his way to the cottage beside his. For that brief moment, he paused, his hand on Karla's door, glancing around the dense wood.

"I'm not sure." He was honest with Karla. Always had been, always would be. And it was that honesty and trust that kept his relationship with Savaria in the early years so easy to conceal. Karla would never betray his trust—she'd always been forthright with him, and kept her lips sealed. It wasn't forbidden for a guard to bed his Lady, or a female guard to bed her Lord, or whichever combination would ever come into question. But Savaria and Rennick agreed it was best for their love to remain a secret from Aellethia because war was coming. And sure enough, that war had come and gone and ended in their downfall.

The discovery of her pregnancy months before the battle horns sounded at their doorstep solidified their act of secrecy. No one had known about the Dragon Heir in her womb, and no one would come for him or his dragon like they had for Savaria and hers.

Aeden would be safe. No matter how hard the rest of them were hunted, his son—their son—would be safe.

Warm fingertips grazed the back of Rennick's neck, followed by soft lips upon his temple. If not for the state of the already overwhelmed stool he sat on, Ren would have pulled her into his lap.

Karla stood and made to bow and Savaria sighed as she took in her movements. "Karla, please. I am hardly your queen anymore. You are my friend. Please act as such."

"As you wish, my queen." Ren could feel Savaria's eyes roll at the term. No matter how hard Savaria tried to change Karla's ways, she'd always see her as her queen.

Their queen.

He reached for Savaria's hand, kissing the back of it. "You will always be our queen, my love. You cannot beat it out of us."

"I can try, my king." The words made a shiver run down his spine. If their kingdom were still—well, if the battle had ended in their favor, he would be king. She would have made it so the very next day, he had no question in his mind of where her loyalties lie.

He would be king, but he only ever desired her heart—not her throne. And now he had that, along with their young heir that stirred gently in the corner of the darkened room.

Savaria made her way to the edge of Aeden's crib, peering down at the little fae prince. Small, chubby arms waved in the air, reaching and calling for his mother.

"Come here, my love." She gathered him from his crib, and Rennick watched as his two loves, his entire world, came together in an embrace. He wanted nothing more than to walk to them, to press his body to theirs and surround them. To keep them safe, as any guard should. As any king should. As any father and husband should.

But the wind beyond the door had ceased entirely, and even Karla had remained standing, making her way to the small lowered window beside the door, peering through it as discreetly as she could. Ren knew the stiffening of her back and the slight twitch of her fingers along her waist where her weapons usually lie could only mean one thing.

Savaria cooed, paying no attention to the two warriors in the cottage across from her. Karla's eyes darted to Ren, then to the baby, then to the window.

And that's when Ren felt it. The intentions of bloodlust, of insatiable hunger. The nagas would be sent first, scoping out areas for their Lord. But Ren knew what would happen once the nagas found them. It wouldn't be long before Gedeon's guards would send word of their location and then—

"My Lady, I fear we are no longer safe here."

Savaria's gaze landed on her husband's taut body, his own eyes moving between hers and the stack of weapons in the corner of the room.

"Nagas," was all Rennick said as he moved to sheath and stash weapons anywhere he could on his body. Taking up a sheath and a sword he wished were a bonded one, he moved to Savaria, securing it over her hips. His fingers slipped along the clasp, his eyes now transfixed on his son in his lover's arms. "We must go. They are close."

"If they make their way here—" Savaria's words were stifled by a brief shudder. "If they make their way—"

Ren's gentle touch landed on his wife's shoulder, his eyes fixed to her golden-brown ones. "We won't let them take him. Remember. As we agreed."

She nodded. And then, they moved. Quickly.

Through the door, down the thick line of brush and trees away from the reek of the naga's desire for blood and misguided vengeance for their Lord—a Lord who granted power to beasts who knew no bounds when it came to flesh.

Karla led the way, cutting down wayward thickets as Savaria clutched onto Aeden with a ferocious desire to protect her son with Rennick at their backs. He'd wanted to burn the brush down, but fire meant smoke, and smoke would bring more nagas than they could fight off all at once.

Yet, the snarling sounds began just as a fog rolled in at the edge of an opening—the very last few warded feet of ground at their heels.

Karla froze as she took in the fog, the growing haze above the ground before them that hovered with lethal intent to seek them out and cut them down, now too close.

"Sav," he whispered from behind her, reaching out to wrap his arm around her. "We have to send him now. He's here. Drawing too close."

Savaria's eyes welled with tears, several rolling down her face as she refused to pull her eyes from her son. Their son. Droplets of water landed on Aeden's forehead as he repeatedly called to her, his own gaze shifting between his parents as if he understood what was to happen. It was possibly the only blessing from the Stars—the fact that he would not remember them. Would never have to relive this day in his memory.

"We have to send you somewhere now, my sweet boy." Savaria's head dipped low, her nose nudging against the tip of Aeden's. "We will always love you."

Ren's hand slid over the crown of Aeden's head, sifting his fingers through the thick brown strands. Aeden began to cry, his face turning a bright red. Karla rushed to his side, sheathing her weapons as she moved. She stretched her arms wide, a slight tremor running through them as she waited to take the babe in her arms, not a single sign of fear in her eyes when they flashed up at her queen.

"You know where to take him, Karla. We can't risk him being captured." Karla's head dipped low in a bow, her arms still outstretched, still empty of the child. "Promise us you will go directly to the portal."

"Yes, my queen." The order was from the crown, and from her friends. Her loyal companions. But Karla addressed them as if it were a direct order, because it had been. Her duty was now solely to the Dragon Heir.

Aeden's cries grew louder, breaking through the snapping and snarling of the fast-approaching nagas and the poisonous fog beyond the tree line. Savaria tried to soothe him, to make the crying cease. But it was no use.

"Run fast, Karla. Don't look back for us. We will hold them back long enough for you to run."

"But, my king—"

Ren held up his hand, stopping her. "This is your most important task. We knew this day was coming, but the visions were never clear on when, and yet, we hoped it would be different." They hoped the Stars would have shifted their desires, had changed the way their family was to separate. But knowing Aeden would have someone in another world, that was enough for them both to live as peacefully as they could in hiding all those months.

Waiting. Wishing. Hoping. And letting their son grow as much as he could with his dragon—wanting nothing more than to see the day beyond the one that the Stars had warned would come. And that final day was now. It ended now. The hoping, the wishing, the waiting. All gone like the ground beneath the encroaching fog.

Savaria took one last glance at her son and then passed the boy to Karla's waiting arms. Rennick held his wife tighter to him and his heart shattered as he bore all of her weight, her legs quickly weakening.

"You must hurry, Karla. The future of everything rests in your very hands. We will never forget what you have done for us." Savaria seemed to fight against every desire in her body as she spoke.

Ren forced a slight smile for his friend, one with too much grief and desperation. "Go. Now."

"My Lady—"

"Go." Ren's voice was hoarse, his own body fighting to not break apart piece by piece as his wife's was in his arms.

The fog and the sounds of the nagas were too close now, and without hesitating again, Karla took off on her fast heels, leaving nothing but a rush of wind behind her.

"We have to fight, my love. We can't let him win," Ren whispered against the crown of her head.

Savaria's eyes locked onto Ren's from where she shuddered into the crook of his arm. Her nod came slowly, but her tears never stopped falling as they both readied their weapons and walked to the edge of the trees.

"I love you. Not even the Stars will part us when we fall," Ren said softly. Not *if*. But when. And that when, they both knew, was coming down to the minutes.

Savaria didn't reach for her tears. She wore them proudly, knowing the love for her son was more than the hatred of a mad king. "Not even the Stars will part us when we fall. Together."

They twined their fingers together, weapons in their other hands as they moved to the very border of the fog, waiting for the figure in purple to emerge. And when he did, when his white-blonde hair peeked through the top of the haze, he stilled.

"Well, well," he drawled, his words sharp and vile. Everything evil that had ever existed lived within those lips, they were certain of it. "It is quite a surprise to see you both so...*alive.*" His grey, steely eyes flared as he took in Ren and Savaria's linked hands, Ren's fingers tightening around the fine earthen ring he'd crafted for his wife the night before.

Gedeon cocked his head. "I did not think it was possible for vermin to love. Tell me, was the wedding a fine celebration? I do not think I received an invitation."

"You are a monster," Sav hissed out through her teeth.

Ren could feel the intent of the man before them, the monster before them. And he wanted nothing more than to rip his head off for it.

A flash of fire spread around them, Savaria's power intensifying to a high wall that reached for the sky.

Gedeon didn't bat a single eyelash. "Without your dragon, you are useless. Those pesky illusions of yours? No longer. Do you want to know how long—"

"Fuck you," Rennick spat as Gedeon waved a finger toward him.

"You are nothing but a guard. A shield for your fallen whore at your side. Worthless. The amount of power in you alone is nothing compared to me." Gedeon's hand flicked beside him, and Rennick was brought to his knees under a heavy force of air. "There. That is much better. Bow before your Mora."

"Ren!" Savaria shouted, the flame wall falling rapidly to the ground. Her attention turned to Gedeon, her words turning vicious as she snarled at him. "We will never bow to you. You may have ruined my lands, but you can not ruin us. And when the Stars send us back, we will kill you first." Savaria spoke as if she were certain the Stars would send them back, but no one, not even the young seer, could tell them that.

"I will wait for that day with a smile on my face, knowing I have destroyed Vizna and their Mora. Whatever is left of your filthy wielders—they will never want for you to return. You failed them all." Gedeon shrugged as Rennick fought to lift from the ground, to straighten his legs. He sent a blast of fire to Gedeon, noticing the way he seemed to favor one side and stiffened on the other.

"You believe you are invincible, but even I can see that you are wounded. What makes you believe we won't win, right here. Right now."

Gedeon's smile fell flat at Ren's acknowledgement. He pushed his shoulders back and cleared his throat. "You can try to fight me, but this?" The fog danced a foot from where Savaria still stood, her weapon on the ground and her hands ready to fight. To wield. She would need an opportunity—a distraction. "This can bring you both down. I'm sure of it."

"Use it on me, then. Go on." Rennick twisted against the air that pressed down on him, waiting for the fog to roll toward him and away from Sav. From his wife. The love that not even the Stars could take from him.

The fog stilled. "You are a delightfully cocky thing, aren't you? Perhaps I should have bought you at Sentra."

"Not even your highest bid could have bought me. I was always meant to be hers." And hers, he had been. Loyally, devotedly, lovingly—hers.

The fog remained as Gedeon's brows furrowed as if he were confused that someone could not simply be bought. Loyalty was earned. And Savaria had earned it far before he was sent to Sentra. He'd always belonged to her—ever since they were children, playing in the back alleys of Vizna and causing too much mischief for a future Mora to cause.

That seemed like a lifetime ago now.

"*I am curious why you believe you are so valuable?*" *Good.* His interest was a good start. The fog inched closer to Rennick just as the sounds of the naga drew closer once more. They hissed at their backs, but neither dared to turn to see the numbers. From the sounds alone, it was dozens.

Gedeon scanned the fog around him, smirking toward the nagas at their backs—waiting. Savaria's eyes were white with fear when she met with Ren's gaze. Her eyes darted back and forth, warning her husband to stop.

He gave her a weak smile, one that would never meet his eyes because of the aching hole that their future was. "I love you," he mouthed, then whipped his head back to Gedeon just before he did the same.

Ren smirked. "I'm more valuable than your piece of shit guard." Ren spat at the Mora of Prydia's feet, making Gedeon's eyes widen in delight. Gedeon hadn't always been a madman, but the past few years before the war had certainly worn on him, turning him into the man that now stood with his lethal fog hovering at his fingertips. Hovering closer to Rennick than Savaria.

That's it, Rennick thought. *Closer, you fucking coward.*

Gedeon snickered, watching with a craze in his eyes as the fog lightly touched Ren's knees that stayed on the ground, making him cry out in agony.

"Ren! Please! Stop this!" Savaria cried. "Please—I'm begging you!"

"Begging? Not even you would stoop low enough to beg *me.*"

The fog pulled away from Ren's knees as Gedeon hummed in amusement. "Look at the mess you have become." Ren's knees were raw, blistering and swollen and bloodied.

Ren turned his cries into laughter. "Fuck. You."

All at once, the fog dissipated. In its place, the clear land sprawled before them, laden with dew drops that glistened against the morning sun like a promise. The Stars were cruel, but perhaps this was their message—Aeden was safe.

He was safe.

Just as quickly as the land had cleared, just as quickly as that one small glance at the sign from the Stars had taken Ren's focus from him, a whip of air followed by a loud crack sounded near him. The fall of Savaria's body was the next sound to ring in his ears, and it sent his body to the ground. He shouted for her as he crawled, elbows biting into the grass as he was no longer bound by the air magic that had pulled his bloodied knees down before, praying and hoping to the Stars that their fate be different. But as he reached out for his wife, his love, and took her limp hand in his, he cried out again. Her unblinking eyes did not respond, and her lips no longer opened to whisper to him.

I love you.

"Savaria!" he wailed, crying out with his head tilting between the skies and her lifeless body, her neck unstable and broken as he lifted her into his lap.

Rage deepened in the now hollow cavity where Ren's heart once existed. His whitened fingers paled further as they gripped onto Savaria's dark hair. His son was gone. His wife—his very existence.

Gone.

He placed a kiss over her still-warm lips, feeling the water rolling down his cheeks and onto hers. His calloused thumb caressed and smoothed the tear along her jaw, feeling her soft skin and savoring it one last time.

Not even the Stars will part us when we fall, my queen.

Ren's head turned as he placed his wife down gently to the ground, then stood to face the man who he'd end. Maybe not by his hands, but if his son were to ever return—if Celine's promise was to be fulfilled—the two of them would end him. Celine's unborn child and his own son would bring about the ruin of the man who had taken everything from the people he loved the most.

"I'll fucking destroy you."

He charged with that thought burning within himself, letting it roar as loudly as it could as his body collided into Gedeon's, every last piece of his soul charging with him.

Chapter One
Aeden

I was death hidden behind the guise of serenity as I reached for one of the arrows resting in the leather quiver slung across my back. The string bit into my cheek as I nocked the arrow into place, the small scar going down just beneath my jaw a firm reminder of how hard *not* to pull the string from nearly two months ago. But the deer that grazed in front of me wouldn't get away like the first ones had.

No. This one was coming back to camp with me.

My shoulder ached as I held the arrow in place, waiting for the perfect moment. An autumn breeze rolled through and the deer lifted its head to look in the opposite direction, ears twitching to listen to each gust as if it held a predator. But the deer was sorely missing the predator hiding behind the trees, tucked away within the tall blades of grasses and flowers.

The deer collapsed on impact moments after I released the arrow from my calloused fingers. Feathers flickered in the breeze as the arrow wedged deep into its heart and lungs, piercing the sweet spot between the ribs. Humane enough. I slung the bow over my shoulder, which honestly, fucking hurt as the thick wood slapped against my shoulder. I'd been training every single day—Seamus doing what he could with my wielding and Murrie training me to fight with as many weapons as she could. I didn't skip any days in my training and my body had become keenly aware.

The lack of sleep didn't help, either.

Inky blood pooled from the mouth of the deer, seeping into the ground, but all I could think about was how excited Murrie would be about the pelt's mostly intact condition. They'd all need it soon. I pushed my tunic sleeves up and yanked my arrow free before I placed it back in my quiver, stood, and flicked my wrist. My neck rolled through the tension as my air and earth magic worked together, uprooting the grass and the deer together, keeping both elevated. Blood droplets leading anything or anyone back to our camp was not what I'd set out to do. With another flick, my air magic propelled the deer and bed of grass forward as I walked back towards that camp. To where she'd be.

Wingbeats sounded above me and my lip curved up as the remnants of white and red fluff that dangled from Varasyn's mouth caught my eye.

"I see you're getting better at using your bow." Varasyn's voice was muffled as she clamped down on her dinner, but her mocking tone came through clear as day. My smile widened.

"I'm surprised this field can keep up with feeding you, Vara. Tell me, is it normal to eat ten sheep in a single day?" It was hard to imagine she was still growing, but seeing as she was the only dragon I'd seen so far, I didn't know just how *big* they grew to be.

She turned and dove down, landing beside me with a thud that wobbled the ground under my boots. She tucked her wings in, slinging her neck with it. *"You're lucky you are bound to me, or it would be ten sheep* and *one fae for today."*

"Seriously, could you not shake your bloody shit all over the place?" I narrowed my eyes, taking in the few hints of red dotting the grass. *"And if you ate me, you wouldn't have any other fae to berate."* I slowed my pace as we crested a hill, spotting a wisp of smoke in the distance.

Varasyn growled through the dead sheep in her mouth. *"I can think of a few other fae to assault at your behest, starting with the girl."*

"Enough of that, Vara. You'll have to get over it."

"Something you're managing quite fine with, aren't you?" I rolled my eyes to her, giving her a look that threatened to burn every last sheep in the Fields. A look that silenced her rather quickly.

Shay waved in the distance from where she sat beside Murrie, who was leaning over the spit of the fire. Murrie's faith in me still hadn't wavered, and I could see that even from where I was—she was always so happy when I returned. Even though Seamus insisted he should be the one hunting while I rested, I'd simply...needed the release. Resting wasn't something that came easily to me anymore, and I needed to get away.

I set the quiver and bow down and sent the deer closer to Seamus so he could skin my kill.

"Great job, Aeden!" Murrie clapped, her face beaming from not just the flames. And then another, more dull clap, came from beside where I'd stopped. Where I always gravitated to.

"Bravo, Fire Boy." Paige clapped her hands together slowly behind her cell made of slim tree trunks, erupting from the ground and arching together well above her head. Pink and white peonies bloomed across the top, dangling upside-down above her, which I thought was a nice touch—adding her favorite flower. But she didn't seem to give a damn about it.

I turned my back to her, ignoring the twinge of pain and guilt in my chest as I did so. We weren't exactly on the best of terms since I put her in a confined living space for her own protection, not that she liked me *before* I did that.

After about a week of her trying to escape, Shay suggested we try something more...inhumane. I was just waiting for the night when her attacks on the cell walls finally gave and I'd have to chase her down. It wasn't like she would be interrupting the sleep that I wasn't getting, but I laid close-by, for more reasons than one.

Just in case.

"Huge beast of a deer, the skin will give ye some gloves and boots for winter. It's fast—"

"Fast approaching, yeah yeah, we know." Murrie waved her hand at him and Seamus grumbled in response before sharpening his blade to skin the deer.

"Do I get any of these clothing items, or are you going to let me freeze to death in here?"

I turned my head over my shoulder, my eyes skimming the flowers before falling to Paige. "I'd never let you freeze to death." I lifted my palm with a ball of fire hovering delicately above it, then closed my fingers one by one, extinguishing the small flame. I'd learned to keep myself warm, but even without that ability, I'd sooner go without clothes if it meant giving each piece to Paige to keep her warm.

"Right, because you *love me*." Paige rolled her eyes, stopping for a brief moment on those pink and white petals before narrowing them back at me. "How stupid of me," she mumbled under her breath.

I could understand her anger. Understood the reasons why that beautiful woman with a fiery soul spit on me when I tried to wish her a happy birthday months ago. It was absolute shit timing on my part, seeing as that was the same day I'd taken her from the arena—not exactly the happiest day in her memories, whatever that was now. But for me, it was definitely one of them.

I turned on my heels and took a few steps closer to her, meeting those piercing green eyes through the trees. "Yeah, actually." I smirked at her, hoping it hid the level of pain I felt every time I thought about the unrequited situation I was in. "I do love you. But I'm also not the complete asshole you think I am." She scoffed, but somewhere within her she had to believe she was safe with us, or at least much better off than she would've been with that sad excuse of a father she had. Yes, my dragon threatened her almost daily by snapping her teeth or snarling at her, and no, I would never tell her just how many times Vara said into my thoughts that she wanted to devour her whole. Yet I knew, without a shadow of a doubt, that if it came down to it, Varasyn would kill *for* her.

"From where I'm standing, you sure do look like one," Paige said, wrapping her hands around the trees, looking all the more like the prisoner I knew she felt like she was. I stared back at her, hesitating on advancing, on making her feel less than the capable and strong woman she was.

Because I fucking loved her.

Paige wanted to escape, I wasn't oblivious to that. But escaping would get her killed at some point. Most of Prydia's territories had turned on her. Paige was seen as a cheat, and several other vile things that only made heat rise to the surface of my skin just thinking about them. Prydia and the rest of Aellethia from what I knew had been out for blood long before she entered that arena, and when they saw my dragon, *my flames,* as I tried to hit Gedeon, it fueled their hatred for fire-wielders even further while giving away exactly who I was.

Gedeon was smart, I had to give him that. He knew she'd only leave that arena in one of two ways—either die in the trial, unable to reach her air magic anymore, and being that she was stubborn as hell she'd stick to the rules, or she'd be rescued by the fire-wielder she came to Aellethia with who he hadn't managed to capture. The one who had slipped into his castle, attended a ball, and gone to a room with his daughter, all unnoticed. But what really got me, the jagged piece of his messed up puzzle that showed me how meticulously calculated and hateful he could be, was wiping her memories of me and her mother as if she'd never lived in the mortal world with either of us.

Although Paige looked nothing like her father, it was obvious who she'd inherited her wits and calculated thoughts and actions from. There was a perk to knowing her so well, knowing the way her mind worked and the way she put things together. It gave me insight into her father's logic, and one day, I'd use that knowledge to end his life.

"If that's what you think of me," I whispered, glancing one more time at her before dropping my head. That twisted, knowing smile Gedeon gave me in the arena—the one that told me I had just played into his game—replayed in my mind before I stepped away from Paige's enclosure and moved to sit next to the others by the fire.

"Drink?" Shay offered a cup and I took it without a second thought, knocking it back and draining the fae wine in big gulps, ignoring the bitter taste that seeped into my bitter feelings. Thank the ever-loving Stars for Murrie, who was not only well versed in healing tonics, but had started honing her craft in making fae wine the moment Paige joined our group. I guess she realized I'd need it eventually.

"That bad, huh?" Shay asked, flicking her eyes over to Paige.

"Yep." I held my cup out for more. "Any news on Prydia?"

"Not much," she replied, filling my cup to the rim and watching me with concern as I knocked it back just as I had done with the first. "Prydian guards are still ransacking villages and small towns, really any congregation of fae outside of the castle in Prydia, and further out in Aerborne territories, searching for the"—she cleared her throat and fumbled for the words I knew were coming—"t*he fire-wielder and the cheat*. But they haven't moved very far into the south yet." *Yet.* But they sure would be soon, especially if they spotted or got wind of Varasyn.

Everyone rotated being on watch for scouts—Prydian and Aerborne guards who were sent out to look for us. Call them whatever you wanted, they belonged to Gedeon and went where he said, just as the rest of the kingdoms had their own guards to command as well. Seamus had said that sending out scouts or the occasional guard or two was a tactic he'd resort to first before extending his wards or taking too many guards from their posts. Gedeon was still, as of now, the Mora of Prydia and ruled unopposed with no remaining children to steal his throne from him. Children that had failed the Triad, unsurprisingly. But I didn't have to grow up here to know that there were more ways to take over a kingdom.

"That's why you either need to fly low to the ground and stay close-by, or well above the clouds and hidden out here," I reminded Vara while she ignored me, digging into her sheep like she hadn't been devouring them all day. Seamus darted his eyes between the sheep and Varasyn, his eyes widening for a moment before settling on the deer carcass again. He was afraid of her, as any normal person would be, but he'd come around a bit and didn't shake every time she came close to the campsite anymore. And that was progress.

"Ye can't drink away yer problems, Lad." Seamus handed a slab of raw meat to Murrie, who put it directly on the spit. They'd been a lot more tolerable since we got back from the arena, easing some of the tension between all of us, but Paige picked up the slack in that department.

I lifted my cup up to Shay, her brow furrowing as she seemed to have those second thoughts I didn't. Paige let out another scoff and I rubbed at my slacked jaw, then reached around to the back of my neck, trying to control the urge I had to remind her of who she really was as I felt the weight of my cup filling again.

She thought I took her chance away at ruling her kingdom, even though Murrie told her she wouldn't have been able to win anyway with the poison *her father* had given to her. Murrie could smell poison on Paige's lips like a hound when I'd asked her to inspect and heal her after we had landed that day. She promised she'd find a cure for what he had done. But she had yet to come up with one. Paige was reluctant to try anything Murrie made, even though I'd taken each tonic and ailment before her to prove it wasn't poison. I trusted Murrie, but Paige most definitely did not. It was becoming all the more apparent the only way we were going to cure Paige was to leave the Fields of Araros, finding other ingredients to test out.

But leaving meant risking all our lives. Gedeon could only portal into areas that were warded by him or not warded at all, and the mountains around where we stayed were, in fact, warded. Secured by Leander Earthborne, the notoriously batshit Mora of Buryon, whom we hadn't had the pleasure of meeting. Not a single person in our group had seen him before, or met someone who had. If Gedeon wanted to find us out here, we'd know about it well before his guards had the chance to come close to us. Our spot on a rather tall hill gave us the better vantage point for miles and miles beyond where we camped. But if Leander managed to come out of hiding and portal to us...well then, I guess we'd be fucked.

Paige flipped through the pages of a book I had Shay give to her, acting like she wasn't listening intently, waiting for more information. I knew she was analyzing everything, taking in everything faster than anyone else I'd ever seen. She was, after all, my best friend before I fell in love with her, before we were separated and put into this world.

She may have forgotten why she read so much—a coping mechanism she picked up in her childhood due to the consequences of her upbringing, but she still did it. She was all around the same Paige, just a little less anxious, a lot more confident, and armed with way more attitude than I was ever on the receiving end of until now. But I still loved her. No amount of poison, or really anything, would ever change that.

I took a deep breath and set my filled cup down. "You last said that Prydian guards were searching Shreeve Port and any Prydian roads of transport. You said last week that an *Easrich captain* told you he was *unable* to travel there. He was worried many towns could starve in the winter if they didn't clear the port and allow passage." I eyed Paige, raising my voice so she could hear me more clearly. She was going to listen regardless, so I decided to make it really obvious that I wanted her to know what was going on. And if she knew something, maybe she'd help. "Why would they search the port if everyone in the arena very clearly saw a dragon? Shouldn't they be looking somewhere more...open?"

Shay shrugged. "No one seems to know where dragons went after the Battle of Vizna. That's one of the only things keeping us so safe right now. That, and the wards." She glanced up at Varasyn, who ripped a leg from the mangled flesh of the sheep, and shuddered.

"Searching the port means searching ships. Cargo. What dragon would fit in a ship, or risk being exposed by so many people? Especially at Shreeve Port, the biggest port in all of Aellethia?" Paige wasn't the only one reading up on Aellethia. Gedeon was either reaching for straws, sorely undermining us, or...or maybe he wasn't too invested in us at all.

Shay looked at Seamus, and then Murrie. Both had nothing to add.

"It just seems futile to waste resources when you're hunting not one, but *two* fae who are at large. And he *definitely* wouldn't want to miss the opportunity to catch Vara."

"He's right," Paige added, flipping through another few pages.

I darted my gaze to her. "Maybe you have something more to share?" My brows shot up, but she spared no glances my way as she thumbed through a few more pages, searching for the spot she so obviously had no intention of reading from.

"Nope." More pages fell.

"Of course not." I turned back to the rest of the group, angled just enough to keep Paige in my periphery. "He isn't searching all those ships for us."

The pages stopped moving, and Paige's feet shuffled in the dirt where she sat with her knees bent up, trying to hide her face behind the book that rested there. And failing.

"What else do ye think he's lookin' for, Lad?" Seamus helped Murrie make room for more meat on the spit. I hadn't eaten yet today, and the smell of cooked game mixed with the thought of whatever the hell Gedeon was searching for was making my stomach churn violently.

My arm wrapped around my stomach. "Not sure. But it can't be good. He's a ruthless bastard." I lifted my cup again, taking smaller sips this time. Fae alcohol was possibly just as ruthless as Gedeon, and I frequently underestimated it. Not tonight.

"*Wise choice,*" Varasyn chided.

I lifted my cup up to her. "If you had just let me complete the Triad, *maybe* you wouldn't be dealing with *him* anymore," Paige suggested from behind her book, where her fingers turned white against the cover they were pressed to.

I cocked my head over my shoulder. "If we let you *try* to complete the Triad, you'd be dead," I quipped.

"Mmm, he's right, Paige. What I told you wasn't a lie. Your father used a poison that is commonly used on fae before they are executed or put on trial to make sure they can't escape, only it somehow only took your original nature from you and didn't leave it grey." Murrie glanced over her covered arms before she gave Paige a smile that said she was done explaining to her just how impossible it had been for her to have won her Triad, yet remained sweet enough to not bark it back to her. Murrie was a lot more patient than Seamus, who was hacking the limb off of the deer and glaring back at Paige with each remark she made.

Her legs stretched out just enough to move the book away from her face. She glared back at all of us. "I would've found a way. The rules didn't state I couldn't fight my way to the door. I'd already used my air magic once, so technically, I was in the clear." Ever logical, Paige. She would no doubt be the best asset to our group *if* she ever wanted to be a part of it.

Seamus' blade stopped mid air before he slammed it down through another limb. "Fight yer way through men of stone? With what, yer daggers? Are ye nuts, girl?" He looked over to the log outside of her cage where each of her twelve daggers lay embedded in the wood, just out of reach from her. Better safe than sorry.

My gaze followed Seamus' before falling back to her.

"No, I'm determined. There's a difference." Paige was defiant. Always had been. But damn if it wasn't hotter the more tipsy I got.

I angled my glass toward her. "There's also a difference between living and dying. Pretty sure I saved you from the second." I said as I took another sip of my drink. If I finished the cup and didn't eat soon, I'd be at the edge of her cage, trying to get her to remember me in more ways than one.

Nope. Shouldn't go there.

I ripped my gaze from her and leaned over the fire, pouring the cup's contents just above the tip of the flames, making them flare up as the alcohol burned.

Chapter Two
PAIGE

Walking through a hallway with walls made of glass, I started to shiver as I heard voices come from a room. The moonlight flooded in through the space where the door ended and the flooring began, light trickling into a path. I reached up on tip-toes to rest my ear against the door just as it flew open, making me stumble forward.

"I *told* you, we should have taken her before he could—"

"Before he could, what? Kill her?" A familiar, yet slightly distorted voice replied from the space where a blue, winged-back chair faced another glass wall, looking out over staggering, snowy mountains.

The other man with icy-blonde hair crossed his arms, the same one that rushed in from behind me and opened the door. The blue, velvet jacket he was wearing brushed the edge of my cheek as I settled to stand beside him. My hand cupped the spot, where a strange sensation came almost as fast as it left, like specks of snow or cool rain falling over where he had touched.

His grey eyes raked over the back of the chair where the other person sat before his gaze jumped over to the glass wall. My steps were light as I moved to stand in front of the man beside me, knowing he couldn't see me—something I'd grown used to in these lucid dreams.

The man now standing before me was beautiful in a striking way—with a thin frame and angled jawline that came to a not-so-abrupt point at his creased, clean-shaven chin. His clothing and body were all straight lines and sharp angles.

All of him seemed to be cut from stone until I gazed up at his bright icy hair that stood in all directions, possibly only brushed loosely by his smooth hands. He looked nothing like the raw and rugged—

Nope. I'm not going to think about him.

I shook my head, clearing it. I wouldn't allow myself to have any thoughts like that about Aeden, not even in my dreams.

"Do you think she's safe?" Concern oozed from the man in front of me as he held his breath, his fingers sliding through his messy hair that was more cool than it was warm, like ice, like...*the walls.* They weren't glass. They were ice. A very solid, thick layer of it. That's why it was so cold.

I wrapped my arms around myself, thankful the floor was tiled and not made of ice as well. How did they live in a place like this?

A tuft of warm, golden hair peeked out from the back of the winged-back chair as the man with the distorted voice rose from his seat—all broad shoulders and perfect posture. I didn't have to see his face to know exactly whose body I was looking at, seeing as it was his that constantly pinned mine to the training deck back in Prydia.

Eoghan's cocky grin was on full display as he turned, the distortion fading as he said, "You don't know the one who saved Paige. *Trust me*, she's safe." A frown tugged on my lips at the word, the realization the *her* in their scenario was *me* sending my gut to my toes. If being caged was *safe*, then yes. I was forcefully that.

The man closer to me started moving, closing the distance between him and Eoghan, and right when that distance no longer existed between them, the icy-blonde man with grey eyes took Eoghan's hands in his. Eoghan's face softened, just as it did when... Ikelos was mentioned.

And then he spoke again, "We need to find her before he does. You understand we can't let—"

Thump, thump, thump

I startled awake, sitting upright and reaching for daggers that weren't sheathed at my hip. My eyes darted around the camp from behind the line of trees that blocked me in. *Where the hell is that sound coming fr—*

Thump, thump

My eyes scanned the camp, counting the lying figures in the grass. Everyone was there *except* for the one I wished would leave me be, for good.

I pushed up to my feet and moved around the prison they kept me locked in. I was trapped in here for the majority of the day, save for bathroom breaks Shay and Murrie escorted me on. My eyes squinted through the darkness of the night, my face pressing against those bar-like trunks, and that's when I saw him.

Switching between the bow and arrows he used to hunt and the hatchets Murrie crafted for him, Aeden was taking up weapons and throwing them with lethal precision, hitting dead-center almost every time. They didn't trust me with freedom *or* weapons. Smart on their end as it was, it was also very shitty on mine. The tree bark started to burn in my tightening grasp as I watched him take aim and hit the target, again and again.

One of the thin trees of the prison wall I leaned on groaned under my weight, drawing his attention to me with cool, lingering eyes before he went to retrieve the hatchets from the middle of the target. I didn't care if he saw me watching him. For all he knew, I was studying my opponent. But as sweat beaded down his toned frame, down the groove covered in marks on his lower back that I hated admitting I'd noticed more than once, I had to question for a second if simply studying him was what I was doing.

He lifted the hatchets, took aim, and let them fly. They landed with another set of *thumps* inches from the center of the target, and as he bent down to pick up his bow and quiver, he looked back at me.

"Like what you see?" he asked, and that second of insane admiration of his body was gone.

Sort of.

He smirked, not bothering to wait for a reply that he knew wasn't coming. If only I could reach my air magic, I'd have my daggers back, and then he wouldn't be looking at me like *that* anymore. But as it was, I could only sense my water magic, and there was no way I'd be able to wedge my daggers out of the log, much less do it discreetly enough to matter, with that power.

I imagined flinging chunks of ice at Aeden's head or trying to see how long I could push him back with blasts of water, but he would have the upper hand. He trained every day, and every day, I got to witness it. Wallow in the shadows of my cell as he got stronger each and every. Single. Day. And those marks, all four of his damn marks, mocked me when his face and words weren't doing the job.

He glanced back at me again, shaking his head like what I was doing was somehow *cute* to him. I decided to keep my mouth shut, turning my focus to the heating of my cheeks and using my water magic to cool them, only to end up freezing the tips of my fingers instead.

Did I enjoy watching him with his shirt off? Yes. I wasn't blind. But did I need to perpetuate that and let him revel in it by showing it all over my face? Nope. I wouldn't give my captor that satisfaction.

He emptied his quiver without another glance my way, then retrieved the arrows and hatchets from the middle of the target. His head dipped down and I squinted again, watching as he rubbed his thumb over the blade of one of the hatchets, checking if it needed to be sharpened or not. It didn't, I could tell from here how sharp they were just by the deep grooves they left on the wooden target. But he slipped the hatchets into his waistband by the handles and walked over to sit on the log where every single one of my daggers were buried halfway to the hilt. The log that was tauntingly close to my cell, yet far enough away to where it was just out of reach.

If I could just get close enough...

Aeden started sharpening, and I moved to sit close to him from the inside of my prison. The trees may have been my physical barricade, but the real thing barring me from any chance of escaping was trust. *He needs to trust me if I want to have the freedom to escape.* "Can't sleep?" I blurted, and he stopped sharpening for a moment before continuing as if I'd startled him. Perhaps I did. I didn't initiate conversation with him unless he provoked me. And he wasn't exactly threatening me with his hatchets.

"Not really," he replied, swiping the stone in his hand down the blade of the hatchet he held in his other.

I nodded even though he wasn't looking and drew my knees to my chest. The skin on my forearms formed goosebumps and I rubbed them against my thighs until something rumbled up from beneath the grass in the center of my cell. I looked over just as a stump of wood and dried grass emerged in a sloped pit of dirt. My jaw tightened as a small ball of fire no larger than my fist rolled in next to the pit, changing form into a small deer made of flames. My lips parted as the deer jumped up into the center of the pit, igniting the grass and logs.

I snapped my unhinged jaw shut again. "Show-off," I murmured into my knees. "But thanks. I guess." I shuffled closer to the flames, almost wishing it would finally grant me the mark that I could use to burn the prison, and every last flower above my head, down.

"Is that a thanks for also saving your life?" He was persistent, even though he knew exactly what I thought about his rescue mission that took away what I'd worked so hard for.

"Not a chance," I replied, keeping my eyes on the fire. He laughed as I warmed my hands by his creation. "Have you been doing that all night?" I asked, trying to gauge exactly how much he'd slept. Maybe I'd get lucky and he'd take a nap during the day instead, if he were tired or depleted enough.

Then I could try my chances at escaping while Murrie was distracted, trying to heal the poor depleted Fire Boy while I went on an urgent bathroom break. Although last time I tried that, Murrie threatened me with her huge battle-ax. So maybe I wasn't going to get anywhere, not with the way she swung that thing around like another limb.

He definitely wouldn't trust me any faster if I tried to escape again.

Aeden's eyes skated over to where Varasyn slept, her body curving in a way that made her seem less deadly than she was. "Yeah, I guess I have." He lodged both hatchets next to my daggers, then took the quiver and bow from his back and laid those down on the log as well.

My stomach gurgled as my eyes fell to the food supply. It wasn't like they never fed me, because they did. Or tried. I refused, more often than I should. He stood abruptly and made his way to the rack that had drying meat splayed out across it, took a few pieces, and walked back over to the edge of my cell.

"Here." He wedged the pieces through the gaps that I could barely fit an arm through. I said nothing, took the pieces, and began eating slowly as I settled back down, shimmying closer to the fire that was no closer to reaching into the well of power I should have had by now than the grass and trees around me were. I felt nothing, and that was possibly more frustrating than being stuck, surrounded by my favorite flowers put up by a lovelorn idiot. I never thought being surrounded by peonies would tick me off as much as it did, but here I was.

At least the fire served another purpose. It was getting cold fast, and soon enough, we'd be covered in snow if we didn't find somewhere else to stay. Aeden sat back on the log and reached a hand over his shoulder. As he rubbed, his corded forearms flexed in a way that sent a shiver down my spine, my food becoming harder to swallow. I silently reasoned it was because of the weather, even though the fire kept me more than warm enough to fight against the cold.

"You know, if you don't sleep, you can't heal as well," I prodded. I bet his muscles were sore beyond belief from more than just his most recent target practice, and that fire he'd made and the way he shaped it...his power was wearing thin.

He stopped rubbing and started rolling his shoulders back. "Hard to sleep when you talk in yours." He knew as well as I did that if you didn't rest, your power wasn't going to regenerate. Yet instead of sleeping, he went back to rubbing.

Heat rose within me. "No one told you to sleep so close to the prison you made." I spread my arms wide. "There's an entire field here. Pick somewhere else to sleep."

He sat upright, then swung his legs over the log to face me, his entire body so clearly in view between the spacing of the trees. I didn't shuffle away, just stared right back at him, raising my chin. He rested his forearms on his knees as he leaned forward and my breath caught in my chest as the light of the burning wood danced in his eyes. His lip curved up to one side. "Not a chance," he said, then he lifted the hatchets from the log and went right back to practicing.

Chapter Three
Aeden

"She was dreaming about Eoghan. *Again.*" My lungs burned, but not as brightly as the knowledge of Eoghan being in her mind and in her thoughts did.

Seamus stopped at the edge where we frequently hunted and craned his head toward me. "Ye can't be serious, Lad. Ye know he doesn't like…ye know." He scratched at his beard. "Women."

I held my arm out in front of Seamus, stopping him in his tracks. I nocked an arrow, the wood warm in my grip as I held it down by my side. Careful not to scare the rabbit before taking aim, I crouched down low, my boots digging into the grass and mud. And then I released it, sending a burst of air behind the feather fletching. That rabbit wouldn't have made it no matter how hard it'd tried to run.

"I don't care what his *preferences* are," I finally let out as Seamus moved to pick up the lifeless animal. "He doesn't deserve to eat up so much of her time." Maybe she wasn't aware that she'd said his name over and over in her sleep. But I painfully was.

The grass shuffled in the distance, and Seamus and I knelt down to watch for whatever animal, or thing, had yet to come out of hiding. A baby deer stepped into view, ambling by alone. I dropped the arrow I'd begun pulling from my quiver across my back and Seamus peered over at me. "Nice to see ye still have a soft spot, Lad."

"Killing kids isn't really my thing." The image of Cyprian, the barely teenaged fire-wielder who was hung in Prydia for simply existing, flitted through my mind. My jaw clenched. "I may have been harder to be near lately, but I'm not a monster." Not like Gedeon. Not like a man who could poison his own daughter.

"Ah." Seamus patted the top of my shoulder as his other hand clutched the very large, very dead rabbit. "Ye don't need to explain it to me. But I think ye could use a break." He jerked his head toward camp. "Let's go."

Varasyn flew above us and Seamus froze in place. "Still gettin' used to 'er." I nudged into him with my shoulder as she circled above us, then took off again toward what I assumed was a herd of sheep in the far distance.

Going to eat more sheep or are you bringing some back? Murrie wanted me to ask for some a little less harmed so she could use the wool. Just a thought. We'd all need the clothing a few sheeps would provide to keep warm in the winter. I'd keep warm just fine, unless my power depleted. Something that may or may not be happening to me anyway with the amount of energy I was putting into training and none whatsoever in sleeping.

I make no promises, but let the tiny one know I will try. I chuckled, knowing damn well Murrie would be mad to know of her nickname by the dragon she so respected.

"You go on ahead," I said to Seamus as I reached down to tie my boots that didn't need to be re-tied. "I'll be there soon." Seamus turned to walk, throwing a hand up as he walked on without me. A wave of dizziness hit me as I looked down, the tied-off remaining ends of two laces in my hands turning to four.

You know, if you don't sleep, you can't heal as well. She knew exactly what me not being able to heal would mean for her. She'd try to run...again.

The wave of dizziness settled just as the grass rustled briskly, then parted in waves. I stood and stared down over the edge of the hill, watching where the grasses grew so tall that I usually struggled to see above it when I was hunting. I only ever walked in if something I shot ran in, or if I needed to cross. Something was there now, and that *something* was *big*.

I readied another arrow, lifting my bow to follow along with the movements of whatever was in the grass. I'd never seen a deer move sporadically in zig-zags, and rabbits and foxes were too small to separate the grass that much. A sharp hissing sound came from the depths as the thing stilled.

I knew that figure would be clad in black scales, with a sharp tongue and fangs ready to devour me.

I dropped the bow and readied my hands instead, sending a blast of air through the grass to flatten it down for good. A single naga stood in those tampered grasses. They usually traveled at night and in packs, but this one was unlucky enough to wander from the rest and find me in broad daylight.

The naga's claws extended toward me as it snarled. It didn't look too startled. No, this one looked hungry. "You're weak," it hissed out, licking its fang-like teeth and thin upper lip. I hadn't encountered a naga since the night I was saved by Murrie, but I was nowhere near the wielder I had become over the past two months.

"And you're dead." I pushed my sleeve up, letting my marks do the talking. The naga's thin and slitted eyes turned steely and wide, but its tongue swiped along those scaly lips before it let loose another snarl. As if their bloodlust would ever be stronger than the weakened state I was in.

The hungry thing took the challenge immediately, attempting to lunge just as I anchored thier legs down to the ground with vines so thick they refused to snap. The naga moved from thrashing to clawing at their legs, but I reinforced the vines with roots, then turned the ground beneath it to a mud that started to devour the beast with every thrash it gave.

The naga shrieked, then turned its head over its shoulder as it sank, as if searching for others that weren't there. Their head swirled back around to face me as another wave of dizziness came and I stumbled forward.

The beast laughed. "Sssso weak. The othersss will come for you," it hissed, those eyes widening more with each glance over its shoulder. Those others it spoke of weren't showing.

I grinned. "Fuck your friends," I said, fighting past the dizziness that was taking me under just as quickly as the mud was devouring the naga. I bent my knees into the grass, not allowing that grin to falter. I wanted that *thing* to know just how much I was enjoying this. Enjoying the kill. Watching its life fade before it would have the chance to do so to me or my friends. I maneuvered my wrist against the grass, sending a rope of air around its neck.

"You can't live out here for long, fire-wielder," the naga let out through wheezing breaths, grasping and clawing for that unseizable rope.

"Longer than you will." I tightened the rope of air, watching until its eyes began to roll to the back of its head that was falling limp. That smile still remained on my face as the mud continued its vengeful gulping of the lifeless body until I forced the earth to stop. I wanted to leave a warning for *the others*, a mark that this would be their end if they even thought about trying to hurt anyone I cared about.

Varasyn dove down as I ripped a fang free from the naga's mouth and stashed it into my pocket, hoping that Murrie would have a use for the poison that once took me down. That day seemed so long ago, and oh, how the cards had turned.

I wobbled backward trying to gain my footing to stand. *"I'm taking you back to camp, where you will sleep,"* she commanded, her voice in my mind making the dizziness worse.

"I'll be alright, I can walk." I waved a dismissive arm at her and tried to steady myself, focusing on the blades of grass beneath my feet that were quickly warping instead of being the one focal point that might keep me still.

"Listen to me or I'll happily knock you out myself." She came closer, craning her neck and nudging into my torso, urging me to climb on. *"Grab on unless you want me to carry you by my teeth."* As much as I wanted to argue that I was fine, that I could make it back by myself, I knew I wasn't going to make it very far.

I patted her neck where she'd swung into me, then wrapped my arms around one of her spines and fought past the intense burn of my muscles to hoist myself between the spine I held onto and another. Her head swiveled to the naga, pushing me the rest of the way up from the ground, and her neck rumbled as she growled. *"More will come. We can't stay in the Fields anymore."*

Her red and golden scales scraped against my cheek as I nodded against her, the effort alone making my entire body ache. *"I know."* I'd hoped leaving a present for the nagas friends would be warning enough, but I couldn't be sure of their numbers. I was careless at times and had risked my own life plenty, but I would never risk the lives of my friends. She stomped through the field, deciding that was safer than flying with the way I was mounted and as we approached camp, I slumped off of Vara and fell to the ground.

The last thing I heard was Shay screaming. I watched through heavy eyes as her blurred frame moved closer and closer until it was lights out for me.

"Only a bleatin' fool would!" Seamus' hushed voice carried to my ears as I moaned and rolled over away from the fire. *Fuck, nighttime already?* My head was throbbing and my arms were pulsing like the magic inside of me was trying to come back to life but was struggling. Murrie appeared in front of me with a cup as I tried to swallow against the dryness that burned my throat. "Drink, and don't try to tell me or anyone else here that you are fine. Varasyn dragged me out to see your little naga display. Seamus is gathering everything now, so we can leave." I reached for the cup and my hand started to tremble. "I'll hold it, you absolute idiot. Why haven't you been sleeping? You know we warn you about draining yourself almost every damn day and—"

I held up a hand to stop her, then sipped from the cup she held up to me. I tried to push my head back to see Paige, making sure she was okay in her 'prison' as she called it, but everything in my body felt so distant and unusable like my mind was stuck in a cloud, my body heavy as if I were sinking underground faster than the naga had. Murrie cleared her throat, not giving a shit if I wanted to hear her thoughts or not. "Right, well." She inclined her head toward Paige, or at least that's the direction it seemed to be moving. My brain was still fucked. "She told us about you refusing to sleep. I guess she still cares about you, in some way."

I let out a breathy laugh that turned into a cough and my body shuddered under the pain in my lungs. "I doubt *that's* why she told you." As much as I wanted for her to remember how much we used to mean to each other, and showed her daily how much she still meant to me, I couldn't quite picture her giving a damn about my health.

"Maybe she's coming around. Sometimes all that is needed is time and patience for these things to wear off." Murrie shrugged and tipped the cup up to my mouth again.

I took another sip, then pulled my head back. "She hated me before we put her in there." I rolled onto my back and looked up at the stars. My eyes were still adjusting, so they looked like little balls of blurry light, but at least I wasn't curled up in pain anymore. "What's in that?" I lifted my brow at her as I slung my arm behind my head in the grass.

"What do you think? I used up what I had left of the potion I gave you last time you went down weeks ago. Thanks for the fang, by the way. I'm sure I will find a use for it." She patted her leather satchel then looked over at Paige who I couldn't see clearly yet from here, but I imagined she was reading a book and ignoring me all the same. "You can't keep this up, Aeden. We need you to live, and as much as she doesn't want to hear it, she needs you, too. She just doesn't remember all of that yet. Have faith, and be patient."

Faith. I looked back up at the Stars, who really had it out for me lately. I kept my eyes on them as I held out my hand for the cup. The potion she made was working wonders, and my body was beginning to feel more grounded and less *in* the ground, while my mind raced to catch up with it, like two pieces of a puzzle merging. She placed the cup in my hand, and I consumed every last drop, then propped myself up to a sitting position.

I looked over my shoulder at Paige, whose eyes were peeking over the edge of her book before she buried her face in it, trying to conceal that she was, in fact, watching me. *Interesting.* "What do ye want to do with 'er?" Seamus asked as he wrapped jerky and bundles of wool in the freshly dried deer hide. Vara must've found the time to get some sheep for Murrie after all.

"She rides with Murrie," I ordered. Murrie nodded her head, dipping down into a slight bow and reached to wrap her fingers around the handle that protruded from where it slung on her back. A show for Paige—I knew she'd never actually use it on her, but she'd damn well scare her enough to let her think that. And after Paige almost jumped off of Vara when I saved her from the Triad, I didn't want to risk her actually doing so again.

"Why can't I ride with Shay?" Paige stood, closing her book and tucking it under her arm.

"Shay rides with me," Seamus said, throwing the wrapped items over one of the horses and securing it down without sparing a single glance at Paige. Besides the terror that Murrie incited in Paige and the way I was certain Shay wouldn't have it in her to hold Paige back from escaping, Seamus would never ride a horse with Murrie. They were civil, but not *that* civil.

Shay gave her a quick look, almost apologetic, but continued helping Seamus pack whatever was left of our belongings. Shay's kind of magic to enchant less powerful fae couldn't be used on Paige to keep her from escaping, and as much as I didn't want to mess up the odd friendship they had formed, I knew Paige had probably targeted her as the weakest of the group when she decided to be nicer to her than the rest of us. I hated thinking she could be so conniving, but Paige losing her memories didn't lessen the survival instincts that were ingrained in her, and I could see right through every lie and ploy she tried to sell.

Paige bit her lip. "When are you letting me out?" The question was solely delivered to me as she met my eyes.

I ran a hand through my hair, contemplating. "I'll have to bind your hands, but not until we have the horses ready for you to get on."

"How am I supposed to fight if we get attacked? There're nagas out there!" Her hands flew to her hips as her attention briefly moved over to the log that held all twelve of her blades. She was good—the queen of manipulation *and* my heart.

I followed her gaze with my own and smirked, then looked to Seamus who just shook his head and continued packing.

"I'll protect you, don't you worry," Murrie said with a grin that begged for Paige to try escaping while in her care.

"What if I fall off, and they come after me?" She feigned fear as if it were a new set of armor. She'd have to try a lot harder than that to convince me of her being afraid of anything, though. Much harder.

I moved to collect her daggers, tossing the last one up in the air by the tip of the blade and catching it along the hilt. "I'll bind your hands, *and* your legs to the horse. Satisfied?" Fuck being the nice guy. *This* version of Paige had forgotten just how *nice* I had always been to her, and I was wielding it as a weapon to pierce through that new armor she'd developed. I wasn't going to let her escape back into the hands of her father, or wherever it was she thought she was going to be safer. No one could keep her safer than I could. One day she was going to see that and stop trying to find opportunities and loopholes to aid in her plans.

Varasyn stalked up to the edge of the trees that caged in Paige and released a slow, steamy cloud over the top that made flower petals fall like rain over her. Sometimes, I was truly thankful that she wasn't able to breathe fire yet. She was too young. If she *were* able to, I'd have to come up with more than confinement to protect Paige from not only herself, but also a dragon who she managed to piss off since day one.

Paige didn't even flinch and only shielded her book from the steam as it blew across her. It was oddly turning me on just how brave she was, even up against a dragon. *Actually, scratch that.* Anything she did was a turn on and it wasn't odd at all because I was so fucking in love with her it was bordering on pathetic. But try telling my dick that.

"Satisfy your needs elsewhere," Varasyn demanded as she stretched her wings, getting ready to fly us to wherever we were heading. I threw her a dark glare. She knew damn well I didn't want anyone else, no matter how much Paige hated me.

Shay struggled to lift her sack up onto the horse, so I rushed to help her lift and secure it. "Thanks," she said, gasping for air. I patted her shoulder, then turned to check if Seamus had the other horse ready. He was finishing some complex sailor's knot, but everything else he'd packed was already lifted and secured. All that remained to pack up on my end was Paige.

I turned and made my way to her, her book pressed tight to her chest as the anger radiated from her. It was the only belonging she had other than the daggers I'd packed away on Seamus' horse, save for a few I tucked into my waistband. No weapons besides Murrie's ax would be traveling with them—and there was no way Murrie would ever give her ax to someone else just to keep it from Paige. "I'll take that," I said, reaching my fingers through the trees to accept the book she had no intention of handing over.

She took two steps back, taunting me with the brightness in her eyes. "You want it"—she took two more steps back into the center of her space—"come get it, then." Her lips curved up, the defiance in her fueling me even more.

Fuck, I love her.

I pulled my hand from the gap, and looked at the others. Seamus scoffed and grumbled something to himself and Shay put her hands on her hips, giving Paige a look to emphasize how little time we had for her games. Murrie tossed her small hand back to clutch her weapon as she scowled, and when I finally looked back at Paige, her cocky smile had faded as mine grew.

I lowered my voice to a tone meant just for the two of us—rough and low. "If you wanted me to come in there with you, to put my *hands* on you, all you had to do was ask." I flicked my wrist and the trees bent to form a larger gap that I slipped through with ease. Her eyes widened as I closed the distance between us, my body burning to rid every inch between us until there was nothing left. I bent in toward her, my lips grazing the edge of her ear and damn if her slight shiver didn't bring me right back to having her on her kitchen counter, a day that felt like years ago with all the shit we'd been through. I wanted to pull her close, make her feel how much I'd missed her. But she didn't want me like she had before, if she ever really did as much as I have always wanted her.

My knuckles grazed gently down her marked forearm in a way that sent my body humming with need.

"Give me the book, Paige," I whispered sweetly into her ear, quite proud that I managed to get the word 'book' from my lips instead of 'your body, your mind, your *everything*.' She mumbled under her breath, something that sounded like 'asshole,' as she slammed the book into my chest.

That's my girl.

I couldn't hide the curve of my mouth as I pulled away from her and tucked her book under my arm. I may have been disappointed at the potential we could have had, to rip into each other and finally give into that temptation that had been boiling over for years, but damn if I wasn't proud of the way she stood her ground. She may not have her original nature to throw at me, or a dagger, but she was still so fucking stubborn it lit a fire in my chest seeing her as she had always been.

Resilient. Stubborn. Head-strong.

She rolled her eyes and looked away. "Better be quick." She held her hands out in front of her and pushed them into my gut, ready to accept that I had to bind her first before I took apart her cell.

"I'd prefer to take my time with you." I felt her wrists go taut as the vines formed around her hands gently, yet tight enough to keep her from breaking free. I was told I was a fool for loving her, and I was okay with that, but I wouldn't be a fool by losing her again. And if she did run, there was nowhere she could go that I wouldn't find her. I'd scour the ends of Aellethia to find her and bring her back to me, where she belonged.

"There, that wasn't so bad, was it?" Her nostrils flared, and she shot her head away from me. "Don't move," I ordered, and in seconds the trees went back into the ground, the roots splaying out like teeth until they, too, sank below the ground. A flower fluttered down to where her hands clasped together beneath the vines, landing on top. I sent a wisp of vine out to pin down the flower above her hands and noticed the tinge of a smile before it faded into malice again as she lifted her brows. I guess she still had an appreciation for the smaller things in life.

"Your weapon, for the ride." I moved beside her, inclining my head toward the horse where Murrie stood waiting for her.

"This isn't much of a weapon. What am I supposed to do, wave the flower around and distract the nagas with beauty?" she asked as her elbows jerked to adjust the vines that weren't giving under her attempts to free herself.

"You already do that to me, why not try it on a naga as well?" I admitted, not at all ashamed at how cheesy that came out.

She scoffed, but her cheeks deceived her as they pinked over. She didn't try to fight me when I lifted her and placed her on the saddle, or when I secured her legs to it, just as I promised I would.

"Where are we going?" she asked, her eyes narrowing as she looked around, possibly scanning the dark for nagas. Maybe she was hoping for an attack, another chance at escaping.

"Easrich is a good start, we can get there in a few hours and it still keeps us within Buryon territories. We should be safe there for a night or two," Shay answered. I swiped my bottom lip with my thumb and nodded. Easrich was the closest, safest option. The further south, the better.

"Vara and I will keep watch from above. You should all be safe." Vara splayed her wings and thrashed her tail on the ground.

"We aren't completely helpless, Lad. Don't go usin' up all yer magic again. Ye may be stronger, but ye can only do so much." Seamus lifted his forearm, showing the current of waves that flared vibrant blue along his skin as each one did on mine. Murrie nodded in agreement as Shay positioned herself in the saddle. Seamus would be riding behind her, and Murrie would be behind Paige, taking the reins.

"You should sleep while I fly. I'll wake you if they are in need of your assistance." I looked up at Vara, cocking my head to the side. *Shit, where was I going to hide her?*

"Don't worry about me, I can stay hidden above the clouds. I've remained hidden for this long." She had a point.

The others were looking at her curiously too. "She's going to stay hidden, and *stay out of trouble,*" I said, hinting that she needed to remain unseen but also keep her meals as inconspicuous as she could to avoid drawing attention. She lifted her lip, showing her rows of deadly sharp teeth.

"I don't think she likes listening to you," Paige chimed in. I shrugged, reaching for the jacket that I wore whenever we took off to fly. I threw it over Paige's shoulders, securing it in place with one of the top buttons.

Paige bit down on her lip and looked me up and down. "I don't need your clothes." She rolled her shoulders back, trying to act like she wasn't getting comfortable in it as she sneered at me.

"You're cold. I'm not. We can just call it yours from now on so you don't have to justify it to yourself."

"Asshole," she mumbled.

Murrie shuffled in closer to Paige, making Paige glare back at her. "I think what she meant to say was 'thank you,' didn't you, Paige?"

She didn't pause for a single second. "No."

"When she wants to thank me, she will." I turned and climbed onto Varasyn's back. "Enjoy the warmth, beautiful!" I hollered just before we launched into the air.

Chapter Four
Paige

I'd seen the desolation of Prydia—the shambles that didn't reach the castle walls my father lived in. I remembered all of it, every inch of his home I walked or trained on since the day I landed in his dining room.

Seeing Easrich for the first time blew the flame from the Prydian wick.

It was beautiful. The town was quaint and serene, with pointed roofs that weren't caved in and even had adornments along the trim in all kinds of colors that were visible at night, unlike Prydia, because of strange, lit orbs that floated in the air. The grass in Easrich was actually bright green moss—I realized after staring at the way it sat like a sponge above the earth—that sprawled just as its people did in the night. And there were *people*. Fae that weren't in poverty, weren't sickly thin and covered in torn rags.

"How..." The words were lost on my tongue and my jaw fell slack. I looked over at Shay as our horses flanked the slim road that led into the town. "I thought most places were...Eoghan said...." *Nope, still no words.*

"Eoghan doesn't know everything," Aeden muttered. I almost jumped against the saddle, forgetting he'd told Varasyn to let him walk the last hour in case anyone was wandering the path at night. He stayed close to Seamus and Shay for most of that time until he shifted to keep stride with our horse. His conversation had been focused toward Murrie for the most part, but his eyes told another story of where that focus of his truly was. One that made shivers roll down my spine again and again each time his eyes raked over me.

"I was surprised too. Most towns aren't quite like this. But people don't know much about Buryon and its territories. At least, not where I'm from." Shay had been here several times for supplies, gathering intel as discreetly as possible at the same time. But she never once spoke about what she saw here. Not to me, anyway.

"What are those lights?" I lowered my voice as a small group of young fae passed us. We were minutes from entering the town, but I was so struck with absolute awe that every second stretched on timelessly.

"Faelights. Usually only used to brighten the darkness of smaller spaces. More for personal use," Shae answered.

"The lights in my father's—in Gedeon's castle—were more like flames trapped in orbs of air."

It was Aeden who spoke before Shay could open her mouth again. "Probably a show of power. Trapping flames within air sounds like it fit that fucking wallpaper perfectly." *That wallpaper.* A very faint whisper of grey trailed my memories when I thought of that wallpaper, as if it were tied to another thought that had involved the man mere feet from me.

"You've seen it?"

Aeden nodded his head, but the look he tossed my way as he did so was confirmation enough, his darkened eyes a mix of recollection and the realization that I hadn't known, hadn't remembered, that he knew of it. Whenever he became acquainted with the inside of my father's castle, I couldn't remember it. But I must've known. At some point, he'd been there, in that hallway. Perhaps even in my bedroom. Yet the idea of Aeden in a room with me in that castle thrust a cloud of grey so thick through my head that it made it throb.

"I'm sure Seamus here can show you how to make faelight one day soon, although last I remembered he was shit at it." Shay tossed her delicate hand in the air.

Seamus' lips curved downward. "I'm not shit at it."

"Last time I asked you to do it, you nearly blinded us both!"

"Faelight is no different than using yer elemental powers. It's driven by yer feelin's, and ye were half-naked and—" Shay shifted and wiggled back against

Seamus, a coy smile spreading along her face. "Woman, are ye tryin' to seduce me?" He arched his back away from her ass and adjusted his crotch.

Aeden cocked his brow toward Seamus. "Do I want to know why you needed a faelight while Shay was half—you know what? No. I don't need to know that."

Given how beautiful both of them were, I didn't need a vast imagination to picture what they were doing. Seamus was just as tall as Aeden, muscles well-defined, and given the rate of how fae aged, it was hard to tell if he were any older than forty-five, although he probably was with all the life experience he seemed to have. And Shay...she was devastatingly beautiful. I doubted she ever needed to use the siren song she could wield—her looks would do enough.

"Get yer head out of the murky bog, Boyo. Shay was swimmin', and it's not like I have flames like ye do. I never taught ye before because ye needed more practice with the fire. Besides, faelight can be faint, but if not careful, it can be too bright. Can kind of give away where ye are more so than a small flame will."

"Sounds like your head was well within that murky bog if you almost blinded Shay," Aeden deadpanned. Shay giggled, flipping her dark black hair over her shoulder and across Seamus' cheeks that had turned bright red before he continued. "Lessons in faelight soon, then." Aeden glanced at me, his gaze roaming down the lengths of my legs, as if confirming I hadn't found a way to run yet. "Teach Paige, too." Seamus' color faded quickly back to normal as he nodded.

If he was looking for gratitude, I wasn't willing to give it to him. Instead, spitting in his face was more tempting than uttering any form of thanks beyond the couple I'd graciously given him already. I wouldn't turn down learning a new ability, a new power, even if it wouldn't aid me in escaping as much as my other powers would, or could, if I had the full use of them. But I also wouldn't let him see how excited I was to learn *something*, to train *something*. Giving a grain of salt wouldn't brine a damn turkey, nor would it make me feel any different toward him.

I only cleared my throat, breaking his gaze from my body and looked down at my hands.

My very bound, very restricted hands. The hands of a prisoner.

Yet being held captive, being restricted and bound and made well-aware of how little freedom I had, didn't seem to affect the way my stomach knotted as he walked beside my horse, the heat of his eyes on me too noticeable—too unavoidable. I sat up straighter in the saddle and pushed it down—way, way down.

I drew my eyes back up, wondering how long I'd been trapped in my thoughts to where I hadn't noticed we'd come to a building. My eyes flashed to the words written on a wooden sign labeling it an inn and bar as Murrie and Seamus slowed the horses down to a stop, allowing Aeden to wrap both reins around a post next to a few other horses—another strange aspect of this town. I never saw a single horse in Prydia.

"Are we not camping...you know, outside?" I asked as Murrie jumped to the ground. The image of a bed was sending my thoughts down a spiral I didn't want to be down right now. Or ever.

Seamus took some pelts from his bundle on the back of the horse and Shay followed him inside. "No, we should have enough to trade for a room or two for at least a night, maybe two tops," Aeden answered as he came up beside my horse. The vines binding my legs disintegrated and before he could offer to help, I swung my leg over and slid down the side, using my elbows to guide me off the horse and to the ground.

"Stay still," Aeden demanded the second my feet hit the ground. He reached for the back of his waistband and I immediately scanned the homes and shops, my heart pounding wildly as I looked for whatever threat there could be that would make him reach for his weapons because I wasn't running, so it wasn't me he was hunting in the dark. Something smooth and hard rubbed up against my finger and I jolted back into the horse, making it snort and stomp its hooves in retaliation.

"Easy." Aeden's head bent, drawing my eyes down.

Nagas weren't attacking. Nothing was. My hands broke free as he pushed the dagger, *my dagger*, through with a final cut. His hand cradled mine, making warmth creep along my fingers as the vines tumbled down to the moss at my feet.

"Don't make me regret this. Please." A calloused thumb grazed the back of my hand and then the heat was gone. But the stupid knot in my gut from the way he looked at me earlier was still twisting as I pushed my arms into the sleeves of his jacket.

Hungry, I'm just hungry. That's all.

I rubbed at my wrists through the jacket. "You won't." And it wasn't a lie. I wouldn't try to go anywhere. Not tonight, at least.

The morning?

That was a different situation entirely.

"Take a seat, lass," Seamus ordered as he passed our table. Shay locked her arm around mine and guided me to sit beside her and I took that time to look around, anywhere but at the man who had bound me to a horse.

The bar below the inn was dimly lit—low lighting playing off green and golden adornments that crawled along the walls, completely unlike the terror of the wallpaper at my father's home. It was breathtaking, with darkly stained wooden tables that were dotted around the room before ending at a long bar that pulsed like the liveliness of the people inside. Just beside the end of the bar was a sweeping, curving staircase leading to the second floor where a balcony gave way to two hallways with what I imagined were rooms.

A room I hopefully would not be sharing with Aeden.

A glass slid down the table sent on a precisely measured gust of wind and I looked up to see a young woman around my age with doe-eyes and short blonde hair and a small, purple mark on her forearm. I wanted to reach out to her, ask her about Prydia, get anything from her. But asking those questions wouldn't look good.

"Those handsome men had this sent over for you." She inclined her head with a knowing smile toward the bar where Seamus and Aeden were talking to a man who held up two keys on leather strips. I smiled back at her crookedly enough to send her away as Seamus heaved his sack of pelts over the bar top. I watched as the man they were talking to beamed and shook both of their hands.

"Cheers." Shay lifted her glass to me. I lifted mine, taking a huge gulp, then two, then three. Shay's dark thin brow arched up before taking her sip. "You okay?"

I nodded before downing the rest of my glass. "Fine." But I wasn't. I wouldn't be *fine* until I could take Prydia from my father—the evil, self-righteous man who didn't even try to stop Aeden from taking me from the arena. And having maybe a few handfuls of guards throw arrows at us as we flew off wasn't exactly settling, either.

I was never truly wanted by him and that was fine. I didn't want to be his daughter just as he didn't want to be the asshole who sired me. But I still had a right to be angry—at my father, at Aeden, and even at myself. I should have run the moment we landed and he cut the damn vines from my hands with my own dagger. I should have blasted him back with all the water magic I could summon from under my flesh and taken one of the horses.

So why the hell didn't I?

My eyes drifted to one of the few skinny windows by the front doors, spotting Murrie through it as she gathered the rest of our belongings strategically to haul them up to the rooms.

"I'm proud of you, you know. For not running." Shay's icy-blue eyes looked over my features like she was searching for some answer, something she couldn't understand as grooves formed between her eyes. I had a firm goal in mind with each conversation I had with Shay over the past several months—use her as a means to get out of my cell and run because she'd be the least-likely to be able to stop me. I wasn't running at the moment, but that didn't mean she should be proud of that fact.

"There's nothing to be proud of," I replied honestly. It simply wasn't a good time to run. That was all.

Seamus slid into the seat next to Shay and my focus immediately shifted to the seat next to mine. Empty. As I took another sip, I flicked my eyes to where Aeden was leaning against the bar, talking to the same blonde girl who slid our glasses to us. She twirled her hair as she handed him his drink from the other side of the bartop, her fingers lingering a little too long as they slid down the cup and brushed over his hand. A hand I knew the exact texture and feel of. I pushed my hands under the table and tried to rub at the backside of them, where his had cupped mine moments before.

"Are ye well, lass? Yer a wee bit red." Seamus flicked his wrist and filled my cup with water, a notion so agitating and yet so familiar I froze before reaching for the glass. I stood from my seat and tilted my chin up and away from Seamus, taking the water with me to the bar. My boots slowed as I approached the other end, seats down from where the woman with short hair was so clearly offering more than just alcohol. I flashed two fingers up to the man behind the bar, hoping that would be enough to get my mind in a better place than wherever it kept traveling to whenever I looked over at *him*.

The red hair of the bartender flashed in my vision as he nodded and drew thoughts of Nya, my trainer and friend, to the surface that I'd pushed down every time they came up. Even seeing Seamus' hair, and sometimes his eyes, made me think of Nya. It was easier when I didn't dream about the people that haunted the past I did remember.

"On the house, traveler," the man said as two glasses slid down the slick wooden top, stopping right before my hands. I flexed my fingers before grabbing hold of both glasses, reveling in the way the man didn't give me a look of concern, knowing I planned to down them both for myself. I'd gotten that concerned look too many times while in the Fields, when golden flecks pierced through the barriers of my prison. I usually ended up refusing just to get the look from his face and out of my thoughts. Just as I lifted the glass to my lips, a familiar shiver rolled down my spine again.

I set the glass down faster than I'd been able to lift it to my lips. "Do you have something you need to say or are you just making sure I'm not trying to make a run for it?" I tucked strands of hair behind my ear then tapped my fingernails on the glass, waiting.

"What if I just wanted some company?" Aeden took a step to the side from behind me, then sat in the stool next to mine. I took a sip from one of the cups, intentionally diverting my eyes from meeting with his. The knotting in my gut was now bordering on furious behavior.

I pushed my palm into my stomach, urging it to stop. "You *had* company." I inclined my head over to where the blonde fae woman was flirting with a different, older man.

I glanced over, seeing Aeden's jaw set as he grated his knuckles along his 5 o'clock shadow that spread down his neck. The moment I noticed his eyes were glued to me, unwavering and unblinking, I shifted in my seat and quickly fixated on my cup again, taking another sip.

I could almost hear the distant smile on his mouth as he said, "Jealousy was always *my* thing when it came to you. Never yours." *Great.* More memories that I didn't have of some relationship I still couldn't fathom. Hooking up with him I could definitely picture. But loving him? No way in damn hell.

I reached up to rub at my temples. "Jealousy? You think I'm *jealous* of some woman? Over *you?*"

Because that certainly wasn't how I was feeling. I reassured the knots in my stomach, but they fought back harder with every inch of skin Aeden soaked in with his stare.

"I think"—he bent in and whispered softly, but loud enough for me to hear over the rest of the fae in the bar—"I *think* that even if you don't remember how great it felt when I had you pinned up against your kitchen counter, when you *begged* me not to stop, when you wanted nothing more for me to fuck your pain away—I think *that feeling* doesn't fade away with the rest of your memories." He pulled back as my heart started to hammer loudly in my chest, the scent of campfire smoke and earth leaving my small bubble of space right as heat built between my thighs.

What the actual *fuck?*

My fingers fumbled against my glass as I lifted it, taking long sips in strides to finish the glass before starting on the next one. I could feel the heat intensifying around me, all of it coming directly from him. He was covered, no one in the bar could see who he was or who I was, but that didn't stop his original nature from flaring. Others would mistake it for the amount of people crowding the room, but not me. I knew what that was because it happened more often than I liked to think about.

"You need to control yourself," I said to him, but also somewhat to myself. My heart wasn't settling even with the help of the alcohol I was consuming like rapid-fire while the remaining magic I had toiled violently under my skin. The air around us cooled almost instantly as he cleared his throat, then took a sip of his drink alongside me, his gaze finally leaving my body. If he were captured, I had no doubt in my mind that I would be captured too, and I couldn't be certain that either of our captures would end well. I needed to escape on my own, to get back to Prydia *not* in chains. It would be moronic if I let his power get us both discovered.

"It's getting harder to control myself around you," he admitted, his words going into his glass before he took another long sip.

The fact that elemental magic was so intertwined in emotions, like a virus feeding off of its host, was something I could relate to. As for the feelings he held for me, as much as I told myself I didn't understand it, some part told me that I did. Looking at Aeden was sometimes painful in the most conflicting of ways possible. I wanted to throttle him, scream at him over and over for taking away the right I had to claim my kingdom properly. He kept me as a prisoner and tied my fucking hands together rather than giving me a weapon to defend myself. But another part of me felt a gnawing, undeniable attraction to him, to his voice, to the way his muscles went taut when he practiced in the early hours of the morning and then softened whenever he approached the trees that I watched him from behind. And the way he made heat spread throughout my body...

Fucking alcohol.

I drained my last cup as we sat in silence. His looks spoke louder than any words could in the growing banter of the room. I needed to be alone, to stop the torturous thoughts that kept spreading. I stretched out my arms and faked a yawn. I'd been so consistently tired, my dreams never allowing a stable night of sleep, that it was believable. Believable enough for Aeden to dig into his pocket and pull out a key.

He jerked his hand back when I reached for it. "Don't. Run. Away." He enunciated each word as he clicked the keys against his palm, then laid it flat on the table with his brows furrowed. "Please."

"Yeah yeah, if I run, you'll find me. Got it." That didn't mean I wouldn't try it eventually, but the town we were in was so secluded from the rest of Aellethia that I truly had nowhere to run to where he or Vara wouldn't find me.

I stood and saluted him like a damn soldier, thanks to the alcohol making my brain a bit fuzzy, and turned on my heels to walk up the stairs, feeling four sets of eyes on my back as Murrie entered the bar and sat across from Shay and Seamus. I could almost sense the unease in each of those eyes, but perhaps proving them wrong by staying would get me closer to the escape I needed to make.

Chapter Five
Aeden

I'm a total, absolute, complete *fucking* idiot.

Hours after I'd given Paige the key to her room—the room meant just for the women because I'm a gentleman, and she deserved her space after everything I'd put her through—she went missing. Something told me to check on her, make sure the alcohol didn't bring up any torturous memories of her mother that had thankfully been wiped with her father's fucked-up poison. Either she learned to lie in a way that I was unfamiliar with, or I'm the fool everyone thinks I am when it comes to her.

Nevertheless, I walked into an empty room.

Everything I'd worked so hard for, to make sure she was safe, was now out the Stars-damned window. I glanced around her room, got on my knees to check under both beds, checked her small bathroom, and found nothing. The sounds of wind gusting snapped my attention to the walls where a thin door was ajar, leading into a closet. As I pulled open the door, a new flood of panic rolled over me, heating the walls as I struggled to contain my original nature.

Who the hell puts a window in the closet?

Of all places for a window, of course she would get a room with one more secluded. I could almost picture her small frame sliding through it with ease, her thinner curves barely touching the edges. There was no way I'd be able to fit through it to follow her.

If I rushed downstairs, I'd signal distress for the rest of our group, and I didn't need to be scolded for being so trusting when it came to her. But I'd had a few drinks, and seeing her get jealous over the girl who was throwing herself at me made me think she'd wanted to stay with me. That somewhere, deep down inside of her, the Paige who loved me back was coming to the surface. I raked a hand through my hair, analyzing the logistics of trying to fit through the window once more before turning and walking as calmly as I could back down to the bar.

I was tipsy after a few glasses of fae beer, but as I rounded the stairs, the sight of Murrie and Seamus singing while Shay danced with other patrons made me halt on the top step before continuing down the stairs. They were trashed and would be back to bickering at each other in the morning, but it made for an easy escape out the front door without so much as a glance from anyone.

Maybe if Paige had seen their behavior, she would've opted for the front door herself instead of climbing through a window to escape.

My hands were shaking as I got to one of the horses, adjusting the reins before hoisting myself over.

"Do you see her anywhere?" I called down the bond, silently scolding myself for triggering Varasyn to hunt for someone she had no interest in saving in the first place.

"Ha. I have not. But if you want me to search the town—"

She wasn't far then. *"No. I can't risk you being seen. Circle the outskirts and alert me if you have a lead."*

"I told you she was trouble. You should have let me scare her more before we left." Her voice was muffled, like she was eating again.

I adjusted myself on the saddle, fitting my feet into the stirrups. *"Keep to the fields. At least there's sheep there for you. Passed a few cows, too. Should be more than enough for you to not get us noticed."* I knew I was insulting her needs. She knew it too by the way she growled in reply. But she had to stop threatening Paige at some point. It was becoming exhausting, getting the people I cared about to care about each other like our little fucked up family was something to be proud of. To cherish.

The family that Paige had just broken.

"Good luck. I'll try not to drop any carcasses on her if I see her."

"You drop anything *on her and I'll have to question whether you really were the dragon hatched for me."* I flinched a little bit and I felt a sliver of tension go down our bond. Living in Aellethia was really doing a number on how callous I could be. In the mortal world, I wore it like a set of armor for protection while in foster care. But here, in my true home, I felt it shift to a weapon like the hatchets tucked into the back of my waistband. I could almost imagine how Eoghan's behavior was justified when he pushed me through the portal. He did what he had to, just like I was doing.

"I'm the best one for you." My head cocked to the side at her slip-up. Her immediate silence afterwards let me know that she hadn't meant to let it out, had let me in on more information than she should have. *So, there are others.*

I tugged on the reins, needing to find Paige before she got too far, before Varasyn was the one who found her and not me. I knew she wouldn't hurt her in reality, or maybe I told myself she wouldn't just to make myself feel better. At this point, I didn't have any other options that wouldn't wreak havoc on our already fragile group. The group that was bonding quite well inside the bar while I hunted down the last member.

A shiver rolled down my spine and the sensation that someone was watching me drew my eyes to a cluster of trees, then another as I searched. My eyes rolled over the streets that few fae walked on as the night turned into early morning, then shifted my gaze to roaming along the roof lines. I froze as I took in a dark figure sitting on the roof of the inn. A small, feminine body, with hair that waved down the curve of their back as they looked up at the stars.

Her.

The panic settled instantly and the horse snorted as I leapt off, tying the reins back to the post it was hitched to. I patted its mane and moved to the side of the building, then used my earth magic to create stumps in a raised spiral. It was draining, but using earth magic in a territory ruled by Buryon, the earth kingdom, seemed less attention-drawing than the rest of my powers would be. And there was no way I'd be able to use my air magic to float me up there. Using it on dead animals after I hunted them to bring them back to camp without leaving a trace? Sure. They were already dead—no harm, no foul. But truthfully, I was absolute shit at air-wielding, and using it to raise my own body was well out of the question.

She didn't move, didn't shift her eyes from the stars as I approached her and took up a position next to her on the roof. "I thought you left." I cleared my throat to cover the quaver in my voice. But she heard how fragile, how scared I'd been at the thought. I couldn't help but be vulnerable when it came to her, and I wasn't the best at concealing it from her, either.

She took in a deep breath, then exhaled and pulled her knees to her chest. I'd noticed her doing that more often here than she did in the mortal world. Like she was hiding, or afraid to uncoil and show who she really was, even though I knew her better than anyone else I'd ever known.

"No, I told you I wouldn't. Remember?" Her eyes flicked to me, then back to the stars. "Do you think—" she began, then wrapped her arms tighter around her legs. "Do you think they will let me try again?"

I followed her gaze up to the stars that winked and shined brighter than any stars ever had in the mortal world. Or maybe I'd never noticed because back in Jessup, the stars were almost irrelevant. Just dimly lit orbs of gas. Here—here, they were gods.

My brows lowered as I looked back at her. "The Triad?" I asked.

She nodded into her knees, then rested her chin and tilted her head toward me. This was the girl who was my best friend. The girl who'd stolen my heart time and time again in Jessup, and every second of every minute in Aellethia. No one questioned the Stars or their behavior here, and I doubted anyone who survived the Triad would ever dream of entering it again. But she would—she would enter in a heartbeat because she was just that stubborn and hated to surrender to anything or anyone in life.

"I think they'd be idiots not to let you try if that's what you want." I wanted to reach out, stroke my hand down her cheek. Anything to reassure her.

Her back stiffened as she laid her legs out flat against the slope of the roof, then put her hands back to brace her weight as she leaned back. Every soft feature of her face turned cold and dark. "Of course, it's what I want. *You* took that from me."

I winced, letting her reality wash over me again. I sympathized with her, I truly did. But the Triad was going to get her killed, and I couldn't let that happen. I couldn't live without her.

"There has to be another way, the Stars—"

"The *Stars* don't give a damn about me, about any of us. They wanted a victor, and I wasn't it."

I rubbed the fire mark under my sleeve. "No," I breathed out. "I didn't enter the Triad. There are ways around the stars."

Her eyes narrowed on me. "Your kingdom is gone. Your people, your *mother*, murdered by my rightful kingdom. If you even have a kingdom left to rule, how do you know they will let you?"

I hadn't thought about anyone being against me taking up the position that was rightfully mine. But she had a point. The Triad showed your worthiness, not only to the Stars themselves but to the people of Aellethia. Seamus, Shay and Murrie were so certain that I'd be welcomed with open arms that they hadn't considered any other possibilities, any animosity toward me ruling a fallen kingdom, if there was anything left of it to rule to begin with. I'd been under the impression that the fae left would, in fact, welcome me without question.

But what if that wasn't the case?

"Fuck," I said.

She nodded. "Fuck is right."

A rustling sound came from the trees beyond the inn, right at the border of the town. I would have shrugged it off as wind, but the lack of a breeze on the roof, where Paige and I sat in silence as I contemplated what the hell I was trying to accomplish in the first place, made me still. Made both of us still.

"You still can't feel your air magic, can you?"

She shook her head, eyes fixed on the trees as she reached for her empty pockets reflexively.

"Aeden, I smell naga. Are you okay?"

"Naga," I whispered, leaping up onto my feet in a crouched position on the slanted roof. The noise from the bar below hummed in the foreground while the hissing noise in the trees intensified.

"How's your water magic?"

"Really?" she replied. "You ask that *now*? If you think I could wield it better than you, don't you think I would have used that to escape?"

Fair point.

"You passed that trial using water magic, right?" My hands reached for the hatchets, my fingers flexing tightly around the handles before pinching my eyes shut, pushing down the doubt that popped up in my head, the voice that called me an idiot for what I was about to do.

Or maybe that was Varasyn, warning me.

"Here. Take this. I assume you know how to use it?" She scoffed, telling me she knew it well enough as I placed one of the hatchets on the roof in the small space between us. Without looking away from the trees, Paige wrapped her fingers around the handle, her nails scraping against the roof. If she decided to lodge the thing in my head, and use it to escape, I'd never hear the end of it. That is, if she used the end of the hatchet that wouldn't instantly kill me, opting to knock me out instead by pure mercy.

"You sure you want to give me this?" she asked.

"I trust you." But I shouldn't.

"You shouldn't," she responded, no doubt contemplating which end to use on me before advancing toward the nagas. I didn't fully trust her thoughts, but I wasn't oblivious to the way she'd been watching me. She may have been analyzing my strategies, perhaps learning how to fight me when the time came. But she was also attracted to me, held *something* for me in her heart with every eye-fuck she laid over me as I trained shirtless. Which is part of the reason I did it daily.

How was I so oblivious to that fact in Jessup?

She won't try to kill me.

Right?

The hissing doubled, tripled, then turned into a menagerie of sounds and snapping teeth as they emerged from the woods. There were at least ten of them.

"Shit," she whispered.

Shit was right. We were outnumbered, and alerting the people inside would cause a frenzy.

"We can do this." My knuckles grazed her hand on the roof, and to my surprise, her finger grazed mine back. Or maybe I imagined it.

Her lips rolled in as the nagas drew eerily close, then without hesitation, she leapt from the roof. I clambered after her, more following to protect her, to be the shield she didn't really look like she needed as she lifted the hatchet at her side.

I knew we'd need a plan. She'd need to work with me, not against me. "We split them down the middle, draw them back into the—"

And then she took off, running for the biggest motherfucker of them all in the center.

Dammit, Paige.

I summoned vines from the ground to anchor the largest one down while the others raced for both of us, spreading their numbers in a circle like the fire that caged in Paige during her last trial. Paige was closing in on the big one, arms raised as she clutched onto the hatchet. She leaned back while running and threw it forward with precision, her training led by another Mora clearly paying off more than I anticipated.

The vines at his feet distracted him long enough for his head to bow, to claw at the vines as the hatchet drove into the middle of his lowered head. He fell to the ground as Paige approached, yanking her hatchet free and moving onto the next without batting an eye as the nagas blood poured into the grass and the others wailed in fury.

I swallowed, watching her move the way she was. We were stronger here, born and bred to be weapons. But she'd fascinated me long before I knew any of that.

Thinking back to that log, where her daggers had been, and the damage she probably dreamed of dealing out to me—

I pushed that down and flicked my wrist, forming a thick wall of ice around us like Seamus had done that day I killed a hag, blocking out the nagas from us, and Paige and I from them.

"What are you doing?" she yelled, halting at the massive wall I'd built and turning on her heels to face me.

"You ran before I could tell you the plan. We need a plan." I folded my arms over my chest, glaring down at her. So many things could go wrong. Too many. She could get hurt, and that was the only wrong thing I cared about.

"We don't *need* a fucking plan, Aeden. We *need* to stop them before they get to the inn!" She forced both arms down to her sides, her fist tightening around the handle of the hatchet. If she was sneering at me, I could all but acknowledge it. I was too focused on the way she looked holding a weapon.

The clawing sounds snapped me back to reality. "With a plan, beautiful." The hissing rolled over the edges of the ice as the nagas continued to claw their fang-like nails in, scaling the wall slower than a hag could.

Paige held her arm out to the wall of ice, her face flushing with anger or maybe it was the way I still found time to flirt with her. "*This* is your plan? To hide behind a wall?"

"Annihilate them, Aeden. The girl is right."

The nagas were reaching the top of the wall finally as I stared down at her, their tongues and teeth focusing on her more than me. I couldn't lose her to them. To anyone. The power under my flesh grew hot as the fire begged to be set free. To protect her at all costs.

The heat in the air spread and Paige grinned up at me, like she'd won. Because she always did, and she always would. "You ready now, Fire Boy?" she taunted.

"For you? Always." With a flick of my wrist I melted the ice with my flames, the change from solid to liquid making the nagas fall on their faces. Paige leaned back and threw her blood-soaked hatchet into the head of another naga that stumbled up first. I did the same to the next. And then there were seven left.

"Vines!" she shouted, and without blinking I braced the legs of the few she was next to. She formed a spear of ice, although small, and threw it like a dagger into the head of another. The look of shock on her face told me she didn't expect to be able to wield that well since being poisoned. But she did.

"Yes!" She punched a fist into the air as I took up the hatchet from the skull of another naga. I turned and saw Paige heading for another, but two were coming up behind her. Too fast.

"Paige!" I shouted, feeling the fear boil over as my fire begged to be released again, to burn all of them to the ground as they neared her, fanged claws raised in the air.

"Are you alright? I'm coming!"

"No!" I shouted back down the bond to Varasyn. She couldn't risk it. *I* couldn't risk it.

I flicked my hand, setting the fire free under the feet of the two nagas, then gusted air into their stomachs, pushing them back while their bodies burned like they were coated in gasoline.

Paige turned, her eyes darting between the two for a split-second before she pulled her hatchet from the one she'd just taken down and leaned back, flinging the hatchet right toward my head.

I ducked, narrowly evading the ax. My brows pinched together as I stood there, tilted over as if the ax was still coming my way. *Did she really just try to kill me?*

A wail erupted behind me and I tossed my head off my shoulder just in time to see a naga clawing at their stomach, innards spilling from the open wound Paige had just sliced open with the hatchet that now lay in the grass further beyond it.

But that couldn't be right. She...she *saved* me.

My jaw slackened a fraction before I righted myself. "You're welcome!" she cried out as she bolted past me to get her weapon.

There was only one left, one terrified naga who began *retreating* back into the woods. I lifted my finger, waving it side to side at the naga before moving my wrist just enough to set it ablaze right at the edge of the woods.

The naga fell to its knees, hissing and wailing in terror as it melted rapidly, flesh falling and sizzling to the ground in chunks. With as many dead naga around as there was, I doubted more would follow. I pushed past the draining feeling in my bones, sending the remaining bodies back to the woods with gusts of air, loving the way their limp bodies slapped against the trees before they fell.

Paige walked up beside me, then reluctantly held out the hatchet for me as I scanned the outside of the inn—not a fae in sight. I was glad for the stupor that fae alcohol put on anyone who drank too much of it, even if that meant I was the victim of it at times.

"How'd you know I'd duck?" I lifted my eyebrow at her as I lifted the hatchet from her splayed hand, not missing the chance to graze my fingers over hers before pulling back and tucking the hatchet back into my waistband. She folded her arms across her chest, then turned to face me after evaluating the inn for herself, and if I wasn't mistaken by the darkness of the field we were in, I'd almost say she was smiling before she hung her head low.

"I just knew." She shrugged, then faced away from me and began walking back toward the inn, avoiding the roof and heading to the front instead. She intended to go back to the room.

She wasn't escaping.

"I'm alright. We're fine. No one was hurt." I rubbed my palms together as the power beneath my flesh began to settle.

"Good." Varasyn's voice was muffled again. She must have a lot of faith in me if she went right back to eating that quickly. I chuckled to myself, then trailed behind Paige, closing the distance as she reached for the door.

"Thank you," I whispered low. She held onto the handle and blinked once. Then twice. Then nodded up at me with her beautiful emerald irises meeting mine for a few blissful seconds.

My heart pounded under my ribs, not just from the adrenaline from the fight and the depletion of power that was setting in fast. But, from her. From *those eyes*. From the pain of not having her like I really wanted her, like I *needed* her. My hands twitched at my sides, longing to draw my fingers through her hair, to pull her close to me and thank her with more than my words.

We were safe. She *was safe. She didn't run.*

She didn't hurt me.

She saved *me.*

Chapter Six

PAIGE

Why did I save him?

It would have been easy to let the nagas get him. To let their fang-like claws sink into him. Poison him. Murrie would've ended up healing him anyway, so why the heck did I save him? My heart fluttered and my stomach knotted violently when he held my gaze, *my gaze*, the one *I initiated*, at the door of the inn instead of just staring at the door like I should have.

Those *damn* golden-flecked, brown eyes.

I tossed and turned a lot that night, thinking about the fact that I saved Aeden from being hurt, and what that meant for me and him. He said he trusted me and handed me a hatchet. The same guy who kept me as a prisoner and took my daggers from me ended up needing my help, and had trusted me enough to let me help him, or hoped that I would help him.

And I did.

I stupidly did.

"Mornin' lass," Seamus hollered up at me as I descended the stairs slowly. A flash of brown, tousled hair beside Seamus made me jerk my head elsewhere as quickly as it had fallen to where it should never go. I needed anywhere to look that wasn't near the man I'd saved the night before. A cloaked figure shuffled in his seat near the window by the door, as if answering my plea. Although I couldn't see his eyes past the black hood he had over his head, I could feel the coldness of them on me, the way they were watching my every move. I rubbed my hand along my sleeve as I continued walking down the last few steps.

I didn't know whose attention to ignore more—the cloaked man's, or the one who made me constantly too aware of his presence. I wished a window were at the end of the stairs, open and waiting. I'd jump through it in a heartbeat. I went from rubbing my arm to rubbing along my waist at the gnawing sensations that toiled beneath as I walked up to the table. To where *he* was.

Shay slid a mug in front of me as I sat down beside her. "I don't drink that crap," I muttered, my nose scrunching up at the smell of what passed as coffee in this world. She just shrugged her shoulders and turned her attention back to whatever Seamus was talking about, continuing to drink from her mug.

As much as I tried not to look right in front of me, I failed entirely as Aeden cocked a grin. He swiped his fingers through his freshly showered hair, still smiling at me with that stupid grin that made his cheek indent before he lifted his mug and took a sip.

His eyes never left me, his mug staying low while he sipped. He pulled the mug from his face, and I continued watching as his lips rolled together. Everything inside of me churned, but I couldn't look away. I folded my arms along the table and threw my head down on top of them when I'd noticed just how long I'd been staring at his mouth for. The others would assume I was hungover—if only that could take the blame for the way my body was reacting to him. Again.

Something was seriously wrong with me.

"The lad here tells me ye had a wee bit o' fun last night?" Seamus cocked a brow at me as I lifted my head, my eyes gluing to the golden specks in Aeden's eyes that seemed to light up more with the reminder.

"Yeah, you could say that." His chin jerked toward me. "Thanks to Paige here, the inn wasn't taken over by more rogue nagas."

Shay breathed out heavily and I didn't have to turn to know that she was smiling because she was clearly proud of me again for all the wrong reasons. "Really?"

I rolled my eyes between her and him. So, that was the story, then. Nothing about him thinking I had escaped and me calling him out about the fact that he didn't have a kingdom like he thought he did.

"Yeah, sure," I said. It seemed like he left out the fact that I saved him, and maybe that was his way of letting me sit with what I'd done on my own. He raised a brow at me and smirked like he was reading my thoughts and I threw my head back down and groaned.

"Aye, the girl still wants ye, Boyo," Seamus said low, forcing my attention back to the man across from me. Seamus tilted the corner of his mouth, nudging Aeden's shoulder with his own as I turned back to see who the *girl* was.

"Don't remind me," he replied, folding an arm and pinching the bridge of his nose as he closed his eyes. I craned my head over my shoulder further until I could see the blonde waitress, her hair mussed and her eyes glassy as she looked over at Aeden. The waitress' gaze flicked between our table and another, prompting my eyes to move from her to the man who was now sliding himself in between Aeden and Seamus, the hood of his cloak now pulled down, resting on his broad shoulders.

He was stunning, with vibrant green eyes that were almost neon, save for the darker circle of evergreen that shone around his pupils, like what the top of a forest would look like until you went below, into the shadows. His russet skin and black, closely cropped, tight curls brought out the intensity of his eyes as they honed in on me, ignoring everyone else at the table.

"Good morning, gorgeous. Can I get you something else to drink? I noticed you didn't like the coffee." He lifted a finger from where they propped his head up beneath his stubbled chin, pointing to my mug that sat in front of Shay.

Aeden cleared his throat and glared at the mystery man under hooded eyes as he took his mug back into his hand. He squeezed so tightly, I thought the cup would shatter.

I blinked away from his whitened fingers just as the man spoke again.

"Oh, how rude of me. I'm Lee." Lee waved at the waitress who grinned back at him like she knew him well.

Seamus' hand flew across the table. "Mornin', I—"

"I don't remember extending an invitation, *Lee*," Aeden interrupted Seamus, deciding against being friendly. Seamus curled his fingers in as he pulled his hand back to his side, looking paler than usual. Aeden fixed his attention on me and cocked his head to the side like he was trying to figure out what I'd do. Seeing if I'd entertain the stranger who'd just called me gorgeous. We hadn't left the Fields—hadn't interacted with other people—before now, but I registered the look on Aeden's face and the way his jaw clenched as Lee got comfortable in his seat. My memories of him were gone, but I remembered other men in the mortal world.

Aeden was jealous.

I let a soft smile curve up as I held out my hand. "Actually, I would love one. That tastes like what I'd imagine horse piss would taste like. I'm—"

"Leaving." Aeden made the table shudder as he thrust his mug down. "We were just leaving. Weren't we, *gorgeous*?" I could feel the heat rising in my cheeks, crawling up from my neck. Lee could have called me gorgeous a thousand times and it wouldn't hold a candle to the effect Aeden's voice had on my body when he nearly purred it. I squeezed my thighs together under the table and shifted in my seat.

Seamus choked on the sip he'd taken, trying to hide his face as he stroked his beard. He nudged his head toward the bar, and without hesitation, Shay gathered both her mug and mine and followed Seamus away from the table.

"Well now, look what you did. You made the whole gang leave." Lee pouted dramatically, watching Seamus and Shay as they moved away from us.

Aeden's knuckles turned white as his fingers curled in along the table and the heat in the room rose in a telling sign. He was jealous *and* annoyed. "What is it that you want?"

Lee let out a low whistle and fanned himself as the table fell silent. "There is no need to simmer, um, what is it you said your name was?"

Shit. He noticed the heat in the room. Aeden adjusted his sleeves, the motion of his hands raking up like he'd chosen against hiding the flames along his arm making my breath hitch. His gaze slid to mine as he held the fabric in his hands, then they softened as he pulled his sleeve down further instead. "I didn't."

"Ah, that's right. My mistake." The way Lee smiled back at us was like he'd come here for the sole purpose of messing with Aeden. He wasn't interested in getting me a drink, or *me*, at all.

"If you'd like to get me a new drink, I'll take a double of whatever you're offering." I needed Lee to leave. No one could know about Aeden, because that would lead them to me. We'd both be captured. Killed.

Lee smirked at Aeden, then cracked his fingers as he stood from the table. "I like a woman who knows what she wants." His black cloak brushed the edges of his ankles, giving way to the well-constructed leather boots that covered his feet. Feet that moved with a stealth I'd witnessed before, as if he'd hinged his life on moving in silence.

Aeden leaned in close over the table, his voice dipping low as he said, "We need to leave. Go meet Murrie out by the horses, and make sure your jacket is on tight."

I scoffed. "Says the man who almost chose his pride over our safety." I stood and adjusted the jacket he'd given me, ignoring the way his guilt had broken our eye contact. "I know what to do," I added. Because I didn't want to go back to Prydia as a prisoner, and we couldn't trust anyone. Especially not the incredibly stealthy man who hinted at knowing exactly why the room was warmer than the season outside allowed for.

He nodded, shifting his weight as he stood, examining my movements and jacket from the corner of his eye like I couldn't see the fear that was clear as day on his face. Lee was deep in conversation with the bartender and the waitress, too engaged to see the nod of Seamus' head as we all worked our way outside.

Aeden didn't bother to bind my hands when we got back on our horses, and my legs were free on the edges of the stirrups. I told myself it was because we were in a hurry, but when he offered the hatchet back to me, I realized maybe he was starting to trust me.

Varasyn flew above us, disguised in the clouds, but if one squinted their eyes hard enough, they'd catch the shadow of her wings rippling in and out of wisps of white where the cotton color warred with the red and gold of her wings. It was faint, but I saw her, and so could Aeden as he walked beside our horses. I silently wondered if she knew that I now had a weapon, and if Aeden was being constantly scolded for giving it to me with every glance he threw to the sky.

Seamus' baritone voice brought me back from the clouds as it carried on the wind back to our horse, which meant I not only overheard we were heading towards Costa, but I also knew that Aeden had been hit on quite a few times by the waitress. So much so that she'd gone to his room at some point in the night and offered herself to him. I couldn't hear what had come of that, because where Seamus was all baritone and breathy, Aeden's voice was softer, gentler and low. Like he knew I'd be listening. I tried to ignore how much I wanted to know that he had rejected her. *If* he had rejected her. Their conversation moved to the man that sat at our table uninvited, the words "fucker" and "gorgeous" quite loud, but when Aeden turned back and saw me leaning over the neck of the horse to hear them both better, he flashed a wink at me. I scowled back at him and moved back to tune him out completely.

When we'd made our way far enough from Easrich, Vara flew down and took up Aeden on her back, the movement so natural to him now, he looked like he'd been born on her back and had never gone a day without her.

And then we fell into painful silence for nearly an hour before I finally gave in. "How far is Costa?" I asked, because that's the only thing that popped into my mind. I didn't really care how far we were from Costa, but I knew they were focusing on that town in particular. Costa was Aerborne territory—my father's lands. It was honestly intriguing they believed it was worth going there in the first place more than it was on the *how* we were going to get there part.

Murrie sighed and answered, "Costa is about a week away at this rate. Maybe more if we have to stop along the Amaliro Mountains. The wards will be up there as well, but not under Buryon's Mora, Leander." She shifted her hold on the reins. "I believe Eoghan Waterborne is someone you know?"

Something snapped, a twig or a branch in the distance by the fading treeline behind us. Perhaps it was just a deer. I doubted any more nagas would try to fight us again anytime soon, and being as there were no hissing noises, I shrugged it off, loosening the fist I held around the handle of my hatchet I kept in my lap.

"He trained me." Our horse slowed from a trot as we continued along a mossy field at the edge of a steep cliff overlooking the ocean just outside of Easrich. "Oh, he's also fucking my brother." Murrie made a garbled sound behind me, spitting with a roaring laugh that I wasn't expecting. He was, in fact, *in bed* with my brother, as my father had put it. But he also loved my brother. My brother who I'd never met, but was quite certain I'd seen before in my dreams more than once.

Find Ikelos. It was the one thing Eoghan told me. The one thing I held on to after waking up from the fitful nights of sleep I'd had. And once I was free, I'd find him. At first, I pushed it aside like he was an unreachable object, and I had accepted that as my new normal. But with this hatchet in my possession and a seed of trust planted, it was beginning to feel more and more possible. A reality I could *see.*

Murrie adjusted herself and her weapon strapped across her back, shifting the saddle I was sitting on until she stopped. "Right, well, Ikelos is a good-looking young man. And so kind. It's a shame he failed his Triad. He would've made a great Mora."

My back went straight as I turned to look at her just over my shoulder. "You know my brother?"

"Not really *know,* more know *of.* But yeah. Everyone knows of him. He competed, after all, and didn't die. That's a feat of its own. I guess it's something you both share in common now." I rubbed at my forehead, looking back up to the clouds where Aeden rode on Varasyn's back, the cloud coverage increasing so much that I could no longer decipher what was a darker cloud or what was her shadow.

The image of my father flashed in my mind. That glass of wine he offered me, hoping I'd end up dead. My fist wrapped back around the handle of the hatchet. "Yeah. We both didn't die. What a feat." I laid the sarcasm on thick and Murrie squeezed either side of my waist as she tugged on the reins. Both horses came to a stop. I looked up again, the darkening clouds spreading as they reached lower.

When did it get so dark?

"We need to stop and make camp!" Murrie called to Seamus, who nodded in response before he jumped off his horse and helped Shay off next. The sounds of wingbeats filled the space above us and right after Murrie and I slid off, Varasyn swooped in to land, making both horses rear up.

"I got it, Seamus." Aeden slid down the side of his dragon, making quick work of his magic to make domes from bent trees and vines that came from the earth, bending however he wanted them to. Seamus threw pelts inside of each dome as I examined the thatching Aeden managed with his magic. It was impeccable, and if I weren't so agitated by him all the time, I'd compliment him for it. But I bit my tongue, and walked up to one of the domes.

A third, smaller dome formed beside the one I approached, and I immediately knew it was his. He always slept just outside of my prison, and although I wasn't being caged in anymore, it didn't seem like he was ready to change that aspect yet. If ever. Shay and Seamus shuffled into their dome as the sky grew black and heavier. Murrie and I went into the other, and the close rustling sound just before the rain hit the ground let me know that Aeden had made his way inside of his. The rain was cold, and just as I rubbed along the sleeves of Aeden's jacket I kept on the entire time to keep hidden and warm, a small fire formed in a ditch in the center of our dome. I looked up, noticing the dome even had a chute for the smoke to seep out through that miraculously didn't accept any water in as the smoke trailed out.

There was no way he'd gotten laid the night before because his magic seemed to be replenished and ready. No, unlike me, he'd gotten decent sleep. That shouldn't have been my first thought, but it was.

He had rejected the doe-eyed blonde.

"He's getting stronger every day, that boy. What a kind gesture," Murrie cooed as she adjusted two pelts on the floor for us to rest on. The rain and wind battered ruthlessly along the walls of the warm dome and the faintest smile spread across my face as I listened to the sounds. I loved rainstorms. "I heard you saved him. We are all grateful that you decided against…you know." She drew a finger across her neck and hung her head to the side with her tongue out.

So he did tell them about what I did. Yet Shay acted as if she didn't know.

Interesting.

"You're welcome, I guess." I laid my head down facing away from her. I couldn't comprehend why I'd saved him in the first place and I knew if I said anything else to Murrie, either with my emotions I struggled to mask on my face or with the words that could spill from my mouth, she'd run it straight to him. So I kept silent after that, trying to keep thoughts of Aeden out of my mind.

As the rain and thunder fell into a rhythm outside, I drifted off to sleep.

Chapter Seven
Aeden

I couldn't sleep.

Again.

Paige continued to whimper in hers, and as much as I needed to rest, to be ready to wield my magic in case we ran into more trouble, I couldn't fall asleep knowing she was in some kind of pain. And I'd had enough of letting her succumb to whatever she was going through on her own.

I bent to exit my dome and entered hers, being vigilant not to stir Murrie awake as she snored. Paige was curled in on herself, her fingers balled into fists as her body twitched over and over. She never spoke of nightmares in Jessup, but ever since I saved her from the arena, there weren't many nights where she didn't have one.

She murmured a name that sounded an awful lot like Hector, the fucker who guarded Gedeon, and let out a small scream, curling into herself more. My head flicked over to Murrie, sleeping soundly as if she'd grown used to the noise and was accustomed to sleeping through it. Something I'd never be able to do, not when it came to her.

I crouched down, uncertain if I should wake her or curl up next to her. One glance at the hatchet tucked into her jacket had me sliding down the edge of her dome next to where she laid, not touching her but close enough to watch over her. Her face contorted in pain and it took every ounce of willpower within me to remain still, to keep my hands off of her as she would want if she were awake.

Her body trembled, her arms shaking for seconds that went on like hours until she finally relaxed against the pelt of one of the animals I'd hunted down. In some way, it eased the tension in my chest just knowing that something I did was helping her, comforting her.

I tilted my head back against the dome, and finally drifted off to sleep.

A sharp blade pressed against my throat, jolting my eyes wide-the-fuck open.

"Why are you in here?" Paige whisper-shouted at me, giving just enough pressure to the hatchet to keep me still, yet not enough to draw blood.

Her green eyes went wide as I leaned into the blade. "Are you going to hurt me, Paige?" It was bold. It was fucking stupid, too. But I had to know if saving me the other night meant something more, that *I* meant something more to her than she cared to let out. And when her eyes dipped down to my lips for a fraction of a second, I couldn't hide the cocky grin from spreading on my face. She let out a huff and pulled the hatchet from my neck, then stormed out of the dome.

It was dark out, water coating the grass making it slick. But that didn't stop Paige from bolting to the cliff's edge. My strides covered the distance in half the time. She turned her head, checking my pace as she ran and then increased her speed.

Was this her attempt at running?

"The girl is getting away, want me to—"

"No. I've got it."

"You never let me finish wh—"

"I said, I've. Got. It."

Varasyn huffed in frustration as the sounds of her wingbeats came in from behind me then faded away again just as quickly.

Paige stopped running right before the edge of the cliff, her shoulders curling in as she watched me catch up to her before she took a seat in the wet grass that was more like moss. More slippery, more unforgiving if one of us got any closer to that ledge.

I stopped beside her, her chest heaving as her fingers clung to the handle of the hatchet. She pulled her knees to her chest. "Why won't you let me leave?" she asked with a twinge of annoyance lacing her words. I sat down next to her, making sure that we were far apart enough that she couldn't press the blade to my neck again but close enough for us to talk.

It was fucking time we talked.

My eyes slid over her, noting the way she was closing herself off the second I got closer. I wanted her to open up to me. I needed her to. Even if that meant I'd have to be more vulnerable than I'd ever been. I exhaled through my nose, feeling that deep weight in my chest sink further. "I can't let you leave when that means you could die."

"I can protect myself," she bit out, raising the hatchet against the moonlight, letting the blade glint as she twisted it in her hand while her other arm held on tightly to her knees.

I let out a laugh. "I know that." How could I not? She'd proven herself in the Triad, and slaughtered nagas like it was just another Monday. Like she'd been born for it, because she was.

"Then why." A demand, not a question.

I pulled my hand down my face, then stared back at her whereas she refused to meet my gaze back. "I can't lose you again." I paused, choosing my next words carefully.

Her arm shifted around her knees, her legs straightening a fraction. Vulnerability didn't exactly come easy to me, either. But around her, I'd turned soft. Malleable. Breakable. "They say if you love something, you should let it go. But that doesn't work for me. I can't let you go, and there was a time you didn't want me to. I've waited years for you, Paige. Sometimes it feels like I've waited my entire life. Just for you. And until you remember that, until you have all the memories back that your shithead father stole from you, I'll keep fighting to keep you close to me. Where you belong. Where we *both* belong. With *each other*."

She twirled the handle again and again, evaluating everything quietly to herself as she often did. I used to think that was part of her trauma from having an absent mother and having no one to vent to until I came along. But she'd forgotten her mother as well, and now I recognized it as her way of making sure whatever came next from her mouth was just the way she wanted it to be. Second guessing herself, always so...unsure.

She looked out beyond the ledge, toward the Stars themselves. "I could run right now." She tossed the hatchet into the air and caught it by the handle again. "I could use this against you and fight my way free." Her fingers flexed around the handle.

"You could," I agreed. "But I don't think you will." The hatchet stilled in her hand right as she was leaning it back to possibly toss it in the air again. I knew she trained in wielding weapons for the Triad. Knew she probably poured every ounce of her being into learning, all to get free. And watching the way she fought the nagas...it was intimidating, to say the least. But some idiotic part of me was certain I'd never be on the receiving end. She'd stop herself before she'd actually wound me.

"You're too confident in that. Giving me *this* just proves that."

"And you've proven that you won't kill me with it. I ducked, and you *still* gave me the hatchet back." I reached a hand to the back of my neck as she shook her head, her shoulders moving with a faint laugh.

"If I *actually* went after you, if I managed to press this into that thick skull of yours, I'm sure I wouldn't get far. Not with your dragon ready to filet me for breakfast."

I shrugged as Vara huffed through my thoughts. "That's how you feel now. I can tell you that you were far from wanting to kill me back in Jessup. In fact, I think you actually l—"

She turned her head, eyes meeting mine finally. "What makes you so certain that even when my memories do return, I'd want to *stay* with you, no matter what happened in the past? How can you possibly believe this is all going to play out in your favor when that day comes?"

The hatchet slicing open my throat would hurt less than the invisible wound she delivered to my chest. The fact was, I couldn't be sure of any of it—the depth of her feelings for me, her memories ever coming back, her trauma taking over again once they did, *if* they did. Just like the realization that my own kingdom, whatever remained of the people of Vizna, might not want me back. I hadn't contemplated the aftermath of Paige's memories returning and it *not* putting us right back to where we were that last day in Jessup.

All I wanted was to keep her closer, yet all I seemed to do was push her farther away.

My silence echoed louder than any words could have, the distance between us more like miles as she nodded her head and turned back to the ocean, to the damn Stars in front of us, reveling in the heartbreak that kept rolling over me.

I didn't know it was possible to hurt so much. That love could be my undoing.

I knew I had to keep fighting for us, fighting for the love that I'd put all hope into. One of us had to, every fiber of my being, every pulse of my power under my skin, told me that this was right. That *we* were right. If I had to wait centuries for her, I would. I would be a patient man. Just for her.

I shook my head, curling my fist in against the mossy grass as she pretended to focus on the handle of the hatchet again. "He may have taken me from your mind, but he can't take the way I know you feel about me from your heart. You just have to stop being so damn stubborn and accept it because pushing you from my mind would almost, *almost*, be a luxury right now, like I know for a fact that you keep doing whenever you catch yourself thinking about me." My hand shook as I pushed it through my hair. "At least then it wouldn't hurt so fucking much to look at you, to know that you hate me and that you think you would be better off somewhere else. Somewhere away from me."

Her eyes narrowed on the Stars as I stood up and left her, my chest aching and tears welling to the surface. I'd never cried over a woman, much less anything, but Paige was always the exception.

She always would be.

CHAPTER EIGHT
PAIGE

I was so screwed.

As soon as Aeden left, I felt the power surge under my flesh. It was uncontrollable, like the air and water had been when they first took root inside me. Like the willow tree that just sprouted and grew rapidly in the exact spot where Aeden had been sitting, spreading its roots in the ground beneath me. The edges of the weeping strands taunted me, brushing over my cheek in a gentle caress as a tear rolled down it.

The earth spread through my veins and across my back, and for a brief moment, a small gust of air weaved its way through my body, the faintest trickle of power reemerging alongside the earth and water before it vanished again. My back stiffened as my head turned over my shoulder to find Varasyn's wings spread out wide as she took off with Aeden on her back, flying over the domes that glowed faintly in the distance.

I wiped at the tear along my jaw. He'd cage me in again if he knew I'd developed another elemental power. Giving me a hatchet was one thing, but gaining more power? That was a threat. My father had taught me that much. There was no other option than to keep it hidden. And I really didn't need to show just how much Aeden had influenced the new development on my back.

I would spend days convincing myself it wasn't because of him. If the mark was of flames across my back, the moss ashen beneath my feet, then I'd have an even bigger problem, knowing one hundred percent that it was all because of him and the way he was working his way under my skin.

I had hurt him.

I'd hurt him and now a tree was there as evidence, showing me that even though I *wanted* to hurt him, actually doing it felt...wrong. I'd hit a nerve—a soft spot that no threats with a hatchet seemed to reach. And knowing that *I* was that soft spot made my stomach twist all over again.

I tried to flick my wrist, send the tree back into the earth like Aeden repeatedly demonstrated mastering, but ended up pulling a singular root up from the ground. It looked as if a crowbar had forced its way underneath and failed pathetically to conquer the entire tree, and I was that crowbar. I was that wedge that just kept lifting and didn't know when to stop.

I raised the hatchet, then glanced back to the tree, then to the hatchet again, and finally to the night sky over the ocean.

"Shit," I murmured to myself.

Chopping it down would be tedious with such a small blade, but if I had to choose between hard work and imprisonment, over showing that some part of me *did* care when I didn't want to acknowledge that at all, I'd choose the first option a thousand times over.

I got to work, chopping at a tree as thick as both my thighs combined as quietly as I could before Aeden and his watchdog in the skies noticed what I was doing. Why couldn't it be flowers, or grass? A small sprig that refused to grow, knowing how much he'd wronged me. Why did it have to be something so obvious as a willow tree in an open field with absolutely no trees? On the edge of a moss-covered rocky cliff where things shouldn't be able to grow, no less.

But that was my luck.

With the tree gone, chopped and kicked over the edge of the cliff and down into the crashing waves below, I sent a silent thanks to the Stars for Aeden's absence. The fact that no one had come to search for me gave me a sliver of hope for an escape, but truly, there wasn't much hope to be had. The sprawling fields of moss and rock, looming mountain tops in the far-off distance...no, any chance of escaping was not in *this* field. It would be too obvious. Varasyn would pick me up by her teeth if I tried.

But the ledge...

My weight shifted to the ledge, my toes inching closer and closer, allowing a glimpse just beyond the rocks. If I jumped, I'd be risking my life. Scratch that, I'd be dead. My power was nowhere near what Aeden could wield. He could go right over this damn ledge and survive the fall somehow, but me? I'd have no hope of surviving that fall, let alone be able to swim in it if I did survive. The hope for an escape crashed just as violently as the water did against the jagged rocks below, my toes receding from the ledge and my arms waving in circles at my sides to find my balance until I stepped back onto the cushy moss again. How Shay managed to confidently dive into those waters was beyond me.

The only thing left of the tree was a small stump that I could've tried to disguise as a block of ice, but knowing our domes were probably too far to pick up on a slight bump coming up from the ground, I decided to leave it as it was.

I made my way back toward the domes, back to Murrie's snoring and the rustling of whatever the hell Seamus and Shay were up to in theirs, and laid back down on the pelt.

Minutes later, the leaves around the dome shook, the undeniable sounds of wings followed by the rattle of the ground beneath my head as Vara landed, making me still, like she'd somehow see me in here. The one who'd just hurt her rider. No wingbeats retreated for minutes after she landed, and several seconds later I could hear Aeden talking low outside.

Curiosity was edging me closer to the opening of the dome to get a better look at the only dragon heir I knew of—the only one left, to my knowledge. Murrie taught him what she knew about dragons and their heirs, and I listened to those lessons like my life depended on it. I'd sit behind my prison walls, hiding behind my book, listening to how he was bound to her in a way that gave them a mental connection and one day he'd get more abilities from her as their connection grew.

But watching them together was a completely different thing.

He wiped his hands roughly over her scales as she let steamy clouds roll from her nostrils, her eyes glazing over as she squinted at him when he stopped and moved to stand in front of her. He chuckled, then cocked his head to the side before he moved to her other side and resumed... petting the very large, very lethal dragon.

That's what he was doing.

Petting her as if she was a dog.

I wasn't scared of her just like I wasn't scared of Aeden, but I was scared of the potential that the two of them had together to stop me from making my way back to Prydia. Their bond was new when they pulled me from the arena. Weak. A shiver moved down my spine at the thought of what they could do now, and in a year, there was no telling what could stop them. If anything could stop them.

"You should have seen the look on her face, Vara." My ears perked up and I jerked my head from the entrance right as he turned to look at my dome. Varasyn couldn't breathe fire yet, but if she caught me eavesdropping—because that was absolutely what I was doing—I was sure she'd find a creative outlet for all the hot steam she *was* able to release.

He continued, letting me know I wasn't spotted just then. Or maybe he didn't care if I was listening. "I know, I know. I can't just make it go away though." A thick plume of steam spread across the top of the dome, seeping in through the few cracks that Fire Boy left in his design.

"You haven't exactly been forthright with me, either." More steam. Whatever questions and accusations Varasyn was laying on Aeden, she wasn't all that happy about it. Aeden sure knew how to piss off the women in his life. It was a miracle that Murrie still praised the ground he walked on knowing what a dipshit he could be.

His cocky grins kept playing over and over in my mind like a broken record, because let's face it, my mind was basically a very piecey, greyed-out record on repeat. With only two month's worth of undisturbed memories with bits and pieces from before I came to Aellethia, there wasn't a whole lot left to keep on my mental rotations. What did find its way in was his grin, his mouth, the hard lines of his stomach and shoulders every time he threw a weapon. The way his eyes always seemed to find mine when I didn't want them to.

"I'm sorry, you're right. I've just had a lot on my mind lately." I peered out through the opening to see Aeden, a six-foot-plus wall of muscle and marks, lifting up on to his tiptoes to hug the neck of his dragon. He was *hugging* his dragon. He reached down and picked up a rabbit, white fur bloodied in one faint spot just like the several that lay along the grass. *Of course that's where he went.* He always hunted, or trained, or wielded against inanimate objects when I lashed out at him, standing my ground. He tossed the rabbit up into the air and Varasyn caught the rabbit between her teeth, blood sliding down the sides of her jaw as she bit into it. Aeden reached up as she bent down, his hands wiping away the bead of blood before she nuzzled into him.

"Atta girl." They rubbed into each other one more time before she walked off to curl up and sleep. I pulled my head back in, then laid on the pelt, wondering what kind of Mora would ever show as much compassion to anyone like that, let alone a dragon. It wasn't just Varasyn he showed it too, either. He was always ready and willing to help others, even if that meant tying me up because his friends requested it, something that I obviously wasn't a fan of but the way he protected those around him more than himself was surprising.

He certainly wasn't like my father, who refused to ward his territories and ruled with a bloodied iron fist, wielding it like a fifth element. Eoghan Waterborne wasn't all too bad, but his habit of bending truths and omitting things left little to be desired. And Leander, well no one knew a thing about the man who ruled over Buryon, but his wards held true in keeping my father from portaling in, which bumped him up on my list.

But Aeden.

Aeden Fireborne was...different. He cared.

I didn't know what kind of a ruler I'd become if I ever got the chance to take Prydia, but I knew the kind of leader Aeden would be.

Those thoughts kept me awake until the sunlight started to shine rays in through the thin cracks of the dome, making me wince back at the brightness. His people might not exist anymore, but I found I hoped they did.

Because Aellethia needed someone kind.

Someone like him.

Chapter Nine
Aeden

The stump I flew over was…interesting.

What was even more interesting was the view of Paige chopping down a tree—a tree that grew spontaneously next to her—with the hatchet I gave her to protect herself with. I couldn't help but stare down at her from above the clouds Varasyn was circling, watching as she hacked at the trunk like it had personally wronged her.

I think in a sense, she *had* used that hatchet to protect herself in the ways she'd always done. I wished she knew she didn't have to push things away from me or try to hide who she was. How she felt, what she was thinking. What she wanted. As if I didn't try to show her enough how anything she did would never change my mind when it came to her.

But why try to hide something we all knew was coming?

I had the chance to connect with the elements the moment I stepped foot in Aellethia, and because of that, I developed my powers pretty quickly while trying to find her. To be with her. My emotions had always been all-consuming even though that emotion hadn't been *love* until recently. Yet, I never considered that facet of myself to be beneficial, but the marks on my body proved otherwise. Now that I had all my marks, it was becoming a burden—*feeling*, like I was. Trying to conceal how strongly I felt about her. Trying not to edge her away from me because of those feelings, and failing in not just one world, but two.

In Jessup, I'd been more concerned with not pulling her from her mother and the dreams she had of turning her life around. *Both* of their lives around. Paige had made it her priority to change her mother. To *fix* Celine. But you couldn't change people. Not really. They'd always be the same person they were before, just dawning a new mask until it would inevitably slip off.

Paige was still the girl I loved even if she didn't remember everything about who she was to begin with. Who her mother was. Who *I* was. If she had her memories back, she'd probably argue that her mother made her temperamental and stubborn, and I'd made her trusting and forgiving and all of that was our doing. But she'd been those things all along, they just shined brighter in our presence. And who she was, and still *is,* would always be the woman I loved.

I'd gotten some practice in with Vara before the others could wake up, and judging by the way Paige hadn't screamed or cried out again in the night, I don't think she ever fell back asleep.

"You are getting better at riding, Aeden."

"Did you just compliment me?" I put a hand on my chest just before she dipped low beneath the clouds, making my stomach rise into my throat.

She laughed, the vibrations strong against my thighs.

"You compliment me and then you plummet. Mixed signals, Vara."

Steam surrounded me as she breathed out, flying right back into it. *"Not any more mixed than the girl gives you. I'm just warming you up for the day."*

"I would love to tell you you're wrong, but after what she said last night...I don't really know what to think anymore."

And the things I said back to her weren't sitting right with me, either. *Pushing you from my mind would almost,* almost, *be a luxury right now.* I was angry when I said it, and I'm not sure who I hurt more when it came from my mouth.

My guess would be me, though that faint shimmer of hope that told me she was awake in that dome thinking it over, thinking *me* over all night, was making my thoughts go even more haywire.

Vara tilted and I gripped on harder to the earthen saddle and one of her spines. Her wings went straight and flat beside me as she spun, then thrust upward into another plume of clouds. I loosened my grip on her spine as she steadied herself, then put my arms out, feeling the rush of adrenaline with only my thighs gripping on. *"Good. Wanted to make sure you were still paying attention."*

"You did say I was getting better," I replied, waiting for her to dive back down but keeping my arms out.

I finally settled them back on the spines. *"I admit, something is odd between you two."* I stiffened, fixating between the next piece of cloud in front of us and the still, open water beneath us. *"Beyond the whole you being obsessed with her bit."* Vara dove, but my heart had already sunk into my stomach at her words. My ass barely left the saddle. Holding on through her motions—chaotic as they were to test me—had become much easier than that first flight we took.

I cleared my throat, croaking when I went to speak again. *"I'm not obsessed,"* was all I had to say back, though what she said did have some truth to it. Something was odd. Different from anything I'd seen before. Paige being near me in Jessup was one thing. But in Aellethia? It was an entirely new playing field. It was like we were tethered together somehow. I couldn't explain it, but as I learned more about my connection with Varasyn, I couldn't shake that Paige and I were more than just two people who happened to become friends. Two people who were also of another world than the one they lived in.

The coincidences just seemed...*too* coincidental.

She laughed again. *"Right."*

"Can people bond to each other here? Like you and me?" I rushed through the question, not thinking about anything beyond that tether I felt between us.

The huff she gave me was more from irritation than it was the amount of flying time we were getting in. *"I don't know. But I don't think so."* Her words were clipped too short. She didn't sound too certain.

"Why not?"

"Because what would be the point of keeping dragons strictly for the Firebornes and binding them together if any other fae could run off and bind themselves to someone else with power?"

I paused, considering it for a moment. *"What if binding wasn't to grant you more power, though. What if you just did it out of lo—"* She dove down, aiming straight for the domes. When she landed, it was rough and she shook until I had to jump from her back before her spines would spear through me. I stomped around to face her. *"What the fuck was that for?"*

"If you want to know how to get that girl to bind herself to you out of a love that she doesn't have for you, you should ask another Fae. We are bound by birth, of fire and blood. Good luck trying to get that one"—she jerked her head toward Paige who was sitting by Shay and Murrie eating breakfast, innocently enough—*"to do the same for you. As if she'd bleed for you to begin with."* Her tail slammed into the moss behind her. *"I'll be back when you're ready to leave. Looks like the red-haired one isn't up yet."*

Before I could try to wrap my mind around why the hell in all of Aellethia my parents bound me to the most jealous, easily angered—

"My thoughts were the same about you. Learn to block me out like I have done for you or I will always know what you are thinking and feeling."

"You guys okay?" Shay asked as I sat down in front of them. Wind whipped at my back, my hair falling in front of my eyes as Vara took off behind me.

Paige's gaze landed on my hand where pieces of vine were woven between my fingers as I pushed them through my hair. I must've ripped a piece of the saddle off when Vara landed and knocked me from her so abruptly.

I shook my hand out. "Fine. I'm just...apparently an idiot."

"So right you are." I could almost feel the tension rolling off of the scales I didn't have.

Paige choked on a laugh and her hand jumped up to block any food from coming out of her mouth. Then she looked at Shay as she swallowed the rest of her food. "I think I need to pee."

I stood and held my hand out to her. "I'll take you."

Her eyes darted between my hand and Shay, who just shrugged her shoulders. Murrie opened her mouth, but I cut her off before she could offer.

"There's no coverage here, save for the very short, very close-by domes. And Seamus isn't awake to make you an ice wall. So unless you want everyone to hear you, I suggest you just let me take you."

She slapped my hand away as she stood, dusting the dirt off of her tight leather pants. "Fine. Just make some trees or something over there and I'll go there myself."

I laughed, crossing my arms over my chest. "If you think for one second that I will let you go over there by yourself, you haven't been paying much attention to the one you think you hate so much."

She scowled. "I'm not going to escape."

I shrugged. "Maybe." I dragged my gaze down the curve of her neck, waiting for her to tell me about the new power she'd gotten. She could try to create another tree, just like the willow. I'd even fucking show her how, if only she'd ask.

But as I waited and her scowl intensified to a sneer, probably her questioning why I was just staring at her, I decided to speak up again. "Look, anything can happen. I don't know this place. What if there's some invisible beast or flying thing waiting to get you?"

Murrie started, "There isn't any—" Shay nudged her elbow into Murrie's side, silencing her.

Paige directed her open hand toward Murrie, her face saying *see?* so obviously.

"Doesn't matter." I reached down to pick up my jacket Paige had discarded on the grass and thrust it toward her. "You either let me take you, or you hold it." I grinned down at her. "I think we have, what, several hours before we hit another town?"

"At least a half-day, actually, if we really hustle," Murrie helpfully supplied.

"There you go, Paige. A half-day." I leaned in closer to her and saw her fingers wringing around the jacket, no doubt picturing the material being my neck.

Her shoulders fell as she grumbled, "Fine. Let's just hurry up and get this over with." I held my arm out, letting her lead the way. After a few steps, she raised her middle finger up at me just over her shoulder. "I can feel you watching my ass from here, Fire Boy."

I chuckled. "I could always lead if you'd rather look at mine."

She didn't respond, but continued to sway her hips as she pushed her arms slowly into each sleeve of my jacket. The bottom hem hit right where her ass continued to curve in those tight pants, but I could still see her moving her hips like she knew I was watching and was trying to mess with me even more.

It was working.

When we were far enough away from everyone else, my mouth had run dry, my mind completely on things it shouldn't be on. I made a string of thick trees and continued to watch her until she made her way behind them. When she was done, I made a small stream of water, somewhere she could wash her hands, and without hesitation she went right to it. She pulled her hands back and peered up at me, shaking her hands out at her side.

"Still can't access your original nature?" Either she was committed to not showing an ounce of her power, or she really couldn't reach her air magic like she should be able to yet. My fists curled in at the knowledge that her father's poison was still somehow affecting her.

Her brow arched up as our eyes locked briefly. "Nope." She averted her gaze almost instantly, focusing more on her hands as she patted them along her sleeves. "I thought it hurt too much to look at me," she continued casually, like she was stating the time or the damn weather.

My voice dropped as guilt burned beneath my ribs. "I didn't mean it like that."

"Really?" She couldn't wield fire, but with a spirit like hers, she burned hotter and brighter than I ever could. She rolled her lips in and then gave me a weak half-shrug. "I'm pretty sure you said it hurt to look at me, and…that…."

Her voice broke as I stepped in closer, my chin tucking down toward my chest to find the best angle to make sure I was the only thing she could see, like she had always been for me.

I reached my hand up to the ends of her soft, wavy hair, spinning it around one of my fingers. Her eyes widened as I said, "You have no idea how much control you have over me, do you?"

Her breathing stilled with those words she'd forgotten. Her chest expanding, undoubtedly holding on to the air she'd use on the words that would take me down next. I was a glutton for pain, apparently. But unlike each time Vara dipped low from the clouds to catch me off guard, I didn't brace for anything.

I'd gladly fall in her presence.

She bit down on her lip, drawing my eyes to the way they rounded over her teeth. "Aeden?" she questioned, her body leaning into mine while mine responded like it was being put under a heavy spell, getting close enough to—"Just wanted to tell you that you stepped in dragon shit." Then she turned and walked away, leaving me in a stupor, my brain unable to process what she'd said but fully able to drown in the sight of her.

Vara burst into a fit of chortles and laughter as the smell shifted my ogling from Paige's tightly-bound ass to my shit-covered boots.

"Fuck."

I couldn't shake the feeling that we were being watched the whole way to the Amaliro Mountains. Adding paranoia to the ever-growing list of shit that Aellethia was doing to me felt like adding a fleck of sand to the expansive shoreline in Costa. I was losing my damn mind, my palms sweating at times as I scanned the open land.

No one disagreed with the way we were heading. Murrie and Shay needed to search the markets of Amaliro for some tonic they didn't want to discuss with me and Seamus didn't seem to care where we went. I was starting to think he'd be fine going anywhere so long as Shay and I were with him.

Paige's quiet demeanor was the only unsettling one. It was suspicious—her tight lips. Almost like she didn't want to say anything that would sway me from changing my mind. She wasn't fighting me on it, so what could she possibly want there other than maybe to see Eoghan again? She heard 'Amaliro' and her attitude seemed to shift. She sat straighter in that saddle and her eyes bore forward to whatever end she was envisioning.

I rubbed my dampened palm together. *"Nothing still?"* I glanced around, walking behind the two horses so no one would see how on edge I was. Maybe it was just the Waterborne wards—as invisible as they were, they still didn't go unnoticed. Not on the back of a dragon, all the way up in the clouds, and definitely not down here on the ground with the others. The wards seemed to call to the power inside of me like an internal alarm system, raising the hairs on my arms and on the back of my neck.

"I can see the mountains up ahead, a bunch of snow, moss below me, and oh yeah, you all on the ground. That's it. Oh, now I see some sheep."

"Be careful here. These are his lands, and I don't want you to get captured."

"I'd like to see him try to get me," she replied, her wings bowing in and out of the clouds.

"Don't, Vara. You need to stay hidden." Her body descended slightly, probably from defiance or maybe it was the winds that had grown harsh and cold, or the clouds that were turning thick and heavy again out of nowhere.

Eoghan was smart. He paid attention to detail. Too much attention. Sure, he'd seen Vara in the arena, but knowing about her and seeing her flying around your land were two very different things. I bit my tongue for several minutes until finally she ascended back up when the mountains became larger, and we could no longer see anything on either side of them.

The weather went from mild fall to full-blown winter once those mountains flanked us, and everyone started shivering and rubbing their arms as they dipped down lower to the back of their horses. I knew, *knew*, Seamus was chanting in his head *I told you so* when he said that winter was fast-approaching back in the Fields.

But. Fuck. Me. I didn't think we'd be trudging right into it as abruptly as we had. Not even the jacket I gave to Paige would keep her warm enough. I'd be fine, but the rest of them didn't have an element that burned throughout their blood and would keep them from freezing.

"How much further?" Shay shouted back to Murrie, her voice quavering in between shivers. Seamus put the reins in her hands and leaned back to grab one of the pelts we used to sleep on. He wrapped it around them both, his arms rubbing up and down her arms underneath it while she settled back against him.

"Maybe an hour?" she replied, picking up the pelts to do the same for her and Paige. But Paige shook her head.

"I'm fine. You need it more than me." She gave Murrie a faint smile over her shoulder, her eyes finding me behind them where I walked. The second I smiled back, she huffed, a small plume of heat escaping her mouth before she faced forward again.

"There's a home hidden in the mountains. Hidden well," Vara acknowledged, her wings dipping briefly, the red and gold more clear against all the white.

"Just one?"

"Yeah. Not very big, either. Looks like it's made of ice or glass."

A singular home of ice high up in the mountains? It was either Eoghan's or another High Fae we didn't want to encounter. But a home made of ice made sense for Eoghan—showing his power in the walls of his home like Gedeon did with his bloody wallpaper. The power alone to build an entire home would knock me out for at least a few days, or take months of building. And on a peak? No, thanks. I'd rather be somewhere warm, with a season I doubted ever came to the Amaliro Mountains.

"Don't get too close." She huffed, like that was obvious. *"I'm serious, Vara. I can't lose you, too."*

"Huh." She paused for a moment before adding, *"Feeling sentimental?"*

"No, I'm just being cautious."

"Imagine, Lord Waterborne: Lover of Paige's brother, hater of Paige's ex-boyfriend. Do you think he could slay a dragon if he tried?" Her sarcastic tone was getting on my last nerve. I just wanted her bright scales to stay out of sight, and *this* was the snark I got in return for caring.

"Someone was clearly capable, otherwise I'd see more dragons. Right?"

That shut her up, making her wings completely disappear again as her tail went vertical into the sky. Part of me wished she'd just tell me about them. I knew she was hiding that information as much as she could from me, but *why*?

A gust of wind pummeled through and sent Murrie teetering off the edge of the horse, snapping me from my thoughts. Her small body seemed to do a complete 180 and righted almost instantly, going the opposite direction of the heavy gust that sent me jolting forward to help her. I came up beside their horse, eyeing over Murrie as she rambled on about the wind and clutched onto the back of Paige for support as she shifted in her spot behind the saddle.

But my sight went to her—to Paige, and that slight tremble I thought I saw right after Murrie fell, or would have fallen. It was as if the air around Murrie cupped her softly, like a conflicting wind gust aimed *just right*. It was almost indecipherable against the already gusting wind that surrounded us as we pressed on, but I noticed. I'd always notice when it came to Paige.

So, she'd either concealed it earlier and lied about it, or this was new to her, too. Paige had not only garnered a new element, but she was, in fact, regaining her original nature as well. What else was she hiding from us, from *me*?

I let my eyes skim over her until she was finished helping Murrie behind her, using her arms for other things to undoubtedly keep the regained power hidden from me. Her hands reached for the pommel while Murrie took hold of the reins, her face furrowing ever so slightly.

No, I don't think she knew she could do that, but I also wouldn't put it past her to lie about it. But if her original nature was back, if the poison was wearing off finally, then maybe the rest of it was coming back to her, too.

So, I baited conversation with Paige, drawing on her memory as gently and inconspicuously as I could. "My old car used to make this terrible rocking sound whenever the wind got too strong before a snowstorm."

Her brow flicked up, like she hadn't noticed me still walking beside their horse. "Mmm," was all Paige said as another gust whipped through the air—an ensuing storm that wouldn't make me stop trying to pry the truth from her. Another gust came and Murrie grabbed onto Paige, who looked down to where Murrie's small fingers clasped around her waist, the pelt shifting to expose those small hands and where they had tightened.

"What's a car?" Murrie questioned, shouting against the whistling sounds that slapped against our ears.

"It's like..." I tried to think of a way to explain it, but Paige took right over, dismissing Murrie's tight grip on her entirely.

"It's like a wagon with better wheels, and has a part called an engine that makes it go without needing something to pull it. It also closes around you so you don't get hit by every weather condition known to man."

She had some sort of memory of the mortal world, that much was clear, but I had to know if she remembered *me*. Had remembered being in my car, sometimes late at night after a long day at work or the hospital. Other more enjoyable times when I'd take her on a ride through the backcountry, even though the car couldn't really handle it. I decided that I could either go with another story, or I could try to see her reaction to me, in general. Surely, if Paige remembered who I was, she'd react differently to me. *Wouldn't she?*

What makes you so certain that even when my memories do return, I'd want to stay with you? Her words hit me like a knife, and I fumbled through my thoughts to try to push it back out as Vara grumbled through those thoughts.

"You used to make fun of the sounds, saying it was like being stuck in a dryer that was breaking from the inside." I chuckled lightly at the memory. And then, because I'm an idiot, I reached my hand out, grazing the back of my finger along her leather-covered calf. When I looked up at her, I couldn't hide the pain of those words, the memory hitting me like I might not ever see a day like that again. I wondered if she noticed that pain, not that I could try to hide it if I wanted to. Her sharp tongue seemed to relish in the way my heart had barricades for everyone else *but* her.

Paige sneered, but her eyes softened as they moved from my finger to the slight smile I managed to give her as I looked up at her. So, maybe she didn't hate me as much as she led on. I had to believe that. I'd caught her looking at me before, but

I wasn't always certain if she was calculating my movements or thinking about me in the ways I thought about her.

Her brows furrowed down at me, her features turning more confused instead of full of hate. It shouldn't have given me hope, especially not when she finally kicked my finger from her leg and shifted her focus back to the mountains instead of me.

But I was hopeless when it came to Paige, and if she thought that a little something like memory loss would stop me from getting her back, she was sorely mistaken.

Chapter Ten
Aeden

My air magic was not equipped to tackle against each gust of wind that came hurling its way through our path. When a small town with homes and shops made of thick logs came into view, buried in between mountain ranges that disappeared behind the thick clouds above, I heard more than one sigh of relief. Including my own. Each building was painted and well-maintained for as far as any of us could see. It was a sea of vibrancy that rivaled Easrich—both starkly different from Prydia and Costa.

Murrie jumped from the back of her horse and the rest followed. She was eager to grab the reins of both horses and lead them to a stable down the snow-covered road barely visible from where we stood. Even as it bit into her ankles, she didn't falter once, her determination always a shining part of her personality. Seamus offered his assistance before she took the reins of his horse, but she denied him, shooing him toward the rest of us and pointing at our slimming cargo she'd just shoved from the horse's backs. I'm pretty sure I heard her calling him a few choice words because it took some time for him to give her the reins and get off her back.

Shay rushed into the nearest shop, presumably asking for directions from anyone she'd be able to find. That was the part about Shay that made her such an essential part of our group. She was always willing to subject herself to the company of fae, knowing she'd be able to sway their opinions with her power, her ability to enchant those who weren't strong enough to fend it off. She could go brazenly where most wouldn't, and in my eyes, that made her just as valuable as the rest of us.

Paige walked up to the shop Shay walked into, where books were stacked behind the windows that looked more like ice than glass, the faint ripples of the light and the bindings of faded books from inside the shop distorted. I moved closer to where Paige stood with her arms wrapped around her waist over my jacket, admiring the books while squinting to read the titles of each through the ice. Just over my shoulder, Seamus was gathering the rest of our belongings from the ground, brushing off snow as he muttered under his breath.

The door of the shop swung open and three sets of boots trailed out from the door.

My jaw flexed, my teeth grinding down impossibly hard as red spots filled my vision before he had a chance to speak. "What a fine coincidence it is to see you again, Princess."

Coincidence my fucking ass. I reached over and reflexively tucked Paige behind me as Eoghan, Shay, and some very light blonde man walked out from the threshold. Paige stepped out from behind me and moved to my side, folding her arms across her chest defiantly as she looked Eoghan up and down.

Her jaw dropped the moment she was done examining him and fixed her attention on the other man, his grey eyes that looked oddly familiar sending a prickle down my arms. He smiled widely at her, grinning ear-to-ear, and to my surprise, she burst forward into him, wrapping her arms around his waist. Shay awkwardly looked over each of us while Seamus dropped our things to the ground and formed a ball of ice in his hands, his stance shifting as he prepared to fight. As if Eoghan could sense the power brewing behind him, he held up a hand near his shoulder, not sparing a single glance to Seamus.

And then the ball of ice dropped. "Ikelos?" Seamus let out, astonishment written on his face. Ikelos turned his head just over his shoulder toward Seamus, keeping most of his focus on Paige who was still holding onto him in a lingering embrace. A deep groove formed between my brows as the memory of a room and the picture of a man resembling Gedeon with softer eyes flashed in my mind. He was slightly older than he was in the portrait but his eyes were still soft, like he hadn't woken up every day of his existence trying to murder innocent people.

Ikelos.

Seamus shook his head as if to clear it, then smiled solemnly at Ikelos. "Aye, ye was but a wee lad when I saw ye last, but seein' yer...the resemblance..." He looked exactly like his father.

Ikelos' jaw hardened at the mention of him. His father had sent him to Sentra after he lost his Triad. Most people would see that as a dressing-down to what he was truly capable of. A way to strip someone of their title, their right, without death. A way to publicly shun your own child and make them regret the day they lost the trial set by the Stars themselves. Death was the swift way to not live for centuries in servitude to someone else. Yet Ikelos didn't look regretful, nor did he seem ridiculed and downcast by society. I stared at his clean face and squared back shoulders, golden-trimmed blue velvet jacket and perfectly tailored pants, and then moved on down to his pristine leather boots—no, everything about him was as if he had indeed won those trials.

Paige unclasped her arms from her brother as he nodded back to Seamus over his shoulder. "Seamus, is it? I think I remember you. You were a guard, right? I remember your kindness. Too kind to be working for my...for Gedeon. It's good to see you again." Seamus inclined his head in silent thanks, almost a slight bow, yet shrugged his shoulders at me when my eyes narrowed back at him. I put my palm to my face and pushed it up and through my hair, shaking my head at him the entire time. It was un-fucking-believable how much Seamus really knew. I never thought he was close to Ikelos, nor had he told me that he had been. Perhaps that was my fault in assuming guards were only close to the High Fae who hired them, not to their families. Not when the head of the house was a power-hungry, murderous tyrant. I heard *guard* from Seamus' mouth and envisioned him gallivanting throughout Prydia and the territories, catching thieves and collecting taxes.

Clearly, I hadn't questioned him enough about it.

Ikelos drew his attention back to Paige and blinked down at her, tugging her close again and squeezing her arms. I didn't know whether I should be defensive, to pull her back to me in case her brother had ill intentions. But the smile that didn't leave his face as he continued searching her over in disbelief had me unfurling my fingers at my side.

"Wise choice. You wouldn't want to give a bad first impression to your girlfriend's brother, would you?" Ikelos groaned and Shay took that opportunity to wiggle herself away from between the two of them, making her way over toward Seamus to help him collect the things he'd dropped.

Paige scowled over at Eoghan, then released her brother and marched up to him, her hair whipping furiously as another gust of wind blew through the street. Paige stopped, standing with her back to me so I couldn't see how she was feeling until her hand slapped across his cheek. I didn't know what it was for, but my heart swelled with pride instantly and the cockiest smile grew on my lips.

That's my girl.

"That's for fucking kissing me." She turned her head back to me, then up at Eoghan again who was rubbing at the red mark that she'd left across his cheek. "And he's not my boyfriend." She tossed a thumb over her shoulder, then glanced back at me once more. But I couldn't focus on that because I was too consumed with images that burned hotter than the blood beneath my skin. Images I'd rather burn over and over again.

But more importantly, I wanted to burn *him*.

My reflexes were faster than my brain could process, all of my focus honing in on Eoghan's lips being on hers when I'd been so sure mine were the last to grace them. She was *mine*. My vision turned completely red, then turned starkly black. Before I knew it, I was tackling Eoghan to the ground, pressing him into the snow as my fist raised above me, aiming for the red mark left by *my girl*.

"You fucking kissed her?" My fingers turned white, the heat that swelled around us signaling that my power was on the precipice of turning him into ash before I would have a chance to allow my body the sweet release of decking him with my fist. "What happened to *she isn't my type*?"

A strong gust of air forced me from Eoghan right as my fist started to come down, sending me rolling into the middle of the street. I stopped the momentum with my own burst of air. "*She* needed protection. Something I'm sure you would have agreed to had you'd been consulted on the matter." It was Ikelos who spoke while glaring over at Eoghan as he righted himself from the ground, stumbling a bit on one of his knees.

Good.

I stood to brush the snow from my body, my attention straying to Paige as a mischievous quirk rested at the corner of her lips. A look meant just for me before her emerald eyes darkened and landed right back on Eoghan.

She was enjoying this? I don't know why that was as hot as it was, but it fucking was.

"*You idiot,*" Vara growled low.

"What protection are you talking about?" Paige directed her question to Ikelos as Eoghan wiped his thumb along his lip where a small bead of blood fell down from a faint, toothy cut. They both fell silent for a beat, Paige glaring at Ikelos who was glaring at Eoghan who was glaring at me, all while I was still fixed on the woman who liked seeing me get a little dirty for her.

Murrie came around a corner from the stalls, fighting the wind with every ounce of strength she could as the handle of her battle-ax waved across her back. Her face turned from surprised and ready-to-fight, to acceptance when I gave her a slight nod and waved my hand down by my side, showing her it was okay.

Seamus let out a loud sigh. "Aye, this is all fun and dandy, but the storm is kickin' up. Do ye 'ave somewhere we can stay or are we not welcome in these parts?" Seamus' beard danced with another gust that sent Shay rocking on her heels as she held onto a bag of herbs Murrie had secured in Easrich.

"After you, then." Eoghan gestured with his hand to no one in particular right as a blue swirling portal formed in the doorway of the bookstore. Murrie stepped forward first, bowed slightly to me, rolled back her shoulders, and turned to face the portal.

Without a single word, her loyalty had her waltzing in first through the blue swirling mass, side-stepping all of us as if it were as normal as entering the bookshop that sat safely beyond it.

"I like that one," Eoghan said.

"I bet you do." I knocked into his shoulder as I walked by him, watching Paige follow in right after Murrie.

"Stay up there, I think we're going up to that house you saw."

"You think?*"* I could almost picture the steam rolling from her mouth. *"You really are an idiot, following that girl—"*

"Vara, that girl has a name," I warned, casting a glare to the skies without shifting my head. *"And I don't have time for this right now."* Eoghan was already giving me odd looks, yet said nothing to rush me through as the others followed in first.

"You're lucky there're peaks for me to rest on."

"Rest up then," I replied curtly.

Eoghan called out from behind me right before I finally stepped up to walk through, "Don't worry. You should both end up in the same place this time!" My body tensed at the reminder right as the blue pulsing waves dragged me in.

Chapter Eleven
PAIGE

Hugging my brother was something I quite literally dreamed about. Seeing him made a well of tears come to the surface that I hadn't expected to come. I was relieved to meet someone related to me who wasn't a monster, yet also shocked at the resemblance he had to said monster. Even in my dreams I hadn't been that aware of it, but in person, it was undeniable. However, I was strangely at ease with him holding me. With those same eyes looking into mine. Each time I met Gedeon's gaze, I could almost feel the physical pain he wanted to put me through. Could feel his desire to end me and watch me die. My brother's eyes were nothing like that.

I glanced around the room we'd portaled to, noting the icy glass walls, shelves of books, the wingback chair, the desk. All so similar to the dream I'd had where Eoghan's affections gave way to who my brother was without even speaking his name. The familiarity was eerie, like I'd been here before, yet all the while being quite certain I'd never set foot in this place, even with the loss of my memory. A shiver rolled down my spine, edging me to pull Aeden's jacket tighter to my body.

A groan came from the corner of the room by the shelves of books, followed by Murrie cursing. Eoghan, Seamus, Ikelos, and I all landed gracefully enough by the door of the room, but as Aeden wobbled to his feet and helped Shay and Murrie up beside him, I couldn't help laugh at the sight of him.

Aeden's eyes darkened as they met mine. "You think that's funny, Paige?" His features turned playful instantly, with a raised brow and a coy smile as he wiped the snow from his knees, sending a small flood of heat through my body that I tamped down just as fast as it came. Eoghan muttered something under his breath before the fallen snow dissipated with a flick of his wrist, like he'd been annoyed by the mess Aeden had somehow brought through the portal with him.

"It is a *little* funny." I pinched my fingers together, showing him the small amount of pleasure it was bringing me, knowing I was surprised that I'd managed to land on my own two feet and didn't end up on the floor like I had before each trial.

Aeden righted himself, all the snow gone from his legs. "It's good to hear you laugh." His smile turned sincere instead of goading and the softness of his voice sent another shiver throughout my body. "It's also nice to see that we both ended up in the same place this time."

I cleared my throat, then fell awkwardly silent as he looked down at me from across the room. I couldn't remember that day, but I'd heard about it enough to know that it tore at him in ways I didn't reciprocate. I remembered being at Gedeon's home just fine, and the few splotches of grey that dotted my memories from that time were just that. Dots. Some I didn't care to ever replace. I angled my body away from him, though I'm sure it did nothing to take his attention from me.

"As I said you would," Eoghan replied as he strode over to the wingback chair and took a seat casually. Ikelos moved to stand beside him, stretching his arm across the back of the chair above where Eoghan's shoulders were. The gesture was so formal, so protective, it made me still for a moment. It was so unlike what my father would have done. He would've forced Eoghan from the chair and made him stand in the far corner, sent to the floor on his knees if he could command him to do so.

Along the window, Seamus, Shay, and Murrie shuffled to gaze out over the mountains to the storm that had rolled in. They usually tried their best to ignore whatever Aeden and I said to each other, and even though we had two others now in our presence, they still acted like we would have it out for each other. Regardless of who was there or who wasn't.

They were right.

I wouldn't care, and I doubted he would either.

Aeden brushed past me as he walked over to the desk, his balance and grace completely righted as if his fall had never happened. He planted his hands down on the wooden surface, turning his steely gaze to Eoghan. "I want to hear your justification for kissing her. Now."

The heat rose in the room, helping me shake off the chill that was slowly leaving my bones, although *this* heat served a different purpose entirely. A certain purpose that also had the tension spiking in the icy room. Something about that never seemed to make my body react the way I wanted it to. No, my body was a traitor, and every time his magic seeped through my skin, it became too warm.

No, *hot*.

Too fast.

My fingers dug into the ends of his jacket along my arms, continuing to ignore that aspect as much as I could.

Ikelos cleared his throat as Eoghan wiped the pad of his thumb across his split lip. He must've cut himself with his teeth, because Aeden was forced off him by my brother before he could land a single punch. Eoghan met Aeden's glare, smirking back at him as he let out cooly, "I think we get to ask some questions first, seeing as you are now under *our* roof."

"Deal," I blurted before processing what Eoghan had said and moved across the room to position myself next to Aeden, the deep grooves and ridges of his forearms flexing as I stood beside him. I'd heard Aeden talking about Eoghan before, but it wasn't clear how or when they'd met. That grey haze floated over my brain again, giving me a sharp headache just from thinking about clearing it.

"Where have you been this whole time?" Ikelos' asked as his cool grey eyes assessed me. I rubbed at my temples, causing his look of concern to deepen, his brows scrunching together. The question was directed at me, meant for *me*. But Aeden felt the need to step in just as my mouth popped open to answer.

"Earthborne territories. Our turn." *Our turn.* Like it was *his* to even have. His jaw worked once, then twice, as his gaze shifted from Ikelos back to Eoghan.

"What protection did you extend to Paige that you couldn't tell me about in that fucked up letter you left me? You know, the one iced to a damn door days after you left me for the nagas."

"A letter?" Murrie let out a hum at my question. I knew I didn't know everything that had happened before I'd been captured. That wasn't exactly news to me, even though I did try to listen as much as I could or pry a few things from Shay whenever she took me out of the prison. But she was mostly tight-lipped, and asking Aeden, as Shay so firmly told me to do over and over again, was out of the question because I wanted nothing more than to ignore him.

Verbally, at least.

A cool grin spread across Eoghan's face. I knew that look. He was like a cat, enjoying the chase of a frantic mouse. That much of my memory was intact. But Aeden wasn't frantic. He was the predator that fed on both the cat and the mouse, leaving nothing but bone. A *jealous* predator. All over a kiss that meant nothing, not that he thought to ask me about it first. The very fact that I felt the need to explain that part of it to him had me rolling my lips in to fight against it.

Aeden lifted his arms from the table and pushed up his sleeves before placing them both down again, drawing Ikelos' eyes to his marks before they flicked back over to me. Here in Eoghan's home, surrounded by those who had been with him for months—there was no need to try to conceal who he was.

It was a power play for the other two men, although it wasn't needed. Aeden was the boy of flames who took the Aerborne girl from the arena on the back of a dragon. But his flames and the mark now exposed along his forearm only showed a part of who he was. The dragon he rode on the back of into the arena on the other hand?

Well, only one family could do that.

"I think we all know that Paige was poisoned, correct?" Suddenly, all eyes fell to me at Eoghan's words. *That's one way of putting it bluntly.* Everyone nodded except for Aeden, who folded his arms over his puffed-out chest, his irritation over the reminder clear as day. "That poison was supposed to take away the use of her magic. I put a tonic on my lips that would protect her water magic, sort of like a seal over it." Eoghan shrugged, looking almost bored. "There was no other way to give it to her that wouldn't raise suspicion. No servants would think twice about me kissing her, and it's not like Gedeon cares if I'm loyal to Ikelos or not."

Ikelos flinched, but righted himself quickly, like he had been prepared to hear about what had happened and how much our father didn't care about him.

I was simply stricken by her beauty, and wanted her to remember me. That's what he'd told the guard right after he kissed me.

Remember me.

He was telling me exactly why he needed to kiss me, I just hadn't mulled over his words. Hadn't considered the hidden truths within them. He had always been enigmatic. Eoghan wasn't telling me to remember *him*, he was telling me to remember the power he'd given me. Alerting me to the danger I so imprudently overlooked that day. Thanks to him, my water magic still hummed freely under my flesh, and unbeknownst to them, my earth, and a sliver of air magic churned there as well. All in unison.

Eoghan's fingers steepled over the desk, waiting for Aeden to reply. But there was nothing as Aeden grazed his knuckles over the curve of his jaw and glared across the desk at Eoghan. It didn't seem to matter what Eoghan's reasoning was—Aeden still burned just as hot, and standing this close to him I could envision him forcing the desk aside or flipping it right over and lunging for Eoghan again.

Ikelos walked over to me and cupped his hands around mine. The act was kind, gentle. Familial. "He wanted you to die in that arena, Paige." I let his words sink in, waiting for a sting, a bitterness to settle into my flesh and bones. But when it didn't come, I just stared down at our hands. I'd known that, after all. The tilt of our glasses together right before the Triad, the sinister look on his face as he took...something I couldn't quite remember from me. The irretrievable memory burned and made my wrist tingle as if something belonged where those tingles spread.

"I'm so sorry I wasn't there to protect you." I nearly jumped when Ikelos continued to talk, forgetting he was still holding my hands in his. Forgetting I was standing in Eoghan's home, not Gedeon's. His fingers were long and soft with little to no calluses, his skin the same pale hue as my father's. I felt the urge to jerk my hands away because those same hands had threatened my life before. Had summoned swells of air against me and sent me against a wall.

His voice pulled my head up, where the eyes that blinked down at me weren't cold like the steel of a blade, but were instead like a peaceful morning sky, just before a lulling storm.

He wasn't the man who'd tried to poison me.

He wasn't Gedeon, *my father,* who wanted me more dead than alive.

He was someone entirely different. He was my brother. "I promise you, I am nothing like him," he whispered, as if he understood the internal struggle I was trapped in for far too long. And I believed him. Something within me snapped, pulling me from that dark place I'd been in. I shook my head and tightened my fingers around his.

"Was it just your air magic that the poison took?" He examined my face as I shook my head again.

"No. I um…" I hesitated as the heat in the room simmered, reducing to a warm caress that prickled along my neck.

"She doesn't remember me. Or…." Aeden's face softened, like I'd crumble under the weight of his next words.

I continued for him, putting all of my strength into my words. "I don't remember *him*"—I inclined my head toward Aeden—"or my mother." Aeden never mentioned her to me. At first I thought that was because he didn't really know her, but his whispers with Seamus one early morning after a hunt changed that thought entirely. He said her name, Celine, and I watched as his muscles went taut in a way I hadn't seen from him before. He looked worried that morning as he glanced over at my prison after saying her name aloud, checking to see if I was still asleep before he continued.

But I wasn't asleep. I hadn't been since he'd woken up and left that morning.

"Was she our mother?" I asked Ikelos, who shook his head immediately in response. I fought the bile rising in my throat, knowing Gedeon had found not only one woman to bear him a child, but two different women.

Those poor, poor women.

Eoghan sucked in a breath through his teeth and put a hand over his heart. "That's gotta suck, huh." He looked between Aeden and I. "I mean, the part about your mother is tragic, but you forgot *him* too? And to think, you were both so...infatuated? Or perhaps lascivious would be a better term for what I witnessed, or rather didn't witness. And to think, you must not remember that part of the night, either." He wasn't wrong. I had no memory of it, as if a majority of the night had revolved around him and was now encased in grey matter.

Aeden's red mark seemed to pulse all the way up to the part that peeked out along the base of his neck that he was no longer concealing, shadowed by his jaw that clenched tightly. The heat in the room stifled dramatically since Eoghan had opened his mouth, so much so that a bead of sweat began to trickle down my face.

The gentle warmth was gone.

"Haven't learned to control that yet, I see." Eoghan relaxed back into his seat and flicked his wrist, leveling out the rising temperature just as easily as he'd cleaned up the mess of snow on the floor. Aeden remained quiet, though his face suggested his thoughts were anything but. It was either because of the taunt in Eoghan's words or because of the mention of the night that seemed to mean more to him than I could understand. Perhaps it was both.

Ikelos moved to stand behind the chair once more and Seamus let out a sigh. "The lads learned 'nough with what little time and resources we've had." If Ikelos were anything like my father, Seamus would be on the ground, gasping for breaths that would never come until the light had begun to fade from his eyes. My toes curled in my boots, daring me to move backward, to avoid any wrath that may have been shared between my brother and my father. But I refused to move. I'd grown past the fear of *his* wrath, leaving nothing left but a fierce desire to end him.

"You've done an excellent job so far, Seamus. Don't listen to this asshole." Aeden's tunic bunched under the tight flexing of his muscles as he glared back at Eoghan, who seemed to get excited every time Aeden looked at him like he was going to maul him over.

"Aye. I don't think controllin' the fire inside of ye was in our best interests these past couple months, anyway." Seamus raised a finger at Eoghan. "And you. Ye try tellin' him to control the fire while ye have a dragon breathin' down yer back."

Ikelos snorted. "I've read dragons can be quite temperamental."

"Perhaps it is a shared trait," Eoghan quipped.

"How did you know where we'd be?" All eyes moved to me, even the pairs that were standing by the icy wall. It was like they hadn't considered it themselves, they'd just accepted that Eoghan and Ikelos were in the bookshop during a snowstorm in the middle of one of the smallest towns I'd seen so far.

"I'm curious about that, as well." I cocked my brow when I noticed the corner of Aeden's mouth lifting after he spoke, as if he'd picked up on it too. I didn't believe in coincidences, and I was willing to bet he was the same way. Murrie's fingers found the handle of her ax, not caring that doing so was threatening the Mora of Hydrasel.

Eoghan and Ikelos shared glances like they were holding a private, unspoken conversation. Eoghan's posture refused to shift as he looked at Murrie, at where her hand was gripping around the handle of her weapon. It was the same position he'd been in when I first met him in Prydia in my father's dining room, and again on the day when my father forced me to fight Nya—the posture that covered any fear that lingered just beneath the surface. But when his eyes darted to Ikelos' for the brief fraction of time they had, I saw through that facade again.

He was scared.

"I'm a Seer." Ikelos loosed a sigh as his shoulders dropped. "It's how I survived so long living within those walls he calls a castle. It's how"—he pushed back a few strands of unruly, light hair as his grey eyes rolled up to the ceiling then fell back to meet mine—"It's how I survived the Triad. Well, that, and Eoghan." Eoghan patted the hand that had slid over his shoulder, giving Ikelos' hand a firm squeeze that pulled a small smile from my brother as their eyes locked. Eoghan told me he loved my brother, but now that I was in the same room as them, there were no words to describe the connection they had. You could almost feel it—their chemistry, their love for one another.

"A Seer? But your father..." Seamus rubbed his hand along his beard as his words left him.

Ikelos shook his head. "He doesn't know. I kept it a secret. I'd been this way for as long as I can remember, possibly even before then."

"Gifts come at any age, and the younger they come, the stronger the gift is said to be. He would've killed you. He would have seen you as the biggest threat to his rule, especially with a gift as rare as that. The kingdoms would be...the Battle of Vizna maybe wouldn't have..." Murrie was so distraught, she turned away from us and stared back out through the window. I hadn't seen Murrie go speechless. Ever.

My brother laughed. "I can't count the amount of times my father, *our* father, tried to kill me. He would have done so without the knowledge of my *gift*, as it's called. But I'm safe here, behind Hydrasel's wards for as long as they extend beyond Hydrasel."

"Which will be always. You will always be safe here, with me." The words shocked me as they rolled from Eoghan's tongue so...easily. I'd seen so many sides of him that it made my head spin just thinking about it.

Aeden's eyes hadn't left me for some time until he looked over at the window where a soft, almost indecipherable shadow moved through the snow-heavy clouds that drifted quickly across the sky. *Varasyn*. He turned his head as mine blinked away from the shadow, the corner of his mouth twisting up again.

That smirk.

Like he knew my thoughts.

The very idea was unnerving—that someone could know me that well, and yet, I didn't remember the first thing about him and his past. I didn't know everything he was thinking when he brushed his finger down my leg earlier, yet I could guess where he wanted that conversation to go. He wanted me to remember. But I couldn't. I wanted to be mad about it, but again, I couldn't. My stomach started to harden like a stone had been put there, my anger unable to fully rise especially when he kept looking at me with *those* eyes.

What was happening to me?

I refocused on my brother, his and Eoghan's moment now well over. "If you're a Seer, why didn't you know where I'd been since I was capt—" I stuttered on the words, the heaviness in my stomach warring against the words that used to come so easily. "Since I'd left Prydia," I finished, deciding on not touching the subject of my capture, or rescue, or whatever it was that Aeden had done for, or to, me.

Aeden's brow raised as he leaned against the edge of the desk and crossed one of his legs over the other. He really did see right into my mind as if he alone held some key and I kept the door to my thoughts unlocked for him, even if I didn't want to. A sliver of grey slid through my mind, blanketing whatever memory that had provoked.

Eoghan pointed to Aeden. "We think dragon boy is the one to blame. We still don't understand it, but seeing as how a dragon is the only thing in the equation that is different from anything or anyone else Ikelos *can* see, I'd be willing to bet that it's something to do with that. The only time he got a glimpse of you, Aeden wasn't there."

Ikelos shrugged. "I saw you briefly and recognized the area. I'm pretty good at what I do."

"Good? You're the best Seer in all of Aellethia." Eoghan winked up at Ikelos and a blush spread across my brother's pale face at the compliment.

"So, when you trained with me...when you...when you...." It was right at the tip of my tongue, but I couldn't reach it. More grey. "I can't remember what you did, but I know you must've used Ikelos' gift on me before, didn't you? You knew more than you could explain."

Eoghan's brows went up before they pressed together. "You really don't remember how I helped you before your first trial?"

I remembered the troll, the wide flare of its eyes as it looked at me before I slashed its neck, the inky red blood pooling around my feet. I remembered Eoghan coming to my room before that trial. Something about...a board? No. That wasn't it. But my head and thoughts were clouded over, and the headache that had started to brew earlier intensified. I rubbed my forehead.

Eoghan's lips rolled in, then popped open. "I gave you Aeden's bracelet, told you it would help, all thanks to your brother. It's the very thing that scared the shit out of the troll, allowing you the time you needed to make your move. It was made of hedonium—a rare element you can't exactly get anywhere."

Murrie cut in as I rubbed my wrist, trying to imagine a bracelet, given to me by the man I couldn't remember loving. I'd worn *his* bracelet into that trial. Had chosen to do so. "Trolls can't mine or forge hedonium, Paige. It's heavily sought after for it's rarity, because it can only be made with—"

"Dragon fire, yes," Eoghan finished, his slitted eyes raking over Murrie. "I'm glad you listened to the advice in my letter. Finding a dwarf was a good choice. You're welcome, by the way." That damn letter. My hands itched to hold it, to read it.

Aeden's very tall frame bent over the desk, but neither Ikelos or Eoghan flinched as he got closer to them. "Murrie found *me* before *we* found your letter. She saved me from the nagas you so carelessly threw me to. You probably had no idea whether I'd survive it or not, did you?" I didn't know how he'd met Murrie, hadn't cared enough to want to know. But I found I really wanted to know now.

"Nope. Sure didn't. But seeing the marks all over your body led me to believe you were more than capable. It was also better than dying at the hands of a Prydian guard, or worse, their father." Eoghan shrugged. "I had no choice." Eoghan waved a hand and stood from his chair.

Aeden pushed back up, standing just as tall as Eoghan. "You could have warned me about the woods."

"Potato, po-tah-toe."

Aeden's fist curled in as Eoghan stepped around his desk, moving in closer, and yet, I took a step toward Aeden, almost defensively.

Was I defending him?

Fuck.

"I'll shove a potato right up your—"

I held a hand up against each of them, making Aeden stop and look down at me. But I'd had enough, and my headache was only getting worse. I squeezed my eyes shut against the pain. "You're both acting like idiots. Just say sorry, it isn't that fucking hard."

The dark blue jacket Eoghan had on cooled my skin whereas the warm, soft tunic Aeden wore only spread more heat through me, slight pulses of warmth spreading along my open palm. My stomach knotted harder, almost unbearably, as his body leaned into my touch, his muscles firm under my fingertips.

I knew getting too close to a Fae whose original nature was fire was dangerous, but I wasn't in the Triad anymore. I'd already failed that. It wouldn't hurt to have the power Aeden's contact might give me...and now I was justifying simply *touching* him.

My power called out and sought for it. That was all it was.

Nothing more.

Ikelos laughed as he moved to stand beside Eoghan and clapped a hand over his shoulder, tugging him away from where my hand kept him at bay. "My sister is right, you know. You both really are acting like complete idiots." Ikelos winked at me and I felt my arm softening so much that it fell against my side, away from Eoghan. My other hand had no intentions of releasing Aeden from where he stood, and whether that was for their protection or the way my body reacted to just touching him—

"What, do you see us becoming friends with that gift of yours if we apologize?" Aeden asked as his body continued to nudge into my touch, though his facial expression told me his thoughts were not in the same gutter as mine. Or perhaps they were and I just couldn't tell because I'd avoided deciphering his thoughts for a while now.

"He can't *see* you anymore since you found your dragon, remember?" But Eoghan cocked a brow at my brother, waiting to hear his response regardless. It was like their testosterone was turning them into neanderthals.

Ikelos thought for a moment, then shrugged. "Honestly, you two are so conflicting in your personalities that even if you did apologize right now you'd be fighting about something new the next minute. It really doesn't take a seer to *see* that." Seamus howled with laughter in the back corner of the room.

"I like your brother," Aeden mumbled, the vibrations of his voice erupting through his chest and onto my fingertips before I finally let my hand fall and turned my back to him. The room had cooled enough that my cheeks shouldn't have been as flush as they were, but there I was, probably redder than the marks along Aeden's rippling arm. I'd kept my hand on his chest for too long. There was no way he wouldn't read into all of that.

"There, Ikelos, see? That's something we can agree on." Eoghan rolled his shoulders back. "Let's eat. I'm sure you're all hungry. Come."

Shay and Seamus eagerly moved from their spots and tailed behind Ikelos and Eoghan while Murrie followed closely behind them. She was fiercely protective and I could see the slight twitch of her fingers every time Eoghan or Ikelos made any sudden movements. I was relieved the attention was diverted from me for once, at least where Murrie was concerned.

Aeden, on the other hand, was proving even more so that he would never divert his attention from me. And yet, those stupid flutters and heat refused to diminish. When his finger gently swiped mine as our arms swayed too closely near each other while we followed behind everyone else, accident or no, my throat went dry and my chest tightened uncomfortably.

I couldn't keep lying to myself, telling myself it was just hunger, just being tired, just…anything. Because it wasn't just anything. Or anyone.

It was him.

The Starsdamned fire-wielder who kept slipping through my defenses. I didn't need a distraction, couldn't afford to be distracted when my purpose was greater than whatever *this* was.

My mind had been set on knowing where we stood to one another, where we *should* stand since he imprisoned me. But my body and my traitorous organs felt otherwise. Now hearing how I'd taken a part of him with me into a trial I thought I'd surely die in? I didn't know what to think anymore.

And it terrified me.

Chapter Twelve
Aeden

Eoghan's house was smaller than the castle in Prydia, more homely. Ikelos prepared dinner while the rest of us waited for the alcohol to take its effect, which I was gauging by the conversation. It was a solid hour of painful small talk. The worst type of conversation.

"So, a bracelet, huh?" Paige and I were two drinks in as we sat around a circular dining table amongst everyone else, her tone uncertain as she glanced at her wrist.

I lowered my voice, using that as an excuse to need to lean in a fraction. "I gave my bracelet to Eoghan to give to you the night of the dance at your...*his* castle. I wanted—" I paused and took another sip, longer this time, because I couldn't stand the thought of looking into her gorgeous green eyes and seeing the blankness that came with the loss of her memory. The loss of us. "I wanted you to know I was there for you during your trials."

She fell silent, twirling the base of her glass between her fingers.

"So, the snow outside. I'm surprised it came this early," Shay said as Seamus downed his entire glass. His body tilted in closer to her, as if the act were to protect her. Although I had yet to see Shay use a weapon of any kind, I knew her words, her tongue, usually worked just fine. But she was surrounded by High Fae, so unless she wanted to siren song Murrie to start swinging her ax at whoever threatened her, Shay's power was of little to no use at this table.

Eoghan propped his head on his hand, his brows drawing together as if he could sense her tension. "You've never been this far south then, have you?"

"Um, no. I mostly stay near Lake Kree." Shay looked down at her lap.

"Right. Of course. Mermaid, right?" She lifted her gaze back to him and nodded, finishing the entirety of her glass swiftly. With her sleeves pushed up as they were, there was no denying she wasn't Fae.

Seamus stretched his arm along the table, his pinky grazing over her forearm. One day they would come clean about their relationship, and perhaps they already had, at least to each other. I envied that. Envied that they could just be together with no repercussions, neither one shying from the other.

I repositioned my body a little closer to Paige, who kept shifting in her seat and then going rigid when I'd move a modicum closer to her. It was intoxicating—the way my power responded to being this close to her. More inebriating than I could ever hope to feel off the wine in front of me. I wondered if she noticed it, too. Could feel that ardent thrumming in her veins, like I could.

Maybe that was why she'd chosen the chair next to me instead of the available one between Shay and Eoghan. Or maybe I was reading way too much into that one small decision, but fuck it, what else did I really have to focus on? It wasn't the weather, or what each one of us were. Perhaps she kept the other chair empty for her brother, but I'd hoped it was more than that.

I took another sip of the wine—sweet and smooth with the slight hint of something floral, reminding me of the way Paige's hair used to smell back in Jessup. On the days when hugging her had been as easy as breathing, when she'd wanted me to be close to her, even if it was just platonically. Something I never should've taken for granted.

I was still waiting for Paige to respond, but wasn't too hopeful that she actually would. She did love to torture me, after all. Murrie was perceptive and took the reins of the conversation, talking about the herbs Ikelos was using in the kitchen, continuing on for a good while and talking for the rest of us who were too uneasy to speak until we were drunk enough to do so.

"I remember the trial, but—" Paige began, but Seamus' laugh cut her words off from across the table, his cheeks burning red from something Ikelos had shouted from the kitchen. Paige continued anyway. "When I try to think about my memories, things that involve you, or her, my mind gets foggy." So she *was* trying to think about me. About us. Her voice cracked when she opened her mouth again. "Sometimes I wish—" Another loud cackle from Seamus, and I had half a mind to send water across his fucking face for interrupting her again. Instead, I raised my glass toward him before finishing it off.

"More?" I asked Paige as I grabbed the bottle from the center of the table, meeting Seamus' glazed over eyes and giving him a look that said he was pissing me off. He grinned back at me as he put his arm around Shay, tugging her closer to him. He knew I'd never actually hurt him, although it wasn't that long ago that I'd promised to do the very thing if he crossed a line.

The bastard.

Paige nodded, rolling her lips in as she scooted her glass toward me. I needed her to get out of her head. It was borderline infuriating that she kept pushing things down. I could tell by the looks she'd give and the short responses, the nervous twirling of the ends of her hair and the way she'd focus on her fingers like they held all the answers. Her tells were the same as they'd always been, except now she had a hatchet and a few of her daggers that I'd given back to her before we left for the mountains, right after she leaned in close enough to wrap me around her finger once more then mocked me for stepping in Vara's shit. I wanted to give her back every last dagger, but Seamus and Varasyn repeatedly told me I was a moron for even giving her one, let alone five *and* a hatchet. *Imagine the ways she could hurt ye, lad* Seamus had reminded me. But she'd already hurt me more than any dagger or blade ever could, what difference would it make if she cut into me physically when inside I was already wounded enough?

"Your poor mortal heart—you grew soft in that world. You were built to be a warrior. A leader." Varasyn. Her voice coming in randomly to my thoughts, my mind, had become so commonplace. Even when it wasn't requested, she would pipe in her two cents. I really needed to figure out how to shield her away.

"I can still be all of that. I think this world could benefit from someone with a heart."

Varasyn let out a chortle, like she was laughing at me or scoffing. *"You won't be there to prove it if you keep getting too caught up with her. She's a distraction."*

"Much like you're being right now. Don't you have something to go hunt down and eat?"

"Oh, sure. Lay on the jokes at my behest. When I'm larger, you won't think twice to joke like that."

My lips turned up at the thought of her being bigger and just as likely to bite my metaphorical head off. *"Oh, I will. That's our dynamic. And you love it."*

Silence filled the space left wide open for our bond, our connection.

Paige sat there, silently watching me, waiting. "Sorry." I filled her glass first, then emptied whatever was left of the bottle into mine. "Cheers." She lifted her glass to her lips, emptying it with several long gulps.

"Woah, Princess. Slow it down a bit or Aeden will have to carry you to your room." Eoghan muttered something to the rest of the table, making Shay throw a wink my way as she slid into Seamus' lap. Didn't matter that Eoghan was The Mora of Hydrasel, one day I'd wail on him the way I wanted to. But ignoring him now was like choosing against escalating things with Dick Little at that party. It came a lot easier with Paige there next to me.

Paige scoffed as she leaned over the table and grabbed another bottle, filling her glass once more. My eyes narrowed at Eoghan as I downed my glass then slid it over to Paige—an open invitation to refill mine, too. If she was going to get trashed, so was I. I'd follow her into the depths of anywhere. She was getting more and more used to that, yet I could feel her eyes roll beside me before she tipped the bottle over my glass.

The winds were whipping violently beyond the ice walls as heavy snowfall rained down through the valleys of the mountains we were on top of. But the rest of the table continued with their conversation, Seamus' stories of his days as a guard for the most hated fae in all of Aellethian history cutting through the harsh sounds from outside.

"Hey," I whispered to Paige and shuffled my foot over to nudge her boot beneath the table. Her head perked up, her cheeks rosy from the wine and eyes glassy as I inclined my head toward Ikelos, who was serving bowls of his soup to each one of us using his air magic from the kitchen. "How'd you know he was your brother?" I didn't want to draw attention to what I was asking her, so I kept my voice low and bent in even closer to her. Closer than she'd normally allow, but she didn't shy from me this time. I breathed in deeply, unintentionally taking in not only the sweet and floral scent of the Paige I knew in Jessup, but now a heavy dose of torrential rain and thunder rushed through the sweet smell, like how storms cut the heat of summer from the air and made it more enjoyable. She smelled like a storm, and that power along her arm and the way she wielded her weapons when we fought naga side-by-side radiated the truth of that.

My girl was a damn storm.

Her shoulder pressed into my tunic as she swirled the wine in her glass, her eyes trained on the stem and the way her fingers pinched together over it. "I've seen him in my dreams. Just like I think I saw her"—she tipped her glass in Shay's direction—"though that has a lot of fog around it, too. The memory, that is. I'm not exactly sure..." She shrugged as her words trailed off, her shoulder moving up against my bicep as she took a sip. Her touch alone made more heat spread over my skin, my magic fighting beneath my flesh to be near her, like it would never be complete without her. I silently threw a praise to the Stars above for making fae alcohol so damn strong.

Ikelos cupped his mouth with his hands, and even though we were maybe six feet apart from each other, he shouted, "Eat, you two! We are going to a party after this. Attendance is mandatory." I looked outside again, wondering how long my air magic would hold before I'd deplete myself if we went out into the storm that was whipping violently against the walls. And partying while we were being actively hunted by the Mora of Prydia didn't sound like a wise choice, either.

I sure as fuck hope his wards are as strong as Buryon's are.

"What do you mean, you *saw* them?" I ignored Ikelos, angling myself toward her and dipping my head lower to shield my words. Everything about what Paige had said didn't sit right with me. Aellethia was weird, but I hadn't heard about anyone who could see people in their dreams before meeting them. But what did

I know, I had lived most of my life not believing in magic or the things that lived here.

She shrugged again and started working on her food idly, her spoon dipping into the soup only to let it fall back into the bowl. "I don't know. There aren't exactly books about it, none in my fath—" She cleared her throat. "None in Gedeon's house, and that one Shay gave me, or you, whoever, gave to me doesn't have anything about dreams. Maybe it's the gift that hag told me tasted so good." She took a small bite, then said, "You know, when it had some of my blood during the second trial." *No. No I did not know that.* She was so nonchalant about it and I knew it was because of the alcohol, but fuck. My head was spinning, the room turning too bright and too loud as Paige started talking to the others.

"Vara, what do you know about Fae with gifts?"

Her voice came out muffled—possibly eating. Again.

"Mmm, not much. I know you don't have one."

"I know that. Fuck."

"Don't be so rude. Why don't you ask the brother since he has *one?"*

"You know I can't trust him with this. It doesn't help that he looks exactly like his father."

"Last I recall, it's also her *father. And you seem to have no issues trusting her."*

As if Eoghan were in on the conversation, his bright blue eyes slid to mine as he took a sip from his still full glass, his brow arching slightly. Varasyn fell silent when I didn't reply and went right back to eating.

I couldn't just come out and ask him about it, who knows what he'd do with the information that his sister might have a gift? I sure as hell couldn't trust it wouldn't go badly, and I didn't want to risk anyone else knowing about it, either. Her brother was a Seer, but perhaps he didn't know or see everything about her because I hadn't

left her alone often in those fields, and every night she slept, I was there, too.

But if Paige was finally talking, maybe I could find out more. Maybe she was finally ready to let me in and help her. So I swallowed the belief that a party in a snowstorm while all of Prydia was undoubtedly hunting for us was a terrible idea and asked, "Where's the party?"

I should've guessed Eoghan and Ikelos would have a plan to wield a massive air shield over the buildings, blocking the snow and wind effectively enough for the few hundred inhabitants to come out and enjoy the party in town. There was a ton of food, alcohol, loud music, and laughter. Paige was thoroughly invested in the drinks and talking with her brother, Shay and Seamus were all over each other, dancing to the music of a band playing. Eoghan lit the town up with dozens of faelights like we saw in Easrich, illuminating how crowded the street had become once the storm was blocked from hitting below the roof lines.

I fell back from the group when I was sure no one would notice or bother to care that I was gone, and most importantly when I was sure Paige was safe, and slipped into the vacant bookshop.

The shop was narrow but long, with six tall rows of bookcases filled to the brim with books, scrolls, random pieces of framed and unframed artwork, and feather pens and inkwells all scattered in an unorganized way. With a simmering flame in hand, I walked slowly down the first shelf. Searching. Some of the books were written in a language I couldn't read, symbols of the elements as my only guide to knowing what they might be about.

"*How many languages are spoken here?*"

Vara's voice came in groggily, as if I'd woken her up. "*One widely used, your mortal tongue that came hundreds of years ago spread like wildfire in popularity. There are dozens of older languages, but being that I haven't listened to them, I wouldn't know how to translate or where to begin.*" As far as I knew, Vara had been mostly hidden for two decades, yet some of the things she did know made it seem like she'd concealed a part of her past from me. But I didn't have time to wonder more about dragons right now.

"I'll figure it out. Get some sleep."

I took her silence as a response, and slowed when I saw a bundle of scrolls that had the same symbol around it—a flame inside of a triangle. I slipped one from the bundle and put it inside of my jacket. I didn't want to have to steal it, but no one was waiting inside the store to take money I didn't have, so stealing it would have to be.

I moved down another row, and then another mostly filled with artwork of the mountains. I found a book with a dagger etched into the spine, and stashed that into my jacket as well. For Paige. I had no idea what it was about, but I didn't have time to flip through anything. I needed to get back out to the party, to make sure she was okay.

At the end of the fifth row was a small book, a title I couldn't understand as it was written in one of the languages Vara told me about. It was faded and torn, covered in a thick layer of dust, and had a picture of two hands touching, meeting fingertip to fingertip on the spine just below the title. As I pulled it from the shelf and slid it between my chest and my jacket, the sounds of footfalls came from behind me. It grew without finesse, then turned faint like a pinprick along the floor. I closed my fingers around the dim flame, diminishing it before whipping my body into whoever was inches from my back.

In two seconds flat, I had them pinned against the shelf with my forearm pressed to their neck, sending a few scrolls rolling to the ground from the shelf in front of me. Behind…her.

"Easy, Fire Boy." Her hair cascaded over my arm, waves thrown in a frenzy while the deepest of green eyes glossed over me, tugging my power to the surface. I eased off her neck as she smiled playfully.

Then, I took a step closer. "Paige." I let my eyes wander, drinking in every piece of skin and leather she'd let me. "What are you doing here?" My boot edged into the inner side of hers, pushing to spread her thighs apart, allowing me to step in closer.

She cocked her brow, her breaths evening. "I should ask you the same question." Paige reached down and tugged at my jacket, exposing the few items I'd taken from the shop. "Looks like you've been…busy." A small flash of pink fell out from behind her jacket—a peony petal. I couldn't adorn the ceiling of her cell anymore, so I'd moved on to putting her favorite flower inside her jacket, *my jacket*, the past two mornings since she'd saved my life. She hadn't said a word about it, but surely she noticed. The scent of her rolled through me again, and Stars I was growing weak just fiending off that. Peonies and storms and sweetness—like an addiction I couldn't shake. Trouble. If Vara was awake, I wouldn't hear the end of what I was thinking—she'd sense it all too easily between our bond.

My fingers trailed to hers, removing them from my jacket and the books I'd taken. I held her delicate, dangerous fingers in mine for two beats before letting them fall to her side. "I have been." I leaned in, brushing my lips against her ear. "Are you going to tell on me?"

I opened my palm and formed a small orb of fire above my flattened palm, hoping I'd find that same desire in her eyes I was feeling as I pulled an inch away from her.

Her wide, glazed over eyes glowed as they darted over to my hand, then lingered on my lips before shifting back up to where I was still staring back at her. She was in a better mood, whether that was from the alcohol, her brother, or both. I wasn't sure.

But I liked it.

"No. Looks like fun though." She lifted both hands up, her fingers walking up the front of my jacket like tiny soldiers on a mission before her palms went flat and pushed me away. Gently, not strong enough to move me, yet I did so. For her, I stepped back. Even when every part of me, especially beneath my waistband, throbbed and told me not to. "Do they have anything on Prydia?" Her voice cracked on the words, although I was certain she could hear my heartbeat, had felt it along with possibly other things before she pushed me away. She knew what I wanted, and she reveled in that power she had over me.

Her eyes roamed around the shelves as I reached into my jacket, pushing through those unwholesome thoughts. "Not sure, but I got this for you." I pulled out the book with a dagger on it and held it out to her. "Looked like something you'd like to read."

Her head tilted slightly. "I like to read just about anything. But you knew that, didn't you?"

I did.

"Yeah, I do." I ran my fingers through my hair to brush it back into place. "I used to give you my books from my classes, even the boring economics and statistical analysis ones. But I figured if I couldn't give you back another dagger just yet, then this might work for now."

She flipped through a few pages. "It works. For now."

We walked slowly as she read a page from the book that was actually some story about a centaur who made bonded weapons for a Mora hundreds of years ago. I was reading over her shoulder when she stopped, and turned her head up at me, then closed the book. "Thank you," she said with a sincerity that had me stiffen.

"You're always welcome. You don't have to thank me. I like doing things for you."

She shook her head. "Not just for this."

"For what, then?"

Her tongue pushed into her cheek. "For saving me. I wouldn't be alive right now without you. Even if I don't remember all the ways that's true." Ikelos. Or maybe Eoghan. I didn't know what they said out there, or if it was about the bracelet, but they had something to do with her change of heart. Or maybe it really was just the alcohol. Nevertheless, Eoghan was officially off my shit list for the rest of the night, and Ikelos was off my radar of skepticism.

Just for the night.

I nodded, too awestruck and filled with warmth to let anything else come from my mouth that I might regret later. I didn't want to ruin the moment. Instead, I asked, "Is that why you followed me in here? To thank me?"

She giggled, fucking *giggled,* and I couldn't breathe right anymore all over again. She looked down at the floor and shook her head. The tip of her tongue graced her bottom lip as she lifted her head again. "No, I wasn't following you.

I just really wanted some more books." She rolled her eyes up to me and started talking faster. "I've read that part in the other book about the group of fae who were ripped apart by nagas so many times, and ever since we'd been attacked by them, it hasn't appealed to me quite so much anymore. And as much as I love to learn about new things, I think I reached my limit on nagas. For now."

"That's understandable." I laughed with her and my fingers ached to pull her in close to me, to wrap them around the back of her neck and find that perfect angle to meet her lips. The lips she was now biting on.

The memory of her pinned up against the shelves and her legs parted for me flitted through my depraved thoughts, the desire to do it again as we walked beside more shelves all too tempting. But she'd probably stab me if I tried that again.

"Aye, Boyo, are ye in 'ere? Get yer fuckin' ass out 'ere and drink yerself blind with the rest of us, would ye?" The door of the shop closed so hard it shuddered through the walls and when I snapped my head back down, Paige was no longer there.

Chapter Thirteen
PAIGE

Aeden's voice came in deep from down the hall. "That was never the plan."

I picked up my pace, moving past the few decorations of mostly seashells and ice. A true testament to whose house we were in.

"Just because it wasn't the plan, doesn't mean it can't be. Try to have an open mind." *My brother.* Still such a foreign thought.

"He can't have an open mind, Ikelos. He doesn't trust us."

Aeden's voice cut through sternly. "How the hell can you expect me to trust you when you—"

"Don't try to begin to understand my methods, Fire—" The room grew silent when I opened the door to Eoghan's office, where apparently a meeting had started before I could make it in time. Or perhaps that had been the plan—to leave the girl missing a chunk of her memories away from the official business.

But I didn't grow up with men in my life, and being pushed aside by them wasn't about to happen. Aeden's brow arched, his examination of me making me shudder. "Where was my invite?" I walked in, closing the door behind me and taking a position along the space in front of Eoghan's desk, where no one sat. They were all standing in different areas of the room—Eoghan leaning against the ice wall, the mountains beautiful and clear, and heavily snow-capped from the storm the night before, Ikelos shifting his weight against the bookshelf, and Aeden standing in the center of the room, his body angled toward the corner which gave him the best vantage point to see all of us, even as he turned his feet until they pointed at me.

Born to lead. It's not like I could deny that.

"Ah, good. Maybe she can talk some sense into him." Ikelos clapped his hands together, pointing his combined index fingers at Aeden but directing his words to me. "He doesn't think it's wise to wait here, in our home, for another two months or so." *Or so?*

I nodded, rubbing my thumb along my bottom lip. "I don't think it's wise to stay anywhere for longer than is needed, given our circumstances. I'm surprised the nagas hadn't come for us sooner in that field we stayed in for far too long. Is there a reason we should stay?"

The hurt on Ikelos face flashed briefly, like his reasons were personal, and I had just demanded a further reason other than familial attachments that should keep us here—*me* here.

Eoghan's eyes darted to Ikelos before landing on me. "We think it would be best to stay here, within our wards, before moving into a territory that is Prydian, and therefore well-known to be...unwarded. Unsafe, as well, with the amount of guards possibly out there looking for the both of you."

"That's your reasoning?" I countered and Aeden chuckled. It wasn't a great reason to keep us here, so I had to side with Fire Boy. The wards would be gone no matter what we did. Costa wasn't going to change, and neither was Prydia or any of the towns ruled by my father. Therefore, if my father was going to portal to us when we crossed into his lands, it wouldn't really matter if the wards existed or didn't. He'd be able to portal in regardless because the wards would be *his* around the Aerborne territories, *if* he finally decided to put them up—which I highly doubted he would do. His wards would only be beneficial to stay behind because they'd protect against other beasts—slightly, sometimes not at all—but it wasn't like Aeden and I couldn't take whatever came for us. We'd already proven that to each other, and damn did I hate how well we fought together.

At least, I told myself I hated it.

"Wards or no, waiting here would give the Prydian guards time to clear out and move away from Costa, where they are still searching. Winter in Costa is like here, and you can be assured no guards would want to trudge through snow storms to search through homes, much less leave the comfort of them. Especially not during the week of Winter Solstice. They aren't exactly strong enough to wield against the winds and snow, like we are. Like you will be." Eoghan nodded his head toward Ikelos, which made Ikelos tense for a moment before he continued, "It would also give you time to train your new element."

Aeden raised both his brows at me, rubbing his knuckles against his jaw. It was still hard for me to understand what was going on in his mind like he'd already mastered when it came to me and mine. But saying he looked surprised, that would be a lie.

The prick knew.

"What is so special about the week of the Winter Solstice?" I deflected, but rubbed my palms up along the sides of my upper arms, the tip of a pink peony poking out from the inside of my jacket as it shifted with the movement. I hurriedly tucked it away, but it was too late. Aeden smiled softly as he glanced at the edge of my sleeve. His eyes never seemed to want to leave me, even if others were keenly aware of it. He never cared to hide it.

I jolted when my brother's voice cut in. "It's the biggest celebration of the year, in all the kingdoms. The only time our dear father requires complete absence inside his castle. All of his guards are sent home. He doesn't do it out of the kindness of his heart, but the guards all flee as if it were one. All except for possibly Hector. His station is far too important for such activities, though how he negates it—"

"That's it? It's just a holiday?" I pressed on, hoping it would distract Aeden from the question he held on the tip of his tongue about what I was trying so hard not to answer. It was the one thing I was sure he was still thinking about as he rubbed the back of his neck, the rounds he was making on my body with his eyes coming close to ten, no, eleven times—each one slower, more languid, than the previous one.

"Well, that, and it's ummm..." Ikelos cleared his throat, and Eoghan took over as Ikelos blushed. "It's the day when all temptations go through the window, and we all fuck like rabbits. Uncontrollably, of course. The Stars want what they want, after all. I guess because it's hard to conceive for all fae, it had to be made into a holiday where everyone is tempted to at least try to procreate." Eoghan shrugged his shoulders, the hint of a smile curving up the corner of his mouth as he looked between Aeden and I. "As many times as they possibly can in the span of a week," he added. My throat went dry and heat coursed through my cheeks, my thighs. "It's nothing to be ashamed of, we all fuck. Just last night, Ikelos was on his knees, and I don't like to make my man beg for too long. Though he is quite good at it."

"Enough, Eoghan." Ikelos' face turned bright red as Eoghan cocked a mischievous grin at him.

But I hadn't fully registered what was said as I cleared my throat, consumed with the image of Aeden's body without clothing and trying to push that away as far away as I could. "So, *if* we stay, we have a better chance of staving off the guards, even the ones near the ports, is what you're saying?" Because everyone would be...*conceiving*.

Eoghan and Ikelos nodded in unison, though Eoghan's brows lifted briefly as if he were surprised at the information we did have.

Costa was close to the biggest port in all of Aellethia. Not so close we could be seen from it, but a dragon flying close by wouldn't be well hidden if there were hundreds of guards outside, ready to search all caravans and ships. Whatever tried to get close or pass through. Which we knew was an active threat because of the intel Shay received from her source in Easrich.

But if the guards were off duty, at home with their husbands or wives...doing...

My voice came out gritty as I asked, "Why can't we go around the other way? Go through Earthborne territories until we hit Fireborne territories?" I knew why, but maybe putting it out there would make Aeden reconsider.

It didn't. "Besides not knowing the Mora of Buryon, much less trusting him, Murrie needs an ingredient she is sure can only be found in Costa and we *are* going there. She'd be lucky to find it elsewhere, but I don't trust luck enough to tempt it," Aeden replied swiftly.

I rolled my eyes. "Yet we stayed within his territories for months."

"We had no other options, unless you expected me to risk traveling all the way to Fireborne territories—*my* territories—immediately after your last trial with everyone in tow, not that Vara could've handled that in one flight much less would have agreed to do it. It could have killed us all. And trusting *him*"—he jerked his chin at Eoghan—"with our location right after everyone in Aellethia discovered my dragon at that arena didn't sit well with me, either."

"You wound me," Eoghan said dramatically while slapping his hand to his chest.

"He had his reasons to not trust us," my brother said, giving a slight nod to Aeden. "I wouldn't have come here or sought us out either knowing our father was friendly with Hydrasel. Well, not with a dragon, not right after that stunt you pulled in the arena." Ikelos smiled faintly at Aeden. Then looked to me. "He did come to see us, you know, in Hydrasel. Right after you left, Gedeon demanded to be hosted in the city. For an entire week, might I add. Yet we all knew who he had come to find. We were both so relieved when you hadn't been reported to be found in any of the Waterborne territories."

Of course Gedeon went straight to Eoghan. He and my father didn't get along, but that didn't break the friendship that had been formed before Eoghan was the Mora. "I guess it's a good thing I was trapped in a cell then, right?" I snapped back, making Aeden flinch. I moved on, not wanting to ask my brother what had happened during that week. The hatred in both of their faces said more than words could. So, I turned to Aeden instead, continuing to poke the rather large, fiery bear. "Has she even said what ingredient it is she is looking for that is so desperately needed?"

Stern, leader-type Aeden was back in full-force at the bitter tone I'd used. "She has not, nor have I dared to ask. If you feel the need to question her, feel free to do so." I pictured her large battle-ax swinging across her back. I wasn't afraid of her, but was it worth asking her what it was she so desperately needed? "Thought so." I thinned my lips and scowled at him. Perhaps I would ask her, then. That, and why the hell it was so important to go there when I could list several other things we should be doing.

Just to spite him.

Eoghan went to open his mouth, but Aeden cut in as he looked at him. "If we stayed, would she get to train here, with you as her trainer again?"

I wondered if he had even heard the fact that we'd be in a situation where it might be hard to keep our hands off of each other. The implication was clear as day on Eoghan's face. A part of me hoped he hadn't, but a larger, more agonizingly undeniable part made heat flare up my neck even as I scowled at him again while he tried to plan out my future as if I wasn't there and able to speak for myself.

I wondered if the Winter Solstice started its magic months in advance, in preparation. That's what all this heat and body tension was, all the strange, unwanted feelings—the damn Stars. It was always them.

Eoghan replied as if I'd asked the question, not Aeden. "Ikelos and I can both help in training you, but wouldn't it be fun if you both trained each other? Think about it—months of getting to know how the other fights, how they wield"—his gaze shifted to Aeden, a smirk tilting his lips—"what they feel like against you as you pin them to the ground." Eoghan was a bastard. He knew exactly what we both wanted. I wanted to learn how to escape by learning his every move, and I'm sure Aeden, well, if what I'd felt when he pressed into me against those bookshelves the night before was any indication...

"Deal. We will stay under your protection, along with my dragon who *will* remain safe, and train. But I want you to help train Paige." I didn't see that coming. Did that mean he didn't want to train with me? Was I really being insecure about it, or was it just curiosity?

"No fun." Eoghan clucked his tongue, then inclined his head. "But, fine by me. Let me know if you change your mind."

I bit down on my lip involuntarily, now dodging another set of questions and diving headfirst into what was already discovered rather than dwell further on him. On us. Because there was no *us*. "How did you know I got a new power?"

Eoghan shrugged again and clasped his hands behind his back, the motion so similar to a memory that faded in and out and probably had something to do with Aeden. "I didn't. But I figured with you being out in nature and all, and with heightened emotions because of…well…you know." His smile lingered between Fire Boy and me. "I guessed."

Dick. He nailed it though, so I had to give him that. I had, in fact, developed a new element, and that had, in fact, been because of those *heightened emotions*.

"What element, Paige?" Ikelos questioned, moving along the books on the shelves, focusing on the titles of each as he went row by row with his finger outstretched.

"Earth," Aeden and I both replied, and my jaw almost fell to the floor. I suspected he knew, but hearing it aloud versus believing it were two very different things. I thought I'd been careful enough to hide it, yet, he'd known.

Of course, he did.

Eoghan let out a low whistle. "Looks like you two still have some work to do on communication, huh?" He turned his head to look out over the mountains. "Don't forget, Winter Solstice is coming. The worst thing that can happen is a lot of hate sex, which would make things—"

"Got it!" Ikelos cut off Eoghan as he pulled a dark green book from the shelf, and thank the Stars above for that. I didn't need to think about Aeden anymore than I already was, but I wasn't alone. Aeden's exposed neck and chest tinged a reddish hue at the idea that he may get lucky because of the Stars and their desires, which I was quite certain matched the hue along my cheeks.

How hard would it be to fight against what the Stars wanted? The image of the Triad, a game I couldn't exactly escape without some dire consequence, flooded my mind and my stomach sank immediately. It would be really damn hard to fight against it. I'd have to make binding myself with vines the top priority of my upcoming training.

Aeden held his hand out as he leaned over the desk to retrieve the book from Ikelos, and then took a few steps closer to me before passing me the book. His fingers brushed mine as I took the book from him, ignoring the electrical current moving through my power under my skin as much as I could at that singular, brief touch. I tipped the book spine-up to attempt to flip through the pages as my fingers fumbled for purchase. I quickly turned the book the correct way and didn't dare look up as I thumbed through what a beginner could learn while wielding earth.

I continued flipping until I reached the end of the book, where the advanced things like shape formation and bending the actual earth beneath our feet were outlined. So Aeden was advanced in his training—he could dip into the ground and form domes out of things that weren't already there. I had a lot of catching up to do if I still planned on escaping. Because that was still my goal, wasn't it?

I snapped the book closed, holding it to my chest, almost crushing the peony I left there. I shifted in my jacket, nudging it deeper inside and away from the weight of the book. Aeden was put in the room next to mine, which wasn't a shocker. But what *was* shocking was his determination to continue putting peonies in my jacket. I couldn't remember ever being so consistently thought of before, unless he'd always been like that and I'd forgotten, or perhaps it was my mother who had been that way.

The pain that cinched in my chest as I tried to think of Celine, the stubborn grey matter fogging over my unreachable memories, was more of an annoyance now as I found I needed the memories that were stolen from me. One day, regardless of what I or anyone else did, they would return. One day, I'd remember everything.

But it wouldn't be just my mother that I'd be remembering. And that was starting to scare me more than it should.

I startled when Aeden started talking again. Or had he been talking the entire time? "What about the others? I need your word that they'll be safe here, too. We are a packaged deal." I had to agree with him. Leaving them to go back to their homes didn't sit right with me, probably because their home was in

Aerborne territory—my father's land. Call it a guilty conscience, or a fear of being discovered. Whatever it was, I nodded my head in agreement.

Eoghan walked up to Aeden, then stopped in front of him, dropping his cocky demeanor and taking up the face of a king. One I'd actually get behind, if he stayed consistently like that. "I expected them to. My home is yours. I do believe I am indebted to you at least that much. Does this make us even?" He stretched out his hand, which Aeden shook readily, two Moras in agreeance.

But the look on Aeden's face was unmistakably resentment as he said, "I'll accept that. But I want the first spar against you. No weapons, just fists." I wasn't entirely sure why, but I kind of really wanted to see that. Maybe it was because they both deserved to be punched in the head a few times or maybe it was because of the idea of watching Aeden spar, in those clothes that—no, it was definitely the first.

Eoghan grinned boyishly and long gone was the king. "I'd expect nothing less from the Dragon Heir."

Aeden rammed into Eoghan, lifting him up in the air before tackling him into the mat like Eoghan weighed nothing more than a sack of flour. Over and over, the two wrestled as Seamus roared for Aeden from the sidelines.

They said it was just going to be a one-and-done type of thing.

Get it out of their systems.

But there we were, on day three of them beating the shit out of each other. Murrie returned with more herbs from the market, and she was setting them up for a brew that I'd seen her make dozens of times by now along with another I didn't recognize. Through the icy glass right beyond Eoghan's smaller, more sensible training deck, I could see her laying out each herb as the water boiled in the stove behind her.

Eoghan landed another punch to Aeden's jaw, and Ikelos all but flinched his fingers at his sides, trying not to intervene when Aeden kneed Eoghan in the groin. The first fight was more elegant, like a play with a script written just for them as they danced around each other with flair. But this fight, and all the ones after the first, threw the finesse of the first over the ice balcony that overlooked the mountains.

Even Varasyn perched up on a nearby mountain peak, probably impatiently awaiting an end to their juvenile ways with a few smatterings of blood around her as she ate, her long neck craning when she looked our way with steam clouds billowing from her nostrils.

"You...suck—" Eoghan held out a hand as Aeden wrapped his forearm around Eoghan's neck, cutting off his words and pinning him against the front of his body as he held him down to the ground.

"I swear to the ever-loving Stars..." my brother muttered beside me. "Tap out!" he hollered through cupped hands. My fingers grazed the hilt of one of my daggers, wanting to throw it close enough to them as a distraction, just to pull them away from each other. It would be good practice—taking aim at moving targets.

"Fuck!" Eoghan's words came out garbled. With no weapons, and no use of power, they were just working the shit out between them that didn't seem to have an end in sight. Eoghan slammed his hand down to the ground, tapping out, and when Aeden released him with a grunt, rolling his forearm away from Eoghan's neck, Eoghan's blonde hair whipped violently as he spun across the mat from the force.

"I think we agreed that it would be Paige who would be training, not two men who aren't even practicing with their powers. What good is this doing for either of you?" Ikelos scolded as he walked up to Eoghan, wiping blood from Eoghan's mouth and cheek and rubbing a thumb over the bruise that Aeden had given him over his left eye. There were so many small motions over the past few days that showed me the stark contrast between my brother and our father. Ikelos cared deeply for others, loved Eoghan fiercely, and smiled. A lot. It made my heart swell with pride.

My brother.

Aeden and Eoghan both glared at each other as their chests heaved, telling me we might be revisiting this same thing tomorrow morning at the crack of dawn. Ikelos placed a kiss on Eoghan's forehead, then slapped his upper arm with the back of his hand. "Let's get you inside, it's my sister's turn to train. And seeing as you need more healing than Aeden—" who had all but two scratches on his neck, and possibly an irritated shoulder muscle that he kept stretching and rolling back between breaths. "I want to see Paige and Aeden training now. Together."

Ikelos rushed Eoghan off the deck, not wanting to hear either of us negate his order. Yet the smirk that curled up on Eoghan's face as Ikelos' arm curled underneath his to guide him from the deck told me Eoghan quite possibly planned the very thing. He *wanted* us to train together. He wanted to be rushed off the deck by Ikelos, leaving just me and Aeden. The image of us pinning each other to the mat that was laid out on the deck, like Eoghan had described us doing, flashed through my mind intrusively. I shook my head to get rid of it. Not that it worked.

Aeden moved his hand through his hair as he stepped off the mat to drink water from his glass. I began removing my jacket. "Sparring first?" I asked, and he looked at me as he tipped his glass back more, then wiped his mouth with the back of his hand as he set the glass back down.

"Your choice." He didn't look too pleased to be told to train with me. He actually looked kind of upset about it. Not hurt, but agitated.

I rolled up my sleeves and started to unsheathe my daggers, placing them on the ground before meeting him at the edge of the mat. Shay finally woke up and meandered her way over to where Seamus stood, tugging on the ends of his beard, seemingly fascinated over what we'd do next. Seamus was a good man, but the way he held Aeden in his heart as if he were his son made me keep my distance.

"Spar first, then I need you to teach me how to bend the earth to get rid of whatever I make. Like, a tree, for instance."

"For instance?"

"Yeah, hypothetically."

"Right. Hypothetically." He smirked like he knew it wasn't just hypothetical. Because that's probably how he knew about my new power. He saw the tree I'd made, probably watched me chop it down too, like a total idiot.

I shrugged, not giving him the satisfaction of taunting me, though under my skin I was anything but calm. I'd gone from picturing his body pressed into mine to thinking of how I could ask how to make vines thick enough to restrain me for whenever the messed up holiday came. "Yeah. Anyway, spar first. Then teach me how to make the things I make go away."

He edged in closer to me. "Spar. And *then* we can focus on making things first. Like this." He opened his palm and I watched with rapt fascination as he grew a yellow peony out of nothing, then held it out for me to accept. I rolled my eyes, taking the flower from his hand while refraining from lifting it to my face.

I pressed on. "Spar, then *you* make more of these and teach *me* how to get rid of them." The flower lifted from my palm right as my fingers moved to close around the delicate petals and crush it in my hand. I turned to watch as it floated over, landing inside of my crumpled jacket on the ground at the edge of the mat.

When I turned back to him, he was smiling. "You need to learn to create first before you can destroy. Logically. That's also what your book says."

Logically, I could just take all of the peonies he made and push them back into the earth with my fists or cut them up with my blades.

"When did you read my book?"

He shrugged. "I asked Ikelos for a copy." I lifted my brow at him and folded my arms across my chest. "I need to learn too, you know." His arm nudged into me as he moved into the middle of the mat.

I met him there, and Seamus and Shay started clapping from where they stood. I could see my brother through the window, taking whatever herbs Murrie was giving him to lay across Eoghan's face and placing them gently over each wound. I hadn't understood how valued Nya was to Gedeon until I realized that Eoghan didn't have a healer. Not one that stayed in the Amaliro Mountains, anyway. He only had the one in his home in Hydrasel, and he said his mother was sick and it was spreading to the staff there and they needed the healer more than we would, especially with Murrie here to help.

"Of course, you did," I muttered.

He smirked at me. "What was that, Princess?" Aeden picked up on the nickname given to me by Eoghan, and had been using it to goad me on whenever he got the chance. I thought the jibe was more meant for Eoghan, but now that Eoghan was out of earshot, I knew I'd been sorely mistaken.

"If you're trying to get a rise out of me, it's working." Our eyes connected from where we stood, mere feet apart on the mat. He raised his hand and I noticed immediately the difference in his stance from the one he used with Eoghan. His loose posture, his smile, and the hands that were nowhere near ready to do any harm. I rolled my neck and put my fists up, my knuckles turning white. "Do you plan to slap me around out here, or are you going to match me?"

I glanced at his hands that slowly curled inward at my remark. "This better, *Princess?*" He laughed, and with that small distraction, that few seconds where he was more focused on my mouth and my chest than he was on my hands, I crossed the few feet separating us and threw my fist into his gut.

The force was enough to send him back a step. A *single* step. But it was something. He let out a low groan. "Well, fuck me."

"You wish." I lunged again, for once hoping he was imagining me and him doing the things he surely thought about with those wayward glances he threw my way. But he was two steps ahead of me. He stepped to the side quickly and turned, wrapping his arm around my waist and tugging me back against his chest.

"Maybe." I could feel the heat of his breath on my neck as he bent down, his nose brushing against the shell of my ear as he whispered, "Would you like that?"

I tensed against him, but then lifted my knee and thrust my leg back, kicking his shin. When he released me, he was smiling. *Fucking smiling.* "I don't think whatever I'm going to fight is going to be trying to get into my pants, Aeden." I crouched just as his fist swung above me. He knew I'd move, he gave me way too much time to see his hand coming at me, but Seamus and Shay whooped for him on the sidelines all the same.

"They better not or it'll be me they'll be fighting. If they aren't a pile of ash by then." Something told me he preferred to watch them burn rather than give anyone a chance at having me. At even considering it.

"I can handle my own." I charged into him, and just when he bent to take in my force, I moved to the side and made him fumble forward. I'd seen him evade the move hundreds of times with Murrie, but with me? With me, he was allowing it. "Can you fight me like I'm not me, for once?"

"I've been fighting with you for the better half of a few months, Paige." I lunged again just as he righted himself. He stepped to the side but left his forearm out, and in my anger, I didn't stop in time to dodge it. I flew over his outstretched arm, and he flipped his arm back, thrusting my back smack into the mat.

My breathing became shallow—the wind knocked from my lungs for several breaths. But he just kept walking away.

"Punch me!" I slammed my hands down into the mat, my words coming out ragged through the pain I felt in my lungs and chest.

He turned his head over his shoulder, his lips cocked to the side, those wayward eyes returning. "I didn't know you liked it like that."

"You know what I mean, dammit. Fight me like I'm him!" I pointed at Eoghan through the icy wall, who wasn't directly watching us at the time but I'd felt his eyes on us since we'd started. He was watching through the herbs that lay plastered to his face, and he was waiting, just as I was.

He turned fully as I stood, then his strides quickened until there was but a few inches of space between us. "*You* didn't send me to my death and *you* are nothing like him."

"What if I am? What if I just haven't made my move because your fucking dragon doesn't let me out of her sight?"

He scoffed. "Oh, we both know you aren't afraid of Varasyn."

"What makes you so sure?"

Aeden bent in lower, his forehead almost touching mine. But then he whipped his head to look over to where Vara was on the peak, probably responding to something she was saying, and I used that moment to duck and spin my leg to the spot right behind his knee, making him buckle to the mat with the hardest kick I could land. And then I moved, sitting with my legs spread over his lower stomach, pinning his arms to his sides. Not that he was fighting it. In fact, he seemed to enjoy it.

Bastard.

He angled his bottom lip, blowing air upward to brush the hair from his eyes. "I don't think you're afraid of anything. Not Vara, not your father—" I was spun, my body pushed into the mat as he shifted our weight and positioned himself above me. His knee inched up my inner thigh, making my breath hitch. It was a lot harder—breathing—when he was pressing into me, making me feel parts of him that were more distracting than they should be. I rolled my lips in and turned my head to the side. Seamus and Shay were ignoring us. Hell, everyone was ignoring us now. This is what they wanted. They wanted us to work out whatever it was that had been between us. "And certainly not me, *My Queen.*" I turned my head back to him with wide eyes. "Do you like that nickname better?" He chuckled low and I felt the rumble of his chest against my stomach as he pressed deeper into me. "I think you do."

"Get off of me."

"Make me. You want a fight, here it is."

"You are so infuriating." I grunted as he pressed in closer than I thought was possible. *At this point, he might as well be inside—no, don't think that.*

"I think you like that, too." He bent down, his breath a too-soft caress against my cheek. "The only thing you're afraid of, Paige, is *this*. Us. That's what you're really scared of." He pulled back and our eyes met, but where mine probably threatened daggers, his were full of...something entirely too sentimental. Too vulnerable. One blink, and it was gone. He shuffled his body against mine, as if I'd ever forget he was above me. I'm pretty sure I heard someone yell for us to get a room, but I couldn't lash out at anyone but the man who had me pinned to the ground.

"There is no *us*. There is only this mat and your technique against mine. That's all *this* is."

He winced and his eyes darkened above me, those glittering flecks of gold standing out even more now as they shined against the dark obsidian haze his irises had turned. His brows furrowed. "You really want me to fight you?"

I nodded.

And then he jerked his elbow back and landed the punch I begged for right into my gut. It wasn't hard, but the way Seamus reacted told me he'd made it *look* hard. I didn't know if I should be angry, or happy he hadn't gone full-force on me. Sure, I wanted him to fight me. But actually receiving a fist to the gut was another thing, even through all the leather I was wearing.

He let us roll, and that's what we ended up doing—weakly punching and nudging and rolling all around the mat, and eventually right off the mat, until we were both out of breath, panting in a tangled mess of limbs and hair. Somehow my corset strings ended up wrapped around his wrist and fingers. Neither of us were bruised, but to say I didn't *feel* bruised would be an utter lie.

I felt something.

And it wasn't good.

Chapter Fourteen
Aeden

I let her get her rage out on me, and later that night was the first night I heard her crying since I'd taken her from the arena. At least when she was still conscious. I knew she wasn't dreaming because the second her door closed, the sniffling began. The sound could be heard easily through the walls and seemed to reach out through them to me. I might've been sensitized to it from living next door to her and our houses being close enough to allow her cries to travel through the thin windows, but hearing it and knowing it was my fault was tearing me up inside.

My paces weren't steady as I moved back and forth in front of the shared wall. Nothing like the stealth I witnessed from Eoghan's footfalls. What I thought was a courtesy to grant us rooms right next to each other, or rather a courtesy for me, ended up being absolute fucking torture. A torture I couldn't take anymore.

I opened my door, and when I got to hers, I knocked gently. The sobbing stopped immediately and her voice cut through the door. "Go away."

I hesitated, then just as my foot turned in the direction of my door, my hand jumped back up and tapped again on her door. I was so conflicted, but I'd hesitated before, during that night at her house when her mother passed away. A time when she needed me. And if she didn't want me then when she actually felt something for me, then why the hell did I think this time would go over any differently?

Yet, I couldn't let it go.

"Paige, I'm..." *What, sorry?* I was sorry for pushing her, but I didn't think a simple word was going to fix it. No, I'd been a total ass out on the mat. Surely, something I said or did triggered her in ways I wasn't anticipating.

The door flung open, revealing Paige in a short silk nightgown and swollen eyes that glared back at me while I remained silent. It took everything in me not to grab her and pull her close, to make her try to remember me as I'd done so often lately. But that would only make everything so much worse.

"You, what, Aeden? You wanted to tell me more of your theories on who *I* am?"

I let out a sound between a groan and a cough, trying to find my voice once more. "I know you, Paige. They aren't theories, I'm just trying to—"

"Help? Do you think you're helping me when you keep telling me I'm...I'm supposed to love someone that I don't?" Her brief pause allowed me to notice the way my chest had started to crumple in on itself. And when she began again, it didn't get any better. "Do you think I enjoy not being able to remember a thing about who we were or who *she* was to me? Do you think I like traveling with someone who tries to remind me of a past I can't remember, no matter how hard I try?" I tried clinging on to that blip of information—she had tried, possibly on more than one occasion, to remember me. Not just her mother.

But grabbing onto that like a lifeline for the ache I felt was useless.

I shook my head as she crossed her arms over her chest. "No. I was only trying to...fuck...I don't know." I dragged my hand through my hair. "Do you know how much it hurts seeing you go from looking at me one way to"—I motioned to the entirety of her face that had gone red with anger—"to that? You hate me now, I get it. Without who we once were, why should you love me? I took you from the arena, I took away your chances. And now I'm towing you along to find my people—" Shit, even saying it aloud from my own mouth, I sounded awful. How had she not stabbed me, yet? And now we were moving beyond how I kept pressing for her memories, into the real reason behind the amount of scorn she so clearly felt at the sight of me. "You have every right to be mad at me. I pulled you from the arena to protect you. As hard as that is to accept, just know that

I was only doing what I thought was right, to keep you alive. The same goes for why I kept you..." *Fuck.* "When I kept you in that cage, it was for your protection. Not for Murrie's, or Seamus' or Shay's. Yours. You were so ready to run back to Prydia, they would have killed you the second you stepped foot into one of his territories." I reached my hand up to cup her cheek on impulse, but she pushed my hand away, that ache in my chest solidifying into a pit that was lodging into my throat as I continued. "I only want to keep you safe. Even if you don't love—even if you don't want me. I know you never asked me to and I do try to fight against it, but I fucking fail. Every. Damn. Time."

She looked me over, her arms tightening around her chest. The thickness in the air around us became palpable—more than just the warmth I emitted. It was pure fury. "Maybe you should try harder."

"I am. Paige, I...fuck, I am. If that's how I can make you stop crying"—she wiped her cheek and shied her head to the side at the acknowledgment—"If it makes you happy, I'll fight against my instincts. As much as I can. And I'll try to stop pressing for your memories beyond what you agreed to let Murrie do. I know it wasn't your fault, Paige. What he did...none of it was your fault."

"So that's why we are heading to Costa, then. Getting my memories back is more important than going where we should be going." A statement, not a question. She analyzed me again, letting the silence stretch on. Then she shook her head and muttered under her breath, "And here I was, thinking it was something to heal you faster when you're so hellbent on depleting yourself." I had assumed she knew or had heard the reason for why we needed to go there. But damn, I was failing there, too.

She moved on. "If I try to leave right now, go wake up Eoghan to get a portal out of here, you won't try to stop me, then? Won't try to protect me and keep me with you until my memories return?"

Until her memories return? I wanted to keep her after that, too. I never wanted to leave her side. But maybe I shouldn't touch on that. I examined her, prying my eyes from hers and moving them down to her bare feet and back up. She was so beautiful, even with a puffy face and swollen lips. I didn't want to lie to her, so it would have to be the truth, and the only truth she was going to accept was, "No. I won't stop you."

Seeing her cry—it was *breaking* me.

Her back straightened and the red began to fade from her cheeks. "Really?"

"Really." I nodded, feeling the strain of my body also not fully on board with the idea, but did it anyway. Let's face it, I'd do anything she wanted me to, even if it went against everything in me. I might follow her instead of stopping her, but she didn't need to hear that, either.

"Are all men so encumbered when they fall in love?" That's why they call it *falling*, isn't it?

I groaned. *"This isn't about you, Vara. Please, just stay out of it."*

"No, it isn't directly about me, but if you can't fight because of her, then it is about me. I become involved in whatever matters of the heart you have because you can't seem to press through without the thing. It makes me feel kind of—"

"Useless?" Paige's head tilted to the side and her brows furrowed together, probably a reaction to whatever my face was doing as Vara crept into my thoughts.

"Sorry, Vara isn't too happy with me or where this is going right now." Or really ever.

"Well, you can tell *Vara...*" I didn't hear what I should be telling Vara, because she cut in. I guess even Paige's words coming into my mind was enough to let Vara in on our conversation.

"I'd love to hear what the girl wants to say to me. Please, let her speak."

"Go back to sleep, Vara. Let me sort this out on my own." She huffed, then something between us, some invisible space I could only sense, seemed to make everything silent once more.

"Vara will be fine," I lied. "And I will be, too." Another lie, but not one that would bother Paige any. "If you need to leave, then do so. But you should take these back first." I pulled out the remaining daggers I'd taken from her, because I'd kept them sheathed in my pants whenever we weren't training ever since we'd arrived at Eoghan's home. I was kind of hoping I'd find her in my room late at night, searching for them. But somehow she'd kept her distance when I seemed to fail at that, too. At least her anger was dissipating faster than I'd hoped at the sight of them in my hands. "I've been wanting to give them back to you. They are yours. Always have been. I'm sorry I took them from you." And that...that wasn't a lie. She'd earned those daggers. The right to carry them had never been mine to decide, much less give.

She nodded, taking the blades and moving them slowly over to a dresser that mirrored the same one I had in my room. Eoghan's taste in furniture was more...plain. More comfortable. The bed was simple, the rugs weren't combatting with golden features everywhere. In fact, I hadn't seen much gold since arriving and it was a relief to not be draped in opulence.

I stood in her doorway, not knowing if I should pass the threshold and walk in to continue our conversation, or if it was over. But then she turned back to me and motioned for me to sit in the chair. To come in.

So I did. I watched her move to sit on the edge of the bed as I slid into the chair, my hands tapping on the armrests as the silence grew.

"I—" we both started, but I held my hand out for her to continue.

"I don't think the other's are going to like hearing that you gave those back to me. And I know how much their opinion matters to you. So...thank you. For giving them back."

I nodded, pausing long enough to know it was my turn to speak. "I care about their opinions, but I care about your safety more. And if you're going to leave, you will need those. I shouldn't have taken them to begin with."

Her interest noticeably peaked. "Why?"

I ran a hand through my hair, pushing my head back in the process. I stared up at the ceiling briefly. *Because I fucking love you,* I wanted to say. But she needed more than that. So I sat there, brushing my fingers down the length of my throat before righting my head to face her again, wondering how I should continue without setting her off again.

"I know you don't remember this, but is it okay if I tell you a story? Something from when we were just friends." She nodded, drawing in her bottom lip. I tried to ignore that subtle movement, ignore how beautiful she was as she was about to rip my heart out all over again with the blank looks that went along with the loss of her memory. I dug my fingertips into the chair and sighed. "When I first moved in next door to you, you rarely came out of your house. I remember seeing you that first time I'd caught you outside, though. I remember what you were wearing, what face you were making as you stepped outside...even the fact that you were barefoot, like you are now." I paused to look at her, to make sure I wasn't treading into unsteady waters before continuing. "I remember thinking, *I want to know what she's thinking. I want to know why she has a book the size of Jupiter in her hands, and what the hell she stepped outside for, in the snow, barefoot and all.* I wanted so badly to storm over to you and throw my coat over you, to pick you up and take you inside my house, because I knew your electricity had been off for several days. And then, you looked at me." I raised my eyes to meet hers, surprised to find her full focus still on me. Her eyes, how they bore into my soul that very first time, I'll never forget it. "You *really* looked at me. Like you were thinking the same things I was—that you wanted to know me, too. That you were curious about what was on my mind as I stared back at you."

"I grew up with no one, Paige. No one who gave a damn about me. And when I went to college, I thought it would get better. But it didn't. Those people looked right through me, saw what value I had to them and ignored who I was as a person. They needed me, in whatever ways they could use me. To their benefit, and sometimes my own. But never the way I craved for."

"That must have been hard," she whispered, her eyes narrowing in on my tapping foot.

"It was. But I'm not done." She nodded again, crossing her legs and adjusting her nightgown. Her fingers edged along the hem, and while to most that would seem like she was disregarding them, I knew she was listening deeply. "Something inside of me turned on the first day I saw you. I'd heard things around town about you both before and after that day, but I never took them to heart. Because, like they did to me, those people saw right through you. They didn't see you like I did. They never saw the selfless, devoted, caring person you are. The girl who could read for hours at a time to get away from the reality the world kept forcing upon her. The girl who wanted nothing more than to make a better life for herself and for her mother. The girl who was so stubborn and headstrong that I was sure she'd make it happen, no matter how much shit life kept throwing at her. So I made myself available shortly after that day, and introduced myself more formally. And then I realized something."

"What?" Her eyes flicked back up to me, her voice breathy as her fingers stilled.

I sucked in a breath through my nose, forcing back the urge to not let this out. But she needed to know how I felt about her. I never got to tell her just how much she meant to me in Jessup, and the second I got a chance to, I was ripped away from her. "I realized that I'd never felt like that with anyone. It was beyond the way we looked at each other. I knew you were special that day, but when I met you, actually *met* you, you…you were like the brightest flame, burning right through me and lighting up even the darkest parts of myself. I realized how empty I'd become, how I'd just allowed myself to wander the world without caring about being loved or loving in return. Not caring enough to change it because I'd never found someone worth changing for. And you were the missing piece.

"I can't fully explain it, but something inside of me changed when you came into my life, and now that I have these"—I motioned at the length of my exposed arm, because I'd forgotten to put a shirt on before walking over to see her—"I know it's more than that. Much more. I know whatever we have—whatever it is, the need to protect you feels no different from the rest of the power that flows through my blood. Maybe you can sympathize with that, knowing your own power and the feeling of it. Or maybe I'm just talking out of my ass. But I did the things I did because I was driven to. Not that I didn't want to save you, but even if it was just a want, my body would've fought me tooth-and-nail to bring you back to me. Both physically and with your memories. My body"—I put a hand to my chest—"My soul. Everything about me craves you."

She paused, glancing at her hem and her fingers and then over to the door. Anywhere that wasn't my eyes until she said, "So…what you feel about me"—she brushed her hand over the length of her arm—"is the same as the power?" Even in the darkness of the room, I could see her cheeks warming, the pale pink color playing off her smooth porcelain skin perfectly.

Stars, she's perfect.

"In a way. I mean, please don't throw a blade at me, I'm sure you keep the rest close by you." Her eyes darted over her shoulder to the nightstand behind her, and then fell back on me as she tucked her hair behind her ear. But she didn't move for them, so I continued. "I love you more than I could ever explain. But the part of me that needed to pull you from the arena and keep you in a fucking cell? The protective part, I guess it is. That part seems to be ingrained in my body. Similar to the marks on my skin. And the man that keeps trying to remind you of who I am, who *we* were, is mixed in there as well. Fighting to bring you back to me." Although perhaps that was mostly all me and just who I had become since I'd come here. I had her ripped quite literally from my arms, and that wasn't something I ever wanted to go through again.

Her brows crinkled together as she looked right back at me, and for the first time in so long, her gaze didn't shift into something full of hate. They remained...almost like they were when she was the girl who had been my friend for so long. It made my heart thunder uncontrollably.

"She could still kill you, you know," Vara reminded me abruptly.

I groaned and rolled my eyes back up to the ceiling.

"Not the time, Vara. Please. I think I'm getting somewhere."

"Is Varasyn making sure I haven't hurt you?" I laughed, because she was right.

Paige was not only deadly accurate with her knives, as I'd been reminded of whenever she went out on the deck to train, but she was also deadly accurate with knowing when I was talking to Vara—with recognizing when my mind drifted. It wasn't from the memories she no longer had of me. She was relearning things about me, and that thought roared in tune with my heavy-beating heart.

I smiled weakly. "Yeah, she's a bit concerned."

"You can tell her I won't hurt you tonight. Not yet, that is." She let out the faintest of smiles. "Is it weird that I can hardly remember my house in Jessup?

There's grey, literal *grey* splotches, over rooms and areas whenever I try to think about it. Like the kitchen, and a portion of the hallway is completely gone."

"I don't think anything about you is weird. Not in a bad way, or a way that would make me love you any less." She sighed, but much less dramatically than she always did whenever I told her I loved her. "I do, however, think what your father did to you was wrong—I can't emphasize that enough. To take a part of who you are, to try to diminish your power? It's nothing short of messed-up."

She rolled her lips in. "I don't want to go to Prydia to go back to him, you know. Well, not in the ways you're thinking. I didn't get the best of fathers. Actually, I really hate him and wish he were dead," she deadpanned.

I chuckled, trying not to get hot over the image of her killing her father. "I know. I didn't quite understand that at first. Hell, I thought you were going to jump off of Varasyn's back that day."

She giggled. "Oh, I was. I was definitely going to try."

I grinned. "I never put it past you."

"I didn't really have a plan, but I knew I didn't want to be trapped anymore than I was before. And then when you ended up putting me in a cage...well, it was almost no different than being in my father's castle. He didn't let me outside unless it was to train. The one time I got out was because of Eoghan. He wanted to show me the way my father maintained his city. Or, rather, didn't maintain it. Maybe that's why Gedeon did this to me. He knew that I wouldn't keep him around if I knew—truly knew—what kind of leader he was, if you can even call him that." *Damn. I might have to thank Eoghan for taking her out of that hellhole.*

My fingers curved too tightly over the arms of the chair. Shay and Seamus had assured me she'd be safe in that castle until we figured something out. But never letting her out?

Then again, I'd been no better.

I wondered what else he might have done to her as I looked over at her. What other ways he'd tried to show her how powerful he believed he was. I swallowed that thought down, unsure if the truth of that would help anything right now.

"You can't blame yourself for what he did to you. He had no reason to do any of that." Neither did I. I stood up and crossed the room to stand in front of her, then took her hands in mine, overcome with the need to touch her and let the truth of what I had to say seep in. She didn't pull back, even though she had every right to. "It's not your fault. None of what he did to you is your fault. He's nothing short of a tyrant and a really bad father. The only thing you can do is move forward. Take back what is yours."

And that's when her features changed, her eyes growing dark and jaw setting like the hate was rising above the surface of everything I'd just spilled to her.

Pouring my heart out was just eating me alive, at this point.

"That's what I was trying to do, the day that you took me from—I can't keep bringing this up. I thanked you for saving me during my trials, but I don't know if I could ever thank you for *saving* me when really what you did was put me in a cell." I could feel my chest sinking as she reached for the words that promised to wound me. No matter how many forms of armor I'd developed over the course of being here, I'd never armor myself against her. "I know you think you saved my life in the only way you thought was possible, but there's a part of me that keeps telling me I could've won. I could've made my way to that door beyond the flames, and the Stars would have opened that door for me. If only I'd been believed in enough to do it." She pulled her hands from mine and the loss felt ten times greater than just the loss of her warmth.

She thought I didn't believe in her?

It hit me hard then—I was the problem. All of this, *us,* where we stood now in whatever relationship we had, if any, was my doing. I pushed my hands into my cold pockets and took a step back. "Right." I took another step back toward the door, watching the space between us grow like jagged mountaintops. "I *do* believe in you. Maybe more than you believe in yourself at times. I know you don't want to forgive me for it, and maybe you never will. If you choose to stay, I'll try harder to stop protecting you—to not act like you *need* my protection. If that's what you need to stay, then I'll do it. But if you leave—"

"I'm not leaving, Aeden." She lifted her head from the shield of her hands and looked me over. "I have nowhere else to go. Finding Ikelos is what Eoghan told me to do. And now...well, I found him and now I don't know what to do next."

"You have a kingdom to take back. Once we find my people, I—"

She shook her head and laughed, though nothing about this was funny. Not to her, or me. *Once we find my people, I'm going to start a war for you, My Queen. I'm going to watch you drive that dagger into his heart.* That's what I wanted to say, but what she heard was me sounding selfish again.

"Just...go. Get out. Please. I can't take much more tonight, and I don't want to argue with you again when I have so little left to give." Whether that meant she had little to give because of her lack of memory, or because she just couldn't anymore, I didn't know, but I could guess because she looked like she was going to start crying again.

I inclined my head one last time, and then left her room, letting those jagged mountaintops peak so high I'd never make it back over them.

Chapter Fifteen

PAIGE

An entire month went by, but the days all seemed the same. I'd wake up, get ready to train, eat breakfast with my brother, and sometimes Eoghan, well before anyone else was downstairs to eat, and then I'd get to work on learning to wield better before Aeden made his way out to spar or train with me. Some days, I didn't see him at all. I wasn't sure where he went, but on the days he missed training, no one seemed to think anything of it.

It shouldn't have bothered me as much as it did, but it did.

Eoghan joined me on the mat on the days when Aeden wasn't there and it made me think about training for the Triad all over again, even wearing a new set of brown leather training gear and a white tunic like I had back in Prydia. The newer leather wasn't broken in yet, and was more uncomfortable than the set I'd been wearing, but Ikelos suggested that getting out of the stained-red tunic I'd been in for months might help my mood.

He was wrong.

In a twisted way, that red had grown on me. That realization only made my stomach twist more uncomfortably than it had every time the red of Aeden's marks sprung up in my mind, or his words repeated nonsensically in my head. Which happened more often than it should have.

When Aeden wasn't there and it was just Eoghan and I, it felt...like everything I didn't want training to ever feel like again. I kept trying to remind myself that I wasn't going into an arena, that I wasn't in Prydia anymore and I wasn't fighting for my life because the Stars demanded it. I was in Waterborne territories now, with my brother, and I was safe. And the next fight—the next battle? That would be for me, for *them*. For the kingdom I was going to take from my father. Whenever that day came.

"If you ask me where my head is at one more time, I swear to the fucking Stars, Eoghan."

"At least I'm trying, which is more than I can say about you." Eoghan held up both hands defensively before I bent over my knees, trying hard not to puke or scream or both and reaching for the too-tight laces of my new boots, pulling on them until they loosened enough to ease the pain in my feet. My eyes squinted, shielding against the way the white tunic reflected the sun above us when I stood back up.

My body would've fought me tooth-and-nail to bring you back to me.

"And, what? You think I'm not?" I fought the urge to heave up my breakfast as that twisting started up again.

You were like the brightest flame, burning right through me.

"I think that you don't want to try, not when he isn't here," he replied, his tone shifting to a level of concern I wasn't used to hearing from him. But that slight change in his voice was marred by the knowing grin he flashed me as I glared back at him.

"Shut up." *You were the missing piece.* "Shut up" I repeated, more to the words in my head than to Eoghan—"before I try this new method I'm learning of blasting giant orbs of water at you. I think you'd go pretty far into those mountains."

"It should be air." His grin faltered as his gaze raked over me, nothing like the way Aeden looked at me. *Stars, what is wrong with me?* "Anything developing with that?"

It's not your fault. None of what he did to you is your fault.

I swallowed the growing lump in my throat. "It's there, barely." I flicked my hair over my shoulder, hoping it would bat Aeden's voice from my mind so I could focus, for once.

"I want to see you trying with whatever you do have," he said sternly. I flipped my finger up at him, knowing my air magic was there enough to practice with, but also acknowledging I hated calling on the power that my father had given to me. Surely Ikelos didn't share the same resentment toward his power because that was the only one I'd seen him use so far, so maybe I was just being too sentimental over the amount of times Gedeon's air magic was used against me. I sighed in frustration as I walked away from Eoghan and moved toward Shay who was holding out a glass for me.

Eoghan continued talking anyway. "Or a break sounds good. Sure, why not. It isn't like we have a schedule or a time-frame—"

"She has plenty of time to learn." I almost dropped my glass to the floor as Aeden strolled out onto the deck, wearing a full set of leather gear. Dragon-riding gear. The way the black leather fit Aeden's body was like every piece had been made for him—the shoulder plates that fit just over his black fabric tunic, the matching leather straps that went over his thighs and back for weapons, and the pants...also leather, with ridges along his knees.

I hadn't even noticed the glass was no longer in my hand as he continued to walk up to Eoghan, undoing leather gloves from his hands. The cords in his arms rippled against the sunlight I'd previously been blinded by that now just illuminated all of *him* instead. I threw a quick glance over to Shay, noting how she'd taken my glass before I let it fall to the floor.

My fingers were spread wide open like a cup still existed there as Eoghan and Aeden started talking, but all I could hear was the blood rushing to my ears as my teeth ground against each other. My hand snapped shut, curling in so tightly, my nails dug into my palm. He'd missed *another* session of training, and I'd had enough with the secrets and the way he was avoiding me. We both needed to train, and it seemed more often than not that my training wasn't worth his time anymore.

Fury filled my vision as I strode up to him. "Where have you been?" I closed the distance between us with a few more quick strides. Eoghan rolled his eyes and stepped to the side, granting me the space to stand where he'd been, right in front of Aeden.

"Has she always been like this?" Eoghan groaned under his breath.

Aeden just stared down at me, then ran a hand through his wet hair. *Sweat.* He was sweating. I had to assume he was flying because of the gear, but in broad daylight? Without telling me he wasn't going to be here for training? Who sweated that much on the back of a dragon with snow surrounding them?

Eoghan let out a low whistle when he received no answer. "Right, well then," he murmured. "Neither one of you wants me here, so I'm just gonna...yeah."

Through the corner of my eye, I could see Eoghan going back inside and taking up a spot against the table, him and Ikelos talking with their hands more than their mouths could keep up with. If not for the amount of movement they were both doing, I wouldn't have registered his absence. I was too focused on the man I needed answers from.

I pressed my boots into the mat, the tightness returning around my feet. "Where. Have. You. Been?"

"Careful, Paige. You wouldn't want to look like you actually care about me." He cocked his head to the side and his face brightened once again under the afternoon sun. "Is that what this is? Have your memories—"

I held up my hand. "No, I don't have my memories back." His face—that shimmer of momentary elation—was gone. I added, "And Murrie shot me down when I suggested Forga Market for whatever it is she needs, but she won't risk the travel, even with a portal. I tried to tell her that whatever she needs is more than likely going to be at the most lucrative and unsolicited trading market in all of Aellethia, but now I have a feeling you're to blame for that request being denied too, aren't you?"

"It's not safe," Aeden said flatly. "Too many factors."

Right. *Factors.* I let out an aggravated sigh and pinched the bridge of my nose. "You didn't answer my question." I put my hands on my hips, a move that felt so foreign I ended up dropping them and then fumbled my arms awkwardly until they ended up crossed over my chest. Why couldn't I figure out what to do with my arms? "Where have you been?"

"Flying." One word. That was it.

"Flying?" My eyes followed the 5 o'clock shadow, and the longer tendrils of hair that stuck to his forehead. He followed my gaze and dragged his hand through his damp brown hair again. "Really?" I didn't believe him. Not with the way he looked. Flight clothes be damned—he was doing something else in them. Perhaps he did fly to do those things, but flying was only a fraction of whatever it was he was up to.

"Yes, flying. Do you need me here for something?"

Did I need him here? Why was I so angry about him disappearing all the time? I quite clearly pushed him further away after he opened up more to me, something he didn't need to do, but he did it anyway because I'd asked. And there I was, fighting with him. Or trying to. Yet again.

"No, I suppose I don't," I finally answered.

He nodded just as Seamus called him over from inside. "Right. I'm going to go where I'm needed, Paige. You seem to be doing fine without me." Instead of watching him wince back, I felt my own.

"Yeah. Go. Not like you weren't going to anyways before Seamus called you."

His eyes narrowed on me before he looked over the edge of the balcony, toward one of the many peaks. "What is that supposed to mean?" He moved his gaze back to me, just as I uncrossed my arms and tried for my pockets instead, and then shifted to touching the hilt of one of my daggers that I kept sheathed beneath my leather corset.

"It means you've missed several days of training. Training that *you* wanted me to be here for."

"With Eoghan," he clarified. Seamus called for him again, but he just put a finger up in the air, not bothering to look over at Seamus as he did it. The same hand that held mine and sent way too many jolts throughout my body right before I sent him out of my room weeks ago.

I weakly cleared my throat. "Well, yes, but I figured..."

He stepped in closer to me, but left a respectable distance between us. I let go of the handle of my dagger and let my arm fall to my side as my body urged me to match his stride, closing that lingering distance. *Closer.* "You figured, what? I have my training, things I need to learn and do, and you have yours." He looked between us, noticing how I did indeed move closer.

Agitation rose in his voice. "Isn't that what you wanted? Space? *Freedom?*"

But the way he said *freedom* didn't make me feel like I was free. It made me feel more trapped, even when I was possibly the most free I'd been in a long time. And I...damn,

I had him to thank for that. I held all twelve blades all around my body at all times, practiced whenever I wanted, ate whenever I wanted, and I went into the town below with my brother whenever I wanted. I even read the books I wanted to read and didn't fight about the ones left outside of my door—books I knew were left by Aeden, who'd grown more distant with each passing day. Yet he still left me flowers in my jacket—*his* jacket that I continued to wear whenever I was cold or in my room alone. Every. Single. Day.

So I just walked away, shoving my shoulder into him as I moved past him. I didn't even bother answering him. If he wanted to see my freedom I'd been granted, just as he had been doing, I'd show him what I intended to do with that freedom.

I started by roping my brother into taking me out to a bar in town. Not a single fae treated us any different, and there was an odd comfort in knowing I wouldn't be ratted out by the people. Not in this town, at least. We were safe, for the most part. I could only imagine the relief Aeden felt being here.

"Is everything okay with you?" Ikelos asked as the bartender slid us two very large glasses full of a dark brown alcohol. *Beer*, I guessed. Until I sipped it. Not exactly the beer I remembered from the mortal world. No, this was stronger.

I pushed the liquid down. "I'm fine."

"You don't seem fine," he said. I shrugged half-heartedly. "Maybe you and him need to talk?"

"This isn't about him, Ikelos." It was, and I was a terrible liar. I took another long sip, draining my whatever-the-hell-I-was-drinking drink. I slammed the glass down a bit too loudly and drew the attention of an older group of...I wasn't even sure what they were. They weren't fae, that much I knew. More dwarves?

"Paige, did Eoghan ever tell you about how we...ended up together?"

I shook my head, then said, "Nope," and popped the 'p' at the end.

"We've known each other for, well, for most of our lives. My fa—our father, and Eoghan's mother were close. Not in the way...they weren't sexually close."

"I get it. We call that *friends* in the mortal world." Not that I could remember having any. Apparently Aeden had filled that role, too. Confirmed by the amount of grey splotches covering my mind at the thought.

He laughed. "Yes, friends. So, you understand. Though their friendship was more of an alliance of kingdoms, so it hinged on a larger scale than what I would consider a friendship to rely on."

"So you and Eoghan were matched to continue an alliance?" My nose scrunched briefly, because I couldn't for the life of me picture my father approving a marriage between them two. He'd want Ikelos to be as isolated and alone as possible, preferably never getting close to anyone. I wondered if he was allowed beyond the castle walls like I wasn't.

"No." He laughed as he shook his head and took a few sips of his drink, his *first* drink, whereas the bartender had just slid another to me. "Not quite."

"So..."

"So, we grew up together. Played together, learned to ride horses and fight together. I guess you could say that part was to keep the alliance strong. We didn't really get along that well when we were kids, though. I actually shot him with an arrow one time because he cheated during a game of chess."

I almost spit my drink out. Something about the visual of a chess board and an arrow going into Eoghan had me laughing hysterically, until the dwarves in the corner made guttural noises toward me. I just waved at them politely and let Ikelos continue.

"When it came time for my Triad, Eoghan had already won his, and that was well after the laws became what they are now. I looked up to him because he did what I believed was impossible. He went through each trial so fucking flawlessly, and when he didn't form the fire mark, I was in awe of his will power. I still don't think it's possible to beat the Triad and not get the fire mark before winning, but Eoghan…he always did the impossible and made it look so…"

"Good? Realistic?" I took another sip as he agreed.

"Exactly. He still does. But then…then it came time for my trials. I watched Eoghan ascend the throne, I watched as his mother accepted a position as his adviser, and his life just fell into place. But mine…I never imagined my life could ever look like his." He grabbed the edge of his blue velvet coat, his thumb grazing it as he smiled down at it.

"Because our father is a huge asshole?" I supplied.

His head snapped back up. "Yeah, that's part of it. The sad part is, I knew what Eoghan's future looked like, months before it even happened. I didn't tell him, because I wasn't sure if that would sway the outcome. He was one of the only people I trusted with my secret, but I couldn't use what I'd been shown in good faith. Looking back, I don't think anything could have swayed him any other way. He was always meant for the throne. But my future? No, the Stars are cruel in that sense." He let out a low chuckle. "Or maybe they know that to be able to see your own future would be a cruelty at the times it most counted." He shrugged with one shoulder, then finished his drink. "I didn't know anything about my Triad. All I knew was that I had this gift and the fucking Stars were going to throw it in my face at every opportunity they got while in that arena." I nodded because it reminded me of the hag that wanted to devour me because of some gift I wasn't even sure I had. I silently wondered if Aeden was doing anything about that information I entrusted to him. "Until the night before my last trial, the Stars finally gave me a sliver, a mere glimpse, at what was to come. I was going to die.

They didn't actually show me dying, but it was pretty clear what was going to happen to me the next day."

"What did you do?" I was gripping the edge of the bar top, waiting to hear what happened next. None of this had been in that book I read of previously failed Triads, and Eoghan...well, Eoghan didn't tell me anything unless he thought I needed to know it. Which was starting to look like he thought I didn't need to know anything. But this was my brother and I *wanted* to know it all.

"I ran to Eoghan." Every time my brother said Eoghan's name, I could hear his tone shift. Like his world revolved around him. It was a lot like the tone Aeden used when he said my name. I took another few long sips. "He was staying in one of the guest rooms in that Stars-damned castle, so I quite literally ran to his room. I didn't even notice I was crying until he wiped my tears away and pulled me to him. It was the first time we ever...embraced, like that. When he offered for me to sleep in his room that night, I didn't refuse."

I swallowed my last sip and nearly choked on it. "I didn't need to know that much."

"We only slept, Paige. He held me all night, but we were clothed. We were friends. He was the only person I had." I shifted uncomfortably in my seat. "Something tells me this isn't the first time you've heard something like that."

My throat became dry, even with the amount I was drinking. I couldn't remember having friends, but I knew without a doubt Aeden had been the only one I did have. Knowing that for a fact was starting to hurt, because we weren't *that* anymore. And maybe it was all my fault at this point.

"Just continue, please? How did you get out of it alive?"

"Eoghan, of course. He asked me what I saw in the vision, and we were able to figure out at what point I was going to be sent to the Stars. And then, we used that to our advantage the only way we could, even if it meant I was going to lose."

"So you were okay with losing?"

He looked me over as he nodded slowly. "I never wanted to sit where our father sits now." *Wait. He didn't want it?* But I thought better of asking him more about that as another glass slid in front of him and I watched as he downed the entirety of its contents before continuing. "Anyway, Eoghan had his family's healer with him. Nya was still too young to use that amount of power—"

"I forgot you knew Nya." *I hope she's okay.*

"She was always so sweet. Truly, too nice to be living in that place." We both tipped our glasses up.

"To Nya," Ikelos said, and I drank several sips to that. "But as I was saying, his healer was able to make something that would make me appear...well, it killed me. Temporarily."

"Excuse me?" I shrieked a little too loudly for the small bar, and the dwarves let me know that I was getting on their last nerve with a series of grunts and groans. But, seriously? We were in a bar.

I ignored them.

"It stopped my heart from beating for one minute, and when the arena faded to nothing but dirt and dust, I rose up from the ground. You should've seen the look on his face, Paige. He was absolutely enraged, and it was one of the most beautiful things I'd ever seen. Well, that, and Eoghan's ass. Top two things I picture when I'm feeling down."

"Okay, that much I really didn't"—I hiccuped as another glass slid into view—"Forget it. You can tell me all about it."

So he did. We talked like we'd known each other our whole lives. Even if my memories did return, none of them would be of him. So I started making the memories that I was lacking, and before I knew it, the sun was setting slowly down the side of the mountain.

Ikelos and I finished our last drink, and then we walked back to where Eoghan left a portal up just for us—hidden within the bookstore that I now understood was more like a public library. The image of Aeden tucking books under his jacket when he believed he was stealing them made me giggle.

"What's so funny?" Ikelos asked as we walked down the same set of shelves that Aeden and I walked between when he gave me one of the books he'd taken.

"Nothing. Just...Aeden believed he was stealing from here, that first night we got here."

"Stealing? It says 'free' in like five places by the front door." I laughed again. *Does it really? I didn't even notice that.*

"Yeah, he took a book, or several, and gave me one." I pulled the book from my back pocket. It was small, so carrying it around on me whenever I left Eoghan's house wasn't a hassle.

"And you carry it around with you?" He smiled, and I took a step back, waving my hands.

"Not what you're thinking. It's a good story, and it fits in my pocket."

"Uh-huh," he said. "I'm sure it's the convenience of its size that makes you keep it so close to you."

If it were anyone other than my brother, I'd throw the book at their face. But it was Ikelos, my brother who I'd gotten really close to over the past month. "Don't tell anyone, okay?"

"I won't say a word. But, Paige?"

I followed him to the portal. "Mmm?"

"You should talk to him. Eoghan says that Aeden has been giving off a vibe that's kind of...well, you just need to talk to him." He stepped through the portal right after, and I stopped for a moment, looking around at the books, the shelves, the area where Aeden had been pressed up against me. I must have stopped by that same shelf nearly a dozen times now, lingering in ways that didn't make a lot of sense to me.

Maybe we did need to talk, but how could I do that when one of us always seemed to push the other away?

Chapter Sixteen
PAIGE

I couldn't sleep. Which wasn't saying a lot because I so rarely slept and if I did, it was usually not as peaceful as other people appeared to be able to sleep. Like Murrie—what I would give to sleep like her. I never felt fully asleep anymore, because each time I closed my eyes, I'd wake up in another place.

Sometimes it was random. People I'd never seen, places I'd never been to before. Sometimes I saw Hector, other times I saw my father. Sometimes I felt a ship rocking beneath my feet, other times I was in a dark chamber that was possibly a cell, the sounds of screaming piercing my ears.

But tonight I wouldn't slip into my dreams. I'd asked Eoghan earlier to open a portal for me in town, knowing I'd be out with my *freedom* on full display. Aeden was probably somewhere *flying,* or maybe he was in his room. I wasn't sure, but I knew if I left late at night, he'd notice.

So, that's what I did.

My brother told me about a stream that branched off into the woods just outside of the mountains we were tucked away in. He said the waters were warmed by the earth, and that a portion of it was secluded from the rest of the town—meant just for Eoghan and Ikelos, and recently Shay, to use. And now me. I must've asked a dozen times, promising I wouldn't run away, before he finally relented and told me how to find the path that would lead me there.

So, I took one of the horses from the stables—Misty, I believe it was that Seamus had named—and took off riding in the direction Ikelos told me to take.

I rode, guided only by the moonlight, the Stars above, and the occasional faelight as I passed several buildings before finding the path. Misty hadn't been taken out much since we'd arrived, but that wasn't the reason we were jerking all along the path. I'd never ridden a horse before on my own, and if I pulled the reins too much in one way, she'd react before I'd know what to do.

But we continued on, even as Misty squealed and snorted back at me and gave me looks like she was about to knock me off of her. Truly, I wouldn't blame her, but I wasn't going to let a thing like not knowing what the fuck I was doing stop me. Not now, most likely not ever.

I let her guide us once we were on the path set in between evergreen trees that hung low with snow-covered branches. There were a few snarls of things that lived in the woods, but I'd been told by Ikelos there was nothing to fear of whatever lay within, so I continued. The secluded section of the stream was just beyond where the path ended, where a thin layer of steam hovered above the waters that sparkled against the stars in the night sky.

I quickly tethered Misty to a tree where she finally appeared at ease and stripped down to nothing before walking in. And it felt incredible. The warm water slid over my skin—the softness unlike anything I'd ever experienced before. The only sounds this deep in the woods were of the trickling water, the occasional chitter of small animals, and the faint rustling of branches each time those animals moved.

The waters were shallow, just as Ikelos said they'd be.

He must've seen me in the second trial with his gift, or perhaps Eoghan told him. Either way, I wouldn't have to worry about drowning.

I tilted my head back, wetting my hair and feeling the warm water against my scalp. Steam rolled off my arms and lifted into the cool breeze. It was the most peace I'd found in...I couldn't even remember how long.

Misty made a snorting sound when a twig snapped, and I quickly sank into the water, leaving just enough of my face exposed to allow me to continue to breathe as I scanned the area around me. But when nothing came out and Misty settled again, I went fully under the surface of the water and let a plume of bubbles rise to the surface with a deep exhale.

Relax, Paige. There's nothing.

My feet dug into the sandy bottom as I pushed back up, breaking the surface of the water only to feel it lapping around my waist, and my eyes widened as I saw—

"This is the least safe thing you could be doing, you know."

Wind rolled across my bare chest and I frantically wrapped my arms across my breasts and sank back into the water. I looked back at him through lowered brows. "Aeden." I paused, trying not to look as disheveled as I felt. "Were you following me?"

The corner of his lips curled up, revealing a dimple on his cheek. One dimple, and the heat of my body rushed to my cheeks. But that could just as easily be from the warm water I was…shit, I was fully naked in. And judging by the pile of clothes next to my own, he was too.

My cheeks warmed even more, and it wasn't at all from the warmth of the water. "I promised I wouldn't stop you from doing anything, but I never agreed to not follow you during said times you chose to do…reckless things." He eyed me over, amusement dancing in his eyes that was so clear even in the dark. "You do remember you can't swim, right?"

"Of course, I remember that." My throat turned dry as he stood up from his crouched position in the shallow water, the fine ridge that trailed from just above his hip and dipped down to places I shouldn't be focusing on….it was all on full display. And he didn't seem to care at all. He *wanted* me to look, even followed my eyes to the same groove I was just trapped in for too many seconds and smirked back at me like he could read my exact thoughts.

Fuck.

"Shouldn't you be flying, or doing something more productive than following me?"

"What else could I possibly be doing past midnight?"

"I don't know. Flying, or fighting something, or fucking someone in town. The world is your oyster." *Stars, here I go again.*

"Paige." He let out a low groan. "I'm clearly not interested in doing any of those things. Especially not with you here, in the dark. Alone."

"Could have fooled me at the inn." My words were coming out of nowhere. True word vomit. The steam was turning my mind to goo, that's what was happening.

He narrowed his eyes, the gold flecks standing to attention against the moonlight. "I'm going to say this once. I haven't touched anyone else or looked at anyone else since well before the night we first kissed. I think we both know the only woman I want in my bed is you."

"Okay..." I swallowed thickly, suddenly wishing I knew what his mouth felt like against mine. At one point, I knew. "But did you really have to get in?" My voice cracked and I sank even lower.

"Why not? It looked rather inviting." He cupped his hands, filling them with water before he poured it down the front of him as if he were cold. We both knew he wasn't, yet I allowed myself to watch as the water rolled down. "I am a man of my word, Paige. I didn't stop you. And if I'm going to follow you here, I might as well follow you *in*, too." He dipped low into the water, edging his way closer to me. I tried moving back a step, but was met with the border of the stream that was flanked with several large stones.

Trapped. Every time I saw this man, he ended up trapping me in one way or another. Yet, this time it was doing things to my body that were getting very hard to ignore. He moved in closer, so close I could reach out and touch him. "This doesn't really feel like the freedom you promised I'd have," I whispered, lacing my fingers behind my back before the urge to pull him to me could become a reality.

"No?" He leaned his head back into the water, the lump on his throat making something faint glisten at the surface of my mind that quickly became grey with the strained memory. I'd experienced glimpses like that before and a lot more often lately, but nothing that ever made me *feel* something like what I was feeling now—not comparably in any way, shape, or form. And that something wasn't exactly the love he mentioned quite a few times that we'd had for each other. It was a burning desire for other things. Things that made me squeeze my thighs tightly beneath the water.

The water rippled around us both as his arms waded under the surface. Not that he needed to be doing that. The water was far too shallow to need to support either of our bodies like that.

"No. It...it doesn't feel like I'm very...um..." I was losing my words the moment they came to my lips, and when he looked at my mouth and didn't bother shifting his gaze away, I lost my train of thought entirely.

"Free? Are you not naked right now?" My fingertips dug into my palms, the rocks biting into my arms as I kept them pinned behind me.

"I think you know the answer to that." My eyes roamed to the piles of clothing, then back to him—to his marks, his chest, even his fucking hair that had water dripping from the ends. He was too devastatingly good-looking to not look at. And it was becoming more and more problematic.

He hummed and took a step closer. Our knees touched under the water and the warmth made my legs tremble. I assumed he felt it, too, because the smirk he was giving me bordered on a line I wasn't going to cross. Absolutely was not going to—

"I can help you feel more free, if you want, My Queen." I didn't even know what to say. I tried to look anywhere other than right back at his mesmerizing eyes, but I couldn't look away. He was like a magnet, a stupid gravitational pull to my body, even if he did make me so angry sometimes. Most times, really.

Everything about me craves you.

His words were working back into my thoughts like his knees were doing to my thighs, pushing my legs further apart. Slowly. Tortuously. Heat pooled within me, low and hungry, that had nothing to do with the water and everything to do with the man covered in flames right in front of me.

"I don't think..." I trailed off as I watched him swipe his tongue over his bottom lip, then sink his teeth into it, undoubtedly holding on to what little restraint he had left. And I was right there, too, my hands and wrists burning with scrapes from the rocks behind me.

His eyes darkened against the starlit waters, his knee reaching dangerously close to the apex of my thighs. "Then don't think."

I wasn't sure when my fingers unlaced, or when my back abandoned the solid rocks behind me. His arms stopped treading the surface the moment my arms wrapped around his neck and I pushed myself into him, our lips colliding in the most predatory way possible.

I could feel every. Single. Part of him. The heat of his mouth on mine, the hardness between my thighs, the defined lines of his muscles that bit into my breasts as we clung to each other like the world was going to end if we let even an inch come between us. He was maddening most of the time—so fucking aggravating—but this? This feeling was something that ate away at the grey splotches in my mind, threatening to take down all the barriers of my lost memory.

My fingers laced into his hair and tugged, making him groan against my lips and into my mouth as he slid his tongue in to meet mine. The rocks bit into my back once more, but I was so far gone into...whatever the hell we were doing, that I didn't flinch. I just used it to my advantage as we eased back more and I ground against him, pulling a moan from me that made him respond eagerly with more rotations of his hips. His cock rubbed against my clit teasingly, driving me further and further into the insanity that was *him*. If it wasn't the reflection of the Stars bouncing off of the water, then I was surely seeing the stars that spotted my vision from within my mind. The ones he was causing.

Everything about me craves you. The words surfaced over and over, as if I could finally reach the same understanding through our bodies. It was too much, too consuming.

Then don't think.

His fingers worked their way into my hair just as his other hand moved up the length of my torso, and I sucked in a sharp breath when his palm cupped my breast and his fingers began working my peaked nipple. He flicked and circled, massaging it with his rough thumb and pushing into me more while his mouth continued to claim mine. I wanted more, *needed* more. I positioned my other hand on his chest and slid down eagerly, the mounds of his stomach muscles turning into the smooth, thin line of hair I'd caught myself more than once wondering what lay just below it.

He groaned again and possibly said my name, but I was gone. I wasn't Paige, I wasn't the heir to the Prydian throne, I wasn't the girl that kept denying the insane attraction I held for the man now so dangerously close to entering me. I was just me, and he was just him.

Then don't think.

My hand followed the length that pulsed against me, and we both let out a ragged moan when I curled my fingers around his thick shaft, his desire for me so clear. I couldn't see it, not that I'd try to stop and look down, but it was...more than I'd experienced before. I had distant, faint memories of losing my virginity to some asshole, but I knew he was nothing in comparison to what I felt in the water. It was as if the memories that were washed away with everything that involved the man now between my thighs had already tried to be rewritten by him before—as if I previously tried to forget losing that virginity to anyone but him.

His kisses trailed down the side of my neck, and he bit softly into the curve right above my collarbone when I pumped his length once, then twice. He groaned low, rumbling against my chest.

"Fuck. Do that again. Don't stop." *His voice.* His voice was the hottest, most gritty thing I'd ever heard. And I wanted to hear it again. So, I continued. I pumped him over and over while his hand continued to knead into my breast.

"You're so fucking perfect." His fingers flicked again over my painfully erect nipple. I let out a strangled moan at the contact just before he dropped his head down and took the bud into his mouth.

"Aeden," I whispered, though it was more of a breath that was stolen from me as he swirled and flicked his tongue. I was dying, surely that's what was happening. Dying, or the Winter Solstice was actually today even though in reality it was a month away. Another...another month. What the hell would we be doing to each other when all of our inhibitions were thrown through the window?

The water began to steam more, my hand working under the water as his mouth ceaselessly sucked, nipped, and played with my nipple, then my other.

Everything was becoming uncomfortably hot. The rocks I believed were scraping against my back turned into a swell of fire that burned up the entirety of my back.

"Oh, fuck," I breathed against the top of Aeden's head as I released his cock. "Aeden, I..." His head lifted, lips slightly swollen but eyes set wide as they met mine, noticing my tone shifting from the lust-heavy craze I'd been in, and turning into something frantic.

He tensed, his hands flying to either side of my shoulders. "What's wrong?" His eyes searched mine, then scanned the rest of my face. The steam was intensifying, and as it pulled his attention away from me and out to the rest of the stream, the top of the water began to boil and bubble around us.

"Shit. Hold on." My legs were already wrapped around him and I didn't let go as he wrapped his arms around me and lifted me from under the water, pulling me closer.

One minute we were in the water, the next we were on land. My breathing was...was I breathing? Aeden was still holding me as I curled into his lap, and through the corner of my eye I saw his wrist move, right before a rush of air entered my lungs.

"You have to breathe, Paige. Just...fuck." Again and again, he repeated the motion until I could breathe again.

"You're shivering." He wrapped his arms around me, and it was the first breath I took on my own that felt... right. Too right. His fingers splayed over my back, brushing down my spine until he reached the spot I was certain had just been on fire.

But as the panic began to ebb away, I knew what it was. Knew what had just spread across my flesh. He didn't need to say anything for the knowledge to wash over me.

"I need to go," was all I said before I pushed myself away from the embrace we were in and stood. I got dressed with my back turned to him, and I could feel the heat of his stare on me during every second that I stayed silent as the cold of the snow around me seeped into my bones.

Yet, he said nothing.

He knew what it meant. He'd caused not just one mark to appear, but now two. Whether he was fully aware that he'd caused the first, he most certainly knew he was the cause of the second.

The grey splotches of my mind settled back in like the plague they were becoming before I took off on Misty's back, leaving Aeden naked in the snow-covered grass. I didn't dare turn around and check to make sure he was okay.

Because I knew he wasn't. Fuck, I wasn't.

Not in the slightest.

Chapter Seventeen
Aeden

"Don't you have better things to do? Seamus said—"

"I don't care what Seamus said, Shay. You needed help, so unless you'd prefer Ikelos over me, I don't know who else would've jumped at the opportunity." She needed help getting supplies, and I needed a distraction. Desperately.

"Alright, then." She let out a faint sound, something like an agreement with a tinge of annoyance.

Maybe that was just how I was starting to view everyone around me. Ever since that night not even a full week ago, I'd received more than a few sideways glances, and heard murmuring that I didn't have to fully be able to hear to know what was being said.

I wasn't sure whether it was because Paige had told her brother, who would have then told Eoghan, or because they noticed I was increasing my distance with each passing day. Maybe it was all because of the mark she was now learning how to wield with. Maybe I was starting to affect her in ways she wouldn't own up to. But that thought seemed so laughable in the most unhumorous way possible.

She couldn't even look at me after what had happened. She hated me.

Varasyn was the only one who didn't seem to have an issue with me lately, beyond the occasional sly remark that I was a dumbass who needed to learn to control my cock. I couldn't help but agree with her, because look where I'd ended up.

Not in Paige's bed, or her good graces.

"Over there, I think I see what Murrie said she needed. One of them, that is. There's a list." I sighed as she passed the paper to me. It would take hours to find everything she needed. Hopefully.

"What exactly is she making that she needs all of this?" Perhaps she'd come up with another way to try to regain Paige's memories, but when Shay spoke, my hopes crashed to the ground.

"Healing, mending whatever it is you've been doing to your body. Some things for me, and I wouldn't be surprised if this one was a request from Paige." Oils and soaps made from roses and lilies. Some part of her was starting to remember her mother, even if she didn't realize it. She'd never been particularly fond of either flower herself, and had hated the last one listed as I finished off the list.

"She asked for lavender?" Shay nodded, tapping the paper where the name of the flower was written. The same scent as her mother's candles she lit each time she holed herself up in her room, bingeing, allowing the wax to drip down the surface of her dresser. The reason Paige wasn't particularly fond of the color that now marked her skin. "She hates lavender."

"Well, she asked for it. Maybe you should ask her about it." I ignored that. She knew it wasn't that simple.

Shay started looking around, flashing her eyes over the paper in my hands and the sea of people around us. People that were moving in every direction holding baskets half-full. Wagons and storefronts packed to the brim with food, weapons, clothing, herbs, and many things I'd never seen before. It was nothing like Costa or Prydia. Eoghan's one town was almost enough to convince me he was different, like the pixies had suggested. That didn't change the fact that I still couldn't stop picturing his lips on hers. My fists curled in while the thought lingered until Shay pulled me to one of the wagons full of a smell that made my stomach churn.

"What the fuck is that?" I pinched my nose and turned with my back to the wagon while she sifted through things that were making slippery, wet noises that only made me queasier.

"It's one of the things on her list." She moved to show me the item listed—*a harrowbocker's lung.* Judging by the smell and the nets, I assumed it was some kind of fish, but I refused to turn to find out.

Shay and the shopkeeper made small talk behind me while I watched everyone else around me. Searching for guards, weapons, people that would be ready to lunge for us. But the looks I was getting back weren't from my marks in this place. Not in the way I expected, at least. Women were blushing as they walked by me, looking me over as they smiled and waved. I'd gone from hunted for my mark to being looked at like a prize, even though inside I felt the complete opposite. I shifted where my sleeve had fallen, hoping the looks would stop. But they didn't.

"Does being a mermaid also mean you're immune to smells like that?" Shay nudged me, laughing when I dropped my hand from my face after we took several paces away from the wagon.

"No, but I grew up eating things with a similar smell, so I guess you could say my senses have… adjusted. I remember being young and hating it." I looked her over, trying to picture a girl with long black hair and bright, shiny blue eyes making faces at the food her parents gave her, her small nose scrunching up in disgust.

The thought made me chuckle as we made our way into a store full of flowers. A store full of things I could try to make for free. But there were people who couldn't. People who needed the income from what their power could provide. Eoghan didn't have the same struggles Paige and I grew up with. He had the means, and it was something I couldn't imagine relating to. I shifted the bulge of coins he'd given us for the trip over in my pocket as we stepped further into the store, making a few girls giggle as we passed. If only they knew the marks on my body didn't equate to wealth, maybe then they'd stop looking at me like I could give them the world when all I possessed was the few things in a room that wasn't even mine.

"What was it like when you were little? Not the kingdoms, just…your life?" I asked, and she turned and quirked a brow at me. A faint smile lifted the corner of her mouth as a memory flitted through her eyes.

"It was beautiful—peaceful. I loved swimming with my family, camping, and learning to cook. My mother used to make the best boiled fish and potatoes." She picked up several stems with semi-wilted petals and walked on to another section of the store.

"Camping? Like in that cave?" She laughed and shook her head.

"No, not in that cave in particular. We preferred to lay out and watch the stars until we drifted off. Mostly in the spring and summer."

"Is that how you met Seamus? Or was that at Forga?" A few fae around us stiffened their necks and glanced our way. Shay waved her hand impassively and let out a nervous laugh. When their heads turned and they resumed their shopping, Shay slapped the back of that same hand to my upper arm.

"Keep quiet about Forga, Aeden. Shit, do you want everyone in here thinking I'm a criminal?"

I knew she was a poacher, but the fire-wielder mark on my arm made me one as well. Not that anyone here seemed to care. I smirked down at her. "Ah, so *that's* how you met, then. I should have guessed you two were thick as thieves."

She slapped my arm again. "It's not exactly a place known for its legal wares," she whispered. "But no, we did not meet *there*."

I crossed my arms over my chest and waited for her to continue. She finally did a few minutes later when there were fewer people around us. I thought only fae were shopping in here, but there were other things I'd also never seen before. But if they were going to ignore the flames on my body, then I was going to ignore whatever it was that they were. Pointy ears, hair covering their limbs, scales fading, smaller, crumpled postures and some that looked more animal than human, like we did, although their winter coats and pants covered most of what I could see beyond their faces. Not that it really mattered to me. One of my best friends was a dwarf, I was shopping with a mermaid, and I rode and talked to a dragon on a daily basis.

"Seamus saved my life one day." Not surprising, but I waited again for her to continue. "I was married before." Now, *that* was surprising. My forehead wrinkled, noticing the slight tremor of her hand. I took the flowers from her palm and watched as she rubbed her hands down the length of her long dress.

"I can carry everything, don't worry about it." The tremor wasn't from the weight of the stems that weighed little to nothing. She knew it, and I knew it. But acknowledging her reaction to recalling whatever fucked-up person she was married to before didn't feel right. We all had our pasts. This was hers. I wasn't ever going to judge her for that, and she needed to know that.

She nodded and gave me a faint smile. I wasn't going to ask her anymore than she was willing to give, but she continued anyway. "He was an evil man. He had some good days, but on days he didn't...when he..." Her hands shook again and I watched as her fingers flexed, steadying the movement.

She didn't need to finish the sentence for me to understand. I'd been through similar things growing up, although it was never people I loved who dealt the blows.

The bastard beat her.

"He had good days, but those started to become outweighed by all the bad. One day we were in Costa at the market, buying fish from Seamus. He saw... well...let's just say, although I'm not a fae like you, I had marks of my own." *Fuck.* Heat simmered along with a cooling sensation that worked in waves to ease the amount of anguish I was feeling for Shay. Anguish and rage, for my friend.

"Whatever he did to you, it wasn't your fault, Shay." What I didn't say was, *I hope Seamus slit his fucking throat in front of you.* Things like that coming from my mouth would only make me seem just as violent as the man she was no longer with. She didn't need that in her life, especially not while she was recounting the horrible acts he did to her.

I'd seen that look before in Paige's eyes whenever people talked shit about her mother. It was like she'd pause and watch her own memories like a twisted movie on replay in her mind. The fight or flight mode going way above the clouds.

It had been months since I'd seen her freeze up like that. Since I'd seen that haunting look on her face. That was until her panic attack when the fire mark spread along her back. And I just sat their pushing air into her and holding her like that was what she'd wanted. That I could ease her pain like I'd done before she'd forgotten who I was to her.

Shay's hand landed along my forearm, breaking me from my thoughts before she moved on with her own torturous past like she was trying to make mine fade into the dark. "Seamus, I'm sure, had seen the marks before. And that day when we both went to the market, Seamus looked at me…and then to my husband."

"They fought?" I supplied, hoping she'd take a few breaths in between, glistening pools of water coming to the surface of her eyes that darkened like Lake Kree.

"I'm sorry, I'm not usually like this." She wiped beneath her eyelid.

"You don't have to apologize. It must've been difficult to live through that."

She nodded and coughed gently into her fist, blinking away the tears. "Seamus and I were on friendly terms, and my husband saw the smile Seamus gave to me and…he snapped. More than he usually did when it was just him and I. He snapped, and Seamus reacted."

"He killed him, right?" Another nod, though this time a faint smile touched her lips. "Thank fuck." I dragged a hand through my hair. If we were in the mortal world, I would've beat the asshole, but here? In Aellethia? I would've done the exact same thing Seamus had done. If anyone ever laid their hands on Paige, I'd rip them apart and then turn those pieces to bone dust, and ash.

Shay passed me herbs that smelled like a mix of cinnamon and basil, and another that was more citrusy. She moved over to another table and picked up three vials—each one meant for Paige. "Agreed. Are you okay, though?" She looked me over as I held out my hands to take whatever she grabbed. "Something's been up with you."

The familiar scent of peonies washed over me as we continued through the store. It was becoming harder and harder not to think about Paige, of the way she used to let me wrap my arms around her. The way that scent would wrap around me with her. That growing ache was spreading everywhere, even when I wasn't close to her. She was everywhere.

"I'm fine." She didn't need to hear what was bothering me. Everyone knew what was wrong with me. It wasn't *something*, it was *someone*.

"Don't give me that. I just told you too much to receive no gossip in return." I knew what she wanted. She wanted to not think about him anymore, and even though it hurt to think about Paige, she never beat me. She never put me through what I could only imagine domestic abuse was like. Sure, she taunted me with daggers, and we rolled on the mat, but that wasn't the same. She would never actually hurt me.

"Pretty sure you've already heard." She nodded, then refused to look at me. So, I added, "Do I need to ask who told you?"

Her eyes slid to me as I reached down and picked up a few more herbs.

"Would it sound better if I said everyone knows?" I groaned. "Give her time to adjust. She will come around. I think it's more about—"

"I know what it's about. Her mark makes her just as hunted as I am. If there was any chance her father was going to let her live...well, I fucking ruined that, too. Didn't I?" It was amazing that Seamus and Shay hadn't been more concerned about Paige getting the mark before at the ball, all those months ago. They simply hadn't considered how far I'd go with her in that room that night...and perhaps if I'd let her have her way with me then, if we'd made love then—

No. I didn't even want to consider what could have happened then.

Her brow creased. "I don't think that's what—"

"I'm sure I transferred it to her, Shay. She doesn't look at me like that and hasn't in a long time." And if she'd loved me at that ball, which I wanted so desperately to believe she had, then surely the fact that she now had the mark was my doing entirely. I had transferred it to her against her will.

"Then how did you two end up being so close that night?"

"*I, for one, don't want to know the* how *part. I'm more concerned with the* why *you felt the need to follow her.*"

"*You helped me get there. Didn't think to ask then now, did you?*"

"*I was tired.*"

I laughed and shook my head as we approached the shop owner and put the items down on the counter. "I'm sure you heard enough details to fill in whatever blanks you're missing." I shuffled a few coins from my pocket and placed them into the woman's waiting hands as Shay grabbed a basket to buy as well. My sleeve lifted, showing a sliver of my mark, and the woman didn't bat a single eyelash as she took my coins and wished us a good day.

A good day.

Imagine.

Shay put everything in the basket before we left. "Surely she considered what she was doing. It doesn't take a genius to see what happened between you two was more than a simple…um…gesture." *We almost made love.* Well, it would have been that way for me. For her, it would've been another way of working through her frustrations. It would have been just sex for her. Just her getting off while I fucked her with everything I could give. My chest was getting so painfully used to the agony she was putting me through, yet somehow the stupid organ found new ways to still hurt every damn time I thought about how differently we viewed each other. I loved her more than anything, and she…didn't.

I dragged my fingers through my hair, settling it at the base of my neck. "No, I think you're wrong about that."

"What? Was she drunk? Did you force yourself on her?"

"Stars, no, Shay. I'm not a fucking monster." I was many things, but I'd never touch a woman unless they wanted me to. And she did want me to. I could see it in her eyes and in the way her cheeks turned pink and adorable. It was the same way she looked at me back in her kitchen that day. I was no fool to the look of desire, though I'd been an expert at ignoring any signs of it from her until recently.

Shay smiled knowingly. "Then, what?" Clearly, more than just a few details were spared by whoever was spreading what had happened between us beyond Paige's words. One, in particular.

"I may have told her not to think."

Shay burst into laughter. So much so, that she bent her body forward, catching the attention of others as she continuously howled. When she stood up again, her face was tinged with red.

"I don't get why that's so funny."

"Oh, Aeden. So, what? You think because you told her not to think, she had to listen to you? That girl is as stubborn as you are blinded by her. She's just as guilty as you are in all of this." Her hand slapped between my shoulders as she pushed me through the crowd to the next building. I let my body be subjected to her light push because honestly, I was dumbfounded. Of course, she didn't need to listen to me. Hell, she never listened to me. But it still made me feel like the villain. It was my fault she had the new mark. My fault there was this wedge between us that I wanted to burn down. Even if she didn't admit to wanting me in any kind of way, her body had done that for her that night. And I'd taken advantage of it.

"She has my mark now, Shay. That *is* all my fault." But honestly, it looked incredibly hot on her. I'd been watching her for days on the deck. Watching her form the same flames I did, trying to work her recovering air magic in when she could to send the fire hurdling into the mountains. I watched, and I wished that she hadn't run off that night. Wished she had let me hold her just a while longer.

Shay shrugged her shoulders. "Again, I'm not a fae. You might need to ask Eoghan about all of this—or maybe not Eoghan if you're going to make that face whenever I mention him. Try her brother or Seamus, then. But transferring your power takes practice, Aeden. You developed your power quickly, and I know Ikelos is giving you books that Paige hasn't touched yet, but to transfer? You think you did that, what, by accident?" She cackled again. *So happy someone can find this so funny.*

"She doesn't love me, Shay. So, yeah. The possibility that I did something advanced is more probable than her loving any part of me." She should have already had the mark by the time we left the Fields of Araros with how many fires I put near her to keep her warm. Perhaps that poison had done more damage to her power than I wanted to believe.

"From what I understand, it's any strong emotion that elicits a new mark. It has a lot to do with the person receiving it. Maybe your mark was reacting to her, and then she...also, reacted. It's natural."

Natural. There was nothing natural about us. And yet my stupid chest combated that thought as well because what was more natural than love? It was complicated between us, and being hunted and the reasons why we were in the first place wasn't making it any better. The feeling of being watched here and there also wasn't helping. I let my eyes skim the bustling streets, but beyond the occasional looks, no one stood out. Paranoia was the cherry on top of the fucking pie.

Shay's waving arms brought me back to reality. "You need to talk to her, you big idiot." Yeah. Okay.

"What, when she's trying to ram into me on the mat?"

"As long as she isn't stabbing you out there, I don't see why you can't try."

I grinned at that. "You know I gave her back all of her daggers, right?"

Shay's shoulders tensed, then relaxed after a few beats with a halfhearted shrug. "I guess that means Murrie won the bet, then."

I stopped walking and turned to face her. "Excuse me?"

"She bet that you'd give them all back before we got to Costa, I said after, and Seamus doubted you ever really took them from her to begin with."

I shook my head. "You're all twisted."

"Twisted *and* now broke, thanks to you."

"Meeting room. Now." Eoghan and Ikelos were waiting on the other end of the portal for Shay and me when we returned. Shay turned away when she wasn't given a moment's glance, but me? All eyes were on me—even Paige's from down the hall.

This can't be good.

"It isn't good news, I'm afraid." The door clicked shut behind Ikelos, and I moved to lean my shoulder against the bookcase along the back wall. I rolled my neck, noticing Eoghan's tense shoulders that crept up to his damn ears, and Paige's lips that not only reminded me of the night we shared but also had me tensing in response as they rolled in, and in.

Eoghan's office had become our unofficial meeting space, where another chunk of Paige and I's training took place. In Eoghan's eyes, I was already the Mora of Vizna, even without the people or kingdom to back up that claim. And Paige? She had the backing of two other kingdoms—one being mine, because of-fucking-course I'd back her claim to that throne, and although Eoghan was keeping it a secret from the rest of the world, he had made it clear that he preferred her in Prydia over her father.

Which only left Buryon unaccounted for. Leander Earthborne, the invisible Mora who clearly hated politics as much as he hated being seen. Not that he'd been helpful towards *my* kingdom in the past.

Not that we'd get an opinion from him on what was to come. He didn't exist as far as I could tell.

"What took you so long today?" Eoghan asked, and I folded my arms in response, because fuck him.

Paige cut in as she glared at me. "Let me guess, you were flying, or training elsewhere?"

My mouth snapped shut, replaced by the curve of my lips. Such vitriol in her tone, but man, it was good to hear her voice after so many days without it. If hate is what she was throwing my way, I'd take it in a heartbeat.

"Actually, I was with Shay," I amended, and she scoffed. "I can take you with next time, if you'd like."

Ikelos snorted behind her, and she slapped his chest with the back of her hand. *Bonus points for the brother.*

"This is serious." Ikelos adjusted his cuffs at Eoghan's tone. I watched as Paige shuffled her feet on the floor. "Your father sent one of his guards here. They were, of course, captured. His body will be discovered in a matter of days, mangled by what we will say was nagas"—Ikelos cleared his throat as Eoghan flexed his fingers, an unmistakable tinge of blood beneath his fingernails catching my eye as I shifted against the wall—"but he will inevitably send more. It's not an act of war. Not yet, at least." Eoghan's eyes slid to Ikelos before he shook his hands out at his sides.

I wouldn't have let the guard live, either. Not if she was in danger. "When was this?"

"Earlier this morning. He was captured by a few of my guards stationed in the woods by the stream."

"You said we'd all be safe here, that your town and the people in it didn't want to draw his attention, so they could be trusted. But it seems a lot like that was a lie," I countered.

Eoghan's jaw worked as he glared at me. "They are all here for asylum, for one reason or another. Trust me, they don't want his guards here." That explained...a lot.

And now I was the asshole.

"He probably still assumes Eoghan had a hand in Paige's Triad because of how close you two seemed to get when you were there and, well, with the way my own Triad ended—and where I ended up afterward." Paige slid her hand over Ikelos' shoulder. It wasn't surprising to see Paige had already known what I recently found out about his Triad. That was her brother, and they had grown close. "With his week-long visit granting him no clarity in finding you—he must be still convinced we are aiding you."

"He assumes fucking right, is the problem," Eoghan said.

Maybe that explains your constant paranoia. Can't go against those instincts.

"Just keep looking out for more guards. He wouldn't send just one." One wouldn't be enough to capture what he was hunting. He'd send skilled guards, and several.

Chewing sounds filled my ears and I rubbed at my temple to dull the crunching noises. *"On it."*

"Varasyn's going to keep an eye out." Eoghan nodded and Ikelos' shoulders fell deeper into Paige's hand that rested there delicately, without the intention of harm. Power hammered beneath my skin—wanting and needing, *craving* the same sensation. I'd take those hands holding a hatchet to my neck again if it meant her hands were on me.

"You don't think a dragon searching for guards is going to alert more guards here?" Paige bit out.

"It's not like she will let them live. It's better than being captured and dying, My Queen." Her cheeks reddened at the nickname while Eoghan smirked in the other corner of the room. I cleared my throat as Ikelos' brows shot up in my direction. "That is, better than *us* dying. And since it's an *us* thing, I'm allowed to protect." She rolled her eyes at me. I jerked my head toward the icy window. "Vara will make sure there aren't any scouts, or guards, or whatever else he sends our way. She won't leave anything behind. It'll be as if they never existed."

"Tell that girl she needs to be nicer to you or I won't be saving her from so much as a fly." There were more pressing issues than the blanketed threats Vara had grown accustomed to giving to Paige without her knowing.

So I threw one back. *"I wonder how you will feel about her when it's my crown she wears. My throne she sits on, with me."* No matter what throne she sat on—hers, or mine with me—she would always be my queen.

"You can't be serious. I told you, getting her to bind herself to you like that would be nearly impossible. You want her to commit to you when she still pictures a dagger going through your head."

I shrugged, my eyes gluing to just beyond the window to the peaks, where red and gold wings were stretching. *"I didn't get a football scholarship for hating a challenge."*

My attention fell back to Paige, where she was already giving me an incredulous look that told me to focus on the room more than my dragon.

"We have no doubts that Vara can and will be of great value, but she does need to stay hidden," Ikelos reminded me for the hundredth time. And counting. Vara's growl was the only response I got before she went back to chewing.

"She knows that." I paused and took a look around the room. It felt like a lifetime ago that standing in *this* room with *these* people seemed impossible. It wasn't even on my radar. "What exactly is the plan with Gedeon? We believe his interests lie beyond finding us. He's looking for something else." There was no point keeping pertinent information from them, especially not when guards were starting to get curious in the right direction.

I watched as Paige started to fiddle with the ends of her fingers, watched as her reddened cheeks paled over. She *did* know something about that. She had to. Whether she learned about it while she was there, or through her gift, I wasn't sure. But when we were talking about it back in the Fields, I *knew* she *knew*. I let my eyes wander to Ikelos, wondering exactly how much information Paige had spilled to her brother. He'd let it out before she ever would.

"I have a few ideas, but I don't really like the way you're looking at my man," Eoghan replied.

I cocked my head to the side. "What does *he* know? He lived there, can see the future, or glimpses of it at least. So, I want to know. Cards on the table. What do you know, Ikelos?"

Ikelos opened his mouth to speak, but Eoghan took wide steps across the room until he was in front of me, and cut him off. He did a lot of that—call it overprotective, or secretive, or both. "You throw out there that you believe he is searching for something possibly more important than a dragon heir and an escapee daughter, and you have the balls to ask *Ikelos* what *he* knows?" He tossed his head over his shoulder to Ikelos, but my eyes stayed on him. Watching his every movement like a hawk. His head snapped back over to me once he was sure Ikelos wasn't going to put in his two cents. Though I wished he would.

I looked down the length of my pants, then slowly back up. "I definitely do have the balls for that." A smile, probably a rather cocky-looking one, spread across my face as that redness that had been missing from Paige's cheeks returned. "Are you telling us you didn't know he was looking for something?"

"We did. But I think it's interesting that you decided to keep that information from us. Maybe we should be asking what it is that you know?"

I pushed off the wall and took a step closer to Eoghan. "Well, I can tell you that him sending one or two guards at a time instead of an entire fleet when he seemed to have plenty to spare would tell me he is sending more elsewhere. He isn't sure we are here, nor are we that important to raid entire towns over. Something I'm sure is more akin to his tastes than simply scouting."

"You think I can't conclude that on my own, Fire Boy?" Eoghan muttered, his brows hanging low as he stared back at me.

My jaw worked. "Conclude or don't, you weren't giving that information willingly either, were you?"

"Did you also *conclude* that she isn't as desirable of a bounty as you are? Sure, he wants you both. But the longer she is gone, the more time the people within the Aerborne territories have to be turned over to his side. The side that views her as a spineless traitor." Eoghan glanced at Ikelos over his shoulder and tossed up his hands. "I'm just stating facts."

"She's not a fucking traitor, and she has more of a spine than you ever will," I said. How Paige felt about that was unclear. Eoghan was now blocking her from my view.

Eoghan refocused on me as my fists curled in. "You, on the other hand, you are the son no one knew about. The one Lady Savaria Fireborne and whatever man sired you seemed to have hidden for long enough to birth you and bond you to your dragon. That is a huge threat."

"Are you hiding that information too? I wouldn't put it past you." Not that I had time to contemplate who my father was, or if it even mattered. Seamus had seemed to take over that role more than anyone else ever had.

"No, I don't know who your father is, but I know that it won't matter if you both keep hiding things that might keep you alive."

I stepped in closer. "You're one to talk."

Paige appeared in the corner of my anger-hazed vision, her hair brushing over my forearms as she tried to put herself between us. Unsuccessfully. "I hate to break up your little squabble or love-fest or whatever the fuck it is you two are doing. But maybe we should be trying to work together instead of questioning each other all the time."

"The Princess may have a point. Though perhaps she should be taking her own advice about the whole *working together* thing. Isn't that what you so desperately tried to do that night in the wa—" My fist met his gut before he could finish and Paige took a broad step back. He was close to not only setting me off more, but also Paige. If she didn't want to think about that night right now, she didn't have to.

"You have problems." Eoghan coughed and then chuckled darkly as he splayed his fingers over his stomach. "You know I was defending your dumb ass this time, right?"

"Yep," I replied. "It wasn't for me." I refrained from looking over at Paige. "I have nothing else to add, nor does she." A lie. As far as I knew, she still concealed her gift. It wasn't something she was ready to share, and it wasn't my place. And if Ikelos did know, I'm sure he would have told Eoghan, and then we would have all been made well aware because the walls were thin and the alcohol was plenty at every meal. Something would have come up by now.

Eoghan sighed, pinching the bridge of his nose. "We have no idea what it is he is looking for, but I've got people investigating. Watching the port, larger trade markets and any shoreline that a Prydian vessel may be docked at. We are careful to never go into his territories—which are all warded now, by the way— without cause. Something he would take heed of if he were wise, but his guards crossing our land is proof that war may be closer than we thought. I take it that's why you were so adamant about avoiding the ports, dragon or no?"

I nodded at the same time Paige did. For the split-second that our gaze met, I could see the worry glossing over her eyes. "So, with the wards up, and when the time comes for us to leave, we will have to travel to Costa on horseback...which is..."

"You are correct, I can't get you there. It would be a few days, but only a day or two at most with the horses if I take you to the border of our lands, though portaling Vara to the border is out of the question. Aeden could get there in a matter of hours if his dragon wanted to go ahead without the rest of—"

"No. We all go together. Including Vara." There was no way I'd risk something happening to them. If guards were already dispersing, who knows what or who we'd encounter on the way there, even if we left on the first day of the Winter Solstice. There wouldn't exactly be a way to communicate with them if I did go ahead, either.

Fuck, I missed phones.

Eoghan glanced between the both of us as he pushed his hands into his pockets. "Wonderful. Once we know something, we might feel—"

"We will tell you as soon as we hear anything. We are a team and if we have any hope of coming out of this in all of our favors, we have to keep remembering that. Don't we, Eoghan?" Ikelos finished and Eoghan sighed again, deeply, but he nodded anyway.

"As for a plan, we have a few ideas. Most of them focus on you rebuilding whatever kingdom it is you have left. We will need allies, beasts and creatures and fae alike. And with Leander continuously refusing to meet with Ikelos and I"—Ikelos cleared his throat and Eoghan looked up to the ceiling briefly before continuing—"with *all of us*, you are our only allies at the moment. And with the Prydian guards moving into our territories, Gedeon will assume one of two things. I'd rather not have him believe I'm an imbecile, but if the alternative is him catching wind of the fact that we are harboring *his* fugitives, then I guess I'll be looking rather docile and moronic to his threats while claiming we have the worst naga problem in existence. Though I'm sure you've both realized by now that his territories are far worse, if your peaceful little trip down the secluded path to the water didn't"—He put up a finger and took a big step back from his position in front of me as my fingers curled in again—"If your time together didn't show you that, then perhaps you are both blinded by each other."

"I noticed," Paige said beside me. "And that was a mistake." She shrugged as if she hadn't just crushed my heart into another thousand pieces. "But at least I'm on the same playing field as him now."

Eoghan cupped his hand around his mouth as he directed an *ouch* my way.

"Are we done?"

"Not really, but—" I didn't hear the rest because I tuned everything out as I walked through the door, slamming it shut behind me.

Chapter Eighteen
Aeden

"I think you're losing touch on that stealth of yours." Boots thudded on the ground, almost clapping out Eoghan's entrance to the training deck. I went to the mat a lot in the night, with only Vara there as a spectator, and sometimes Murrie if she was still awake. This was the only time that neither had been there because I'd wanted to be alone. Not that Eoghan got that hint. I was nothing more than a mistake to her, and every time those words thrust through the silence of the night, it tore me apart again and again.

A mistake.

I thought having her think about me in any way would be good for us. Because her mind would be on me. But her thinking I was a mistake? Nothing felt good about being that.

"I wanted you to hear me coming. If I snuck up on you now, while you're all broody and pissed off, you'd probably make good on that promise to try to burn me down. You remember making that promise to me in those gardens, don't you?"

I dropped the hatchets I'd been throwing and leaned back against the balcony. "What is it that you want now?"

He clasped his hands together in front of him. "So I was right then, you are brooding out here. Alone."

I sighed. "Do you need something or are you just here to point out what everyone else already tells me?"

He looked me over as his nails scraped down his clean-shaven jawline. Then he shrugged. "I figured you needed a better outlet for all that emotion you keep bottled up inside of you."

"A better outlet than those?" I jerked my chin to the slew of weapons that flanked my hatchets—swords, daggers, my bow and arrows, all littered the stony floor.

His nose scrunched up as he looked at the weapons. "Yes. You make quite the mess, has anyone ever told you that?"

"You know I leave nothing when I'm done." I rolled up my sleeves, feeling the cold winter air glide right off my skin as the flames beneath flared to life.

Eoghan pointed down at my arm. "That's why I came here. For that very aspect, and the one about your anger needing to be let out. I think what I have to offer you can benefit us both. If you are interested, that is."

I arched a brow, waiting. "Go on."

"I think it's better if I show you." A blue portal formed between us. He took a few inaudible steps toward it and held out his hand, guiding me closer. "I think you know I won't send you to the nagas, not that we have many in these parts to begin with. You'd be more likely to run into wraiths with the cold, but we keep those at bay as much as we can."

"So I've heard." I pushed off the balcony, walking up to him. "I don't care where it is you take me. Just know I will make it back here if it's anywhere that—"

Eoghan placed a splayed hand across his chest. "I promise, Lord Aeden Fireborne, on my very life that where I am about to take you will not cause you any physical harm."

I walked back over to one of the hatchets, tucking it into the back of my waistband. Just in case. Eoghan took another step closer to the portal, his golden hair whipping violently to one side. "I suppose you want me to go first."

I held out my arm. "After you."

We landed on our feet in a dark hall, bricked in from the floor to the low-arched ceiling with several doors squeezed between dimly lit sconces. From the far end, I could hear a song being whistled with bouts of cackling mixed in. I reached to the back of my waistband, ready to grip the handle of the hatchet.

"Down, boy," Eoghan purred as he kicked off the wall behind me, then moved to walk in front of me, urging for me to follow.

My fingers wrapped around the handle anyway. "What is this place?"

Eoghan spread his arms wide as he turned to face me. "This is my dungeon. Or, I believe as you refer to it as a jail. Prison. Whatever. It's where we keep the ones too evil to let roam around our land."

"And what, you plan to put me in a cell with my emotions?"

He scratched the side of his head as he continued walking backward. "The thought did cross my mind—but no. As I said, this will benefit both of us. And if I left you in a dungeon, I don't think it would be very long before Paige tried to throw me over the balcony." I scoffed, because she wouldn't give a damn if I wasn't there. She'd made that quite clear.

Eoghan's brow furrowed and he stopped walking. "Maybe we need to do some team building exercises or some—"

"We can't be a *team*. She wants nothing to do with me and thinks I'm a mistake, remember?" The second he opened his mouth, I added, "You already made it look like I was supposed to be the one training her when I explicitly said for you to do it, knowing I'd end up in this position I'm fucking trapped in."

His jaw worked as he glanced at the floor, mirroring something close to guilt. "Huh." He scrubbed along his cheek before continuing his backward steps. "I guess I'll just have to fix that whole refusal to work together thing then, won't I?"

"What—"

"It's just beyond this door. Here." He reached for his pocket and pulled out a key, then unlocked the door and pushed it wide open, silencing me.

I glared at him, then decided it was best to ignore whatever antics Eoghan had planned before following him in, the dark room illuminating with a faelight he produced and hovered along the wall. Just under the light sat a man, wearing a purple tunic and shredded black pants. His arms were bound behind his back and his legs were tied to the legs of the wooden chair. His head hung low and his black hair fell just below his forehead to cover his facial features. As Eoghan stepped in closer, the man's whistling stopped and his head lulled to the side.

The man smiled cruelly, his split lip dripping blood down his chin. He spat on the floor toward Eoghan's boots. "The fucker is back." His body jerked as he tried to break his bindings to no avail.

As his arms swayed behind him with every yank and tug he tried to free himself with, I noticed the faded purple color along his arm—not quite grey, but not nearly as vibrant as it should be.

"His arms. I've only seen something like that on the dead." I moved in a little closer, granting me a wad of spit by my boot.

"I gave him a little tonic that nullifies his power—temporarily." Paige's mark never faded when she couldn't use it. I wondered if that was because of the poison that was used or if she was just that powerful. "Nothing like the one his lord used," Eoghan added as he took in the deep groove that formed between my brows.

"Come back for more, have you?" the man in the chair shouted, spittle and blood splattering along the floor. "Who is this little shit?" The guy eyed me up and down, then dropped his head as if realizing I was in fact not little at all.

Eoghan leaned against the wall, pushing his hands into his pockets and finally answered. "I brought a friend. Aeden, this is the guard we discovered. Let's call him Ash, since that's what you will want to leave him as when we are through. Ash, this is Aeden *big shit* F–"

I pointed down at him and cut off Eoghan before he could finish. "I thought you said there was only one."

"I did say that, yes. We caught *this* one snooping around just days before the one we *did* kill crossed over my wards. Ikelos demanded we save him for questioning, and who am I to deny him that?"

I looked at him incredulously. "Ikelos knows about this?" I had a hard time picturing Ikelos being one for this kind of treatment.

"Ikelos knows everything. I don't keep secrets from the man I love." The truth. No grin, no sleight of hand or twisted remark. This was the man I preferred talking to—the one too struck by love, like I was.

Ash cackled, dark and wicked, as he finally rolled his eyes up to take me in. "What, you've brought a filthy fire-wielder here to do your dirty work?" His eyes grew wider as they moved from my exposed forearm, up to the edge of my neck.

Filthy fire-wielder.

I reached up to my collar and tugged it lower, then grabbed the empty chair beside me and spun it around so my legs straddled around the back, facing him. As my chest dipped over the chair, I made sure to angle my body just enough to show the blue cresting the top of my shoulder, tangling with the red. As if the size of my flames didn't expose me enough.

I believe Ash tried to gasp, but it came out like a cough. "He's the one we're looking for, isn't he?"

Eoghan shrugged. "I wouldn't be surprised if he is."

My eyes didn't move from him and the way his jaw muscle worked beneath his blood-stained, bruised face. He truly hated fire-wielders. And, for what? Because he was told to do so? Flames rose beneath the surface of my skin, begging to be released.

"Well, you have me now, Ash," I said dismissively, as if my entire core wasn't alight with fire. I could see where this was going. Eoghan brought me here to end him. End his life. *Ash.* Because that's what he'd be a pile of when I was through.

The smirk I gave to Eoghan felt impure—full of an evil I was ready to welcome. I'd only killed beasts before. Never a man. Eoghan wanted me to prove I could do it, and with the way my magic hummed at the thought of ending his life, I wouldn't put it past myself to do it with ease.

He had come into Waterborne territories to find me. To find *her.*

To *hurt* her.

Ash's twisted, bloodied lip curved up to the side.

"Where's that bitch of yours? The traitor." My smirk fell to a sneer as I released my flames, letting them spread along my arms. When my skin was coated up to my forearms, hot and searing and ready, I sent a blast of them in the shape of a fist across his cheek. His body jerked, trying to move the chair away from the fire but the chair was bolted to the floor. He yelped out in pain, the flames dancing over his skin and only snuffing out when his flesh was scorched and burnt.

"Keep her out of your mouth," I growled.

Eoghan clucked his tongue as the man's cries changed to whimpers of pain. "Now, Ash. Surely I told you to not mention her in front of him, didn't I? No? Oh, that's right, I forgot to tell you he was coming entirely. My mistake."

"I'd rather die than talk to him and his kind." He mustered up enough spit to aim for me, but a shield of air spread around me, and I watched in amusement as the glob slid down that shield.

"Well, that sucks, because I have some questions for you."

"I already told him"—he swung his head to Eoghan, the scorched skin dripping blood, exposing muscle—"I know nothing."

"You seemed to know enough to find your way here. To know who I am, and where *your queen* is."

Eoghan's eyes lit up at the words as he waited for Ash's wheezing laughter to die down. "Queen? She's nothing more than a fire-wielder's whore."

Blood and power and heat and fire raged beneath my skin until it broke through the surface once more, illuminating the entire top portion of my body. The chair I sat in burst into flames before I stood and kicked it back.

Eoghan's voice turned darker, deeper than I was used to hearing. "Oh, no, Ash. I know for sure I did warn you just now. And I'm pretty sure he said to keep her out of that rotten mouth of yours."

My flaming fist tucked under Ash's chin and lifted his head enough to make him meet my eyes. He cried in agony as my flames worked their way through his skin, down to his tendons and muscles, mirroring the injury along his cheek. I removed my fist as fear and horror and pain filled those eyes, while mine soaked them in.

The flames dissipated almost as quickly as they had formed. "Where else is he searching? How many of you has he sent? Tell me."

"I don't know!" he cried out, unable to open his lips enough without moving his face—that melted face.

"I did question him, Aeden. I know that he truly knows nothing."

My eyes snapped to Eoghan. "Then why bring me here?"

"I wanted to show you this"—Eoghan strode to Ash and removed a fragment of torn clothing that covered his thigh. Red slashes were sliced into him like…tally marks. "This is their way of keeping track of how many fire-wielders they kill. How many they take to the platforms or murder before getting there."

Twenty-eight. He had twenty-eight lives on his hands. "And this"—Eoghan pushed his finger into a section of the mark where the tally bisected a circle—"this symbolizes the fire-wielder was pregnant."

Ash muttered under his breath, "You were going to be the mark that brought me to twenty-nine, and with your whore, maybe thirty. If you put your filthy seed in her."

I saw red. Red and black and flames and shadows and then darkness as the faelight and Eoghan moved away from the fire that engulfed Ash. Ash, who was surely now nothing but a pile of exactly what Eoghan promised he would be.

When the faelight returned, I tried to steady my breaths, to ease the burning in my lungs as I stared down at that pile of what couldn't even be called a man or a fae. Eoghan's hand clapped over my shoulder, then squeezed. "If you weren't going to end him, I was. Either way, he was a dead man. Men like him don't deserve to live. I could have handled the back-talk and the hatred, but the killing?

Who knows how many children were part of those marks besides the ones that were in the womb. Fae who never lived—got to truly live—because they simply existed as a fire-wielder."

He was going to kill me, to kill her. Kill Paige. He was hoping I'd have her pregnant and ready for another tally with a fucking circle around it for him. Because our child—if I'd ever get lucky enough to see the day—would be like us. They would wield all of the elements—including fire. Possibly fire first, or air. Not that it would matter to me one bit.

But that didn't stop the thoughts that kept pushing toward the edge of my mind, quickly eating away everything else. "I...I killed him." As if struck through with an arrow, the realization sent me to my knees. He was vulgar. He deserved it, in every way he could have gotten it. Death was coming his way. But I had caused that death. His blood was on my hands now. The hands of a killer.

"I know," was all Eoghan said.

I knew it was only a matter of time before I'd take a life, had felt it in my bones that I would possibly end hundreds as we fought for a future we all dared to envision. But actually ending a life—that was a harder pill to swallow.

"Take pride in knowing you wiped him from the face of Aellethia. He will never harm another fire-wielder, born or no, again."

"He's right, Aeden. That is the side of war you need to be prepared for." Her words came into my thoughts gently, soothingly.

I stood, moving to stand over the ash of someone who didn't deserve to be pitied. If it wasn't the first life I'd ever taken, I'd be more at ease over ending his life. "How did you know he knew nothing?"

"I'm an Empath. I can read the emotions of others—their pain, their fears, their happiness." His voice softened. "Their love."

My head tilted over my shoulder. "A gift. Of course, the Stars gave you one as well."

He nodded warily. "She is starting to feel something for you, you know. I can feel it every time your name is mentioned. And when you aren't on the deck on days she thought you'd be there to train, her worry flows from her more than anything else. Worry and fear and when you show up, that all goes away. And then she becomes afraid once more when you are too close—when you make her forget the reasons why she won't admit to herself how she is feeling. There is lust in there as well, but I think that part is obvious."

I thought for a moment. Tried to take in every word—but all I could picture was the hatred in her eyes every time she looked my way. "Does she know you can feel her? Feel us?"

He shook his head. "No, I didn't think she would like to know that I have that much access to how she is feeling without even trying. Normally, I have to seek out the feelings. But, hers? They have always been so clear, like she feels too much. I can hardly block it out when she's in the same room."

I couldn't help but smile at that. "That does sound like the Paige I knew."

"She is still the same woman you loved. Be patient with her."

I dragged my hand down the length of my face. "I can't believe I'm taking advice from you right now."

"Believe it, Fire Boy." He winked, and when my head swirled back down to the ground, to stare at the ashen pile of the man whose life I took, it was gone. "I'll bring you back now. If I could sense people this far away, I'm sure I'd be awash with her worry at this very moment. Even in her dreams, she worries about you."

My shoulders tensed. Could he feel, or sense, her gift? I redirected him. "And what do you sense from me?"

"Right now?" I followed him slowly back down the hall. "You are a bit harder to read. Sometimes I have to focus on you too hard to know exactly what it is that I'm getting from you. But mostly, I've picked up way too much heartbreak to endure lately. It feels like my chest is bleeding, sometimes so much that I have to run to Ikelos to fill it back up and patch it back together again."

"Try living with it. At least you have your person."

"You do, too. She's just being more stubborn about it." That sounded like her, too. My stubborn, strong-willed Paige.

An idea flitted through my mind. "You weren't lying about the Winter Solstice thing, were you?"

Eoghan laughed so loud it echoed off the brick walls and ceiling. "Oh, I wish I was. But, no. That day is coming, I just hope you are both ready for the consequences afterward." For the way that would open us up to each other in ways she might not be ready for.

Fuck. "I hope so, too." The portal formed in front of us, but just as he made a move to walk in, I put my hand on his shoulder. "Thank you," I said.

And I meant it.

Chapter Nineteen
PAIGE

"Welcome to the Isles of Avicante." Eoghan spread his arms wide as I shrugged out of my heavy coat. I looked over as Aeden tossed his bow and quiver to the sandy ground and started removing his coat as well. I could've sworn I heard him muttering something about teamwork but maybe I was just being paranoid that Eoghan had ulterior motives in putting us on the hottest pit of sand he could find.

"You couldn't tell us it wouldn't be cold here?" I wanted to shred more clothing, but after what happened the last time I'd removed my clothes, I clung to the rest of them instead.

"It's an island further north than where we just were. If you couldn't conclude for yourself that it would be warm here at the beginning of December, then your observation skills are slipping through the cracks, Princess." I ignored the fact that Aellethia was backwards. North meant *cold* where I came from, not hot as hell.

He turned his attention to Aeden, who was leaning against a palm tree. "As for you, have you not learned enough in the geography lessons?"

"You mean the one you had Murrie give me yesterday? Yeah, I learned all about Vizna and my territories." His eyes squinted against the harsh sunlight as he looked back at Eoghan. "She didn't touch on yours."

I sighed, realizing Eoghan was right. I knew Vizna was indeed hotter *and* north. But still, I asked, "Why wasn't I included in these lessons?" I crossed my arms over my chest which was starting to sweat. If we were going to be hunting here for a full day and camping here as well, I would have to push decency and modesty aside. Aeden was already taking his shirt off before he picked his bow back up.

"Because you were learning how to wield your last element that your Fire Boy here gave you," Eoghan replied all too quickly. Aeden's eyes scanned my face like he'd repeatedly done anytime someone brought up that night or the new mark on my skin. Which had been a daily occurrence. I shouldn't have talked to my brother about it as loudly as I had, but I was angry and scared and shaking with every emotion that ripped through me. And he'd been there to calm me down and talk me through it after I pushed the one man away who'd probably be just as equally comforting—though I struggled to allow that.

It was *okay* to become more powerful, even if the circumstances around how that happened shook my entire core. And now, each time I stole a glance at Aeden, my entire body flared like I was on fire all over again. I could almost feel his hands stroking my back, his voice breathing new life into me again, like they did that night.

I began rolling my sleeves and pant legs up as Murrie stepped onto the sand last, her battleax swinging under the turbulence she had just gone through inside the blue portal. "Well, nice to see you're ready, Aeden. Paige, do you have your daggers?"

"All twelve." I reached for one of them along my waistband as Aeden smirked at me. He was so damn proud of himself for giving them back that it almost made me want to start throwing them all back at him. He didn't need more leverage over my emotions than he was already getting. I was just biding my time until the Winter Solstice, and afterward, I'd be able to get him out of my mind. Then at least I could use the day as an excuse as to why I'd lost it—my mind, my will, my hold on the reality of us.

Eoghan walked to the portal and stood with his back to it, facing us. "I know we already briefed this before to you both separately, but I'll go ahead and repeat it: This is my island. No guards will be here. I will be back in the morning and expect to see how well you both were able to survive, catch your own food, and use your power to create a shelter." I rolled my eyes. That *teamwork* Aeden grumbled about was making more sense now. It *was* a ploy. "Murrie will be here as a guide, but nothing more. She will not interfere with your abilities. And remember"—his eyes narrowed on me as I used a blast of air to clean the sand from my arms—"Your power will deplete faster if you aren't sustaining your body, so it is imperative that you don't exceed what your body can do." He swiveled on his feet. "Oh, and most importantly, you will both have to work together. That is an order." *Yep. There it is.*

Eoghan walked through the portal and it disappeared on a gust of ocean breeze. We weren't being put on this island to practice hunting and basic survival. It wasn't that anyone believed our powers wouldn't be enough to get us through the night. They expected us to fail because we wouldn't want to work together. Or rather, I wouldn't.

Teamwork.

But I loved to prove people wrong.

Aeden stalked closer to me, with Murrie in between us. I looked up at him, his broad shoulders blocking the sunlight from my eyes. "We should decide which elements to use between us, so we don't wear ourselves thin," I suggested. Thin was putting it loosely. Without proper sleep, I was already worn thinner than I should be. I kept my tone neutral, which was easy at the moment, but later I was sure I'd be biting my tongue.

"Agreed." His arms folded over his chest and I watched as several beads of sweat moved between his thick forearms. "I'll take fire and water," he said.

"No." *Here we go.* "*I'll* take water. And air."

"And why is that?" he shot back. He knew why. He was fishing for compliments. I'd give him the first one, but after that, I couldn't promise I'd be so generous.

I exhaled deeply before admitting, "Because you're better at fire and earth. Everyone knows that."

Murrie's eyes danced between us. "She's right, Aeden. Your water-wielding is great, too, but she needs the practice."

I scoffed. "At least I don't accidentally shoot orbs of air back into my body."

Aeden's dark brow raised, highlighting the slightly darker shading that lay just under his eyes. He shrugged, his smile curving up to one side. "I did do that, didn't I?"

"You did," I replied pointedly.

His eyes lit up, but not as bright as they normally did whenever I struck up any banter with him. Something about him...shifted. Recently. "I'm surprised you were watching me."

He stared down at me, and for a moment, no one spoke as I held that stare. Until Murrie cut in. "Right, well then, let's get you both ready to go hunting first. We should walk further north along the sand until we find the path Eoghan described before and—"

"We should be making a shelter first. And then hunt when the sun starts to go down and it gets cooler, or we might overexert ourselves," I suggested, stealing another glance at the way Aeden seemed more off than usual. It was beyond not getting enough rest. Something happened to him.

"And where would My Queen like her shelter to be?" Aeden tossed his head over his shoulder, scanning the woods as if wherever I directed, he'd make it happen.

So I pointed to the forest behind him. "In there, somewhere. Definitely in the shade. Let's go to where Murrie is talking about, and then we can find a spot."

"*We.*" He bent down, his voice too sweet, too tempting against my ear. "I like the sound of that." Something may have been off with him, but that voice? My body shouldn't have been responding to him like that with just his voice in my ear.

I gave him a weak shove back. "I'm sure you do." He hummed in acknowledgment, just like he had in the water all those nights ago. My stomach clenched and the feeling moved further down as I started walking away from them both, leading the way north.

I bent down and cut the extra fabric from my legs until I was left with a pair of entirely too-short shorts right before we began hunting. I simply couldn't do it anymore, and minutes later, my sleeves were gone as well. The air was thick and sticky and clung to me as if I were swimming. I desperately wished I could swim because if so, I'd be diving into the ocean once we killed something large enough to call dinner.

Aeden handed Murrie a small snake he shot down from a tree branch with his arrows almost as fast as we entered the area we were to hunt in. I had yet to catch anything because, if I was being honest with myself, I was too distracted by the half-naked man to my left. He had also cut his pants to just above his knee, and the way that his back muscles went taut every time he nocked an arrow back...my mind couldn't seem to focus on any sounds or movements within the forest. And the idea of sharing our singular shelter he'd built—because building two meant further depleting himself—continued to weigh heavily on my mind.

At least Murrie would also be stuck in that dome with us.

"Paige?" Aeden waved his hand. "Paige. I asked if you wanted to get that. Over there?" He pushed his hand through his damp hair as he eyed somewhere in the distance.

I shook my head to clear it. "Yeah. Sure." I paused and scanned the area, eyes narrowing to find what and where he was talking about.

His voice softened to a whisper just above my shoulder as he stepped in close behind me. "There." His arm raised as he pointed at the bird resting on a branch in the distance. The inside of his bicep brushed my hair, red flames and sun-kissed skin. I moved to reposition my hair to the other shoulder, then lifted my blade and took a few steps, avoiding crunching the leaves and sticks beneath my boots. "It's all you," Aeden said softly as he stepped in sync with me, trailing behind but not too far to where I could no longer feel his warmth along my back.

I waved my hand in the space to my side. "Then get back. You're going to make it—" And then the bird took off. I turned and furrowed my brow. "See what you did? I was—"

His focus hadn't moved from the area now behind me, and then in a flash, his arm wrapped around my waist and jerked me behind him. I turned back around just as a loud snarl ripped through the air. A bear stood on its hind legs, claws stretched out, reaching for exactly where I'd just been.

I didn't wait—I leaned my body slightly over Aeden's side and flicked my wrist, sending the dagger I still held in my hand flying with a burst of air behind it. The dagger sliced into the bear's flesh and didn't stop until it had made its way through the other end—tearing through the bear's heart. The ground shuddered under the weight of the beast as it crashed to the ground. The bear was massive, with a large tongue that drooped out from behind its sharp teeth as it slumped into the dirt.

"You're still holding me." Aeden turned and looked down at where his arm was indeed still bracing me back from the bear. But he didn't pull back. And neither did I. His arm shifted around me as he turned to face me, his warm hands touching the small curve of my back.

"Aeden," I murmured, waiting for him to move. For *me* to move. For me to run. Someone needed to break this... whatever this was. Some of my hair had fallen in front of my eyes, and just when I tilted my chin up at him, he moved his hand from my waist and instead grazed it across my cheek slowly. He wrapped my hair around his finger, then guided it behind my ear.

All of the sounds around us were snuffed out. His breathing, or mine, I wasn't sure, was all I could hear. My heartrate kicked up to meet those breaths like I was trapped in a competition, seeing which part of my body would react the most around him.

I was so fucked.

"You're incredible, you know that?" His eyes searched mine, and then time seemed to warp until he was kneeling down beside the bear, preparing to move it. I didn't know how long I stood there, unable to pull away from that magnetic force he seemed to have on me. How long had I been silent for, just staring back at him? Seconds, minutes...had he been aware of how long I stood there for?

I moved to collect my dagger, trying to push the thoughts from my mind. "Thanks. But you could've told me instead of grabbing me." One step closer, two steps back.

And I knew it was my doing. But is that what I really wanted anymore? I wasn't even sure. By the time I turned back to him, he had the bear tied up. I flicked my wrist, making it hover just above the ground.

"And risk you getting hurt?" He righted himself and wiped the bear's blood from his hands along his pants—or what was left of them. I struggled not to picture him in his leather riding gear, knowing how he wouldn't have cut those. He would've been...shit. He would have gone completely naked and not thought twice about it.

"You did promise to stop protecting me." That dagger I picked back up? Yeah, I still couldn't find a slot for it, although there were several. My fingers fumbled against my waistband, instead of reaching down further to straps on my legs, or shoving it into the corset I refused to strip off.

"If I see you're about to get mauled by a bear, of course I'm going to put myself in front of you." He spoke with such certainty, like he'd never have to think twice about whose life he'd choose to protect if it came down to it. He'd choose my life over his own.

"You can't just...you can't keep flipping that switch of yours on or off like—"
"What switch?"

I sighed and waved my hand in the air. "The whole 'knight in shining armor' one." Though, lately, he had stayed true to his word, his promise to fight against what he felt to do to protect me.

He froze and assessed me, then seemed to shake whatever thoughts he had away. "It's a little different if you're about to get hurt and I'm just standing there."

"I don't see how that's different." Splotches of grey wrinkled to the surface of a distant memory, one I couldn't get past the fog of. Because I'd started fighting that grey—that fog—as much as I could whenever it surfaced. Ever since that night in the water with him, I'd fought it.

It was then that I noticed Murrie was nowhere in sight. She'd probably made her way back when we spotted the bird. When *he* spotted the bird and came up from behind me. Aeden must've noticed Murrie's absence at the same time because he looked around briefly before trudging on.

"So you would rather have me watch as you get injured, or worse, die?" If I wasn't mistaken, he shuddered slightly as he spoke. His eyes darkened then, as if the thought of me dying had sent him to another place.

My shoulders sagged. "No, I suppose I wouldn't." I really couldn't fault him for saving me, not when I'd do the same for...for him. *Shit.* I would have done the same thing. "You're right. Thanks for saving me." I didn't have whatever protective instinct he described having over me, but I would've tried to come between him and the bear if I'd seen it before he had. I wasn't that cruel.

He stopped walking. "I'm either having a heat stroke right now, or maybe a bug flew into my ear. Can you repeat that?" He cupped his ear and leaned in toward me.

I huffed and faced him, putting my hands along my hips. "Are you really going to make me repeat myself?"

"Yes. Yes, I am."

I dropped my hands, and said with as much clarity and seriousness as I could muster, "Thanks for saving me, Aeden." It still came out with a tinge of annoyance, like it had become a part of who I was around him. Like the last bit of armor I could manage to have before it would all inevitably come tumbling off.

He dragged his hand through his hair again and smiled. "Maybe a hug, too?"

"You're covered in sweat. Don't push it." He instantly flicked his wrist and a shower of cool water fell over us that made me shiver at the contact. Then with another flick, we were dried. My hair wasn't glued to my forehead and my neck anymore, and his skin looked so deliciously clean and golden that I had to bite my tongue. Like I knew I'd be doing eventually, though now it was for all the wrong reasons.

He swung his arms wide. "What about now?" His smile turned to a grin, the same one that always made his dimple pop.

"Thank you for saving me. Again. But I'm not touching you, so you might as well put your arms down and pick up the pace. It's getting dark." He pouted as his arms fell to his sides. "I'm also not thrilled that you decided to use the two elements that we agreed I'd be in control of."

"If it makes you feel any better, you can help me take a real shower when we get back." I froze as he walked on ahead with the bear at his side. His voice carried through the trees when he shouted back, "That body of yours against mine in the water right now does sound much more appealing than skinning this bear."

The image of him naked under a stream of water didn't leave my mind until later that night, after we'd eaten and drank close to a gallon of water each. I should've been focusing on other things—like how to make my way back into Prydia and take the throne from my father, or if that meant we were going to be waging a war soon or if there was a better way to avoid starting one. We were at a standstill for the most part, though my mind felt like anything but.

"You did so wonderful today, you two. I half expected one of you to come back with bruises and cuts all over you." Murrie's voice snapped me back to reality. "And that bear! Great kill! You know, back in..." Murrie went off on a tangent about the first time she ever hunted a bear, not that I heard a thing beyond the first sentence because Aeden was sitting with his back against the dome and was still shirtless. And clean. And staring at me intently.

"...and that's when I learned how to make this one mixture that my friend—" Aeden cleared his throat and rolled his head toward her, his eyes never leaving mine.

"I think we're getting tired, Murrie. It's been a long day." Really the day breezed by. It was the days he wasn't there that seemed to stretch on for weeks. But I stretched my arms out and yawned, then curled into one of the leafy beds he'd made for each of us without a word.

A few minutes later, Murrie was fast asleep. But the rustling of leaves close by told me Aeden had not drifted off yet.

"Are you awake?" I whispered.

"Mhm," he replied. "You should really sleep."

"You know I don't sleep that well." I turned on my back, catching him doing the same from the corner of my eye. "Are you reading?"

He glanced at me as he placed the book on his chest. "Yeah. I was."

"What's it about?" I inclined my head toward the book. "I've seen you reading that one before." I shouldn't have told him I'd noticed him that closely. That I'd been watching him from time to time. Most times, really.

His brow arched up, matching the smile on his face. "I don't really know. I can't read most of it. I think someone tried to translate it, or maybe they just wrote gibberish."

"There were a lot of books in Gedeon's library that I couldn't read, either. I wonder how hard learning those languages would be." I paused as he tapped his fingers on the book, then added, "I could look at it sometime, if you want."

His fingers stopped tapping. "I'd like that. I tried asking your brother if he could read it, but he said he couldn't. Said most wouldn't be able to. But feel free to try piecing together the gibberish with me." *With him.*

We were silent for a bit, our eyes occasionally meeting from across the dome. He went to pick up his book again, until I blurted, "So, what do you think we'd be like if we were raised here?" I frequently thought about it, I'd just never voiced it before. And for some reason, I wanted to keep talking to him.

He put the book down on the floor and turned again, propping his head up on his knuckles to face me. "Well...I'd probably be dead. But you? You'd be the Mora of Prydia. Perhaps helping rebuild my fallen kingdom after putting your father in the ground."

"Why do you think you'd be dead?" I couldn't picture him not being able to survive. He was too strong, too smart, and too *good* to not.

"Honestly?" I nodded, then waited. "I've always felt like I wouldn't live long. And if I'd been here, my life would have been cut short much faster. You know, with the laws and living a life on the run."

Our eyes locked before mine flitted up to the ceiling. "You can't think like that. Your lifespan is literally thousands of years long."

He chuckled. "Yeah. Yours is too, you know."

I swallowed and kept my eyes up. This thing between us, it wasn't going anywhere. If we stayed close by, we would be doing this for possibly hundreds of years.

How I was going to keep denying every feeling that came to the surface for that long, I had no idea. My power was ebbing beneath my skin just thinking about separating from him.

And I thought I could escape.

"If I grew up here, I'd like to think I could've prevented a lot of the lives my father stole after the war. I wasn't alive yet when the war happened, but I know the real loss of life came after, when he started pillaging towns, and when he enacted that fucking law. So you definitely would've lived once I'd taken my place."

"It's good to know I'll have your backing in some way."

I shuffled to face him. Our eyes locked again, and this time it didn't affect my stomach or...other places of desire. It hit my chest. Hard. "I'm nothing like him, just as my brother isn't. Once he's gone, your kingdom—your people—will be free. When Eoghan walked me through Prydia that one night, I couldn't believe my eyes. Do you know about that platform? What he did in that town?"

He nodded. "Yeah. Saw it before I came to find you at the dance."

I leaned up on my elbow. "You went inside that castle knowing what he did to people like you?"

"Like *us*, you mean. And yes, of course, I did." He rolled onto his back, breaking our eye contact. That hurt my chest more.

"Why—why would you risk your life like that?"

"Trust me, it was worth it." The edge of his lips lifted as he recalled a memory I didn't have.

I placed my head back down, my entire focus on him as I laid facing him from across the room. "How so?"

Aeden angled his head to the side as his brown eyes found mine. Those golden flecks were shimmering against the few beams of moonlight that pooled in through the cracks of the dome. His voice lowered with his brows as he stared right through me, finding the deepest parts of myself I couldn't even reach.

"That was the night I told you I loved you."

Chapter Twenty
PAIGE

That was the night I told you I loved you.

Even the lapping of the water against my ears couldn't drown out the words, the sweet hum of his voice reverberating and piercing into every piece of me.

Annoyingly so.

"Keep your hands only where they need to be," I directed as Aeden slid his hands along my thin shirt and bare legs, doing exactly like I'd asked and never touching where he wasn't supposed to.

Also, annoyingly so.

Stars, I was so conflicted.

"I wouldn't touch you if you didn't want me to. You should know that by now," he said calmly.

I was at constant war within myself. Moments where all I could think about was his body pressed into mine, his warmth, his Stars-damned smile, and the way he smelled when he was so close—too inviting, too musky and earthy and ashen. Other times, I was more stable. More like how I'd felt during all that time in the cell—well, most of the time, that is. When I'd see him and want to throw him across the Fields, or after I was released and I'd wanted nothing more than to aim my daggers at him—not that I'd done that yet, but I had the weapons to do that now.

All thanks to him.

My daggers glinted mockingly from the shoreline where I left them displayed. Something that I did to give Aeden heed during the lesson, but he paid no attention to the pointless metal blades that continued to scorn me in the sunlight.

Weak.

That's what it felt like to be around him ever since those words.

That was the night I told you I loved you.

My stomach tightened. "When did you learn to swim?" I asked as one of his hands held the bend in my legs, and the other, the place between my shoulder blades, lifting only when I couldn't support myself.

He looked down at me, the shadow of his body blocking out the harsh sun from the island we'd hunted on before. We hadn't said much to each other since that day, but I noticed a lot of my tension disappearing in his presence, while other things were rising to the surface.

"I was forced to learn when I was around nine."

I cocked a brow at him. "In the mortal world, someone…forced you?"

His stubbled jaw held oceany water droplets and I watched too intently as his lips rolled in, his tongue moving to lick the few drops that had fallen there. He hummed in agreement. "No matter what world you're in, people have their own agendas." His fingers tapped beneath me, urging my body to keep afloat when all it wanted to do was sink. "I was pushed into a lake by the kids in my foster home. They heard I couldn't swim from one of the few friends I'd confided in at school, and they used that to their advantage."

My throat turned dry. "Oh. That must've been…"

"Hard?" He tightened his grip on my legs. "It was. But I learned to swim…among other things."

One of my outstretched arms bumped into his forearm, sending pinpricks along my skin up to my neck. "I bet that's why you don't trust often."

"Probably." A sly smile spread across his face—at the question or perhaps he noticed my skin's reaction to yet another touch.

"So why trust me?" I was aware that I'd frequently trusted people even if I shouldn't—I *remembered* that, although that had shifted recently. But, him? He wasn't the trusting kind. I saw the way he watched people like a hawk and he didn't seem keen on forgiving Eoghan even after all the time we'd spent at his house. And the looks he gave to my brother?

No, trust wasn't just handed out by Aeden Fireborne.

"Why shouldn't I trust you?" I rolled my eyes dramatically, but he didn't laugh. He was serious.

"Besides the time I threw an ax towards your head?" I asked.

Eoghan's voice carried across the water from where he and Ikelos stood along the shore. "When was the first bonded sword made?" *Right.* I'd almost forgotten that not only was I learning to swim today, we were also being subjected to questioning—things we'd been learning since arriving, either via books, talk, or the lessons we received.

Aeden looked down at me before answering, no doubt remembering the book he gave me in the library that day. The one I still carried with me everywhere I went. The one on the shoreline with my daggers right now. When I didn't answer, he shouted, "About three thousand years ago, made by Garrentis Forrow the Centaur and Helix Earthborne, the Mora of Buryon. They combined Helix's metal-bending power along with Garrentis' smithing abilities and made the first Earthborne bonded sword. Because he was a Mora, he continued with the rest of the elements and presented them as gifts to the other kingdoms."

"One point to House Dragon!" Eoghan shouted while drawing another line in the sand next to his three others that shrank my singular one down to nothing. It was the first time I could ever remember struggling with classes. It was new, and I didn't like it. But Aeden—he was learning so fast that it should've been threatening. Yet it wasn't.

Aeden resumed our conversation, whispering, "What if I enjoyed watching you throw your weapon at me?"

"I'd call you a masochist," I said flatly.

"Call me whatever you want, My Queen. As long as you are the one calling it, it will do no wrong."

"Asshole." But the grin that pinched my cheeks begged to differ.

"I can be that, for you."

"Give my sister a chance at this one, would you?" Ikelos cupped his hands around his mouth and raised his voice as if that were the reason I hadn't been able to answer their questions. "The Fae of the Fireborne line all inherit powers from their dragon. Name a power that is most common."

My body tensed. I could name dozens of the powers that Aeden might develop, had researched it endlessly in the hours of the night where I'd wake up, unable to fall back asleep again. Unlike my father's library, Eoghan's didn't limit the information that could be found on the Fireborne line.

"We are waiting!" Eoghan hollered from the shoreline, and I threw him a look that said I was more than well aware.

I don't know why it made me so nervous to think about. It wasn't because I was afraid of the ways he could use that power. I knew he would do well with whatever was gifted to him by Varasyn, by their bond. But the knowledge that I'd focused on him and his line suddenly struck something within me, something I wasn't ready to acknowledge.

Aeden cleared his throat. "I could always tell them to fuck off, if you want. I doubt they would continue to press."

Varasyn circled above, having finally made her way to the island. Eoghan was able to portal fae, but dragons? He simply said she was too large, and if she wanted to join, she'd have to fly well above the clouds that were plenty in the south with all the snow storms that kept rolling in until she'd hit the ocean. Even within his own territories, it was a risk to be seen by any scouts that were making their way through. A risk she was clearly willing to take. I wondered if she was waiting for me to drown, hoping for it.

I finally spoke up. "All dragon heirs have a telepathic connection to their dragon. But once that settles, they can expect other powers, such as superior strength, smell, or sight." Lesser common ones tended to be more deadly like the one Aeden's mother could wield—illusions. She could make people see things, hear things, smell things, that weren't really there. Some of his ancestors had quite extraordinary powers that were equally just as terrifying. I wondered if the knowledge of those powers—the abilities that the Stars had no say in—was a driving force for Gedeon's insanity.

As if he could sense my thoughts, he said, "I doubt I will get anything like the one she had. Vara will probably only allow sight, if anything. She's stubborn."

"You seem to have a thing for the stubborn ones." The words slipped through my lips before I could stop them.

He smiled. "You could say that. I'd be more interested in seeing what it is that you develop though."

"What...what do you mean?"

His brows furrowed. "Well, Firebornes have their dragons and the power they get from them, and Earthbornes, as I said earlier like Helix in the story, had metal-bending, but really it can be anything earthen—like earthquakes or tremors or craters. Some kind of increased capability to their original...you really didn't know? You look very confused right now."

I was. I was very confused. He continued, "Eoghan clearly has some affinity for ice, hence his house, and I read somewhere that your father used a poisonous fog on more than one occasion. Ah fuck, you really don't know, do you?"

"Aeden, it would be nice if you continued. Please." I was aware I had fallen through the cracks on my studies, but—

"Sometime after your marks settle, for Moras and their direct descendants, you are granted a power from the Stars. Not quite a gift, more like an enhancement of your original nature. It can be days after, or years. I'm not even sure if your brother has one yet, but if I had to guess, I'd say he does." His face was full of concern, and he took a breath as he hesitated on the next words. "And now that you have your last mark..."

"I get it. I just...didn't know. I hadn't read or heard of that yet."

"I wasn't told, either. I read it in one of the books in the library. More like connected the dots. I can lend you the book, if you'd like."

I nodded several times. "Yeah. Yes, that would be great. Thank you."

"No problem." Some of his fingers had fallen from where my clothing bunched up above my skin, leaving only a few for support whenever my back dipped. The callouses along his palms felt smooth beneath the water. "Okay. I think you have floating down. Are you ready to try something else?"

I kept my gaze to the skies, watching the red and gold dip below the scattered clouds freely. "I think so." I hadn't noticed if my brother had responded or not, or if Eoghan had said anything from where he stood. But through the corner of my vision, I saw another line drawn in the sand beneath my name and tried not to focus too much on how I had another power to adjust to coming my way. Stars-be-damned.

"I'm going to let you turn over by yourself and then I'll hold onto your arms while you stabilize yourself. If you feel unsteady, let me know." I tried rolling from my back without his help and instantly went under. His hands were under my arms, lifting me in less than a second. "You won't drown, Paige. I've got you."

I nodded, blowing water out through my nose and coughing whatever else I'd managed to take in during that short time. His thumb rubbed my skin where he held me above the water. "You can do this."

I nodded again and his hands moved down to my forearms while I made use of my legs and kicked behind me. But my torso and hips still dipped too low in the water and I knew if he were to let go, I'd go under again.

"Is it okay if I hold you lower?" There was no mischief in his eyes, and I trusted him. I so stupidly trusted him.

So I said, "Yes."

He moved down lower and I looked over at Eoghan and Ikelos who had grown silent. Both were watching intently, both waiting for me to finish the lesson before they threw more questions our way. They looked...amused. And it didn't seem to be over anything other than the way Aeden must've been looking as his forearm slid underneath my hips, lifting me.

But Aeden's focus never left me. "Is this okay?" His voice was shaky, like he would break if I said no.

"It's okay." My voice was equally shaky.

His fingers brushed my hips in acknowledgment. "Start moving your arms and legs like you want to push the water away from you. Kind of like a frog."

I snorted at the imagery of him holding a giant frog in the water but I did as he said. The water glided over my body while Aeden praised me for the simple movement.

I kept my movements frog-like as he walked, making it seem like I was actually swimming. His praise quickly became distant as my arms and legs waded and kicked and when I angled my head past my shoulder in the water to see him, he was well behind me.

And then the water claimed me again.

A force wrapped around my torso and suddenly I was guided back up above the water and back into Aeden's arms. "That was good. You just need to work on... distractions." His smirk faltered as he looked me over, lying face-up toward him. When his hand came up to brush some of my wet hair from my face, my lungs seemed to stop working. "I should have warned you. That wasn't fair."

I shook my head rapidly. "I'm fine." I took a few breaths and felt him watching me, assuming the water had taken the air right from me.

"I'm sorry, Paige. I..." His jaw flexed as he looked down at me, his fingers digging in softly to my flesh. "Do you want to take a break?"

I shook my head again. "No. Let's do that again. I just wasn't prepared but I guess I should have seen that coming. It's not like you'll be there every time I need to swim."

He was quiet, like he wanted to say something but rolled his lips in to avoid letting it out. Finally he said, "Right." But it came out all wrong.

His arms still supported me around my waist, waiting. For me to move, or maybe for more questions to come—more things that would be a distraction, as if his presence wasn't the worst one of them all.

The silence was stretching, and with his hands on me, I wasn't sure if or when I should move or if he was going to flip me back over so I could start again. I turned my attention away from Aeden, feeling the water slap against the side of my cheek as I looked at my brother along the shore. I felt wobbly, and if whenever I did choose to move, I'd just sink to the bottom.

You won't drown, Paige. I've got you.

"You're doing great, Paige!" My brother hollered.

Eoghan piped in as well. "We are enjoying the view!" Ikelos shouldered Eoghan as my cheeks reddened beyond what the sun was doing to them.

"Asshole," Aeden and I mumbled at the same time.

I didn't even question them when they told me I was to practice swimming with Aeden. To learn with him. That's what I'd been doing all these weeks and months anyway. We pushed each other and it seemed to be working. Even when he pushed away, or I did. And on the days he missed practicing with me, I had become a force on the mat against Eoghan, sometimes leaving him speechless. Proud, but unable to declare it anytime I bested him.

I was just shocked they didn't force me, or us rather, to revisit the water for these lessons, where we almost—

Aeden's voice came softly through my clouded thoughts. "He's right. You are doing great. Much better than my first time."

I latched right onto more conversation. "Hmm. Did anyone come to help you after they pushed you in?" I knew the answer before he spoke. Could tell in the way his eyes dimmed and shifted to a shade darker than the deep golden brown they normally were.

"No." My chest tightened under a different kind of pressure—one that aligned more with rage than anything else. "But that wasn't anything new. I remember sinking to the bottom and pushing up as hard as I could with my legs." He paused and squeezed gently along my hip. "Turn over again, if you're ready."

So I did. I turned with his help and started moving again as my arms and legs went to work robotically, no longer entirely focused on the movements, but more so on his words. The way no one was there for him...

I made light of it, not wanting to see those eyes darken anymore beyond my shoulder. "Isn't that more like hopping rather than swimming?" I asked.

"It was." He shuffled under the water, walking into a deeper area where his chest began to disappear. "Until I kept going back every day for months teaching myself to be better. Less hopping, more swimming."

That was admirable. Too admirable. "And no one ever helped?"

"Nope. I didn't ask, and no one ever noticed me leaving for hours every day. Or if they did, they didn't care enough to ask about it."

"But you were nine...a child..." I fought the urge to move my wading arms backward enough to brush over his flame-covered forearm.

"Paige, I've been doing things on my own for my entire life. A lot of it went unnoticed and uncared for. Just like you."

I could remember doing things on my own. I could remember working a job, grocery shopping, paying bills. I just couldn't fathom why. Like a purpose in my life was absent. Greyed over in a familiar hue that used to settle comfortably and unashamedly over my mind.

"My mother...she wasn't very good to me, was she?"

He shook his head, but then added, "I think she wanted to be, more than she realized. But she wasn't able to. She was as much in another world as we are now, hers was just of her own making, in her mind."

Aeden turned, walking us back in the direction we'd come from, where Eoghan and Ikelos were nothing but small specks of blue along a golden and cream-colored bank. "I wish I could remember her."

A pained expression flickered over his features. "I believed that, too. But now—"

A blast of air sent a question bursting through the ocean breeze. "When were the territories formed?"

We both answered, adding onto one-another's reply that the territories weren't formed in a single day but rather shifted as allegiances fell or were gained during times of war. Two lines were drawn in the sand—one under each of our names.

Aeden started letting me go in short intervals, each time sending a faintly noticeable flow of water beneath my stomach that I scoffed at initially, but as my confidence grew and the flow faded, I cursed under my breath at the way he was always so...right, about what I needed. Even when I didn't want to admit what I needed. What I wanted.

Then don't think.

I reached the shallower waters until I could stand, where the tide was starting to recede under the fading sun. Water drops fell beside me and I turned my head to find Aeden, pushing his hair back and looking down at me.

"You were saying something before. Back there." I nudged my chin in the direction of the lapping waves in the distance.

He nodded his head once, glancing over to where Eoghan and Ikelos stood waiting for us before his eyes fell back to me. To my lips, my hair, my wet clothing that gave little left to be imagined—not that he hadn't already seen or felt most of it. But he wasn't looking at me like he did so often. Playful, cocky, always-smirking Aeden was replaced by the somber one—the more contemplative and reflective one. I was learning his emotions just as well as he'd known mine all this time—and the fear of that sent a ripple down my spine.

"Letting go was never easy for you. But seeing you let her go—seeing you forget her—might just be the best thing I've ever seen happen to you. Even if that means you forgot me, too. I've always been selfish, so selfish when it comes to you. Wanting you. But the things that plagued you back in Jessup—they don't torment you here. Not anymore. And for that, I'm grateful." His hand moved toward mine as if he wanted to meet my hand at my side, and for a moment, I wanted the same thing. But he let it fall back to his side. My gaze didn't leave that hand as he continued, "I don't want your memories back, Paige. And if that makes me even more selfish in your eyes, then so be it." And then he just left and walked up the shore, leaving nothing more than the cold, idle waves to caress me.

Chapter Twenty-One

Aeden

Fire spread along my arm as I paced the wall that divided our bedrooms. And I just let it. Because I couldn't focus beyond the recollection of words blaring through my mind. My confession.

I didn't want her memories to return. Something within me snapped as I watched Paige conquer yet another fear. Nothing seemed to haunt her in her waking life anymore. The anxiety, the panic attacks, the fear of never being good enough or doing enough—it was all gone. She still had an urgency about her to do more, and train harder than me, but it wasn't out of fear. Fear was no longer her driving force. To think I wanted that all to return, all so she could possibly love me again—I had been so foolish.

But I couldn't stand there any longer and admit to myself that was what I truly wanted anymore. I had pushed her so much to remember before she called me out on it. Had wanted her to push beyond the haze in her mind and try to remember me. But that would require her to remember everything that pulled her down before. The way she used to feel like a heavy burden, the way she used to try to save everyone from themselves, the way she used to believe no one was listening.

Anything that had pertained to her mother was simply gone—all the town's gossip, all the criticism from any of her peers in school, the reason she couldn't go to college or live a normal life, one where she didn't have to become the parent of the household at such an early age. She described it as *greyed over* in her mind. I would now describe it as a fucking blessing from the Stars. One Gedeon unwittingly bestowed upon her. He'd probably shit himself if he could see her now.

I could find another way for her and me to rekindle what we had. But I wouldn't push anymore. I wouldn't beg the Stars for her memories to return and I wouldn't push Murrie to come up with another way to right her mind, because it *was* righted, although to me it was never truly wronged, either. But she'd see it another way—the worst way. I'd love her all the same no matter what fears or thoughts weighed on her, but would she love herself? Would she want the memories back once they returned?

I knew she didn't much like the thought of remembering me, but she'd made it quite clear that she wished for some knowledge of her mother. Had asked about her, even though I had little to give where that was concerned. I never knew the woman she was before the alcohol took hold, but Paige had spoken of a time when, although brief, her mother was coherent.

A parent.

A loving one, too.

The fire crawled up in a caress around my neck and shoulders in an attempt to blanket the loss. I would never stop fighting for her, for us, but I wouldn't rely on the missing memories returning to change the way she looked at me.

She is starting to feel something for you, you know.

I still slept facing the door, waiting like a madman for a knock, a shuffle, anything that would tell me she was waiting beyond the door for me. Hoping she was ready to tell me everything she had been feeling lately. The few times a shadow had moved by, I'd run and throw the door open, only to find Ikelos wandering the halls late at night like he had his own demons to conquer.

We all had our inner demons, and we all coped with them in different ways. And with his ability to glimpse the future—I could only imagine the terrors that lie ahead if he couldn't so much as sleep in his own home with his lover at his side.

A scream—no, *her* scream, cut through the crackling sounds of the flames along my skin. In seconds, I was at her door, throwing it open. The flames retreated back beneath my flesh right as I reached her, where she curled along her bed under her sheets and blanket. She screamed again and again, clawing at the bed, her pillows, and then my chest as I rushed beside her, laid down and pulled her close to my body. Her screams turned into whimpers as she turned and nuzzled into the crook of my shoulder, the warmth of her soft skin replacing the heat of the foregone flames.

The flooring creaked and my gaze shot to the doorway. Ikelos. His hand was pressed to the door as he leaned against it, peering at his sister and examining her before meeting my eyes.

His brow furrowed with worry. "Is she alright?" he whispered.

I gave a slight nod, being careful not to wake her. "She will be." Because whenever I was that close to her, touching her, the nightmares seemed to hurt less. This wasn't the first time I rushed beside her in her sleep. She'd probably hate to know that. My fingers wrapped around her delicate arms, tracing the purple marks idly. Minutes passed, and when I checked for Ikelos at the door again, he was gone and the door was closed.

I tucked my chin in and stared down at her as she slept, wondering where she was at with the gift I still had no answers for. The one currently tormenting her. And the fae called these things *gifts*. I felt like I was failing her. It was worse than the new blood on my hands. Yet, having her in my arms made that night feel even more righteous than it had before.

I could stop the evil of this world for coming for her, but I couldn't help wherever her mind took her in the late hours of the night beyond simply being there for her. I gently pulled my body from hers once her breathing remained steady for longer than a few minutes, but the moment I made to leave, her hand reached out for mine.

"Stay," she whispered, whimpering slightly. Her eyes remained closed and her voice was a distant, soft murmur—she was still asleep. If I did as she asked, she'd more than likely regret her decision in the morning. But I held onto her hand and waited for her to pull her hand back, to wake up and tell me to get the fuck out of her room, to fight me with the many daggers stashed in her room or the bonded one underneath her pillow that only I'd be able to bond to. The same one I helped pull from her shoulder the day of her third trial.

But her hand never pulled back, and neither did mine.

"Stay. Please." Her tone turned pleading. Dreamlike, but in the most subtle way. Perhaps she wanted someone in her dreams, and was reaching for them. Had mistaken me for them, whoever it was. Her hand tugged on mine and I let my body fall back down as I laid beside her once more, facing her, watching her face relax as I unlinked our fingers and placed my arm around her. I pulled her into me and her body molded against mine, accepting the curve of my forearm around her waist and the lazy circles of my fingers along her exposed spine where her nightshirt rose just enough to bare her body to me.

This is what I killed that man for. This is what I held most dear to me, even beyond my own kingdom. If the rest of Aellethia had to fall for us to be together, I'd let it fall. I waited for the sounds of a certain female dragon to invade my thoughts, but nothing came. No remark about how moronic I was or how love had made me weak. Nothing but silence.

I watched her sleep soundlessly for what must have been an hour, if not more, before a faint knock pulled me from her. Her whimpers and grimacing didn't return as I got up and opened the door.

Ikelos was standing beyond the threshold. He jerked his head, motioning for me to join him in the hallway. "I won't keep you long." I turned my head over my shoulder to check on Paige once more, then followed him into the hallway where the way he leaned against the wall said otherwise.

I crossed my arms over my chest. "What is it?"

"I think we need to talk." His fingers raked through his disheveled, icy-white hair.

"Alright." The word came out clipped.

He expelled a long sigh through his nose. "I won't pretend I don't know about her gift. She hasn't told me about it, but something tells me she has told you." I pressed my lips together and glared back at him. I didn't dislike Ikelos, but that didn't mean I trusted him, either. And with the way they'd hidden Eoghan's gift from us—

"You should answer him, Aeden. His insight could be of great value." Ah, there she is.

"It isn't my place to tell him, just like it wasn't his place to tell me about Eoghan. Or did you forget they hid that, too?"

Varasyn growled. *"There will always be secrets, Aeden. Out of all the fae I could've bonded with, it had to be the one too stricken with love to see beyond it."*

"So sorry to disappoint you."

"You should be."

Ikelos reached for the back of his neck. "I didn't expect you to answer. She probably told you to keep it a secret, so I can't fault you there, because I did the same. Just know that I saw her during her second trial, heard the hag tell her she had a gift, and before you were in the picture, it was Eoghan who came to her when her nightmares became too real. The amount of fear he felt was unparalleled."

My jaw clenched and I looked away from him, trying to diminish the flames that crept along my skin. It was beyond irrational at this point to keep getting jealous over Eoghan's relationship with Paige when she had to go through what she did. Still, it should have been me who was there for her.

Ikelos rolled his thin lips in. "If you aren't in the mood to discuss gifts, then I guess this conversation won't go very far."

"Speak up, you idiot."

"Remind me to torch your sheep as you eat them."

Vara gasped. *"You wouldn't."*

"I hope you like burnt meat."

Varasyn growled again and I could see her bright red and golden wings flash just beyond the ice wall down the hall, pulling Ikelos' gaze to where mine fell briefly.

He cleared his throat. "I think someone else agrees with me that this can't go on much longer." He pushed off the wall, taking a step closer to me. "I can help, but only if you let me. I love her too, you know. Not in the ways you do, but if you love her as much as I can see you do, you'd want to help."

"I don't need to prove anything to you," I scoffed at his attempt to make me feel guilty. Keeping her secret, the one she trusted me to know, made me feel needed. Like I'd finally served a better purpose for her. I'd read through dozens of books about what her gift could be, all with no answers, no guidance on what to expect, or if this was the extent of it or only the beginning. I'd never read so much in my life.

"Tell him now, Aeden." A loud thud sounded above our heads and Ikelos flinched as sharp claws scraped against the roof.

The door creaked open behind me and Paige shuffled to stand beside me. Not her brother. *Me.* I uncrossed my arms and pushed my hands into my pockets. "I didn't want to wake you."

Her brows scrunched together as if she was confused as to why I would have tried to wake her in the first place, as if she didn't remember that she'd pulled me into her bed and had been nestled into me minutes before. She pointed up with a single finger. "I think Vara is on the roof. I keep hearing that chortling sound she makes whenever Seamus gets too close. She doesn't sound happy."

"No. She's not," I admitted.

Paige nodded, then looked at her brother. "I heard you asking about my gift." Ikelos raised his brow. "I asked him not to say anything because honestly, I'm not even sure it's a gift."

"You don't have to tell him anything if you don't want to." She didn't owe anyone an explanation.

"I'm listening, Paige. You know you can trust me, right?" The sincerity in Ikelos' voice was enviable. They had a connection from the start. I wondered why she chose me to keep her secret safe if she barely tolerated my presence most days and not her brother.

"I know. I do trust you, I just—we've been so focused on training and learning everything we can before we leave that I didn't want to be a burden."

"You have never been, nor will you ever be, a burden," he replied quickly. Her gaze stayed fixed on him but her hand grazed the edge of my pocket as I looked down at her. So I slid my hand out and twined my fingers with hers.

She didn't pull back, and as I moved my thumb up along hers, I could feel her pulse beating just as rapidly as my own.

"I have these dreams that feel as if I'm still awake. I've seen places I've never been, people I've never met before, and I used to feel like a passenger. Like my body wasn't mine when I slept. That's how I knew who you were when we first arrived." Right as my thumb started making longer strides along her skin where our hands linked, she pulled her hand from mine as if she realized the touch had grown too intimate.

As if the admission of her gift had left no room for other admissions to pass.

"It appears one of you has some sense."

"Don't forget, I've kept your secret as well. The one about there being more dragons. Even if you never outright said it was a secret. Don't forget this bond flows both ways. I can feel what you feel, too."

Varasyn took off from the roof, making the hallway, and Ikelos, shudder. But not Paige.

"Secrecy can be admirable, but not if it hinders your, or even her, progress."

The muscle in my cheek twitched. *"Glad to see she's growing on you."*

Vara only huffed in response.

"I always assumed you found my old bed chamber in that...that prison. Eoghan let me know it remained untouched, including my portrait. That Stars-damned portrait." A shadow began moving closer from down the hallway. Ikelos' lips turned up into a smile as Eoghan approached and slid his hand into Ikelos' with ease.

"You weren't in bed," Eoghan said as he brushed his lips against the crown of Ikelos' head.

Paige sighed, her eyes also lingering on their linked fingers as her teeth dug into her bottom lip. "We should move this to the meeting room."

"What's going on?" Eoghan questioned, glancing between the three of us. "Oh."

I rubbed my palm along my jaw. "I take it this has been pillow talk for a while now. Paige and her gift," I clarified smoothly, enough to let Eoghan know this wasn't about his—I hadn't told her about his. As much as I hated keeping things from her, I doubt it would do her any good to know how much Eoghan knew about her feelings. About all the things she was pushing down.

He inclined his head toward me in silent thanks, which he made look like an agreement. "Something like that," Eoghan mumbled.

Paige glanced between Eoghan and I, probably questioning why we were being cordial. But that look went away as Ikelos led us down the hall, his fingers still wrapped around Eoghan's.

Chapter Twenty-Two
PAIGE

"So, this all started when you got here?" Eoghan had been pacing the entire time I spoke, like the weight of my dreams was suddenly being shared between us. Aeden leaned against the bookcase, watching me closely as I told them everything I'd seen so far, every place I'd been to before. I even told them about the bright light that I couldn't explain when I watched a shifted form of Hector in a darkened room. The entire time I talked, I couldn't stop rubbing my thumb along my fingers, missing the comforting heat that had been there minutes before.

"As far as I remember, I didn't have them in Jessup—in the mortal world." Aeden shook his head, confirming he'd never seen or heard of it happening before, either. Not like it had been happening here, anyway. He also kept glancing at Eoghan, as if he were waiting for something. "All I know is that when I sleep, I feel like...like I'm traveling. Not really in someone else's body, either. It's like I'm a ghost. I only recently was able to pick up something but it slipped through my fingers just as fast as I was able to grab it."

"What was it?" Ikelos asked, his intrigue and the memory of it making me smile. Not that anyone else was. Eoghan and Aeden looked unnerved.

"A seashell. I think I was in Lystos." It was a day I'd been so exhausted after sparring with Eoghan that I fell asleep in the middle of the day, right when I got back to my room. It was one of the deepest naps I'd ever taken.

Eoghan stopped pacing. "One of my towns."

"Yes. So I've learned. I know all of your towns, as well as the rest of the major ones all throughout Aellethia. Even Vizna's fallen ones."

Aeden smiled at my remark.

"Why were you there? What else did you see there?" Ikelos asked.

The amount of attention would have been unsettling had I not been subjected to the Triad and had thousands upon thousands of fae staring me down as they waited for my death. The only thing unsettling now was the way Aeden kept his eyes on me, like doing so was helping. It wasn't.

"I never know why I end up where I do. Not really. I don't know if I'm the pilot or if I'm the passenger, or if I'm just imagining it all. It was a cute town, though. The people seemed happy. Well fed." In comparison to what I'd witnessed in Prydia, it was almost night and day.

"They are," Eoghan said flatly. "Any building most notable?" *He wants me to prove I'd been there.*

I thought for a moment. "A large circular one in the center, made of white stone and a blue roof that appeared to be made of scales and shells. I saw several older fae walking through the doors before it shut."

Eoghan nodded. "The town hall." His finger tucked beneath his chin as he added, "It seems as if you've truly been there." His brows rose. "Is that all you saw?"

"There? Yes. For the most part. I saw your guards in all blue, children playing by the water and near the shell I collected. I felt a liveliness there that I didn't feel in...in Prydia. But I also sensed some kind of...I don't know how to explain it. Urgency?"

Ikelos and Eoghan both nodded. Eoghan said, "A lot of the people there remember what it is to be at war. I believe many can see it coming. Gedeon hasn't only sent spies and scouts and guards this way." *Spies, scouts, and guards. All plural.* To my knowledge, there had only been one. Ikelos didn't look surprised by what Eoghan had said, but neither did Aeden. *He knew?*

Eoghan hadn't stopped talking through my thoughts, yet somehow I'd managed to focus on everything, tunneling even past the golden flecks lingering on me.

"We've caught a few elsewhere as well, but we don't kill the one's sent there. Not in Lystos. It's too close to Costa, sometimes fishing from the same areas." Costa was given to the Aerbornes as a gift of peace nearly a century ago, but it didn't seem to sit well with Eoghan that so many of his people were being led by my father, *watched* by my father's guards. "What you witnessed was most likely a meeting to discuss that very matter. I have an adviser stationed in Lystos now, mostly managing food and clothing rations because of the hold up at Shreeve Port. Thankfully the town can survive off what the ocean provides, but without trade, they are lacking in monetary support." His face turned weary. Drained. As if he'd given a lot of effort in simply feeding and clothing his people and keeping them away from harm recently, and it was wearing him thin.

"So it is a gift, then. She really is traveling to these places," Aeden said.

"I believe so, and if the amount of books you are blowing through is any indication, I'd be inclined to guess that you have yet to read anything similar to it. Correct?"

Aeden shook his head and my stomach sank. "No, I haven't found anything quite like what she says is happening." He had been trying so hard to find an answer—for me.

"Well, it's clear that when you dream, you can go places, see things, hear things...it's as if you've been there.

But, touching? Being able to grab hold of something...the amount of ways you could use that gift..." My brother trailed off and Eoghan stopped pacing just for a moment to stare back at Ikelos.

Eoghan's head cocked toward me as Aeden's cocked at my brother. "Do you remember what it was that Hector held?"

"No, I couldn't see it. I only know that he seemed pretty scared that he'd lost it, or maybe he was scared *of* it. I think he shifted afterward so he could go back into town with it or maybe he wanted to move around the castle with it undetected. Who knows with him."

Eoghan resumed pacing. "I can't imagine what it would be like if you were the incapable girl your father described to me. It still surprises me that he hired Hector—he's not exactly the strongest or smartest guard there is. Gedeon clearly only values his gift. And if he knew about yours—"

"I'd never let him find out about her." Aeden's brows dipped low. "It's best if he keeps his focus on me. If I need to fly over his castle with Vara to grab his attention from her, I will."

My mouth fell open. "Why would you—"

"Honestly, Paige. If you can't see how much he loves you, then you might be at least half of what your father claimed you were. I should have told you both I only had one guest room for the both—" Ikelos had moved from one corner of the room to the other, faster than I'd ever seen anyone move. One moment, he was searching the library, the next, he had his palm over Eoghan's mouth. I guess that answered what special power he'd received—being able to blast enough air behind him that he could run faster than the eye could see.

Ikelos' eyes flashed to Aeden and I. "Excuse Eoghan, he's cranky when he doesn't sleep enough. We'd never hole you up in a room together unless that's what you wanted."

Ikelos gave Eoghan a nod before he dropped his palm, but Eoghan was quick to add, "They both seemed to like that idea, I promise you, babe."

His eyes met mine almost magnetically as heat flooded my cheeks. But it wasn't from what Eoghan had just blurted—well, not entirely. It was from the realization of exactly why Eoghan wore so many masks. My gaze shot back to Eoghan through narrowed slits. "You're an Empath."

Eoghan clapped slowly. "So you have been studying gifts, then."

"I studied them enough in Prydia. I just never thought the Stars would be dumb enough to grant that gift to you, of all people." Aeden snickered from where he stood. "And you knew, didn't you?" I crossed my arms and glared at Aeden as he held up both hands.

"I found out recently. I was in the dark as much as you were." He'd actually kept a secret for Eoghan. I don't know when it happened, but at some point, those two went from fighting all the time to being...friends? Maybe friends was a strong word to use for someone with as many trust issues as Aeden had.

"If you must know, Princess, I don't sit there evaluating your emotions every hour of the day. I have more important matters to attend to than feeling everything that you do, which recently, has been more than I can take. And when you both reek of lust, I find it hard to focus. So please, control yourselves while we are having such a serious conversation." Aeden smirked slightly. He rather enjoyed hearing how I felt about him, yet remained completely unbothered that I'd heard the same about how he felt.

My mouth must've become agape at some point. I snapped it shut and refrained from hurling something at Eoghan. "Oh, don't look at me like that. It's not like I got to pick my gift, and your brother's gift is as much a secret from your father as mine is. Most fae in a position of power don't admit to having a gift, just as you didn't so freely admit to having one, either." The sad thing was, Eoghan was right.

"That's much better. See? She does understand. I swear, having you two in a room sometimes is just too much." *Asshole.*

"Eoghan..." Ikelos warned.

"As if him telling me how I used to feel wasn't too much, now I have you actually *reading* them aloud to me. Please tell me you aren't coming with us to Costa." I raised my folded arms higher, suddenly aware of the sheerness of my nightgown and the way Aeden's eyes hadn't left my body for several minutes now. As if the invasion of my current feelings hadn't been enough, now my body and my stupid fucking nipples were clearly reacting to him.

It couldn't be ignored for much longer. Besides the way my body kept visibly reacting, the way my chest kept tightening when I was around him...and the grey...the sheer amount of grey, could only mean he had meant something to me before. Something far greater than I had first believed. And now, I could actually *picture* what it was like.

To want him. To love him.

I was starting to understand why. He'd kept my secret, even if it undoubtedly hindered how much we could find out with the time we had. He was kind and soft to those he loved but nothing but pure stone and fire to those he didn't. He worked harder than anyone I'd ever seen before, giving up sleep most nights probably because of me. And he...he had risked his life, just to tell me he loved me.

And what had I done in return?

"I think we all need to go back to sleep. We can discuss this more in the morning." Aeden's voice broke the thoughts in my mind, keeping me from spiraling any further down the hole I steered so clear from. More like the gaping crater of my body and mind that he was starting to fill.

When I finally looked around the now quiet room, it was just him and I.

"Where'd—"

"They left. Everyone needs their sleep if we are going to be leaving tomorrow morning." Aeden gave me a look of concern. "You don't need to listen to Eoghan, Paige. I'm sure he's just reading Ikelos and not you." What should have made us both chuckle awkwardly ended up steering us toward awkward silence instead. Both of us evaluating the other on exactly how much of what he just said that we truly believed.

Neither of us believed it.

I shrugged, my arms still covering my breasts. "It's the Winter Solstice soon. And I'm not going to lie and say you aren't...you know." I waved a finger from where my arms remained clamped together.

I expected a grin. But what I got was...well, not that. "I'll find a way to stay away from you. If I have to tie myself down, or make Vara keep me contained, I'll do it. I don't want to force you into anything you don't want."

"I think Eoghan broke the seal on exactly how I feel about that," I blurted.

"And what about after?" Still no grin. No flaring eyes that circled my body. I recognized the way he looked, even if it pained me to recognize it. He was putting up a shield—a wall. He expected me to hurt him with my next words. I'd never seen him do it before to me and it sent another jab right in my chest.

I rolled my lips, eyes drawn to the darkness beyond the windows. He wanted words of promise, something that showed once we spent the night together, that we'd be moving in the direction of loving each other. He wanted me in ways I didn't know how to respond to.

His head dipped down with my growing silence, and when he picked it up again, he dragged his palms down his face. "Just, forget it. I'm going back to bed."

As he moved past me, I reached out for his forearm. He stopped, looking down at me with furrowed brows. Something had been eating at me since the night his mark spread over my flesh and the way Shay had pulled me aside one day to ask about it told me it had been eating him alive, too. And that didn't feel right. I didn't have an answer to what we'd be to each other in a week, but I knew that he didn't deserve to sit with something that heavy on his conscience.

"You didn't transfer your mark to me."

The color on his face drained. "What do you mean?"

"Eoghan transferred his mark to me, and I know what that feels like. It feels like an invasion, like a force not of my own. But…that's not how it felt with you. I could feel it coming from within me." I squeezed his forearm as his hand fell over mine. "I just wanted you to know that it wasn't your fault."

His eyes softened. "I—Are you sure?"

Admitting it would become my undoing. But he already seemed to have a weight lifted from his shoulders as his eyes circled mine, trying to find the truth of what I'd just told him. But I wasn't lying, not at all. I nodded, squeezing his forearm gently again. "I'm sure, Aeden."

As much as I didn't want to admit it to myself, telling him about the mark was as close as I could get to an admission, even if I struggled to get the words out. And whether he took that as I had wanted him that night, or more, I knew what it meant for me as the words passed my lips. Knew the way I was trying to comfort him could only mean one thing.

I was falling for him.

Chapter Twenty-Three
PAIGE

Eoghan and Ikelos, were in fact, coming along with us.

We'd been making our way to Costa for almost two days now, only stopping when we needed to rest or give the horses and Vara a break. I doubted she asked for one, though. I supposed being in the sky and away from the rest of us wasn't something she was so strongly against.

That was all her rider.

Prynn Springs was the last stop before we made it through the newly constructed wards my father had placed. I could almost sense it as we kept nearing it—that familiar power. Ikelos could, too. I could tell by the way he kept tensing and staring off into the distance.

"Not to say that I'm not happy you came, but you didn't have to," I said to my brother as we led our horses to the edge of the spring. It was still light out, but as soon as the sun started to move toward the west, we were going to gun it for Costa. At least Eoghan had more horses so we didn't have to ride in twos. I needed to be with my thoughts, and riding with Murrie made it quite difficult to do so before.

"I'm happy I did. Hopefully I can be of use to you all. And this way I'll actually be able to see what is happening to all of you and I won't be blocked by her." He pointed to the sky where Vara was closing in on the ground fast, her wings angled back as Aeden stood up on her back, preparing to jump and roll. I would have seen that as him showing off before, but now he just looked even more so the Mora he was destined to be. A slight curve touched my lips as I watched him. "Maybe not all things I should be seeing, but—"

I nudged into him and he let out a laugh. "It was just a joke, Paige. Trust me, Eoghan berates someone almost every year during this time. Even a few children have been named in his honor because of the way he'd push people together. Possibly more than I should try to count."

My throat turned dry. *Children?* "Um...I'm not...I don't..."

"Relax, sis. I already asked Murrie to make you what she's been making for Shay all these months. You won't have to worry about that for the week, at least."

"How...how many of those do you have?"

My brother's eyes squinted, but he still answered. "If you need more, you let me know. Wait...no. Ask Shay or Murrie. I don't know if I need to know how much of this you're taking."

I chuckled and nodded, but then looked over to where Shay and Seamus were, splashing in the near-frozen water, acting like children. "So, they really are together, then?" A shudder hit the ground as Vara landed, Aeden already rebounding from his leap and jogging to the spring. Toward...me.

"It would appear they are. I wonder if either of them is aware just how difficult it would be to produce an offspring between the two, seeing as she isn't fae. Not impossible, but fae having children is hard enough. For them? It would be a one in a million chance."

"Shay's cautious. I wouldn't be surprised if Seamus found it pointless, but she chose to do it anyway." It shocked me that I'd paid that much attention to them. The ones I only thought of as his friends, my captors, were now becoming...well, whatever Eoghan and Aeden were to each other now, that's how we were. I didn't lean on them, but I wouldn't hurt them, either. And to think, I'd planned to escape before. That thought hadn't crossed my mind since Aeden offered it to me, and even before then it had been some time since I truly had considered it.

Aeden slowed beside my brother, his breathing trying to steady as he bent over, that newly fastened sword on his back swaying as he braced himself on his legs. My brother slapped a hand to his shoulder when he stood back up. "I'm going to go check on Eoghan and Murrie, they seem to be tiffing over something." Eoghan and Murrie didn't look too flustered as they talked beside the edge of the spring, but when I turned my head from them, Ikelos was gone.

"How are you doing?"

I shrugged, flicking my wrist to clear the snow from the grass before taking a seat right where I'd stood. Aeden did the same and sat beside me, but left a solid foot of space between us. I wanted that space gone, but made no effort to do so.

"I'm okay. Though, I don't know how Seamus is swimming in that." Right as I mentioned it, Seamus flocked to the snow-covered grass, cradling Shay in his arms as she laughed while he called for Aeden to make a fire. Aeden's shoulders shuddered with his laughter as a fire-pit formed near Seamus, Ikelos rushing over with several blankets, him and Murrie and Eoghan all shouting at Seamus for being an idiot.

Aeden's attention fell back to me, his forearms resting over his knees. "Are you cold?"

"I could be warmer, honestly." He took that as an invitation, shuffling in closer to me and the warmth of his body started to ease the shiver that was spreading down my legs and arms.

"Is that...better?" His breath hit my cheek, warming my face as well. I should've pushed him away, denied the feelings that were growing too rapidly to be able to process. I'd been on the back of a horse for days, but my thoughts had been in the clouds. With him.

"It is. Thank you." The others were so caught up in thawing out Seamus and getting food ready before we'd head out again that no one seemed to notice or care about how close we were. Except for maybe Varasyn, because I saw that look he always made when they were discussing something—the slight twitch of his lips and the unease in his eyes as they focused on the clouds. I decided against prying, unsure if I really wanted to know what her thoughts were. They probably weren't good.

His arm lifted, and just before he put it around my shoulders, I blurted, "Eoghan said there were wraiths out here." His arm froze in the air, and I watched as his hand fell to the back of his head instead, sweeping down along his hair.

"Yeah. I uh...I heard."

I bit the inside of my cheek, now feeling too warm. Too close.

"Paige?" Every time he said my name was like a knife twisting in my chest. I knew how he felt about me, but once I showed him I was starting to feel the same, would it all be over? Would he still want someone as damaged as I was?

"Hmm?" Was all I could get out.

"I know you're feeling anxious about...fuck. I know you don't want to talk about this."

"No, I think we should." Our faces were inches from each other, it would be so easy to just reach out and drag my fingers along that stubble on his jaw, to pull his face in close to mine.

"I want you to know that no matter what happens, and whatever comes afterward, I will never expect anything from you. I may hope for it, but I won't be foolish enough to think that a night with me will—if that even happens—that it will change how you see me."

I wondered if he could hear the thundering of my heart, trapped in a fit beneath my ribs. An entirely new kind of caged feeling. "I know," I said, my voice a little too breathy but I played that off with a shiver.

I wasn't cold in the slightest anymore.

He scooted in closer, keeping his arms to himself. "And if you want me to, I'll completely drain myself to keep away from you. Just say the words, and I'll make roots spread around my entire body with a ring of fire around that."

I laughed and his lips quirked up. "You'd fight that hard against something that affects me too?" Because I'd have to do the same to keep from him. I'd have to wall myself within a shield of air and coat it in ice, and even then I'm sure I'd push through that and break free to get to him.

"I would. I'd fight every last Star in the sky if you wanted me to." The sun was falling rapidly now, and the way his body shimmered against it was too breathtaking. His eyes seemed to shift with the setting sun, blazing hot yet darkening like the night sky. "But if you don't want me to fight, and if you don't want to fight against it either, then make no mistake, My Queen—I will fuck you until the Stars force us apart."

I whipped air into my lungs to steady the rapidity of my thrashing heart, the heat of his body seeping into mine, pooling between my thighs like it had that night when we had almost done just that.

"Might need some of this food over here if you want to be ready for tomorrow, you two!" Eoghan hollered from where the rest of our group was gathered.

"Ignore him," Aeden murmured.

Using Eoghan's interruption to my advantage, I tried to regain some semblance of composure, but it was like building a brick wall with no mortar in a wind storm. Nothing worked to keep those walls up anymore. "Why don't you hate him so much anymore?"

"Eoghan?" I nodded, waiting for him to continue. *Please, continue.* "Let's just say, he helped to open my eyes. So much so, that fucker made me thankful for him. I still don't trust him fully, but I sure as hell respect him."

I let his words mull over in my mind, wondering if I should ask him more about whatever had happened between them. But between the separate training and classes we were each given, I hadn't really seen just how much time they had been spending together. At some point, it must've been Eoghan that had crossed that barrier they built between each other. Crossed it and helped Aeden do *something* in the process.

And I found I was thankful for that, too.

The next morning, although still dark out, we rode. Fast. I felt as if I was panting just as much as my horse was. The Winter Solstice officially hits tonight whenever the moon decides to rear its ugly head, and for once, my mind wasn't filled with the question of what I would do. I knew what was to come. I had come to terms with it. And kind of...looked forward to it.

I will fuck you until the Stars force us apart.

My body shivered in response as the snow slapped around the shield of air I supplied to block from the storm. I'd grown strong enough to block my own horse, but as for Seamus and Shay and Murrie, each of their horses had a shield of air supplied by one of the three other men. One of which I kept checking for in the skies above, but with the clouds and the snow and the darkness, it was hard to see.

That's a good thing, I reminded myself, even if it meant I couldn't make sure he was okay as much as I wanted to.

We hit my father's wards rather abruptly, and the anticipation of being in Aerborne territories again made my adrenaline spike. My hands raked over my body, feeling and counting out each of the twelve blades I kept on me. Murrie must've felt the same because when I looked over, her battle-ax was no longer slung across her back. The blade now bumped along her lap, her small fists curving around the handle as if we were heading into battle.

No one really knew what we were rushing into, but we all knew that this was a monumental moment. One that could end in our deaths if we were wrong about the guards.

The rooftops, flat and staggered as they were, filled the space at the bottom of a hill possibly a mile out. They rolled into view and all of our horses fell to a slow canter as we moved forward. Eoghan had been right about the snow and the weather—it was unrelenting. From where we were, the dingy cottages more resembled what I expected from a town within my father's control as we trudged slowly through what must have been close to a foot of snow.

Seamus fell into place in front of us, leading the way. There was no way to see what lay beneath the snow, if we hit a body of water or a large ditch, we wouldn't know until it was too late. We all moved slowly, our horses tiring faster now as the snow continued to climb up their limbs.

And the snow kept falling.

We made our way to where a few homes dotted the landscape beside us, but still not a soul ran around.

Eoghan sent a flare of faelight into the air, signaling for Aeden to land quickly before anyone in the town below could see, before the sun could rise high enough to show a dragon on the horizon.

With her wings tucked in close, she darted from a spot above the clouds and let Aeden spring from her back moments before she'd hit the ground, then swooped back into the air and above the clouds. My breath caught in my chest and I hurriedly sent a cushion of air beneath him just before he landed on his feet. It was dumb, and impulsive. I knew he could do it on his own like he did the night before, but I couldn't just let him fall. Not without trying to catch him first.

"Thanks for the assist," he said with a grin that made his dimple pop. Even in the moonlight, that damn face of his shone so bright, the light bouncing off of him and into my chest. "You alright there, Seamus?"

Seamus righted himself from where he was pressed flat against his horse, visibly terrified and trying to dodge the dragon that had descended from the sky. He huffed out a shaky laugh. "Boyo, ye tryin' to kill me with that dragon of yers, aren't ye? Can ye at least wait 'til after this week is over?"

I laughed nervously from my horse, glancing between him and Shay as Shay swatted the air in his direction from her horse's back. "I'm not affected by the Stars and their desires, you idiot. The holiday is for Fae breeding, not merpeople."

He scowled over at her, clearly biting his tongue from saying just how much he didn't care whether she was fae or not. She winked back at him, and he relaxed back into his saddle.

The way they could just be together, not caring about the rest of the world or their duties within it, almost made me...jealous.

A deathly shriek burst through the silence, and within seconds, the home in front of us became alight with flames as if kerosene had been poured on every square inch. Everyone jumped to the ground, but Eoghan held out his arms and darted in front of us, moving the snow from his path as he ran.

"That's—"

But it was too late. Aeden was already closer and started running inside the building faster than Eoghan could stop him.

"—a wraith," he finished from behind me.

My boots pushed through the heavy snow, my air shield thickening as I ran after him. "Aeden!" I shouted from the doorway, my heart sinking into my stomach. "Aeden! Get out of there!" The shriek sounded again as a section of the roof caved in, closing off the entrance to the home.

Ikelos ran to my side and wrapped his arm around me, holding me back from dismantling the barricade with my bare hands and running inside the empty home. Then Eoghan stepped in on my other side with his arm extended. Blocking me. They were keeping me from him, from saving him. Water fell in buckets around the space, the men holding me back murmuring something inaudible around me about the flames while trying to dilute the fire—to extinguish it. But, it was no use. The flames emerged again and again, roaring back to life each time.

"Aeden!" I cried out, my ears ringing and my legs growing weak.

He was dead. There was no way—

The shrieking intensified, followed by gurgling sounds that mixed in with the crackling of the flames. Someone threw up another shield of air over my weakened one—I wasn't even trying to keep it in place anymore. My body was going numb.

He was dead. He's dead.

He's dead.

A blur of blue shot around to the side of the house—Eoghan, or maybe Ikelos, but I couldn't focus or hear anything beyond the dread that was taking over, weakening all my senses. Hollowness took over as I squeezed snow into my hands, melting it over and over. Blue returned by my side, along with voices that I couldn't focus on enough to decipher.

And then the air shield fell apart the moment a blackened blur fell to his knees beside me, his hatchet in his...no, *Aeden's* hands covered in black and red—blood? My mind was trying to still from the intense wave of dizziness that started taking over, my stomach—bile—moving up until—

I turned and hurled. Right by my brother's boots. Wiping my mouth with the back of my hand, I turned my attention back to Aeden who was stark naked, covered in a thick layer of soot and ash.

"What the fuck were you thinking?" The rumbling in my chest wasn't just from the way I'd just shouted at him. My heart was pounding so loud, my ears hurt.

"I was thinking someone needed help. I guess I was wrong." Aeden, the leader. The caring fucking asshole.

It didn't ease any ache inside of me. In fact, it ignited it further, grounding it deeper into my core. "You guess?" I buried my face in my hands and laughed, although not a single part of him *guessing* about his life was funny. "If you didn't run into there as fast as you did, you would've heard Eoghan say what it was. You could've burned to death over a Stars-damned wraith"—my head lulled to the side as I peered at him—"and I thought you—I thought..." *I thought you were dead.*

He smirked and tossed his hatchet to the ground as my words trailed, my focus drifting to where one of his hands was cupping his—I tried to ignore the way that his large hand could hardly cover the space between his thighs and darted my eyes away. But it was too late.

Eoghan cut in, letting out a low whistle. "Fire-resistant? How long have you been like that?"

Aeden shrugged as I tried to will my breathing to slow enough to listen to him. He chuckled, and the urge to slap him had possibly never been stronger. "First of all, wraiths are way worse than hags. Holy fuck." His free hand pushed his hair back, his fingers making lines across his forehead from where he wiped away the ash that coated his skin. "I did think it was another fae, but I guess I was wrong. Man, am I glad I read up about those fucking things."

"Are you okay?" Murrie shouted from where she stood mostly covered in snow beside her horse. Aeden shot his thumb up into the air signaling he was okay, but kept his eyes on me.

Eoghan and Ikelos and I stared back at him, all probably for very different reasons entirely. He pushed his shoulders back as he looked between the three of us. "Does anyone have an extra pair of pants? Mine kind of—well, you know." When his eyes locked on mine once more, he winked.

Fucking *winked*.

I lost it.

"I thought you were dead!" I slapped him with a whip of air, turning his cheek and shooting a thin cloud of ash into the air from the force. When he turned back to me, he was grinning again as he rubbed his hand along his jaw where his skin had gone from black to red.

"He should be dead, Princess. Being a fire-wielder doesn't mean he's fire-resistant, just like I could still drown in the ocean, or you and Ikelos could still die without air in your lungs. Sure, he can take his own fire along his skin, to an extent, but—" Eoghan's eyebrows furrowed as he examined him more, his mouth going taut and thin like he was putting together pieces in his mind. "How long, Aeden?"

Aeden shrugged half heartedly as Seamus tossed a pair of pants into his lap. He stood, giving me a suggestive look right before he removed his hand. I jerked my head away, my eyes falling back to the pile of discarded dinner from the night before, making bile rise in my throat again. I shifted against the snow-covered ground, trying to move away from it and knowing if I turned back around I wouldn't feel the least bit nauseous over the sight I'd take in.

"You can look now, Paige. I'm decent." If not for the amount of ash covering his skin, I'd be scolding him again for not trying to cover up faster, even though covering his legs was the least of his worries—yet possibly the majority of mine. His marks would've been on full-display, and yet he moved as if he wasn't in Aerborne territories.

Ballsy.

"When," Eoghan reiterated, his tone increasingly stern.

Aeden finally gave in. "When you portaled me over the wall, I practically covered my body in flames to fight those nagas. Figured it was a fire-wielder thing and just went with it." He buttoned his pants, tucking the hatchet into the back of his waistband, clearly trying to make light of him turning into a literal ball of flames. And it made me even more mad. How could he be so careless with his life when I cared so deeply about it?

"And you had all your elements then..." Eoghan stared back at Aeden like he was the strangest thing he'd ever seen. "Fire-wielders don't get a power from the Stars. They only get it from the dragons they are bound to. You would have had to have been within your wards at some point to get anything from Vara like that...how old were you when you went to the mortal world?" My brother took over, asking the questions for Eoghan. I hadn't even noticed the quelling of the flames inside the house until my gaze raked up Aeden's body once more, where heavy plumes of steam and smoke seemed to frame him against the falling snow.

"A little over a year, maybe. I just know that foster care had to guess my age. I don't even know my real birthday." He let out a laugh that sounded rehearsed, like he'd gone so long without anyone caring about it—about *him*—that he figured humor was an easier way to go about it. It tore into the ever-growing pit in my chest—the one that was starting to feel a lot like it was just for him.

I stood and dusted the snow from the legs I forgot I owned. "Perhaps your mother stayed hidden within your territories, then, instead of somewhere further away. The rest of your people probably didn't go far, either. It means us going there next might help find some answers." And suddenly the *us* part became a known. He deserved to know every part of his past and what that might mean for his future. And I wanted to be there with him.

A soft, gentle caress of warmth spread over the back of my neck as he gave a single nod back to me, his eyes unwavering from mine. I'd felt hundreds of eyes on me before—while training, during the Triad, and at every meal we ate at Eoghan's. But none ever seared into me the way his did in that moment. Saying so much with so little.

"Shay and I are going to head to Lake Kree from here." Murrie's small shuffling strides and low voice came from behind Eoghan as she took the path he carved into the snow, breaking everyone's eyes from me as they turned to her and the way her body shivered in her fur coat.

"We'll go, too. Eoghan and I." Murrie's brow raised as if to say *what makes you think I need your help?* My brother noticed immediately, waving his hands in the air. "You'll need some air-shields, is all, to block out the snow and storm if it comes back. I meant no offense."

She huffed in response as Seamus walked over with a tunic in his hand and held it out for Aeden. I scanned the buildings, any and all we could see from where we stood on the small hill, trying not to watch him as he got dressed—at the way no layer of ash could cover the muscles I'd memorized every single line of.

I walked up to him, legs becoming possessed the moment he was done with his shirt, and took one of his hands in both of mine. My fingers squeezed his, not aiming for gentleness like the warmth he sent over me. No. My hands were rigid and hard and had every intention to send more air across his stupid beautiful face. He blinked down at me, amusement fading and confusion filling his features.

"Don't you ever run into danger like that again. Okay?"

He blinked several more times, then dipped his head down, his breath brushing over the shell of my ear. "Is that an order from My Queen?"

I shuddered, relaxing my grip at the paleness of his fingers then flashed my gaze back up to him. "Yes. It is." My stomach had butterflies, damn *butterflies*, fluttering around just as wildly as the fire that blazed inside the house a moment before. The Winter Solstice was one thing, but it hadn't officially started yet. Had it?

I looked down again to where my hands were now being held, covered in warmth like the rest of my body was. Perhaps it had started, then. Perhaps that's why every nerve in my body was firing off like fireworks.

Seamus cleared his throat and I pulled my hands away, unsure of how long I'd stood there, letting him hold me. "Right, well. Let's get the horses out of the snow 'nd make our way to me house. I think he can make it there without disobeyin', can't ye Boyo?" Ikelos snorted and I glared over at my brother, hoping the way I was looking at him made him second guess the close relationship we'd formed.

"Have a good night, you two." Eoghan winked, moving over to where Ikelos stood and whispering something in his ear that made my brother blush furiously. "Don't do anything we wouldn't!"

We walked the horses down to where the buildings clustered tightly together, each step further reminding me of Prydia and the dilapidated homes there. But Seamus' frown as we walked through made me question if it had always been like this.

Reins in both hands and snow now only an inch up to my boots, I finally asked what had weighed on my mind, breaking the silence. "How did that fire start like that, out of nowhere?"

"Wraith probably started it from the inside," Seamus said, stepping quietly and looking in through every window we passed.

"I don't—" Aeden and I both started at the same time, but when he didn't open his mouth again, I continued. "I don't think a wraith would start a fire like that with it still inside." Aeden's eyes locked on me, his knuckles turning white against the reins as we walked on.

Aeden added, "That, and the way it grew like it was out of control."

"And you still ran in?" Incredulity spilled from me while the image of him emerging from that house eased the ache inside, if only a fraction.

He smirked. "Yeah. I didn't think I would burn in the first place, but I also didn't think you'd care that much if I actually had burned to death."

"Well I do care." I kept my focus on Seamus as he checked yet another empty window space. He sighed when he found no one, yet again. That warm caress over my neck seemed to expand. I didn't dare look at Aeden to see what my admission was doing to him. I didn't have to. I could *feel* it.

"I care 'bout ye too, Lad. Would've been nice to know you wouldn't catch fire. I nearly shit meself." He clapped his hand over Aeden's shoulder, loose rein in his hand while some form of communication between them that didn't require words made them linger in silence for a moment.

"Maybe you should stop trying to save everyone except for yourself." They both turned to face me and I tugged on the reins to walk in front of them, but instead they both picked up their pace, matching mine. I really needed to keep my mouth shut.

Seamus and Aeden stopped abruptly at a door, and I watched as Seamus began to reach into his pockets, then halted as his eyes narrowed on the open space between the door frame and the door itself. Aeden gave the door a slight push and rushed in before Seamus could, and I had half a mind to shout after him again. Why did he keep insisting on running into buildings that he could die in?

Seamus' pointer finger stopped me from doing so as he held it up to me, urging me to follow him quietly like I wasn't strong enough to blast him through the door and chase after Aeden.

Yet, I kept my hands at my sides, because everything was so *still*. The home was torn to pieces—a couch and table and chair were all flipped and tossed around, a closet door hung from the hinges that exposed the mess of clothes and shoes behind it, and heaps of ceramic and glass were shattered along the floors.

"What…" Seamus fell to his knees as he took in the state of the portraits along his walls—or, the few that remained hanging. Most, if not all, were ripped and shredded like sharp claws had made their way through. My mind went straight to nagas, although we had heard or seen none so far—this was the type of destruction they were known for, only it was usually reserved for bodies. My fingers trailed over one of the delicate canvases and pushed a few scraps back together, hoping they'd stay put with little effort.

"Me wife. And me little girl." Tears welled in his eyes as I continued to push pieces back together, but when I moved on to the next piece, the first began to fall back down.

"I'm…so sorry, Seamus," I whispered, and I meant it. Truly, I did. He didn't deserve to have this happen to him. Not Seamus. He'd always been the one Aeden looked to for guidance, almost like a father figure. And Seamus never backed down from that position for as long as I'd seen them together—not once.

Footsteps clattered above us, then a faint shout of a woman before scuffling sounded along the floor. Aeden came down from a spiral staircase, holding on tightly to a woman with blazing, fiery hair and a set of familiar marks. "I caught her upstairs. What do you want to do with her?" He turned and faced me, Seamus' head still hanging toward the floor. He slowly raised his head and turned, his eyes growing wide as Aeden pressed his palm over her mouth, her hair in a wild frenzy around her face.

But I'd know her anywhere. My mouth dropped open, maybe to speak or maybe to gasp, but Seamus cut me off before I could form a thought beyond what I was seeing.

Who I was seeing.

"Aanya?" Seamus stood as I froze, the look of stark confusion spreading over Aeden's face, and possibly mine. Because that was Nya, not Aanya. Although the last time I'd seen her, she wasn't *her*. But this time— her eyes were undeniably ocean blue, not the black onyx of Hector's. Aeden removed his hand and I watched in shock as Seamus rushed over and moved her hair from her face.

Her cheeks had sunken in slightly, and her frame was less built than I remembered her being, but those blue eyes. I stayed fixed on them, telling myself over and over—it's her.

It's her.

It's really *her*.

Seamus' face paled over, his matching fiery hair melding into hers in the unlit room. My eyes narrowed on them—the way each of their noses curved to the same point, and then back to their eyes, and that hair...

When she finally spoke, the shock intensified. "Dad?"

Chapter Twenty-Four
Aeden

The moment I released the woman from my hold, she threw her body into Seamus.

"My girl..." He took several steps back with her in his arms, the color slowly coming back to his face.

I didn't know what to do, so I just stood there, watching as he pushed her back and cleared her face of the matted mess of hair and tears. My eyes swept over to Paige, who was also as stunned as I was. Her mouth kept opening, then snapping shut as if she wasn't sure when to cut in or if she even should.

The words that she finally got out made me still more. "How did you get out?"

Out? "You know her?"

Aanya and Seamus fell from their embrace, Seamus wiping at his own tears as the tops of his reddened cheeks plumped up in the biggest smile I'd seen yet. He didn't seem to be listening to anything, just staring at the woman. Aanya looked over Seamus once more, then rushed into Paige, who was now also crying.

Paige buried her face into Aanya's shoulder and I took the time to look at her. Really look at her.

She called him *dad*.

But that little girl had died in a raid. A fire. Hadn't she? Her body found burned in the ashes of the very house we all stood in now before it was rebuilt. Her marks—earth and water, and a few other ones that weren't of the elemental kind, drew Seamus' attention at the same time they did mine.

"What the fuck happened to ye? Where've ye been? Who—" He reached over to take her back into his arms from Paige's hold—"Who did this, Aanya?"

Her smile fell immediately as she looked back over her shoulder at Paige, then back at her father. "I thought you were dead. I—he...he told me you both—"

"Ye can see I'm well 'nough alive, baby girl. Who told ye—oh, I'm gonna fuckin' kill 'im." His fingers curled around the tops of his daughter's shoulders, and that's when it dawned on me. That's how Paige seemed to know her. To care about her enough to cry over her being here. "Gedeon did this to ye, didn't he? It was 'im." She recoiled slightly at the mention of him, but Seamus fixed his hold on her, pulling her to him again. "That fuckin' bastard." His hand reached up to brush down the back of Nya's head as she leaned into him.

She looked around the disheveled home, then cocked her head up to meet Seamus' eyes. "What about mom?" That vibrancy in Seamus' face died instantly.

"No, Aanya." His gaze shifted to the portrait of the woman along the walls and mine snapped back to Paige. Her memory would be back any day now if Murrie's new mix would actually work. The same pain that lingered on Aanya's and Seamus' face—that would be Paige's soon. That would be her anguish to relive all over again.

And I hoped to the Stars whatever Murrie made wouldn't work.

The silence stretched on painfully until Aanya looked back at me. "And this is..."

"Aeden. Lad's name is Aeden."

Aanya's blue eyes grew wide as they danced between Paige and I. She fixed on Paige for a minute, her brows furrowing along with mine as I considered exactly why she looked so concerned for Paige. And then she hesitated, looking over my ashen skin along my neck and most likely my face, like she was at war with herself on what exactly to say next.

Paige spoke instead, "I thought your name was Nya?"

Aanya nodded. "I told your father that was my name when he came to take me in. But feel free to still call me that. I have been Nya for longer than I was Aanya."

"He didn't take you in, Aanya." Her father disregarded her preference to Nya entirely. "He fuckin' stole you from under me very nose. He knew I wasn't dead." Seamus had been out at sea fishing when his family was attacked, when Costa was raided by Prydian guards who came looking for fire-wielders. "He came because he knew what yer mother was." A fire-wielder. His wife had the mark, but had kept it hidden. He had hoped Gedeon had forgotten that part about his wife, and they had lived quietly for some time before the guards had come, which only made him believe that his wife had been overlooked by the new law and the crazed king—thinking his service had done some justice to keeping his family safe. But that hadn't been the case. He'd spent years believing his daughter was caught up in the crossfire—killed because of the mark she could potentially form. "And he knew what you could do, Aanya. I don't know how he discovered it, but he must have found out."

"Her healing gift," Paige breathed out as her fists curled in at her sides. "My father," she spat the words and then continued, "he made you believe your father was dead all over a gift?"

Gift? Every time I heard that word now, it hit me just how much they weren't gifts at all. They led to nothing but being hunted, abused, or dead. "He could have killed her," I deadpanned, and Seamus' brow furrowed. I held up my hands. "If your wife was a fire-wielder, then—"

Aanya cut me off by slapping her hand down along her arm. "I ended up not being one, clearly," she seethed as she stared at me like I'd insulted her. The waves and vines along her arm shone brightly in the dim room. She must've inherited the earth-wielding from her mother instead of the flames. It made me equal parts relieved for her and sick to my stomach thinking of the way the guards marked their flesh with circles, pridefully displaying how they killed pregnant fire-wielders. Babies who might not even bear the same marks—Nya was proof of that—not that it fucking mattered what they wielded, in my opinion.

"I meant no offense." I flicked my eyes to Seamus, then breathed out heavily before I reached my arm up and pulled my tunic off, taking ash along with it. Her gasp as I took a slow three-sixty spin made my lips form a crooked smile. "See?

I'm no better." If she weren't Seamus' daughter, I wouldn't have thought twice about staying concealed. Paige seemed to be thinking the same thing as a look of confusion took over, her mouth popping open, then snapping shut again. I pushed my arms back through my sleeves.

"First you run into flames and then you show your marks? I knew the Solstice made your kind weak, but I thought you were better."

"It's not a weakness to try to save lives and show an ounce of trust in Seamus' daughter." Vara snarled back at me, letting me know she didn't agree at all. I decided against fighting with her, and instead asked, *"Are you safe? Have you passed the springs yet?"*

"You forget how fast I am. I'm here. You don't need to worry about me."

"Is he okay?" I heard Aanya whisper to Paige as she followed my gaze and leaned back to look beyond the window.

I focused back on Varasyn. *"I will always worry about you. Bonded—remember?"*

"Yeah. He does that." Paige made a gesture around her ear to show that I was crazy and Aanya turned to look at her father.

Seamus clicked his tongue and shook his head. "Boyo is not crazy, he's—"

"A dragon heir. Though I'm sure the marks and the show at the arena already told you that." Aanya nodded as Paige folded her arms across her chest. "And you"—I pointed a finger at Paige—"you know the only thing I'm crazy about is you." Her cheeks reddened instantly.

"I wasn't in the arena for her third trial, but I heard about how…well, how Paige escaped." She turned to face Paige and took her hands in hers. "I'm sorry about what Hector did. And Gedeon. The second they took me before your trial, they put me in a holding cell and didn't let me out until…" She looked down at her wrists, where bruises shaped like cuffs left heavy purple marks on her skin. "I didn't tell him anything. I didn't know he was successful in giving you that poison until I heard Hector boasting about it with the other guards outside of my cell." Paige's eyes watered and I took a step closer to her. Aanya looked at us both. "I made it, Paige. The poison. It was me. I did it, and I wasn't strong enough to fight him back. I should have never made it. I should have found a way out the moment he ordered me to make it. I'm so sorry."

"It wasn't your fault," Paige whispered.

"Do you know how to reverse it?" I asked. Aanya shook her head and my hopes raised as I watched Paige's fall, her shoulders dipping inward. Guilt washed over me—I was being fucking selfish again. But she didn't know what she was forgetting, the horrible things her mother made her feel while neglecting her, sinking further into her addictions while doing so. The few moments she would cherish having back would never outweigh the pain she was missing. Stars knew she wasn't trying to remember *me* that hard.

"I only learned how to make it from a book. It said nothing about reversal. It was intended to do a lot of harm, so perhaps I didn't make it right, thank the damn Stars."

"No, I think you did. Eoghan um..." Paige looked up at me and I tried to tuck in the onset of anger I knew was going to come with the mention of what he had to do. "Eoghan kissed me before I drank it and that saved my water magic, at least. It wasn't until we made our way to the Amaliro Mountains that he told me Ikelos warned him, and—"

"You found your brother? What do you mean he warned him?"

Seamus and I exchanged looks, and I knew exactly where his mind was, because I was about there, too. "I think we should all go get a drink," he suggested. "'ave ye been anywhere outside the house, yet?"

"I try not to go out. Costa was evacuated, due to the uh...threat."

"What threat?" Paige asked right before I could open my mouth to ask the same thing.

"Gedeon was tipped off by a guard shortly after your last trial. He said that a retired guard from Costa asked for their uniforms back the day before the ball. That's when Hector was sent here to force everyone out, saying the guy was a threat. They searched all the homes and questioned most—I didn't know when they were talking about it...that the guard was you, dad." She looked back at Seamus. "I'm sorry. I should have found a way out sooner..."

"Bastard," Seamus grumbled under his breath.

"Yeah, I think that drink sounds great right about now. There's probably still barrels at the bar, might be fun to show Paige where I ended up, especially if it's as empty as the rest of Costa." I grinned down at her, waiting for her to be snarky or snap back at me with some quick-witted response. Instead, a wave of water poured over me, blackened water seeping in through the floorboards just like that first night at this very house. A moment later, I was completely dry.

"There. Now you are at least presentable." Aanya's eyes lit up as she watched Paige use the power that was supposed to be dormant. But Paige was a fighter—shame on Aanya to doubt her.

My grin turned playful. "I don't mind being dirty." The wink I gave her made Seamus groan behind his daughter.

"Come on, then. Best be goin' 'fore the stars 'nd moon 'nd whatever else is supposed to come out, does so. Keep it in yer pants a bit longer, would ye Lad?"

Aanya choked on a cough or a laugh, I wasn't sure. "Winter Solstice is tonight?" she asked, glancing between Paige and I both again.

Paige didn't bother answering as she walked past her friend with beet red cheeks and made her way through the front door, her boots scuttling away as fast as they could.

Aanya caught my arm as I tried to follow her out. "I know she doesn't remember you, and I'm sorry that I did that. My apology wasn't just meant for her, though. She told me a lot about you. I don't know what she thinks about you now, but I'm guessing it isn't quite the same without the memories of you." She looked back to where Paige had just stormed out to at the mention of the Solstice again.

"I wouldn't let her hear you mention how she used to feel about me. It can really get her going sometimes. But thank you, Nya."

I walked past the doorway and stopped in my tracks. My breath faltered as I took in the sight before me—Paige, her brown leather clothes molding perfectly to her body and her hair blowing through the slight breeze while the snow fell down in small steadying drops around her, dotting her hair and clothes with white. Like a Stars-damned angel.

She turned, her fingers fumbling around what looked like a small empty tube before putting it into her pocket as I approached.

"Ready?"

Most of the homes were destroyed. Broken pieces and shards of wood lined the areas where doors, walls, and window spaces used to be. No one was in any of them, and after checking the first few that had blood staining the entryways, Paige pulled me back, before I could try to enter another.

"Stop. Running. Into. Danger."

"Does running into you count?" I cocked a smile down at her, and she scoffed, but I didn't miss the smile she tried to hide.

"Did they teach you how to flirt so terribly in the mortal world?"

I checked Paige's features again, noting the soft blush tinging her cheeks and the airiness about her presence. *"She likes it. That's all that matters."* I shrugged, even though Vara wouldn't be able to see it. She could probably feel it through our bond—the way I tried to act like everything was so easily shrugged off. She knew I was spiraling. Fuck, I knew it, too. I was either going to destroy everything I'd been working so hard to rekindle, or I was going to mess everything up because we wouldn't be able to control the urge to sleep with each other. Oh, and her memories were going to come back and her gift she couldn't yet control, or what to expect from that control, was still looming on the edge. Throw in the fact that her father was out for our blood...

Everything was absolute shit right now.

"You're playing with fire."

"Maybe. But at least I know I can't burn." Vara fell silent, and I felt, for the briefest of moments, as if she had actually laughed at that.

"You're welcome, for that."

"You couldn't have told me that was what was happening every time I surrounded myself with fire? A heads up, or something, would have been nice. Now I look like I lied to her about my power in the water." When I told her I doubted I'd get something like my mother, I didn't know I already *had* something.

"Which time?" She chuckled and I glared south, hoping she could feel just how not funny that was. *"Honestly, I thought you knew."* She let out a huff. *"It's not my fault you keep getting distracted and don't pay enough attention to yourself. You could still develop something else, I'm not an adult yet."*

"What—" I lost my thoughts as I snapped back to our surroundings. I hadn't realized we'd gotten to the path where the bar was. It looked so vastly different in the morning light, but sure enough—the small, ramshackle building sat at the end of it, absent of sound.

"Fuck me," Seamus whispered as he took Nya's hand in his. "Stay behind me."

"Let me go first, Seamus."

"The hell you will," Paige snapped back, pulling me back by my arm as I brushed by her.

I cocked my brow at her. "Why the sudden desire to keep me safe?"

Paige bit down on her lip, then played it off like she was pouting. I wasn't fooled, and it was adorable. "Who…else would train me to wield fire?" she asked, and the stammer in her words made me chuckle. Nya spun and forced Seamus to stop.

"Wield *fire*?" Nya nearly shrieked.

I smirked at Paige, waiting for her to explain just how she got that mark. She folded her arms across her chest, shuffling to stick a finger out at me. "It's his fault." So, we were back to this again.

I rolled my eyes over from Nya to Paige. "Right. All my fault. You felt absolutely nothing when we—" A whip of air snapped my mouth closed and I grinned down at her, making sure my dimple popped enough to drive her mad. She seemed to fluster more when I did that, and I loved watching her squirm.

Nya's cheeks pinked over. "I'm sure the lass can tell ye more when she has a drink or two in 'er. Come on. I don't want to run into another wraith." Nya's eyes widened at the mention of a wraith and their steps quickened.

I fell back to match strides with Paige, allowing my arm to brush the edge of hers, my magic roaring to the surface more violently than it normally did whenever we touched. It was intoxicating being in her presence already, but touching her? Not a soul could ever tell me anything was better than touching Paige Aerborne. I wondered if she felt it too—the way my magic surged couldn't just be me, could it?

"What?"

"What, what?" I asked.

She sighed through her nose. "What is it, Aeden?"

"I'm just trying to figure out when you're going to go from cold to hot again." I shouldn't have said it, and I braced for the verbal assault that was inevitably coming my way.

She shook her head. "I'm just tired."

Shit. Of course, she was. We'd been traveling for days. "I can walk you back to the house, I'm sure they wouldn't mind if you wanted to rest."

"Not like that. I'm tired of—"

Seamus shouted as he ran inside the bar in the distance, and Paige and I sprinted ahead just as Seamus came back out, hauling a near-naked man that looked very familiar.

"Tom?" I bent down, lifting the mans limp arm. His marks…they were completely grey. Just like those along the platform turned the moment the life faded from them.

But Tom was not dead. Tom was breathing. Raggedly, but breathing.

"Tom. Lad." Seamus shook his friend, trying to make his eyes stop rolling toward the back of his head. Tom was muttering something under his breath, over and over. Paige knelt down beside me as Nya covered her mouth with her hands, tears threatening to roll down her face.

"What's he saying?" Paige whispered in close to my ear while keeping her focus on the muttering man on the ground.

"I—I don't know."

"Tom! Tom, my man. Snap out of it!" Seamus raised his hands, waving them above Tom.

Nya moved her hands from her face. "Stripped."

Paige's face went pale as her hands fell to her knees.

"That's real? I thought that was a lie." Tom's eyes went wide, and he lurched forward into me, clutching my tunic and pulling me close to his face.

"You can't win! You can't beat the evil! Run! Run while you still can!" He fell back into the snow, his eyelids moving like rapid-fire.

Nya shook her head, ignoring Tom as he released me and fell back to the ground. "It's not a lie, Aeden. It's archaic, and highly unethical. But some still know the methods of how to do it." I could guess who those *some* were.

I thought back to Cyprian as I fell back on the heels of my feet. The boy who begged to be stripped—for them to take it all away. And they had chosen death for him over it. "Being stripped is more than likely a death sentence.

Most, well really all, go mad. It's better to die," Nya said, her fingers still hovering over her chin.

I snapped my attention to her. "And who says that? Gedeon? If it's so archaic and rarely practiced anymore, how could you possibly know that's what happens?"

"Aeden—" Paige's fingers wrapped gently around my hand. "I've read about it, too. She's not lying to you."

"Aye, madness is no way to live. To be here, without power…yer body starts to weaken and it just isn't good."

I looked down at Tom, who had finally stopped muttering and had fallen asleep on the snow in nothing but his underwear. The man had given me the shirt off his back the first night I arrived, and I couldn't fix the grey mark along his forearm. The same one I once thought was because they were all in some twisted cult together.

So much had changed since then.

Tom was better off dead. He was in agony being stripped, possibly unable to function on his own already. Seamus seemed to watch as I mulled over my thoughts and nodded as I reached into my waistband for my hatchet. Paige glanced down at the weapon on my lap, then squeezed my fingers and pulled out a dagger from her corset.

"Let me help you," she whispered to Tom as she moved her dagger to the side of his neck.

"Stop. Let me—"

"I thought you said you'd stop trying to protect me," she said low, as if she'd startle Tom before she had a chance to…to do what she shouldn't have to do.

"This is different, Paige. Have you killed someone before?" I knew her trials made her kill a troll, and I'd seen her slice through naga, but another fae?

Her eyes slid to mine. "Have you?" Her words were hardly a question as her voice rose, those unwavering, sharp eyes waiting for me to admit what I'd done. But I'd do it again a thousand times over. I'd kill anyone for her.

"Please, Paige. Just let me help you. You don't have to—"

Her eyes narrowed at me as she shook her head. "And who's going to help you?" Her dagger drove into Tom's chest as she shouted her last word and I tried to not flinch back as hard as I wanted to. Tom's face eased, his mouth curling into a smile as the light faded too quickly from his eyes.

Paige's gaze never left mine, but they were now wide with shock. I didn't dare pull my eyes from hers, even though it hurt to think about just how much pain she was in. From the corner of my eye, I could see her hand shaking against the hilt—the only movement since Tom's chest had stopped rising and falling with every labored breath.

"I—I just…" Nya knelt down beside her, taking Paige's trembling hands in hers and pulling her up to stand.

"Let's go inside, yeah?" Nya eyed Seamus, both of them nodding to each other in silent agreement.

Seamus' lips turned thin and his brows dipped low. "Ye did good, Lass." Paige's darkened emerald eyes stayed locked on mine for as long as they could until Nya pulled her completely behind the walls of the bar. But even with her gone, I couldn't get the image of how she looked out of my mind. How her hand trembled against the weapons she so confidently wielded each and every day. The same ones I was sure she was plotting to use against me months ago.

I sighed, reaching over for the dagger and pulling it from Tom's chest.

"Ye did good too, Aeden." I stood, flicking my wrist as my boots settled back on the snow. I watched as my earth magic swallowed Tom's body whole before more blood could seep into the ground—before I could think twice about asking whether he had a family left or not. Something told me not many people that'd been in Costa had much of a family left.

I peered over at Seamus. "No, I didn't. I failed her."

"What she did is no different from whatever trainin' it was that made you believe you should have taken the life for her. She thought she had to do it, 'nd so, she did it." Seamus eyed me with that paternal look he gave when he was waiting for me to talk.

I groaned, raking my hand down my face. "Why couldn't she just let me handle it?"

"Aye, probably for the same reason you didn't want her to do it. She loves ye, Boyo. She just has a real funny way of showin' it."

I snorted. "You and Eoghan have been talking, haven't you?"

"He may have said a thing or two about bein' an Empath. Trust me, he's not only screwin' with yer love life."

I cocked my brow at him. "Shay?"

"Mhm. Nosey lil bastard that Mora of Hydrasel is. Those Stars must love watchin' us suffer—it isn't 'nough to feel the things we do, but to hear it from Eoghan? Oh, that's a whole 'nother set of torture."

My back stiffened at the word and Seamus took note of it immediately. "Ye're alright, right, Lad? Ye know I'm good for more than just me mouth. Me ears work perfectly fine, too."

"I'm as good as I can be. Trying to focus on becoming who I need to be—"

"I'm gonna stop ye right there. Ye already are everythin' ye need to be. Yer mother was a fabulous leader. I have no doubt ye're no different."

"Thanks. Never thought I'd say this, but I'm really glad it was you who was trying to beat my ass at this bar all those months ago." I smiled and patted his shoulder. "Come on. Let's get that drink."

Chapter Twenty-Five
PAIGE

I couldn't stop the ringing in my ears. The sounds of my dagger piercing through Tom's flesh. The feel of it parting through his ribs, sliding and grinding against his bones—I couldn't stop replaying it all in my head.

Nya was talking to me, but about what, I had no idea. Seconds passed like hours, the same sound and feeling on an endless, torturous loop. I kept my head low, looking at the grooves of the brown table trying not to imagine them filling with the river of blood I saw coming from Tom's body.

I couldn't stop fixating on it.

I killed him. It was my doing. I ended his life. I—

"Paige." Aeden's voice broke through those thoughts and the pain in my chest, but my eyes remained trained on those bleeding cracks in the wood.

Tight, everything felt tight. It was hard to breathe, it was hard to think, it was too damn hard to focus on anything—

"Paige. Look at me." A warm hand slid into mine. I was registering the voices around me, but I was frozen to the spot, unable to move. Like bolts of lightning forcing their way through clouds and the earth below, I was the space between, bursting at the center. I wanted to look up, but the cracks in the wood turned more and more red, and the blood... there had been so much blood around Tom's body. The snow was red, my hands were...my *hands* were...

I yanked my hand back, rubbing both along the slick leather covering my thighs as hard as I could. There was so much of it—the blood. Everywhere. Blood was *everywhere*.

Warm breath spilled along my neck and I flinched back, then froze, watching as broad hands slid down the length of my arms, pressing down firmly until they met with my fingers and curled around them.

"There's nothing there, Paige. Nothing." My fingers lifted, my arms going weightless as they moved and tilted against the dim light. "See? No blood. There's no blood." I stared down at my hands, blinking as the blood and the red and the gore began to vanish from sight. On the last blink, my eyes moved from my fingers, to Aeden's. "Your hands are clean."

"How..." Shock mixed with the sound of my own voice startled me, making me jolt back more into the hardened chest and arms that encompassed me. "Fuck. I—" My eyes sought out Seamus and Nya, both sporting concerned looks they tried to conceal with slight smiles. Both failing terribly at it. "I'm so sorry, I—I had to."

I had to. I had to. I knew what I did was necessary, but saying it aloud made me feel insane. I'd killed a man because *I had to*. But the reason why I had to, why it had to be *me* and not *him*...I didn't know what to do with the reason why *I* had to do it.

But I did it all the same.

I killed a man for him. So that the blood that now stained my hands wouldn't be on *his* hands. Wouldn't be his weight to bear. So much had gone wrong in his life and I couldn't allow more sadness to enter those golden brown eyes. Couldn't bear the thought of him adding more on those broad shoulders that held up the weight of not just one world, but two. Two worlds had mistreated him, had never showed him that he was worth what I knew he was. And that hurt me more than killing Tom did.

"Hey, shhh. It's okay." I didn't notice I'd curled back into him and tears had begun to stream down my face. Aeden cupped my chin and tilted my head back, and when I looked up, everything else faded away. "You didn't have to do that,

Paige. But I'm really fucking proud of you for doing it." *For me* were the words I knew were at the edge of his mouth. He knew—they all knew—I'd killed Tom so he wouldn't have to.

I had to.

And now it was my burden, more guilt that I would wear like another set of leather armor over my chest, as if I hadn't armored myself up enough over the past few months and then tried to break through it every time those beautiful eyes and gentle, calloused hands met mine.

Oh man, I was so gone.

"You're so strong. And brave. And so damn selfless." His smile grew weakly as he spoke and I just stared up at him as he leaned over me, unsure if I was breathing or blinking or still within my own body.

The force he used to push my face up to meet him was soft, his fingers tracing my jaw like *I* was the most delicate thing he'd ever touched. It was so unlike how he wielded any weapon during training, and I realized the me from months ago would have used this as an opportunity to lunge backward into him, jab him in his groin or stomach and take off while he was weak and distracted. To escape. But there was nowhere I'd rather be than with him, and I think he started to notice that as his smile grew to pop that damn dimple on his face though his eyes remained dark and filled with worry. His thumb brushed the side of my cheek, wiping away the wetness and replacing it with the gentle warmth of *him*, and I couldn't tell how long I sat there, staring up at the man who made everything else fade away.

"We got ye a drink, Paige," Seamus said before the sounds of glass sliding on wood shifted my attention back to the rest of the room, my eyes blinking rapidly to take in Nya and Seamus and the light and the table that was just brown. Just brown and wooden and grooved. "Aye, there she is. Welcome back, Lass."

Aeden moved to sit across from me and I watched as his legs swung over the seat and his body folded along the table. Every move he made was so effortless, like any and every space around him was made to have him in it. The world bent around him, molding and adjusting because his presence was that powerful.

I couldn't remember him from the time before he saved me in the arena, but I really wanted to. I wanted to know if he'd always moved like that—like he'd been born to rule over an entire kingdom. I wanted to know if he'd always smiled at me like that, and if I'd always reacted to him the way I was starting to. His frame leaned over the tabletop toward me and everything stilled once more. He was the earth and the ground, and I was the storm in the clouds, and between us that lightning finally had a place to meet and just be.

I wanted to know how long I loved him for, and what had finally made me break, because I was starting to break again.

Stars, I was breaking again.

"Paige, did you hear me?"

"Hmm?" My eyes slid over to Nya, who had the concern wiped clean from her face and was now giving me a knowing look, one with wide eyes and a crooked smile. A look I knew because I could remember her. Easily. My father hadn't thought to take everyone from me, and for that, I was almost thankful to the bastard.

Almost.

"I asked if you wanted to eat something. There's not much left in the back, but—"

My brow furrowed. "When did you go to the back?"

She blinked once, then again. "Oh. I sat you down here first, then I went to go scope out the rest of the bar to make sure no one else was here. And then I found the pantry that was mostly raided, but some things they stored for winter were saved—like potatoes and onions and dried meats. I found a brick of cheese, too. I don't really know how to cook though."

"I can do it," Aeden said, taking a sip from his drink and setting it back down. "I'm not the best, but..." He eyed me over, considering his next words. He did that too much around me, and suddenly I realized I wanted to know every single thing that came to his mind. "I used to cook a lot." Something tells me I knew that before. Of course, I had. I was his best friend. Before we were whatever it was that we became to each other now, we were friends.

"I'm not too hungry right now." Food actually sounded quite terrible. The thought of the dried meats Nya mentioned alone made bile rise into my throat. I swallowed that down with a sip of my drink, my hands shaking slightly as I set the glass back on the table.

Shock. That's what this was. Shock and a heady rush of adrenaline that made me freeze up and then try to ignore it in some sick kind of fight or flight response mode I wasn't used to. I couldn't remember ever feeling this hectic. My thoughts were muddled between the man's life I'd just taken and the fact that I did it for another man—the one still in front of me.

"I'm fine, too. I actually grew used to not eating for—" Nya stopped when she saw the way her father's face had twisted at the words she didn't finish her sentence with—*days, hours*. Long enough to make her appear frail. Yet, I couldn't recall seeing her eat besides the few times we were in the dining room together. She hadn't eaten really then, either, and I had mistaken that for her eating separately. Had mistaken that bowl of soup she sent me along with the note for the way she ate regularly. In peace, with comforting foods that filled her as it did me that night.

Had I been that ignorant to not see the pain she was in?

Seamus muttered under his breath, something that sounded an awful lot like *fucking bastard* with a few other choice words thrown in there. If I didn't get to my father first, Seamus or Aeden would be ready to do it themselves.

I pushed aside my own feelings as hard as I could to be there for her now that my body had stopped going between bouts of trembling and freezing and reached my hand over to hers, taking it in mine and squeezing her thin fingers. My voice came out shaky and uneven. "I'm so sorry he was so terrible to you and that I didn't realize it before it was too late." The thought had crossed my mind. She had been taken in after her parents were thought to be dead—which I knew was an utter fucking lie now—but that didn't mean the violent tendencies of my father were abandoned by that singular generosity, if it can even be called that. But I was so focused on getting through the trials, on making it out of there, that the thought didn't last long.

I'd been so focused on what now appeared as another huge grey wall in my mind, covering what was most likely the larger driving force of that strong desire to win and be free. *Him.* I spent so long thinking about myself and what I wanted, I hadn't put enough thought into what would come of my friend in any of those circumstances. I'd even threatened her, telling her it was unwise to turn me into an enemy by hiding things from me, hiding the knowledge of my brother.

I'd been cruel, like him.

Why didn't I try harder to help her? I should have tried harder.

Aeden's booted foot slid against mine and I peeked over at him right as he mouthed, "Not your fault." But it sure as hell felt like it was my fault. Nya was thin before, but never as gaunt as she was now, and after going through what she did...I couldn't even imagine the horrors he put her through.

"I'm just so sorry, Nya." That same foot pressed harder, both of his boots closing in on mine and pressing them together beneath the table. I didn't have to turn from Nya to see he was trying to remind me that it wasn't my fault. But honestly if I had stolen a glance at him in the moment, I would have started to cry again. It was too much to feel all at one time. My mind didn't know where or how to settle or whether to abandon all thoughts or not.

Nya's hand slid out from my hold, and then she tapped the top of my hand. "You did your best, Paige. Nothing he did was on you. Never was, and never will be. You *always* tried your best. And when you found out just how cruel he was to not only you, but to his kingdom, you kept fighting. Even harder, I would say. And hey, look. I'm free now." She held up her wrists and rotated them to show she was unchained, but all I saw were the bruises. I frowned and she pushed them beneath the table. "I got out, and I'm back here with you and my father. I was hoping I'd find a lead here back to you, knowing that the retired guard who reclaimed his uniforms was from Costa originally and that your man, here"—she inclined her head toward Aeden, who appeared calmer than I knew the way he was analyzing me should have allowed him to look—"wore a uniform and was definitely not a guard. Didn't really take a genius to put that together." She chuckled. "I just wish Gedeon hadn't put the two together once he got word, but here we are. He is, unfortunately, very logical and quick to weed things out. Just thank the Stars his guard Hector is an imbecile, otherwise Aeden would have been captured at the ball the moment he saw him climbing down the trellis."

"He saw me?" Aeden was grinning at Nya like he'd just been told he got picked for first place in a swimming competition or something and suddenly all of my thoughts stilled again on him and that smile that was stealing every part of whatever was left of my heart.

"Yeah, he saw you climbing down from Ikelos' room in his owl form or whatever he chose to shift into that night. But he didn't have the balls to go up against you and Eoghan, so he just ran back to Gedeon and told him the next day. The fact that he waited—well, Gedeon wasn't happy with him. Pretty sure he beat him bloody. But I didn't find out about it until Paige told me and then Gedeon made us fight and then I was interrogated and—" She put a hand to her chest, taking several deep breaths between how fast she had been talking and probably a surge of anxiety. Half of what she said was nothing but grey matter. "I'm sorry I'm talking so much. I've been here alone for a while now and never really dared to leave the house beyond hunting and I swear I picked up the place but one day I came back and it had been raided again and—"

"Fuckin' Stars, Aanya. Please—I just got ye back, 'nd now I'm thinkin' of all the ways I could've lost ye all over again and I don't know if me heart can take much more today." *Not with the way I'd just killed his fri—*

"Paige," Aeden growled low. "Don't finish that thought."

I straightened, taking a sip of my drink and staring at him the entire time. I set the glass down when there was nothing left to drink. "I'll get you more, girl. Hang tight." Nya moved quickly, busying herself and calming her nerves that we could all feel from the way she'd just spoken so rapidly, not even pausing to breathe.

"You." I lifted a slightly buzzed finger to Aeden, still amazed at how quickly fae alcohol worked through my veins. I must not have ever drank in the mortal world, or if I did, it had been with Aeden because even thinking about it brought up more grey. I'd never built a tolerance, and now I was in a world where the alcohol was made to make even the most powerful of fae nothing more than drunken idiots. Add that to the fact that I'd thrown up every last thing in my stomach when I thought Aeden had burned to death, and I was well on my way to numbing thoughts I didn't want numbed. "How did you know what I was thinking? How do you always know?"

"I know you." His lip curved up to the side, though it didn't fully reach his eyes, then drank the rest of his glass, too. Nya came back with two full glasses and sat back down.

My hand trembled as I reached for the ruby-tinged drink, the thoughts of Tom's blood rushing to the surface again like the pull of a tide I was doomed to forever be taken under by. Aeden's face turned more serious when he reached for his glass, mirroring my motions. If I were to drink ten of these, he'd be right there with me. He'd do anything to make me feel safe. And it was working. My shoulders eased and the liquid stopped rippling inside the glass just before I set it down.

"Did I ever tell you the story about what I did when I got here?"

My eyes squinted, the mess of my mind mulling over his words like he'd just said the craziest thing. "If you had... I wouldn't remember."

"Ah." He reached up to scratch the back of his neck. "Yeah. I may have glazed over it by telling you I torched a bar." *Not that I'd remember.* "Well, this is the bar I almost torched." He pointed over to Seamus, who was gently sipping on his drink. "And I almost beat the shit out of him."

I would have spit my drink on the table had I not already swallowed it. Picturing the two of them fighting—well, I'd pay good money to see that.

"Aye, Lad. But I almost got ye, too."

Aeden's eyebrow cocked amusingly. "That's not how I remember it, old man."

A small smile cracked my lips, then I threw a finger over the edge of them to cover it. Aeden smirked at me and then continued, directing his words to Seamus but looking at me. "You know I had you." *At least, I think those words were for Seamus.* The glint in his eyes told me he could have very-well meant the words for me though, and I felt heat rise into my cheeks and ears.

"What happened?" Nya asked.

"Well, the Boyo 'ere landed in this bar, disturbin' the peace with a bleatin' portal above his head. He crashed into the ground and started slurin' up nonsense, so the whole bar rallied for me to get 'im the hell out. But when I went to do so…"

Aeden's head rolled to Nya, his muscles loosening under the memory and possibly the alcohol. "Your father, here, tried to attack me and then I got this"—he pushed up his sleeve and showed her the mark again like he had to prove who and what he was, even to himself—"and everyone lost their damn minds. Everyone except for him." His fingers raked up along the flames smoothly. "He was the only idiot to offer to take me under his wing, and then he took me outside."

"And I told ye we could look for yer lass in the mornin' but I had to get ye away from here 'fore someone came for ye."

"You know," Nya said, shaking her curly hair out behind her with both hands, "I think it's great that you two found each other. But I also think it's odd."

Aeden's eyebrow quirked up, but Seamus' lack of reaction had me focusing more on him than Aeden. I swear, people here were always hiding shit and I completely understood why Aeden had a hard time trusting others. I'd always been so quick to give trust to anyone who gave me an ounce of attention, but him? He saw through others immediately, and guarded himself like three layers of a stone wall and a ring of fire wasn't enough. Unless it was me—he trusted me.

He *loved* me.

"Because usually you go to where the Mora directs you to go. Gedeon knew you landed in Costa, but I don't think he knew why because I heard him talking about how it didn't matter much where the mortal boy landed because he was as good as dead here without any powers."

"Good thing he was fucking wrong," Aeden said.

"Yeah, you're telling me," she replied.

I glanced between Nya and Aeden, waiting. After a few seconds, I couldn't take it anymore and threw my hand up. "Why did he end up here, then?"

Nya shrugged. "Don't know. He wasn't summoned through the portal, Gedeon was only looking for you. Hector knew you"—She pointed at Aeden—"Came through too and that you were holding her—"

"You were holding me?"

Aeden didn't hesitate as he said, "Of course, I was. You didn't want me to let you go."

"I didn't?" I squeaked out.

"No, Paige. You wanted to walk in together and I told you I'd never let you go. I promised I wouldn't and I didn't keep that promise."

"That's an insane promise to make."

"I'd like another portal to try and rip you from my arms again. I'd never break another promise to you like that ever again. I'd fight the Stars to keep you in my arms, to keep any future promises to you." I gulped. Too audibly. I took another sip to cover it up. "But I think she's wrong about not being summoned. We both heard and felt a pull to it, and felt damn crazy about just the feeling of it and being close to it."

I could feel my forehead furrowing together uncomfortably. "So, he and I felt like we had to come, but if he wasn't summoned and more just allowed through—"

"Your father didn't summon him through. Just you."

I didn't know portals worked like that. I figured if you saw it and you walked through, it would just let you. But that made a lot of sense as to why Eoghan usually left a portal open in the back of the bookshop with no thoughts about it. I wondered if anyone ever tried to walk through and where they would have ended up if they had tried.

"I thought 'bout it, but figured he was just thrown as close to the sea as Gedeon could throw him. Mortals have been summoned by him before at random, landin' wherever. It's not everyday ye see someone who was meant to be 'ere, *born here*, comin' through like that." Seamus rubbed his beard. "Why do ye think he ended up here in Costa, Aanya?"

"Honestly?" She looked over Aeden's exposed arm, and searched his face. Hard. Like she was analyzing every feature of him down to the curve of his jaw and angles of his posture. "Maybe he has a relative here."

Aeden's raised glass froze in the air on the way to his mouth. "What?"

Nya shrugged again and I felt my mouth slipping open, unable to comprehend what she was implying. "I don't know. Maybe someone distant, who knows." She tapped her fingers on her glass. "I mean, you both saw how many fae were at the ball. Every kingdom's family tree can branch so far because…well, most aren't really *loyal* to their spouses or lovers, and we can live for so long and—"

Aeden cut her off. "Murrie said no one knew who my father was, and that my mother was dead." His glass slid back to the table, not a drop spilling down his throat since Nya had said those words. *Relative.* He had someone. Maybe.

Nya snapped back from her rant and nodded. "True. Lady Savaria Fireborne was very secretive. No one, including myself, considered she may have been pregnant, much less that she lived after the battle and was able to give birth. But, here you are."

"Here I am," Aeden reiterated, his tone flat and his eyes going distant, focusing on those grooves in the wood like I had been doing.

"Anyway, it's just a thought. Who knows, maybe the Stars just wanted you here to help you find my dad, knowing he would help you or that someone here would have since Costa used to be a Waterborne territory and their allegiance to the Aerborne line is less than elsewhere. But, I shouldn't have brought it up. It could have been a coincidence."

"Right. A coincidence." I reached my boot up along Aeden's legs where they still flanked mine. Our eyes locked, and then he slid them to the spot behind me where the long bar top was. "I think I'm going to go cook now. I'll make enough for you guys for whenever you're hungry."

He stood, and although my feet begged for me to follow, and everything inside of me told me to go make sure he was okay, my brain fought harder against it. He hadn't needed me like that, to console him, since I'd been back with him. He'd often gone out hunting, or flying, or training whenever he had a lot on his mind.

Nya said it could be nothing, but I think all Aeden heard was that he could have a relative out there and now he was stuck in an endless cycle of thoughts about if that were true or could have been before the town became an empty wasteland.

Most Mora's would probably jump to the idea that maybe the claim to the throne wouldn't be just theirs. That maybe they'd have to fight someone over that claim. But Aeden wasn't that kind of person. He wanted a family. He wanted to be loved. And it was sending my heart into my throat to think that he believed no one loved him. To *know* that he believed that. Because not only had I grown to know what every look on his face meant and what every tone of his voice implied even if he didn't mean them to, I'd also started to notice the change in the way his warmth spread over me in response to the ways we interacted and had grown to care about what it meant when that warmth faded and abandoned me.

Caring about him was putting it loosely. I cared. A lot.

Aeden came out from the back with plates of food that smelled just as amazing as it looked after many minutes of Seamus and Nya talking amongst themselves, but I couldn't focus on the plate so much as the person who was carrying them out to us. He looked distraught. Not as badly as he had when he first stood from the table, but the grim smile he returned to me told me he wasn't in the mood to talk much more.

So he and I ate in silence, sharing a few glances between each other and a few foot nudges from my boot against his as Nya and Seamus continued to catch up on the years they'd missed. They were still talking as Aeden collected our two plates, leaving Nya's and Seamus' because they'd eaten much slower between talking and laughing and crying.

I just wanted to talk to him, to let him know I did care, to reach my hand over the damn table and to hold onto some part of him. But I let the time slip and never opened my mouth or caressed him further beyond the slight nudges of my boot and the faint glances we shared, because unlike him, I was a coward.

He came back to the table and inclined his head toward the door. "I'm going to go back to your house, Seamus. Clean it up a bit for you while you finish here. Take your time."

I stupidly took that moment to stand. Abruptly. The table shook as my body wiggled between it like I hadn't had legs for ages before this very second. "I'm going to go, too."

Nya's brows rose at me and I'm pretty sure Aeden's rose too beside me, but Seamus only threw his hand up in the air. "Thanks. I appreciate the help." Seamus continued on talking, bringing Nya's full attention back to her father.

"You don't have to help me. If you want to stay here and talk—"

"I don't want to stay here." I looked down at my hands, noticing how stable they were now. I wasn't thinking about the fresh blood on my hands anymore. I was only thinking about him.

"Okay. It's going to be dark soon. Shortest day of the year and all."

"Yeah. I know. Good thing I know a really good fire- wielder, then." I smirked up at him, and he grinned down at me, popping that dimple that I wanted to brush my thumb over. He opened his palm once we got outside, and even though it wasn't completely dark out yet, he lit an orb the size of his fist and sent it out to float in front of us, then made another to keep on his palm. Not a faelight like we'd both learned to make, but flames.

I turned to see the spot where I expected Tom's body to still be, turned and expected nothing but red and blood and a pale body, but somehow wasn't all too surprised to find a small mound of dirt on the ground instead. Aeden had buried Tom, and had left a marker of wildflowers above him that fresh snow started to fall upon.

I never knew Tom, but I didn't have to in order to know that he was with the Stars now. He wouldn't go insane—driven mad, powerless in a world so full of it that to be without was worse than death itself. Aeden's eyes darkened against the small orb he held, but he wasn't looking to where Tom was. He was looking at me, waiting for me to go into shock again. He had just heard the possibility of a relative being the reason why he ended up in Costa, but that look of sadness left his face the second I offered to go with him, like I was such a simple solution to every problem he had.

Yet that darkened look I'd noticed for a while now that played upon a face that shouldn't have any darkness? The one that mirrored the one I now felt inside of me, didn't make him stop looking at me like I'd hung the very moon and cleared every cloud beneath it. His eyes could turn obsidian, his soul sludgier than any dark water and blacker than any night sky—and he would have been the brightness that fought through it all. For me, he would have been the glow on that stone, the beauty beneath the water, and the stars filling the sky.

So instead of running, instead of falling back into the cycle of why and how and what if—I just *was*. *With him, I could* just *be*.

I was allowed that tonight. I was allowed to put aside all the little things that made me want to refute and negate and ignore what I felt, and just let it be. Let *us* be.

I straightened my back, squared my shoulders and started walking toward him. He took note of it quickly. I didn't want to think about blood and kingdoms and wars and my past or any reason I'd pushed him away. And he knew. He would always know.

He inclined his head toward the other orb moving steadily in front of us. "I don't think I'll ever use faelights," he said just as delicately as his boots trudged through snow beside me.

I took the bait happily. We could have talked about the amount of snow we saw falling, I didn't care. "I think I will, but only because my fire-magic is kind of sporadic, at the moment."

His eyes landed on me as they narrowed. "I've watched you use it during your training sessions. It doesn't look sporadic to me. It looks…"

"Like I have no idea what I'm doing?" *I don't*. Not with my wielding. Not with us.

"It looks incredibly hot. You look like you could burn down an entire kingdom and walk across the ash with flames still burning in your hands. Incredible *and* hot."

So, he had been watching me? I snorted and noticed his shoulders dropping down, his body easing as we walked. I ignored the fact that I'd burn with that much fire around me because I wasn't like him. Not in the slightest. "That's because you can't hear what Eoghan is telling me to do out there. I don't think throwing a giant fire orb toward the mountains and causing an avalanche was ever part of the agenda."

He laughed and it warmed me up from the inside. "I figured he was pushing you."

"He was. But to make it smaller. To contain it. Not to blow everything up." Fire, my attitude, the way I treated him. Eoghan, and my brother, too, had been on me about a lot of things. And they were right.

"You always were an overachiever."

"Tell that to Eoghan. He thinks if I don't learn how to control it, then I will burn down an entire town if you and I"—I stuttered, changing the phrasing Eoghan had used—"If you and I fight. He's worried I'll burn down an entire town if we fight." *Fuck.*

The moment I changed that word, the *real* word Eoghan had said, I knew I'd messed up. I shouldn't have brought it up at all. Tonight was the first night of the Solstice, and the Stars were bringing a lot more than just lust to the surface. But Aeden nodded slowly as we veered off the thin path and started to pass the few buildings we had passed earlier and said, "Well, I guess it's a good thing I can't burn then, right?" The smile he gave me could outshine any star in the sky. Easily.

I snorted again, trying not to laugh at the image of him running through a burning town in the nude. And then my laughter died on my tongue as the image seemed to stick, and that hand that covered his cock earlier was nowhere in sight. My throat turned thick and I tried to swallow past it. Unsuccessfully.

"Paige?"

I cleared the urge to choke, forcing it down my throat. "Y-Yeah?"

For a moment, I thought he'd bring up Tom again, picking up on my silence the wrong way. But I'd already settled it in my mind—I wasn't going to regret doing it ever again. I couldn't think of a better reason—a better person—to do that for than Aeden Fireborne.

His arm swept wide in front of me and stopped me in my tracks. "We're here."

Chapter Twenty-Six
Aeden

It had been months since I'd seen Paige go through the range of emotions that I'd seen tonight.

Months.

I hadn't seen her cry since the day her mother died, and I certainly hadn't seen her look at me like she used to. Like she finally knew me and understood me. I wanted to ask if her memories were back—but if they were, she'd tell me.

No, this was new to her. The fear in her eyes wasn't just from taking Tom's life. Honestly, I think she justified what she did rather quickly, and even though it was so damn clear why she had done it, I couldn't wrap my head around it.

She is starting to feel something for you.

I just hoped I wouldn't fuck it up.

"Where should we start?" Paige asked as she made her way to the portraits, holding up one of a young Aanya and her mother, gently pushing the pieces back together. Her heart was never missing at all. It was just hidden beneath every wall she continued to build. The walls that were maybe finally coming down.

"You can work on those. I'll get the furniture and the floors." Seamus' biggest pet peeve of the cleanliness of his floors made me chuckle, although nothing about the sight of his home was funny. Everything was trashed. Nya apparently hadn't had it in her to clean it up, but I couldn't exactly blame her. She thought both of her parents were dead, so she probably avoided any reminders of them and stayed in that room I'd dragged her down from.

We worked silently for about an hour as the darkness swept in beyond the open windowless space. I fashioned a window made of ice, blurring the outside from our view and sealing out a lot of the cold. But the darkness still seeped on through, and the moonlight that hung above it all was making the power beneath my skin go rabid, along with other parts of me that made me stare at Paige's curves like she was something to be devoured. I'd caught her looking a few times back at me, but they were quick and her lips remained pressed down into thin lines.

"Are you okay?" *Dumb.* So dumb to ask if she was fine.

Of course, she wasn't.

But she nodded as her small fingers pressed cloth back together, her earth magic threading the backs of each portrait together again. "Are you?"

I was working through cleaning out whatever was left of his kitchen, trying to use my air magic to get the dents out of his stove. "Not really."

Paige glanced at the door, biting on her bottom lip. I wanted to bite it, too. Instead, I said, "Yeah, I don't think they will be coming back anytime soon." She just nodded again, and I tried to keep from blasting the air into the stove too hard, sending it across the room. I wasn't angry, but the power beneath my skin was pulling me toward her, and I knew she could feel it, too. It was getting harder to control with every passing second.

And yet, she told me she was okay.

I stood, brushing my hands along a pair of pants I borrowed from the closet to replace my leather riding gear with for the night. The fire I'd started in the hearth in the corner was heating up the room, or maybe it was my power. I lifted my sheathed sword up and off first, then reached my hand over the back of my head to remove my tunic, not missing the way Paige was trying so hard not to look at me.

"Why aren't you okay?" she asked, her voice low and strained as her fingers moved along the surface of another portrait.

"I think the better question is *how* are you okay?" I leaned against the counter top, trying not to think of the way I'd once had her moaning my name and spreading her legs for me back in Jessup on a surface similar. That day felt like ages ago now. "None of this is okay, Paige. Not one damn thing. You just aren't admitting to it." I kicked a few shards of ceramic toward the pile I'd made, focusing on the way each shard crumbled further along the ground with the movement.

"*Careful,*" Vara chided in my thoughts. "*What if she kills you next?*"

"*Let her.*" I reached for that threaded bond and tugged on it, and I swore I could feel the rumble of her scaly chest through my thoughts right before I slammed some wall between us down, finally figuring out how to shut her off from my thoughts. How convenient—I just needed to be maddened by desire and the image of Paige naked to find that barrier once and for all. Vara was going to be pissed whenever I decided to lift it again.

"What do you mean?" No inflection in her tone, and by the way she was folding her arms, I'd just hit a nerve. *Good.*

"You tell me. What were you going to say before Seamus ran out of the bar with Tom in his arms?"

She looked away too quickly, searching for another portrait on the floor although there were several by her feet already. "Nothing."

"It clearly wasn't nothing. You said you were tired of something, and it wasn't the journey to get here." I folded my arms over my chest, waiting.

She reached for another portrait, repeating the same thing she'd been doing since we got here and I wanted to walk over to her and take it from her hands just so she would look at me.

"You know what? I'm tired, too." I pushed off the counter instead, grabbed my discarded leather clothes and made my way to the stairs. "I'm going to go fix up the upstairs, and then I'll take the couch. Seamus has three rooms upstairs, so the last one can be yours."

I didn't turn to see whatever way she was looking at me, and didn't stop when a brush of cool wind rippled across my back. A popping noise rang out, similar to the sounds of the stove dents being removed by my air magic. Then clanking against wood, possibly the shards I'd left in a pile dragging across the floor, and I hesitated on a step for a moment before continuing up like I couldn't hear her reacting downstairs.

A few seconds later, I could hear her footsteps moving up the stairs, and as I approached the furthest room in the back corner, I left the door open, just in case she was coming up to finally talk. To let me in.

The room was small with a few pieces of furniture—a bed pushed into the corner, a dresser on one wall and a small desk against another, both pressing into the floor at an angle because of the state of the legs beneath them. I moved to flick my wrist to make new legs for both with my earth magic, but stopped as a rush of air met my back once more, slightly aggressive this time.

Her boots gave one final thud along the floor before stopping. "Do you have something you want to talk about?" I didn't turn as I spoke, just got to work on making the new legs. When I finished, I got up and turned to find her staring at me as she pressed the side of her body against the wall.

"Um...no." She turned her head just over her shoulder, biting her lip again. "Maybe I should just go down the hall and fix up the other room. Seamus', or Nya's."

My eyes moved slowly from the untidy and disheveled laces of her boots up to the curves of her thighs and hips. "You sure?" I got to her corset, envisioning the laces wrapped around my fingers. How easy it would be to tug them and make them as out of control as her boots were. I got to her face, those freckles, the piercing green eyes that were being taken over by her blown pupils, and her slightly parted lips—those *lips*.

She let out a breathy exhale, rolling those lips I was still staring at in and wetting them with that tongue I loved to goad so much. I wanted that tongue everywhere. "Mhm...I mean...I think..." She glanced at the door, fixating on the knob. "Yeah. No. Yes. I'll just go—"

"Stop doing that. Stop pushing away every thought and every feeling. Stop keeping it all inside." I snapped, every ounce of restraint within me breaking faster than I'd ever felt before. The doorknob popped and cracked under a pressure that I wasn't sure whether it was from my power or not. It was hard to tell what the hell was going on under my flesh when I was so consumed with every inch of her. "You don't need to hide anything from me, and it's driving me insane to see you refusing to open up to me. In-fucking-sane, Paige. Do you know what it's like to be driven absolutely insane by you?" I chuckled, wiping my bottom lip with my thumb and swiping across as she watched the movement with rapt fascination. "You make me feel like I'm drowning in a pool of fire, and I can't burn. I have no way to release the way that you are making me feel—to end it. I need to hear what you aren't saying just as badly as you need to let it out."

I stepped in closer to her, taking strides until the distance between us was so thin that I could feel the power between us humming, charged like an electrical current. Pinning her against the wall of Seamus' house was not what I had in mind when we left the bar, but here we are. To say I was upset about it would be an utter lie. I was a lot of things, but a liar wasn't one of them. Neither was being a coward, and I'd about had it up to the fucking Stars with being patient.

My fingers splayed along the wall as she put her hand to my chest, a glimmer showing in her gorgeous green eyes that begged me to come one step closer, one more step, and she'd destroy me with her power that called to my own. I held her eyes with mine, and took another step into her warm palm that held little to no restraint, the tips of her fingers trembling against my skin. A step that allowed my lips to hover just over her ear if I bent in.

Which I did.

"Tell me what it is you want, and say the things you need to say the moment it comes into that beautiful head of yours. I need to hear it all, even if it's bad. Even if it destroys me. Just tell me what it is you want from me." My hand trailed down of its own volition, reaching for the hair that had fallen across her cheek, brushing over my chin. I heard her gasp at the touch, a breathy sound that had my cock twitching against my pants. "I'll give you anything you want, Paige. You want me to burn down an entire city for you? Done. You want me to kill anyone that threatens the crown I already picture you wearing? I'll deliver their ashes to your feet. You want me on my knees for you, kneeling and begging? I'll make sure there are bruises there every night. Just for you."

I pulled my head back, desperate to know what she was thinking—what she was feeling. Her teeth kept her bottom lip pinned just as my body was doing to her against the wall, the flush spreading along her cheeks making them pink over, illuminating each and every single one of the freckles that dotted her cheeks and nose.

"Say you don't feel the same way I do right now." I pushed my forehead to hers and a shudder ripped through me as she moved her hand from pushing against my chest, sliding it slowly up and over my shoulder and then resting along my bicep. "Say you don't want me," I whispered as my heart clawed into my throat. Every touch, every inch between us was driving me closer to the edge of a cliff I was waiting for her to jump off with me. I couldn't think about what would happen if she didn't jump. I knew how far I'd go into the jagged depths below, and I'd keep going with no end in sight. Without her pressing a single toe over that ledge, I'd press further into those depths until the blackness swallowed me whole.

"Fuck, Paige. If you don't want what I do, say the words and I'll go back downstairs and leave you alone the second it leaves your lips."

A second passed, then two. Her fingers tightened around my muscle as her teeth continued their torment on her bottom lip. Any harder and she'd shed blood. I shouldn't have loved the way I could feel her trembling against me like I was a predator, and she was my prey.

But I did.

"I can't," she finally let out on a breath, her voice trailing and uneasy. I could see my reflection in her eyes—a tortured man at his wits end about to shatter.

I could feel my body heating, could feel the flames roaring within me. "You can't, what?" I let my nose tip down against hers for a moment that sent another shudder through her. I found I really fucking liked those shudders, so I moved my hand slowly up against her spine, lingering in the space that curved into my body. "I'm going to need you to use your words, Paige. What is it that you can't do? Because I've always believed there wasn't a damn thing you couldn't do." Her fingers dug into the flames on my bicep more, but didn't push me away. No. My girl tugged me in, her fingers pressing deeper.

"I can't want you." The words a soft whimper, a demand and a plea. Her eyes darted down to my lips, then flared as they lifted slowly, meeting mine again.

I brushed my lips lightly over hers, so lightly that I felt her body move forward to catch them with hers.

But I pulled back.

"Can't." I let the word sit like poison on my tongue, tasting the bitter-sweetness of it.

It tasted like pleasure, and fear, and wanting. So much damn wanting.

And it was a poison I was more than willing to drink.

I paused, looking at those beautiful emerald eyes where black threatened to swallow them into darkness. Our breaths were heavy and shallow through our parted mouths—hers plush, and red, and waiting.

"Can't I can work with."

And I jumped right over that fucking ledge.

I slammed into her lips, and she pushed just as hard back into mine. We were feral as we tried to stake our claims on each other. My fingers dug into her back, tugging at the fabric that concealed parts of her flesh that had kept me awake ever since that night in the water. But tonight, I'd finally put those thoughts to rest and turn them into a reality.

The Stars had their own demands, but this? This was all ours. She was mine and I was hers.

Her tongue met mine, ebbing and flowing like we always had for each other. I reached another hand behind her, cupping the back of her head before pushing her deeper into the wall, giving me the leverage I needed to lift her with my other hand by her perfectly round ass that had been teasing me for months beneath all the leather she always wore.

I made a mental note to spend time there, claiming that spot for myself as well. Every inch and part she covered with leather, I wanted to replace with a part of me, whether it was with my mouth, or my tongue, or my cock. I'd give it all to her, and she wasn't slowing me down, or telling me to stop.

Finally.

My hips kept her pinned against the wall while my hands pulled at her hair, my fingers twisting and curling into the base of her scalp that had her moaning. The moan that played on repeat in my mind when I was envisioning doing just what we were doing now—and more. That sound was in the arrows I pulled back before hunting, in the water that crashed around me when I bathed. In everything. She was everywhere, and everything, and so—"*Mine.*"

My words were lost to her lips, yet the way her fingers laced behind my neck and her tongue slowed in my mouth told me she'd heard. And she didn't unleash that power that was surging between us. She'd never have to unleash an ounce of her power to destroy me. I was already obliterated by her.

Her fingers reached behind her, trying to find the strings of her corset but meeting with my hand instead. "Let me," I said against her lips as I pulled those strings and ground further into her hips. She pulled the leather above her head once it was loose enough and my hand reached up to palm her breast. She gasped, then took my bottom lip into her mouth.

"These fucking tits, Paige. I need to see them. To see you." Bed. We needed a bed. I wanted to do too many things to her, *needed* to do *all* the things to her. *With* her. Her back arched above the sheet as I laid her down, our movements slowing as I reached under her tunic while her fingers slowly trailed down every exposed curve of muscle along my stomach, like she was trying to replace my clothing with her touch as well, inking every groan it dragged from me into her memory.

I stopped, propping myself on my knees between her spread legs as she lifted on her elbows just enough to continue swirling around the lines of my muscles, shifting higher to move onto my chest, then slowly, agonizingly, moved down, following the line of hair to the curve on my waist that led to exactly where I needed her most. I sucked in a breath through my teeth, the touch so intoxicating that I felt like I was getting high off of it alone.

Every girl before her was nothing. Meant nothing. No one was ever going to compare. No one could. I could die happy with just the touch of her fingers against my skin.

My hands slid up and down her thighs, brushing her soft skin. She edged further and further down and then back up, drawing a circle around the grooves by my navel. But because I'm a gentleman, because I was so lost in the heady way her eyes had shifted, I hesitated and asked, "Is this okay?"

Like a fool.

My thumb rubbed small circles against her thighs as I stayed between them. I was a gentleman, but that didn't stop the way I wanted to spread her pretty legs apart further, to put my face where I'd get to hear her moan more and more.

She nodded, murmuring something about a tonic she'd taken that told me she had the foresight to protect herself, *us*, in case this ever happened. I groaned, knowing I'd be free inside of her, to feel her come undone around me as I filled her. I changed thoughts into action as I unbuttoned and removed her pants, tugging down what little lace had covered her as well and admired her as she lay bare to me.

She worked on her shirt, pulling the fabric above her head and tossing it to the floor, along with the small lace bra that tried to cover her there, as well. I'd never been so jealous of a piece of cloth in all of my life, but knowing that lace rested across her breasts all day sent me into a momentary lapse of jealousy. Jealousy that had my thumbs sliding up from her thighs, moving up to her nipples to roll them between the rough pads of my fingers. Another breathy moan left Paige's lips, her head lulling back into the sheet, bowing her chest up as I bent down to take them each, one by one, into my mouth.

Her hand splayed into my hair as she pulled me closer to her, making the power within me rush again and again in devastating waves. The room heated, but the air within her sent a gust throughout the room almost as quickly as my flames rose. She lifted her head and pulled mine back, cocking a brow at me. "Control yourself, Fire Boy."

"There is no controlling *anything* when I'm around you," I growled, taking her nipple back into my mouth as she watched me slowly lick and suck and swirl my tongue there.

"Fuck," she moaned, her fingers digging into the sheets as her thighs tried to press together with my body between them.

I sat back up on my knees and leaned back, watching her release her head back down onto the bed as her lips popped open. A grin spread across my face, taking in her body, letting my eyes claim all of her first, drinking her in like the poison she was.

She was utter perfection. If clothed Paige sent my heart beating like a rabid animal, naked Paige had it stopping completely, then bursting into flames that could burn an entire town to ash. Her nipples were swollen and pinked over from my mouth, and I quickly got lost in the way her soft and delicate skin—save for the sprawling marks of all four elements—would have anyone convinced she wasn't lethal. That she wasn't a weapon.

But I knew better. I gripped for that thread in my mind that walled out Vara, and tugged it down further. No one would be warning me about the way she could hurt me tonight. Tonight, I was at her mercy. If she wanted to stab me in the morning, it would all be worth it.

"What are you—"

"Shhh." I put a finger to my lips, then pressed my knees into her thighs, slowly spreading them wider and wider. "Let me see you."

She drew a shaky hand through her hair, splaying it out from behind her to try to cover her chest, then had the audacity to wrap an arm around her breasts when it didn't work, like she was taking back the visual my eyes were so hungry for. It had been dark in the water that night, but I wouldn't let anything come between us tonight. I tsked and flicked my wrist, sending a small burst of air underneath her palm and pushing it back to the sheets. There was something about using her original nature against her that had my own power swelling inside of me and my dick growing uncomfortably beneath the thin fabric of my pants.

"Don't hide from me. Not now, Paige. You can't take back what you've already given, and I'm too far gone to chase you anymore tonight. Didn't you hear me say you were mine?"

Before my eyes could land back on the spot between her thighs, to her core that pulsed with my words and the wetness I knew I'd find there once my fingers got the chance to stake their claim there as well, I was flipped and pulled into the sheet, my back anchored flat against the bed as my wrists fought, albeit not too aggressively, against a twine of vines that held my hands captive above my head. Teaching her how to make those vines had been the best decision of my life.

"Stay." And stay, I did. Paige pushed her knees into the sheet between my thighs like I'd done to her, then with another flick of her wrist she lifted my hands up higher above my head, dragging them up and up against the sheet. My lips curved, mirroring her expression with my own. I'd seen that look before—the one that showed me just how much more control she had over her original nature than I did over my own at times. She was focused, but not on how to escape, or how to hurt or kill me. Little did she know she'd already ruined me for anyone else without lifting a single hand. There was no one more absolutely perfect than Paige Aerborne.

Her eyes lingered down, down, down until the slight flare of her eyes made the grin spread wider across my face when they stopped roaming and froze just below my waistband. She only got to wrap her fingers around my length before, and felt it pressed up against her, but clearly the mental image and the actuality of seeing it so close still needed some... adjusting to. There was no concealing the desire I had for her, and the thin borrowed pants weren't fighting against the strain. After tonight, I'd be willing to bet she was going to be thinking about just how disappointed every other man had left her before I came into the picture.

A picture I was never leaving.

I was no Dick Little, after all.

"Control yourself, Paige," I taunted, my wrists twisting under the vines that kept me from tossing her back underneath me. Sure, I had the power to burn them, to wither the thin vines into nothing. But it was so hot the way she'd taken control, almost losing it completely.

"I'm not sure I have any control left, Aeden." She tried to work my pants loose, but was struggling with the shake of her fingers. *So eager.*

"Burn them."

"What?"

"My pants. Burn them."

She sat back on the heels of her feet, looking at the bed sheets and then at the fabric of my pants.

"You have me tied up, sweetheart. Burn my fucking pants or I'll be forced to break these vines and burn them myself." Her wrist moved, sending a steady wave of flames down the length of my thighs, the flames catching in her eyes as she watched while my skin refused to burn.

"Good fucking girl, Paige. Look at what you do to me—how hard I am just thinking about you." I watched as her mouth dropped open slightly more, taking in the way my thick cock was bobbing. I knew immediately that I'd made the right choice in keeping the restraints in place, because watching her use the fire I'd given her was lighting the fire inside of me, too. Those vines were staying put, for now.

"Fuck, you're hot," she said softly.

She has no idea.

Her hair brushed against my skin as she leaned down, her eyes flicking up to mine the moment she dragged her tongue across the head of my cock, licking and swirling the precum off the top like a damn expert.

I silently cursed the memories I had of her, the ones where she'd left parties with other guys before or had come home late in the night, headlights flashing in through my window signaling she'd gotten a ride back. The window I'd sat by, waiting for her. Making sure she was safe had always been my top priority. But as she sat there licking and teasing me, there was only one thing that I was focusing on more than her safety, and it had a lot to do with hearing that moan of hers again and again until the walls shattered down into the snowy, moonlit ground.

Chapter Twenty-Seven
PAIGE

Out of all the times in my life that I had no idea what the hell I was doing, this time took the cake.

And no, I hadn't forgotten that it was Winter Solstice. That we had been warned about this happening, but even with that, the Stars had no real sway in what *this* was.

It wasn't that I didn't want him. The Stars knew it, and I knew it, too. There was no one I'd wanted more. It was actually becoming more and more difficult to deny the very fact. It could've been any plain night of the year as far as wanting Aeden Fireborne went and it had nothing to do with the shining assholes above.

I lifted my gaze back to him, his chin dipping into his chest to give him a better view of my naked body and my tongue that stroked every inch of his length, moaning with each swipe. Releasing the tension, the desire I had for him, was making my body feel light. Weightless. Like my power struggled to anchor me, yet had never been so in harmony, all at once. The power pulled me closer to him, and I wasn't fighting it anymore.

My lips replaced my tongue and a moan came from his chest as I slid down, dragging my teeth gently against his cock. "Fuck, Paige."—he seethed through his teeth as I went down further, letting him hit the back of my throat as I fought the urge to gag—"Choking on your words is one thing, but if you choke on my cock, I might lose it." He sucked in a breath through his teeth again as I continued my torment back up and down, inch by inch, trying to take what I could into the back of my throat more and more and damn near failing every time.

A burning smell drew my eyes back up to him, to his hands that were now freed from the flimsy vines I'd tied him back with. The same method he used to keep me in place on a damn horse got a new meaning the second I restrained him on the bed. I used to want to tie him up to escape, to give him a taste of his own medicine, but now the only escape I wanted was right here, with him, and the only taste I wanted was at the tip of his cock and on his tongue and lips as they kissed me back with everything he had.

I shrieked as my body was whipped around and positioned back like he'd had me before I took over, my back arching above the warmth of the sheets. And I let it happen. There was never a power play between us, both acknowledging we were equals in a sense that we were both destined to rule kingdoms and become a Mora. But within these four walls, I'd let him use whatever element he wanted on me, and I had a feeling that was reciprocated by the smirk he gave as he pushed himself between my legs again.

"You're absolutely beautiful, do you know that?" His eyes grew hungry as he raked them up and down my body, a look I wasn't sure I'd ever received from anyone else before. I didn't care to know about those parts of my past. The only part I desperately needed right now was the Aeden and Paige we were before coming here. The people who loved each other, who'd do anything for each other. I didn't remember it, but it wasn't hard to picture just how I'd ended up in that position to begin with. And as he bent down and scraped his lips and then his teeth over my clit, I found all of that remorse I held was more than justifiable.

"So. Fucking. Perfect." He stippled each word with a kiss across my center, then swiped his tongue back up to a spot that made goosebumps flood over my skin. My knees started to quake as the pressure built inside of me, pushing my elements to their limits under my flesh with every teasing lick and kiss he planted.

He sucked my clit into his mouth and a burst of air sent something clattering in the space beside the bed. He slowed his torments until I lifted my hips up to meet his mouth again. It felt too fucking good to stop, and Aeden seemed to agree as he pulled me closer, his hands sliding under my thighs and up to my ass, lifting my hips even more as he continued claiming me with his mouth.

"Aeden," I breathed, not sure what was so important that I had to interrupt the man who was worshiping my body and enjoying it more than I'd seen him enjoy anything before.

"Paige." He held up a finger, which I thought meant he was signaling me to wait a moment, and perhaps he was. But when another finger joined the first, time seemed to slow around us as he flicked and swept his tongue in slow circles around my clit. His eyes met mine through fallen strands of hair just as he thrust both fingers into me, stealing any words I might've said from my mouth as his pressed deeper into me, devouring me. His fingers curved, pressing into a spot I never knew existed until now. Did I have something to say? I wasn't sure. I was melting.

He flicked his wrist, coating the walls and door in ice as I moaned louder. "I've dreamt about the way you taste, Paige. But fuck, it just doesn't compare."

My fingers reached out to run through his hair, pulling him in closer as his fingers curled up into that same spot again and again with every thrust and pump of his fingers into me, making my legs go weak as he continued to lick and swirl that amazing tongue of his over my clit. He dragged his teeth gently over the sensitive bud and then removed his fingers and swiped his tongue down to fill me with it there, too.

"Fucking St—" I gasped as he bit down gently on my clit again, then licked the spot like it was wounded when it was anything but.

He chuckled, making a curse leave my lips as his fingers filled me again. "The Stars may want this for us Paige, but trust me when I say they are not the ones devouring every last drop of cum from your beautiful pussy right now." His fingers slammed into me, making my back arch under the pressure. "That's all me." His lips and tongue worked me over together, bringing me up and then slowing down, each time just moments before I'd explode.

If the stars were the gods of Aellethia, then Aeden was their king. And they knew exactly what they were doing on this night, as did he. Fuck being just the

Mora of Vizna, this man between my legs was as holy as any fae could get. My panting, because Stars I was panting now, stifled as I lifted my fist up to cover my mouth, fighting back words that would sound a lot like worship if I were to let them free.

The pressure became too much to bear, his fingers and tongue making my legs tremble like the ground was quaking beneath it, because it quite possibly was, and with one final curve of his fingers, I broke and swore I was being sent to the very Stars themselves. One of his hands reached up to press my hips down as he lapped and sucked and took everything from me until my hips stopped bucking and shaking and fighting against his hand. He lifted himself above me as my world tried to settle, my breaths stuttering as out of control as my heart was beating beneath my ribs.

"Paige." He bent down and placed soft kisses in a trail up my neck until he found my lips. I could taste what he'd done to me, could taste *me*, but I didn't care. I needed *more*.

"You're so damn pretty when you come, did you know that?" His nose grazed the tip of mine as the corner of his mouth quirked up into a smirk. I shook my head, my nose flicking against his. I had no words for him, nothing that would make sense. So I kept my mouth shut and shook my head again, hoping he'd take that for an answer and go back down between my thighs that were already aching for him to return.

"Tell me you want me. I don't need to hear that you love me to sink my cock into you. Just tell me you want some part of me, and I'll be yours. No can'ts, no won'ts." His words were soft, the muscles of his forearms shaking as he kept himself lifted above me. My eyes swept over the red marks along his skin, the ones that started as burning flames and ended with the purple mark I'd given him, the one I couldn't see as he hovered above me. The mark he'd developed because he loved me—something I wasn't sure I'd be able to own up to yet, although the twinge in my heart at the thought of losing him, of losing this, was too much.

But was I ready to admit that I wanted him? Did I want him to bury himself inside of me, make me forget all the shit I'd been through, that *we'd* been through, and just be with who I was tonight?

I wasn't the same Paige he'd known, the one he loved before, but why should that stop me anymore? Why should I fight the feelings that were so close to the surface even before the sun fell beyond the walls and the moon took up the space in the sky.

Aeden swept the tip of his nose against my cheek, continuing up until his warm breath was along my ear. "Let me make you see stars, beautiful. Let me hear that beautiful moan of yours as I make you come again."

I will fuck you until the Stars force us apart.

I turned to him, meeting his eyes. "Stars, huh?" I let out weakly.

He pressed his forehead to mine. "All of them. Every single one in the sky is yours to bask in tonight. I'm just here for the show."

I flicked my wrist gently along his arm, sending a gentle roll of air behind his back and between his shoulder blades. I swirled my hips against the tip of his cock as his back bowed toward me, pushing my knees to the sides by the sheets. "I want you, Aeden Fireborne. Now, please, make me see stars and fuck me."

He chuckled and I could feel the vibrations in my core through his cock that jumped against my aching slit, his eyes flaring with desire as he grinned down at me. One second, he was above me, the next, I felt the tightness of my body taking him in and in. I gasped as he sank into me, holding my gaze with his own, watching as I crumbled around him.

"Fuck, I didn't think you could get anymore perfect." He slid out slowly, hanging his head to look down and adjusting himself before sliding in again, taking whatever allowance my body gave him. "I don't think anything could be more beautiful than you taking my cock right now. Look at you, how well you take me." He rolled his stomach up as I looked down. He wasn't even halfway in yet and already I was so full. *So. Damn. Full.*

He kissed my neck gently as his hips rocked, trying to find the perfect angle. It was pushing me to the edge already. "You're so damn tight, and so fucking mine," he whispered against my neck, his warm breath making me arch into him. Then all of him slammed into me all at once, stealing the breath from my lungs and the words from my throat.

He pulled out all the way, then drove right back in, dropping his lips and sweeping them gently over mine before I lunged up and sucked his bottom lip into my mouth, driving him wild enough to slam into me again and again and again, each thrust pushing me further up the bed.

He stilled once more, rocking in circles, teasing every inch of my body. "You're going to destroy me, Paige," he said through heavy pants of his breath. I'd seen him run and swim and watched him throw hatchets for hours. His stamina wasn't peaking—it was the surge of his power. Our power. Because I felt it, too.

"Please..." I begged. "Don't stop, Aeden." My fingers dug into his skin, giving him new marks to wear. "You feel so good."

His brow furrowed briefly as if he were contemplating saying something, his face softening as he looked down at me. I wasn't sure what to do with that look, so I lifted and sucked on his lip once more, hoping I'd get the same response as before.

His arm shook, bearing his weight as one hand swept down along my ribs, stopping just underneath my breast and cupping it to take my peaked nipple into his mouth. He was gentle for a second, slowly thrusting in and out as he kissed my breast, and then not, like he was at war with the Stars themselves on how he wanted to be with me.

My nails clawed up to bite into his shoulders as a breathy moan escaped me at the torment he was spreading throughout my body as his pubic bone rubbed over my clit at a torturously slow pace.

"More," I begged. "Please. I need—I need more of you."

And more he gave. His hips started to pound into me once more, my moans mixing with the air around us that grew hotter as his original nature threatened to burn the house down with the orgasm that was building within us both. He slowed again, possessively taking a nip at my nose, then my cheek, then my ear, making me groan in frustration. I didn't have words, but my lungs definitely had enough air for sounds to sate us both. If he was hungry, I was ravenous.

"Please..." I wriggled my hips underneath him, begging him to push back into me.

His chest rumbled again with laughter. "You're getting greedy, aren't you, My Queen?" Another inch retreated, then another as he continued to pull out without the sweet release of pushing back in. "You like the feel of me inside of you, like the idea of coming all over my cock, don't you?"

I slammed my fist down on the sheet. "You're trying to kill me, aren't you?"

He chuckled, his thumb brushing just under my bottom lip before he sucked it into his mouth like I did to him. "No, baby. I just want to hear my name on these lips before I take your breath away again."

Without hesitating, I replied, "Aeden," in the most exhaustive way I could because all self-restraint and dignity left within me were tossed to the floor, along with the rest of my clothes. He smiled wide then he thrust himself to the hilt, pulling a moan from so deep down within me that another gust of air surged in the house, making the walls and floors groan under the pressure.

He slowed again, as he had with every surge of power from either of us. He was considerate in not wanting to ruin his friends house. As for me? I'd let it all fall to the dirt around us in heaps before I ever let him stop. He swept his hand up to my shoulder, to the faintly raised mark left by a dagger during the last trial, and brushed his lips over it before moving down along my ribs with his fingers, trailing them down like molten lava that warmed every inch of my skin until they disappeared between us.

"Is this where you want me? You want my fingers on your clit?" I gasped and nodded, moving my legs to wrap around his back as the heat moved to the apex of my thighs, his thumb working the delicate flesh there, pushing me to the edge of oblivion.

"And my mouth. Here." His head bent to take in my nipple between his lips, rolling and sucking just as tenderly as he'd caressed my ribs.

"Yes," I breathed in a gasp as his thumb and fingers continued their torture, rubbing as his hips drove into me with powerful thrusts, his skin growing slick with sweat at the force of his movements while he circled my clit again and again.

"I'm going to—" His mouth moved from my nipple and shot up to my mouth as the rough texture of his fingers intensified against my core with every throbbing pulse. The words were stolen from me as he kissed me like the world would end if we weren't connected in every way possible while I came undone around him. His hips jerked harder through the tightness of my impending orgasm with a ferocity that sent me over the edge. My muscles clenched right before a release hit me and as I screamed his name, he swept his tongue into my mouth.

"Fuck the Stars, sweetheart. You should see what you look like right now." He removed his hand and reached under to grip my shoulders, pounding harder, not relenting for a moment as his pace intensified and the room heated rapidly around us. "Absolutely beautiful. Hold on tight and take everything I give you." My body was going numb as I tried to hold onto him harder, my power humming like it had been sent over the edge with the rest of my soul. Stars danced in my vision as he kissed me with a tenderness that didn't match the ferocity of what he was doing to me. He moved down to my neck as he pumped into me harder, each thrust harder and faster than the last as he sucked on the delicate skin between my neck and collarbone.

His release came as I wrapped my arms tighter around his back and dragged my fingernails down his marks, feeling the shudder of his spine as he spilled into me with my name nothing more than a garbled mess of words against my neck from his lips.

And holy shit if that wasn't the best sex I'd ever had, or remembered ever having. What we did in the water was earth-shattering and sent my mind in a tailspin, but actually having him inside of me? Being that intimate with him? How would I ever go without him again?

He rolled to the side of me, his tattooed arm draping over my stomach as his breathing evened out while the weight of what we'd just done crashed in on me.

I rolled into his chest, his arm tightening around my back and I felt him go rigid beside me.

"Don't go anywhere, okay?" His golden-flecked eyes blinked down at me. "Just give me one night. Just like this." Part of me screamed and cried out that it was too much—being with him like that would break me further than I was already breaking for him. But he cut into my thoughts before I could spiral, because he always knew what I was thinking before I could even process it.

"Please, Paige." He kissed my forehead. "Please stay with me." His thumb grazed my back and I didn't have the heart to leave him anymore, so I nodded against his chest and wriggled in closer to him, feeling him release a shaky breath over my hair while his arm curled tighter around my waist, pressing me into his warmth.

He fell asleep a few minutes later, his arm wrapped around me and my leg thrown over his—both of us trapped in our weaknesses. Because that's what he'd become to me—my weakness. The once-hollow cavity of my heart started to fill as I watched him sleep, his wavy brown hair falling over his closed eyes that I reached up to brush back. I traced the lines of his face from there, then the stubble along his sharp jawline, and the muscles and curves between his shoulder and neck—taking my time to ink every inch of him into my mind. As my fingers slowed, my eyes grew heavy and the grey fog in my mind began to slowly lift just as I drifted off to sleep.

Chapter Twenty-Eight
Aeden

Warm, honey-brown tendrils of hair laid out in waves down my arm and across my chest. I didn't know it was possible to wake up and be this immensely happy before today. Her breathing was even and soft, her breaths making goosebumps form on my skin. She hadn't cried out once throughout the night, hadn't screamed or even moved from my arms.

I figured she'd be gone in the morning. But the golden part of her hair was catching the morning sun through the window beside the bed. She hadn't left, hadn't run away after I begged her to stay.

Her breathing picked up and I could feel her heart beating more firmly against my side. Thudding, actually, a little too frantically.

"Paige?" I whispered, unsure if she was slipping into a dream or was starting to wake up, and with the way her heart was hammering and her breathing had stopped completely—

"A—Aeden?" Her voice was soft, but alarmed. Her head angled up until her bright green eyes caught mine. "Aeden… oh my…"

I wasn't sure if she was about to run now that'd she'd given me the night I'd asked for, finally coming to her senses, or if she was about to cry right then and there. My arm tightened instinctively around her.

"What's wrong?"

Her eyes swept around my face like she was framing the image of me just as a tear fell from her eye and rolled down the side of her temple.

"Hey, hey, I'm here." Although maybe that was the problem. "Fuck, I'm an idiot. This is my fault, isn't it. I fucked it all up ag—"

"I remember."

My body turned cold like ice was spreading through my limbs. I swallowed, rubbing the back of her hair as I pressed her against me. "You remember...me?" More tears fell against my chest as she buried into me further.

No, it wasn't me she remembered. I never made her cry like that.

"Her. My mother. How...she just..." I flicked her hair away and pressed my palm into her back, feeling her breath turn ragged and raw and then it was deepening, like she was gasping.

"Paige. You have to breathe. Focus on my breathing." I took in deep breaths and exhaled, letting her head rise and fall as she curled up more against me, her heart hammering faster and faster and her breathing hitching more and more. "Fuck, baby. You have to breathe. Please."

"I...can't—" Her hand flew to her chest as she sat up, her skin going pale and damp with sweat.

"You're having a panic attack. You used to get these a lot. Let me help you. Listen to my voice. We are going to count, okay?" She nodded, her hair rising and falling down her back which was all I could see. But I didn't need to see her face to know the panic that was written all over it.

All over her.

"One."

"O-One..." She sucked in a deep breath and I moved to shuffle the fabric of the sheets away from her. I remembered that triggering her further before—unwanted added sensations against her skin.

Sensations that would lead to more thoughts and make her spiral further.

"Two."

"Two."

"That's it. Keep going. Let's breathe with every count. Three, inhale, baby."

"Three."

"Four."

"F-Four." Another breath in, longer this time. It was working.

"You're doing so good. Five."

"Five."

"Keep going. I'll be right back." I leaned up, gathered her hair and formed a vine around it to keep it together and pushed it over her shoulder. I could hear her counting as I left the room and not a minute later I returned with a wet, warmed towel I found in the singular bathroom upstairs.

"Here." Her body was hunched over as she sat with her knees pressed into the bed, the color slowly coming back to her face. "This usually helps you, too."

She nodded. "I remember. Thank you."

Fuck, she did remember. She took it and spread it over her open palms, then pressed it gently to her face and neck.

I sat back down on the edge of the bed, unsure of how much distance I should be giving her, but I wasn't going to leave her. Not like this.

"Aeden?" She turned, curling her body around to face me and grabbing the sheets to cover her naked body. Her hands shook as she pulled the fabric tight around her.

I got up to grab my clothes, but she reached out to tug me back by my hand. I looked down, watching as her thumb rubbed along my fingers.

"I don't want you to go." Her brows pinched together, like she was wondering if I was leaving because I had wanted to, not because I thought she needed space. I was only going to get dressed and then help her get dressed right after, if she wanted me to.

"I'm not going anywhere. I'm here. Always."

She didn't let go of my hand, but looked at the mess we made of the room the night before. Furniture was broken, hanging. Those legs I'd made to fix the desk and dresser? Shattered all over again. "Because you love me, right?"

I sat back down, resting our joined hands on her sheet-covered thigh. "That is one of the reasons, yes."

"You love me...like this?"

I chuckled weakly. "Like this?" I waved my other hand around her. "Why would that stop me?"

Her lips rolled in as she breathed out shakily. "I'm weak like this. I can already feel it. I feel like I'm nothing. Worthless. Unloved and unwanted. How could she...how could she choose all of that over me? Was I that undesirable? Did it hurt her so much to look at me? Maybe she saw my father when she looked at me, maybe it pained her too much to even—" She sucked in another breath and I could almost sense her heart beating out of control again.

"Hey, hey. Shhh. You're okay. I'm still here. You can let it out. I don't want to tell you what's on my mind until you're more calm. Breathe."

"How did you put up with this? I can't even imagine all the times this happened to me without my mind going grey—I'm so sorry. I was really hoping I'd remember you, too. Please, talk. Keep me from thinking more about how absolutely pathetic I—"

"Stop. You aren't pathetic." My hand slid up and down her thigh, still holding onto her hand. "You are the strongest woman I know. You fought through all of that and kept your chin up as much as you could. Not many people would still be fighting in your shoes, Paige. Many others would have given up. You just needed the support to push through the hard days."

"And that was you, wasn't it?"

I nodded. "It was, at first. I learned all about panic attacks and anxiety to help you get through it. We meditated together, did breath work, went on long walks. Anything I could find to help, we tried until you found a rhythm of what worked best for you."

"And I refused medication because of her, didn't I?" Her breath was still uneven, but she was at least breathing more normally.

I nodded again. "Yeah. I think you did beautifully without it. But I would have loved you no matter what decision you made with that. I would have been on your team no matter what."

"How did you fall in love with someone like that?"

"Someone like, what? A fighter? A believer? A rebellious, stubborn woman who reads to still the swirling thoughts, yet still had time to try to care about her mother like she wasn't the reason for why you were feeling like that to begin with?" I smiled, making her smile with me. "How could I not love you?"

Chapter Twenty-Nine
PAIGE

I'd gone from a full-blown panic attack to smiling at the man who helped me through it. The man who shattered my world beyond the amazing night we had just hours before. He held me all night long, and knew exactly what was happening to me when I woke up and how to care for me and get me through it.

My smile grew into laughter. "I wouldn't love me, if I were you."

"You aren't me. You're you. And I love you even more for it."

"Now you're just saying everything about me and making it a reason to love me."

"And?" His brow arched, looking at me like I was crazy for even suggesting that had been wrong to do. He really did love me. It didn't matter what I did at this point, he was as gone for me as I was for him. But I'd never told him that before, not that I could remember.

"Did I...did I ever say it back? Did I ever tell you that I..."

"Loved me?" His eyes moved to the back wall for a moment and then met with mine again. "No. You never did say it back to me. I think you were about to, the night that..." *That was the night I told you I loved you.* "The night of the ball. But Eoghan came in the room and...and I had to leave before your father's guards caught on to who and where I was."

"So, you've loved me all this time and I haven't once said it back to you. And you still love me?"

"Loving doesn't need love in return for it to be justified or right. I could love you for thousands of years without ever hearing it once from you. Love is cruel in a lot of ways, and I think maybe that is the one that is most cruel. But, it won't ever make me love you less." He leaned in, brushing a few strands of hair away from my face that hadn't made it into his makeshift ponytail. He tucked the hair behind my ear, and whispered, "If anything, since I'm a masochist and all, it would make me love you more having to wait that long."

I shrugged and blurted, "What if you didn't wait that long?"

Shit. His hand stopped moving along my thigh and his eyes went amusingly wide. "Are you saying that one night with me was all it took for you to realize that you love me, too?"

I squeezed on his fingers. "I'm not saying that."

"So, I didn't fuck you hard enough then." I swallowed, unsure if I should just say it and be done with it. *I love you. I love you.* Even without the sex, I loved him before that. I didn't need my memories back to know that I loved him. I'd probably loved him even when I was in that flower-filled cell he locked me in. Maybe that made me a masochist, too.

"You know, the Winter Solstice does last a week. It's not over yet."

"So now you're blaming the Stars for the way we were last night?" He laughed and shook his head. "Doubtful. I don't think the Stars had any real say in what I was doing to you. What I've been imagining doing to you for years."

Cold swept over my body and as I looked down, I noticed at some point I'd dropped the sheet from my other hand. I was naked, not that Aeden seemed to mind. Maybe that's why he'd started believing it was the way we'd been together that was making me question whether he had to wait a thousand plus years to hear the words that were etched all throughout my body. When I raised my gaze back to meet his, my mind screamed at me to let it out.

I love you.

"Years?" I choked out.

"Yes. Years. Not months, not days or hours, although all of those being used as time indicators would only make me seem like the most foolish person ever because they'd be so much longer than stating the years it has been. But, fuck it. Let's see...about four years would be how many hours?"

I squeezed his fingers again. "You don't need to count. I get it."

"But I can, you know. Count." He started lifting his fingers along my thigh, counting all the way up to five.

I laughed again, feeling the waves of anxiety and the rush of memories of my mother fade into the background. That's what he was doing—he was purposefully talking about absolutely nothing. And I loved him even more for it. "I know you can count, Aeden. You're very smart." I didn't need my memory to know that. I'd seen him learn alongside me, blowing my studies out of the water, quite literally.

"If you need me to, I'll happily look like an idiot. For you."

"You'd apparently bruise your knees every night if I asked you to."

His voice turned rough. "Is that what you need from me? You want me to beg to hear you say that you feel something for me?" He released my hand and slid off the bed, landing on his knees on the floor below me. I looked down at him, staring into his eyes and looking over the lines of his naked body. "I'm fine having waited all those years to hear you say what I think you're holding out on saying."

"Then why are you on your knees?" I whispered down to him.

"Because what better thing to beg for, to bruise my knees for, than this?"

"What do you—" My back was pressed into the mattress by a gust of air, and another threw my legs over the edge. He lifted my legs, putting one on each shoulder, then pulled me along the sheets until my butt was resting at the very edge of the bed.

"This." He didn't hesitate, his mouth and fingers moving up my thigh. "This, Paige, is what I'm going to beg you for. Let me taste you again."

He didn't wait for an answer as he shoved his fingers deep inside of me, curving them again and pressing. Hard. I moaned, tossing my head back. "Fuck, keep making those noises, baby. I'm going to watch you come again at least two more times before we leave this bedroom. If you want to start hating me again, wait until I'm done here."

"I don't—" I breathed in deeply. "Hate you."

"No?" His tongue swept up, using the tip of it to flick my clit several times, each time making my legs jolt and my breath stutter.

"Damn you. Y-you know I don't."

The way he laughed sent waves of air—his breath—along my thighs as he moved down to kiss them, his fingers moving languidly inside of me, still curving up like a hook, possibly to keep me there more so than for the insane amount of pleasure it made me feel.

"Do I? I don't know...maybe..." Several more thrusts of his fingers—more, because the stretch was becoming too much. Along with more brushes of his lips and breath along my clit, and I was already about to come undone all over again. He said he'd let me go after one more, but maybe I could hold him here for more than that. Several more. Including some just for him.

Hopefully no armies were about to storm Costa. We'd be too gone to give a damn.

He titled his head, his soft hair brushing against my thigh. "Maybe I don't know what you're thinking at all." His thumb replaced his tongue as he watched me squirm on the bed.

"You...do..." I threw my hand over my eyes, rehearsing the words in my mind before they'd reach my tongue and—and now I was starting to see those stars again. Little dances of light between the inability to breathe, my eyes squeezing shut as my thighs tried to press together against the building pressure.

"You're making a mess of my hand, Paige." He pulled his fingers out and grabbed my ass, pulling me so close I wasn't sure he had room for breathing with the way his mouth was now buried in my—

"I love you!" He pushed away from my body, and right as I was missing his warmth, he bent over me and pushed me back further along the mattress with a large force of air, making room for him to lay above me on the bed. His length slid into me as he settled back between my legs, pushing through the tightness that came with my orgasm.

"Say it again," he demanded, driving further into me, making me want to moan even louder than I already was before his hips picked up the pace.

I wrapped my hands around the tops of his shoulders and stared up at him as I rode out the remnants of my release, watching him chase his own as he came apart above me with several hard thrusts. He was beautiful, and he was kind. Selfless and deserving. And he was mine. "I love you, Aeden." No one had ever told him that before. Until now. And I'd remind him of it every day, for the rest of our days, however long they may be.

His head fell into the crook of my neck, where he planted small, lazy kisses along my dampened skin.

"I love you too, Paige." His lips brushed my collar bone softly. "Thank you for not making me wait anymore."

***

I shook my head as I looked around the room. "Seamus is going to kill us."

Aeden smirked up at me from the floor as he pushed his foot back into his boot. "We can rebuild it. He'll be fine." The desk, chair, and dresser could all be mended, but the charred rug...there wasn't much we could do there.

I slipped my clothes back on and watched him admire the burn marks along the floor. Because of course, they hadn't stopped at the rug.

"He'll be fine," he reiterated. "If anything, he will be so happy about the work you did on his portraits downstairs that he won't think twice about the burn marks up here."

I nodded from where I sat on the bed and pulled my boots on. I lifted one of the charred laces and waved it at him. "Those flames didn't seem to stop at the furniture and floor." My chin jutted toward the bottom hem of his tunic.

He grinned and shrugged as he stood, pushing the charred end into his waistband. "We could always take all of our clothes off again. If we're lucky, they'll all burn and then I never have to see you covering an inch of your skin again."

I giggled as I finished lacing up my boots with whatever laces were left and his grin grew. Who knew he could smile like that? "We have a lot of other, more important things to focus on."

"Are you trying to tell me that the Stars are wrong?" He feigned a gasp as he looked up at the ceiling. "Do you hear this woman?"

I flicked my wrist and sent cold water droplets over him, swearing for a moment that his skin steamed from the contact. He shook out his hair, then stalked up to me as I stood. "That wasn't very nice, Paige."

I stared up at him, watching the way my face lit up in the reflection of his eyes. "Neither is taunting the Stars." I didn't give a damn about the Stars. I just wanted to see him wet. Playful us was a lot more fun than I imagined it could be. And we could finally be that.

He raised his hand, his gaze not moving from mine as he dispelled the ice from the door. I quirked my brow up at him. "What about the walls?" I went to raise my hand, imitating him, but before I could move it and take care of the ice, his finger tucked in beneath my chin. His thumb dragged over my bottom lip as I lowered my hand.

"Leave it," he whispered.

"Shouldn't we finish cleaning this up before leaving it like this?" I whispered back, fighting the urge to pull him back down onto the bed with me. Apparently that thought was obvious, because he smirked down at me and glanced behind me at the bed. Somehow it was intact, yet nothing else in the room was.

"No."

"And why not?" I could feel my cheeks blushing over, because I knew the answer already. My body hummed at the thought.

He lowered down to my ear, his nose brushing the shell, sending goosebumps down my neck. "Because no one else is going to take this room from us. And when I'm done making you breakfast and checking up on Seamus and Nya, I'm going to throw you over my shoulder, take you back upstairs, and lay you right back down on this bed."

"What if the others are back?" My fingers laced into the hair at the nape of his neck, pulling him in closer.

"Doesn't matter, but I highly doubt that they are."

"Why?"

He kissed my neck and I leaned into his touch. "If Eoghan was here, he wouldn't be waiting downstairs. He'd be storming up here to try to barge in on us."

I snorted. "Yeah. You're probably right."

"It also takes longer than that to make it to Shay's house from here unless they went without sleep."

I pulled my head back and he groaned.

"What's wrong?" he asked, his brows pinching together.

"Just...you. Us." My teeth dug into my bottom lip as I looked up at him. "I wonder why only part of it came back."

He paused, worry filling his features. "Your memory, you mean?"

"Yeah." I nodded. "It just doesn't seem fair to you—"

"Me?" He blinked. "Paige, you told me you love me. You gave me an incredible night that I won't ever forget. And don't even get me started on this morning. What part of that seems unfair?"

I shrugged, pushing back the well of tears that threatened to break through, already starting to blur my vision. His thumb swept over my cheek and I darted my eyes to the side, trying not to let my thoughts get the better of me.

"Hey, look at me." His voice was soft, cracking a little. I turned back to him. "Don't feel bad for me. Everything that got us to this moment was well worth it. I'd do it all over again if I could."

"No, you wouldn't."

His hand cupped my jaw. "Yes, I would. And when or if your memories of me ever come back, you can just add it all to the reasons why you love me. Because you do. Love me."

I smiled and batted his hand away. "You're pretty confident about that, huh?"

"I may be an overbearing asshole at times, but I'm pretty sure that doesn't affect my hearing. You said you loved me. More than once." He lifted two fingers between us, and my throat went dry, thinking about where that hand had been moments before. "I think it was twice now, wasn't it?"

I gave a halfhearted shrug with one shoulder. "Maybe."

"Yeah, don't feel sorry for me at all, Paige. You made my entire existence when you said it the first time."

"Then why'd you make me repeat myself if your hearing is so good and you only needed it once?"

His arms wrapped around my back as he pulled me closer to him. "Because I'm not only an overbearing asshole, I'm also greedy."

I laughed, my cheek pressing into his chest where I could feel the vibrations of his laughter, too.

"Come on, I really want to make you some food. You'll need your energy for later when you tell me you love me a few more times."

The house was quiet downstairs, with morning sun streaming through the icy window Aeden had put in the night before. Nya and Seamus were probably still at the bar, and with the way Aeden didn't seem alarmed by the stillness in the home, I was betting on him thinking the same thing. He made his way over to the kitchen and started digging through drawers and the small pantry. I could hear him muttering something about the way Nya had stayed in a house like this, but I was too focused on watching the way he moved, soaking in the way I could just stare at him now without any repercussions.

Because we loved each other, and that was normal. I'd seen Ikelos and Eoghan do it enough lately to know that it was okay.

"You okay?" He asked, pausing to look up at me with his hand deep in a drawer that looked empty.

"Yeah, it's nothing. Just hungry," I lied, taking a seat in one of the small yellow chairs we already fixed. I'm pretty sure he knew it too because his brows lifted, but he chose against saying anything as he turned and kept searching.

I loved him, I knew I did. I knew he loved me, too. Could tell in everything he'd done since I'd first seen him in the arena, although I knew that wasn't the real first time I'd seen him. He'd already told me that story. But I'd never actually been in love before. Never got to experience what that was like. I'd jump in front of a sword for him and kill for him, but holding his hand? Kissing him when we weren't in the bedroom? How exactly did that work?

"I'm not finding much here. We might have to walk back to the bar." He held up a rotten...I'm not even sure what it was. Something green, but I wasn't sure if it had always been green. He burst it into flames in his hands and continued on looking through the final few drawers. Something about that made a lot of grey come up in my mind, but I wasn't sure if I should ask about it, or ask what our relationship was, or what we were doing in general. Did being in love mean being completely open with each other and asking whatever came to our minds? I knew for him, that answer was easy. Yes. Undeniably, yes.

Say the things you need to say the moment it comes into that beautiful head of yours.

I opened my mouth, but the second his body turned away from the kitchen, I snapped it shut again.

I need to hear it all, even if it's bad.

"Paige."

"Hmm?" How had he already gotten to the edge of the table from where he was seconds before? The home wasn't big, but—

"You're making that face."

"What face?" My fingers reached for the ends of my hair. I was fine, everything was fine. Nothing was wrong. We were just being hunted, the house was too quiet for Nya and Seamus to be here, my brother hadn't returned yet, and now we had to go back to where we were last night when I—

"You need to calm down, baby." The furniture started moving, the few forgotten shards on the floor quaking. "Breathe, Paige." His hand reached for mine, and the second his warmth met my skin, my power ceased its frenzy on Seamus' house.

One. Two. Three. Four. Five. Six. Seven.

"That's it. Keep going. Deeper breaths, slower on the counting." *Was I counting aloud?*

Eight. Nine. Ten. Eleven.

"Do I keep going?"

"You go for as long as you need. Don't think I've ever seen you go past thirty, though."

I exhaled a deep breath out, not missing the way my other hand had slid into his at some point as well. *Twelve. Thirteen.* Another deep breath in and my mind stilled again. "Fuck. How many times does this normally happen to me?"

He looked over my shoulder, then hung his head low before lifting it back up to meet my gaze. "Would it be bad if I said *often*?" His tongue swept over his bottom lip. "I'm trying to go for honesty here. So… often. But much less after we used the new ways to cope."

"And you said walking—that helped? I remember being on track and going running a lot. And hearing what all the people in Jessup were saying about me as I was running. People were awful there, weren't they? Why did I…" I looked at him, visibly seeing his eyes take on a shade or two darker than they normally were. "Oh. I stayed for you. Didn't I."

"It appears that way."

"Well then, I must have loved you a lot, because the pain of reliving that right now…it's a lot. I'm not going to lie."

He smiled weakly. "Hey, I told you to tell me whatever comes to your mind, no matter if you think it will hurt me or not." Clearly, I just had. "But let's try walking first, then I have a feeling I know something else that may ease your anxiety while we're outside."

"What?" I looked around the room, thinking Nya had just walked in, and she could heal me. But then I remembered her gift didn't quite work like that. If she couldn't heal hunger, I doubted anxiety and panic attacks were on the table. Maybe she could do something temporary, but how long would that last?

He moved to collect his sword and place it into the sheath on his back before he came back to me. "You don't remember having panic attacks in Prydia, do you?"

I thought for a moment, noting the few, grey splotches in my mind at the thought. "I think I did, but not a lot. I'm guessing the few I did have were more about you than anything else."

He flicked the tip of my nose with his finger and grinned. "That's what I thought. Still have all of your daggers?" I nodded, my hands searching my corset because I hadn't fully remembered putting them all back into place. It had become second nature, something I did without thinking about doing it, apparently.

"Perfect."

Chapter Thirty
Aeden

We made it about halfway to the bar before I made her stop walking. Paige crossed her arms over her chest, making two of her daggers shift up. "Grab those two"—I pointed at her chest, and she cocked her brow up at me—"Not your tits, Paige. I can grab those later." I winked at her, but she didn't look that amused. "Your daggers. Take them out."

She shook her head and pulled them free while glaring at me, but at least she was smiling. Vara would shit herself if—fuck, I was still walling her off.

"Are you proud of yourself, Aeden?"

I'd left her waiting for too long. It probably wasn't the right time for her to know what was going on either. She still didn't exactly get along with Paige that well.

"I can feel your hormones. You're...relaxed. Too relaxed. You do know there is an entire kingdom out for your head right now?"

Paige was digging the tip of her blade into the tip of her finger, spinning it slowly and watching me. "Sorry. I walled off Vara, and—"

"You *walled* her off?" she asked, her mouth gaping open slightly like she was shocked...and possibly angry.

"Mmm. Seems the girl isn't too happy to hear about that, is she?"

"Yeah. I did."

"She's going to be angry," she said, but I couldn't help the smile growing on my face because the amount of focus she was putting into the act of just holding her daggers was exactly what I was hoping for. This was definitely going to work. It had to.

"*Smart girl. Maybe we will get along, since it seems I'm as stuck with her as I am with you. You must've had a good night if you're just now opening that wall of yours back up to me. Wouldn't kill you to ask how I've been. Make sure my head isn't on a pike and all.*"

I sighed through my nose. "*How are you?*"

"*Fine.*" She paused, then added, "*At least tell me next time you're going to wall me off.*"

"*Missed you too, Vara. Costa is pretty dead. I'll try to see if you can stay closer tonight.*"

She huffed in response. "*Pretty dead is never a good thing. Keep your guard up. With her, too.*" My guard was already well into the dirt when it came to her. Pretty much non-existent.

"Close your eyes," I directed and Paige gave me a look of incredulity. "Trust me?"

She rolled her eyes, then smiled again as she closed them. "You know I do. What are we doing?" I spun her by her shoulders until she was facing one of the dilapidated, empty homes then I pulled her back, making her take several steps back with me. "Aeden…"

"Yes, My Queen," I taunted. She had all of her daggers on her, and two waiting in her hands. I grinned before saying, "Open."

"A house." She turned on her heels to face me with her brows lowered. "You wanted to show me the house we were just standing in front of?"

"No." I grabbed her shoulders and turned her back around. Then, I flicked my wrist, framing a large circular target in lilies and roses along the outer wall. I slid my hand down the length of her arm, and she shuddered against my touch. Stars, she was so perfect, *so mine*. "This." My hand reached for hers, my fingers wrapping around hers where she weakly held one of her daggers. I pulled her arm back, letting her arm bend naturally like I'd seen her do so many times. "I want you to throw."

She turned her head just slightly over her shoulder as I held her from behind, pressing my stomach into her back. I tugged under the hem of her corset with my other hand, making a breathy sound escape her. "Throw it as hard as you can. Don't stop until every flower is ruined."

"The flowers...they're..."

My cheek grazed hers as she faced the torturous petals. "Your mother's favorites."

"I shouldn't," she breathed.

"It's okay to be angry at her. It's a natural part of grief. I want you to get angry, Paige." I pressed deeper into her, molding my body to hers, acting like a willing piece of armor she could wear instead of every piece she'd made for herself. "Get fucking enraged and pierce every single one of those flowers."

"But—"

"No." I squeezed my hand around hers, feeling her muscles take over to support the weight of her arm as her hold on the dagger tightened. She was ready to throw, she just needed a push. "You need this."

She paused, then whispered, "Does that make me a bad person?"

"No. It makes you *strong*," I purred into her ear.

"But, I loved her." Her voice quavered, but her arm stiffened more, rearing back further without my guidance.

"You will always love her." I wrapped my other arm gently around her waist, drawing her even closer to me. "But you can love someone and still acknowledge all the wrong they did to you. She didn't treat you well, Paige. She gave you so much to worry about, and even in her death, you are still tormented by her choices. And it's completely normal to feel that way. You can be mad at her and still love her."

She laughed, though it was forced. "Kind of like how I hated you, but now I don't."

"And now you don't." She was trying to ignore it. Trying not to focus on going through her grief like I knew she needed to. Like *she* knew she needed to. My fingers splayed across her stomach while my other arm let go of hers, allowing her to take the weight of the dagger on her own.

"Throw, Paige. As hard as you can. Drive it through the damn wall. And when you run out of daggers, use your power. Whatever one you feel coming to the surface—use it. And don't hold back."

She threw the first few daggers with precision, but with each passing dagger that moved from her hands and into the flowers, she grew more and more sloppy. When she had no daggers left, she moved on to making them out of the elements that bloomed along her skin. She started with air, making tornado-shaped blades and forcing them through the wall, taking a chunk of wood out with it. Next, was water that turned to ice, but she quickly moved on to spears of wood, jagged and rough. I could feel her tears dripping onto my arm as I held onto her waist. I brushed my fingers along her stomach through her clothing, her heart beating like ravenous thunder with every burst of power she released onto the desolate house.

A giant orb of flames grew in the space in front of us, and I envisioned what the firelight looked like as it danced in her eyes. *Beautiful.* She combined the fire with air, forming a large swirling vortex that looked like a miniature hurricane on fire, and thrust it through the house. Fiery petals danced to the snow-covered ground in the wake of her storm, releasing embers into the air above.

I waited for her tears to stop before turning her and taking her into my arms once more.

"You're a Starsdamned storm, Paige, and so strong. You're a fighter, through and through. Don't ever believe you aren't enough, not for one single second. You are more than enough." I pulled her head from my chest with both hands cupping her face and stared into those bright, green eyes. "I love you," I whispered. "And you will always be enough for me."

"You aren't worried about them?" she asked as the dim lighting from inside the bar came into view.

"No. They were most likely too caught up in their reunion and ended up crashing there." Seamus probably had minimal desire to walk in on us as well, but I didn't want to draw attention to something that could make her pull away. Unsure if the acknowledgment of us, *together*, would make her think twice. I felt like I was free-diving, falling blissfully through a cloudless sky. But the ground was approaching. At some point, it would have to. Maybe it's because I'd never been this happy in all my life, but I felt like I was just waiting for the rug to be pulled from underneath me.

Pretty dead around here is never a good thing. Keep your guard up.

Vara's words played on repeat in my mind as we walked, and as the silence stretched, I knew I'd inadvertently put her on edge as well.

Yet, Costa remained silent. No sounds came from inside the bar as we reached the swinging doors—no heavy, boisterous laughter, no sounds of movement or glasses clinking or sliding across the wood. Nothing.

"Stay right here." I stretched my arm across the doorway to bar her from entering.

"Fuck no. I'm coming." She put her hands on her hips, fingers sliding to where I assumed more daggers were.

"You—"

"Can, and will, Aeden. I told you to stop trying to protect me, and I also told you to stop running into danger. You're doing both. Right now." I did promise her both of those things, but I couldn't get past the way every part of me refused to let that happen. She needed to stay safe. Every ounce of power within me raged, desperately clawing against my better judgment to trust that she would be okay in there. But I needed her safe and alive, and walking into somewhere that could lead to either of those being disrupted was simply not going to happen.

Until it did. A gust of swirling air pushed my arm up, sending me to the snowy ground. Paige's leather-clad leg stepped right over me, and as my head turned to face her from the ground, she smiled down at me and waved. She walked through the swinging doors confidently before I could get up again and pull her back, because she had put up a wall of air around me to prevent the very thing.

Clever, beautiful, infuriating woman.

The moment I pushed through the same doors, my entire body went from raging against my power to falling utterly still. The bar was empty. Pin-pricks spread down my back as my eyes darted around the space, taking in nothing but firelight and vacant tables, save for the half-eaten plates of food and glasses where we sat last night. I wanted to yell for her, but if she was in danger and not messing with me, that would...no. I couldn't think like that. Not when we had finally—

A slow clap sounded beside me. An eerie sound, filling the deteriorating walls with an echo that drew out the emptiness. I turned my head slowly, lighting a fire orb in my palm.

Paige was plastered to the wall beside Nya and Seamus, each of them covered in thick vines with large thorns threateningly close to piercing their skin. "Why is it whenever we are in the same room, you are *leaking* heat?"

My orb grew at my side as I took in the tawny man with eyes like dark trees covered in neon lights and a cloak that floated down to the cracks on the floor, covering them like a dark shroud. "Lee," I growled, my eyes fixed on him, but my power solely focused on Paige and my friend and his daughter. "Let them go."

Lee examined me, cocking his head to the side. A wicked grin spread across his face. "I will. But first, put away your flames." I responded by making it bigger, glaring back at him and sneering. "Fireborne, right?" He looked behind him, pointing at Paige and then turned, raising his left brow back at me. "And... Aerborne." He went back to Paige, walking up to her and tucking her hair behind her ear. That's when I saw the sheen of air clamped over her mouth, but Nya and Seamus—they had shields of ice over theirs. Earth, water...air... "You did so well in those trials, too. It's a shame, really. My bets were on you winning."

My eyes raked down the length of his covered arms, but I knew what was hidden beneath. *Lee.* I should have seen right through that. "Not going to use your flames on me then, huh?" I taunted, my orb now dangerously close to half the size of my body. I brought it closer, letting it cover my side until my tunic started to burn off in a circle there. Yet his eyes widened in amusement, like he was watching a circus performance, and I was the monkey, while Paige's widened in fear.

"You don't want them. You want me. So let's take this outside and you can let them go." I wanted to burn him where he stood, but he was too close to Paige. I remembered the way I had let my fire engulf a man before—it ran too hot and rampant, and she'd get caught in that crossfire if I dared to do it now.

"Aeden! What's going on?" Vara shouted through my thoughts, ricocheting through the narrowed focus I had on the woman I loved and the man who promised to make himself my number one enemy if he didn't release them all.

"It's—"

"Completely unnecessary." His hand extended into the space between us as all three sets of thorny cocoons shriveled to nothing. Paige fell to the ground and gasped, her fingernails scraping against the floor as she curled her fists in. She bared her teeth up at Lee, then looked at me questioningly as her brows furrowed together. Because she had put it together, too.

"Names Leander Earthborne. I've been dying to officially meet you." He bent down, taking Paige's wrists into his hands, but she jerked them back and reached for her daggers, still on her knees. "Well, now. That's not very kind of you, dear. I did save your hide after your second trial"—He stood and pointed down at her, looking at me through lowered brows—"Or does she not remember that, either?" He curled his hand into a fist and looked down at Paige again, making me close all the distance between us. But I froze, inches from Paige, as a peony unfurled from his fingers. He dropped it to the ground in front of her and grinned.

The flames vanished at my side. "It's been you, then." I bent down, easing Paige up to her feet and wrapping her in my arms. Nya and Seamus stood at that moment and rushed to the other side of the room, talking quickly in hushed voices as they each examined each other for injuries like I was doing now with my hands on Paige. But my eyes never left Leander. "You've been the one I felt watching us all along."

He nodded, his wicked grin returning, but then he coughed into his fist. When his hand moved into the space between us once more, a sickly sweet smile had taken over. One aiming for sincerity rather than violence, but it looked like he practiced the very face in the mirror more-so than pulling it from his emotional state—which was also questionable. His fingers wiggled in the air awkwardly, waiting.

"You just put Paige on a wall, threatening her and my friends. What the fuck makes you think I want to shake your hand?" Paige's arms slid comfortably around my waist before she turned and sneered at him, too. I had a feeling she was using the act of putting her hands together behind my back as a way to keep her wrists from sending Leander across the room, much like I was hesitating in doing something tastefully similar.

His hands went up in the air as he shrugged. "Sorry." He didn't sound that apologetic. "My apologies to Lady Aerborne and her protec…" He looked me over and smirked. "Apologies again. Lord Fireborne."

Lord. Lady.

I pulled her tighter to me.

"For how long, exactly, have you been following us?" Paige asked, her voice one of authority, stern and clear. "And don't give me any bullshit about it being since the inn." Her chin jutted to the floor where the pink peony lay crushed into the floor. At some point when she moved, she'd stomped on it and ground it deep into the grooves.

She shifted in my hold, and even though I knew she wanted me to let her go by the way she had unlinked her arms and was shimmying against me, I refused. I thought I was about to lose her—she'd have to fight me a lot harder than that for me to even think about letting her go. Her nails scraped along my forearm in warning.

"It's a pesky thing, isn't it? Love, that is." Lee moved with ease over to the closest table, taking a relaxed position on the bench as he sat and hung his head down between his spread knees. "Powerful, too. Almost as powerful as—"

"Uh, no. You need to answer my question, first. I'm not interested in listening to your tangents about our relationship when you don't even know us," Paige snapped out, her boots fighting to get closer to him while her arms wriggled in my hold. "Let me go, or your bed will be empty tonight," she whisper-shouted up at me loud enough for Seamus and Nya to hear. I was sure of it.

"Paige..." I groaned, mostly because she was shifting against me in a way that reminded me of the way she felt without her clothes on, and now was not the time for the Winter Solstice and the damn Stars to be interfering with the way I wanted to wipe the smug look off of Leander's face.

"I told you to stop—"

"Protecting you?" Lee's head snapped to full attention as he smirked at us. "Yeah, okay, *fine*. I've been watching since he stepped foot into my territories. When you're as old as I am, you start to learn the ins-and-outs of the energy moving between your wards. A dragon heir *and* their dragon *combined* is kind of hard to miss."

"Aeden, what's going on? Are you alright?"

"Fine, for now. It's Leander Earthborne. He's here, says he's been watching us since I entered the Fields of Araros, but I'm pretty sure he's insane." More like positive of it.

"He's much older, Aeden. Be careful. He's had centuries of practice."

I knew he was old. But— *"How many centuries?"*

Vara went quiet. *"Vara."* I growled.

"What's the word for 'in the thousands' again...millennia? Yeah. He's that."

Fuck.

He didn't look a day over thirty.

"Are you asking your dragon about me? Where is he?" Vara snarled through my mental walls, making me pinch the bridge of my nose in pain. It was getting hard to manage the pull of my own power, the emotions and thoughts I had flooding in from Vara, and the crazy sensation of Paige's as I held onto her. I looked down at her again, noticing the way she had stopped jerking against me. She'd gone completely still.

"You saved me after the trial. You voted for me to live, basically. Why?"

He tsked, then laughed, slapping his knee. He craned his head to look past us, his vibrant eyes fixating on Seamus...no, Nya. He was staring at Nya with too-wistful eyes. Then he sat upright and snapped his eyes back to us. "Because, dear. You are a piece of the larger puzzle that is the outcome of this war."

"War?" Paige feigned ignorance. It didn't suit her. "What war?"

"*The* war." He swirled his fingers in the air. "It has begun. Since about..." He looked around the room like he'd find a clock or a calendar. Then he shrugged again and looked at his nails. "Well...in *my mind*, it's been waging on since The Battle of Vizna. Your poor, darling parents..." he hissed the last word while glaring at me.

I squared my shoulders back. "You knew them?" My arms foolishly loosened, but Paige didn't move. I felt her arms slide back around my waist as her chin dug into my chest while she strained to look up at me. I could *feel* her worry, could feel her heart rate picking up and the intensity of whatever it was our power did whenever we were this close. Of all the things that were spiraling, my mind was at the pinnacle of it all, yet I kept my face as relaxed and uninterested as I could. "How?"

He nodded, smiling somewhat sorrowfully. "How did they pass, or how did I know them?"

Seamus walked up beside me with his finger raised to Leander's chest while Nya struggled behind him, tugging him back by anything she could hold on to. "Ye'll tell this lad everythin' you fuckin' know or I'll spend each of me last dyin' breaths beatin' the shit outta ye." He was trying to be strong, but his face was a bit paler than usual.

Leander looked at Nya and his smile fell. He didn't even try to taunt her father back. He could probably decimate Seamus on the spot, but he just nodded and drew his lips thin. "Of course." He looked at me and Paige, then spread his arm over the length of the table. "You might want to sit, though."

Chapter Thirty-One
PAIGE

Aeden and I sat side by side, and when his hand slid into mine, relief washed over me. Seamus sat beside him and Nya sat beside me, all of us positioned across from the Mora of Buryon who'd just had me tacked to the damn wall.

I shouldn't have let my guard down. I'd planned to go into the bar and sit wherever Nya was. But they were already plastered to the wall when I walked in, and before I could breathe in a gasp, he had me whipped around with air sealed over my mouth, dragging me back with the force of his power until I met with the wall. I wasn't even sure which one he used—my mind went into instant panic. And then I watched as Aeden entered the room and I...I couldn't stop him.

I could've lost him. All because I didn't want to listen to him and the way he thought I needed to be protected from everyone and everything. He didn't always treat me like I was delicate—not when he showed me how to get past my anxious thoughts, or when he fought side-by-side with me in Easrich. And certainly not in bed. But then there were moments when something seemed to get the better of him, and he just couldn't control it anymore.

I nearly jolted against Aeden's side when Leander started talking. "Let me just say, again, how nice it is to finally sit down with you. Both of you. I feel like I've waited so, so long." He started counting with his fingers, flicking them up slowly as his lips moved with the words he was whispering. When he went to raise another hand, my brows furrowed. *Was he counting weeks? Months?*

Aeden let out an agitated breath. "Tell me about my parents, and then I'll decide from there if I want to keep listening to what you have to say. Because, quite honestly, I don't like you, and I don't appreciate the way you keep looking at us. If it wouldn't threaten her life—*their* lives—I would've already burned you to the ground."

"Aeden…" I squeezed his hand under the table, turning toward him and covering my mouth with my other hand. "He did save me. Maybe we should listen and *not* threaten him." I'd heard enough about Leander to know that anyone who was still in power for that long must not only be childless, but also insanely talented and powerful with all the years of practice they'd had with all four elements. Or, they'd be completely deranged and feared for good reason. Leander smirked at me when I turned back to face him. *No, he was all of those things.* My skin grew cold even with the warm caress of Aeden's magic across my neck and shoulders.

"Stars, talk, man!" Seamus' fist slammed onto the surface of the table, sending me sideways into Nya. "And don't keep stealin' glances at Aanya. She won't be interested in the likes of you, even with the Soltice goin' on." Seamus spit across the table as Leander's eyes flicked over to Nya, then to her father. His brows crinkled, like he didn't quite understand what set people off and what didn't. Not exactly the best type of person for Aeden to be sitting directly across from. I squeezed his hand more, noting the spike in temperature along his skin.

"Aanya," Leander mimicked her name like he was sipping on a fine wine. His eyes illuminated, somehow brighter than before. His lips curved up. "Lovely to officially meet you, beautiful."

Seamus lifted a finger to him accusingly. "Ye already met her when ye threw her against the wall! Now, answer Aeden's questions." Seamus pushed back from the table in his seat, his gaze wandering over his motionless daughter before he darted his attention back to Leander. "Out with it!"

"Right." Leander laced his fingers together on top of the table, looking once more at Nya. She hadn't tried to lash out at him once, which I found…odd. Maybe her time in my father's cell had dwindled the spark I'd seen in her. On the days we trained and talked and laughed. Days when she didn't hesitate to lash out at

Eoghan. Now, she was more like a sullen wallflower, losing all of her color as she stared back at Leander and twiddled her thumbs together on top of the table.

Seamus held up his hand over the table and circled it in place, coaxing Leander to continue. Leander cleared his throat, stole yet again another glance at Nya, then said, "Your mother, I'm sure you know by now, was Lady Savaria Fireborne." Leander's tone shifted when he said Aeden's mother's name—a hollowed tone. I now remembered that tone well, unable to even think about my mother without that hollowness spreading everywhere.

Aeden raised the hand that wasn't holding mine, lighting fire along his fingers and down to his wrist, watching as it burned off just enough of his tunic sleeve to show the edge of his mark. At this point, he wouldn't have a shirt left by the time we left, not that I could complain about that all too much. "Think I figured that one out already."

Firelight glowed against Leander's skin as he stared at Aeden's fingertips, still simmering with the remnants of flames. "You look so much like her. Your father, too, with the hair and the"—he gestured at him, drawing a line up and down in the air—"height. Definitely the same height as him." That wasn't saying much. Most men I'd seen here were as tall as Aeden, if not, close to it.

"Who is he." Aeden wasn't going to last much longer. He had far passed the end of his rope when he saw me against the wall. Leander was pushing him even further and it made my palm damp under the heat of Aeden's.

Leander swallowed and looked at Seamus, smiling faintly. "A guard, actually."

"A guard?" Aeden's voice lowered two octaves from the angry tone he had before. Then it rose back up again. "What do you mean?"

"I *mean*, dear boy, your father was her guard. It's really quite simple. You know." Leander motioned toward our obviously linked hands beneath the table, mirroring our hands with his on top of the table. Aeden's fingers tightened around mine, but that seemed more in response to the use of the word *was* than any motion Leander made in front of us. "She fell in love with the guard that watched and protected her every move. And he fell in love with the woman he was hell-bent on protecting. Surely, you of all people can see how that can happen."

"*Who*. A name."

"Ah. Yes. We are not the sum of what we do in life, are we? A *name*—now *that's* who we are." Leander tapped his fingers on the table. Without any movement of his wrists, five glasses filled behind the bar and were brought to the table on nothing more than air, each one settling in smoothly in front of us. "His *name* was Rennick. Ren, for short." Leander smirked behind his glass, then took a small sip. "Nicky, if you got him drunk enough." He let out a low chuckle. "I guess names do tell a bit about a person. Huh. Funny."

"Was." Someone could be a guard, and retire. Seamus was proof of that. But Leander had just made it clear—Aeden's dad wasn't alive anymore. "So, he's gone, too." Aeden's voice was back to being low, and somewhat distant. I slid my fingers out from his and swept my hand in soothing strokes up and down his thigh. I knew what it was like to find out who your father was, but mine was a monster. A monster that I wished was dead.

Rennick didn't sound like a monster.

Leander nodded, taking another sip and glancing at Nya just over the lip of his glass. Seamus huffed as he took up the glass in front of him and chugged it down until nothing was left, then slammed the glass down and folded his arms across his chest, the movement making the bench groan beneath us. "Never heard of him," Seamus said, jealousy pouring from each word.

Leander's eyes narrowed on Seamus. "You can't possibly know everyone in Aellethia. It doesn't surprise me that you didn't know Savaria's guard in the slightest."

"Would've met him or heard about him in Sentra. All guards go there." That was true. It was where they all trained and swore their oaths to whoever purchased them.

"Ah. But he wasn't there long. He was young when he became a guard and left, and not much older when he... died. Perhaps you were purchased well before he even arrived." Leander fixated on Seamus' fingers where they tapped along his empty glass in agitation. Agitation that more than likely didn't stem from what

Leander had said. It was more the way he spoke—flippant and so unaware of what people might take his words to mean.

Seamus looked slightly older than Leander, but that didn't necessarily mean Seamus *was* older. Especially not when Seamus turned to alcohol for so many years.

Leander took several sips from his own glass, but ended up choking on it. He coughed, then wiped his chin and continued. "Rennick loved Savaria since the day they met when they were children. When he went to Sentra, guess who swooped in and bought him right up?" He muttered something under his breath—inaudible, save for the word *waited* which he pushed out loudly.

"If you were such good friends with him, where were you when they died?" Leander paused, staring back at me like he'd forgotten I was there entirely.

He blinked several times, each time making his neon eyes shine a little less. "Well, dear girl, not everyone can be the hero of the story. Not like this boy here." Right. The trial. He spun, looking at the door, then turned back. "Where is the other Mora? Waterborne?"

"We're not finished talking about my parents," Aeden bit out, his jaw working so much that I slowed my hand along his leg.

"No, I think we are, for now." Leander stood, shaking out his cloak. He let out a ragged huff of breath then ripped the black fabric clean from his shoulders, revealing a faded green jacket. He could've been anyone from Earthborne territories. That's exactly what we believed when we first met him at the inn in Easrich. And we'd been so wrong. Aeden moved to stand, but I forced him down with an air shield above his head. He let out a grunt when he hit it and stared down at me, then adjusted back into his seat under the pressure of the air magic I was putting on his shoulders.

"Please," I said to Leander, hating the tone of my own voice as I begged for him to continue. Aeden needed more, *deserved* more.

"I don't mind answering all of your questions, Aeden, but I prefer less of an audience. Maybe just you and I can talk in a bit, without your watchful friends and lover in tow. Sound like a deal?"

"Deal," I said without hesitation. Aeden's fingers balled into fists on the table as he glared at me again, those golden flecks darkening more and more the longer we stayed in Leander's presence. "Stop that. I know you want to know more, and it's not like anyone else seems to know a thing about them like he does."

"Oh, so right you are, dear." Leander raised his hand, flashing the back of his hand at us. A gold ring with a small engraving waved in front of us. A diamond? No. A triangle. With a single flame inside of it.

I wrapped my arm around his, noting the thrum of his pulse. It had picked up. A lot. "Fine," he muttered under his breath, giving Leander a stare that promised to burn him down to nothing if he made one wrong move. It didn't matter if Leander held all the secrets of Aellethia in his mind, Aeden would turn him to nothing but bone dust and ash in seconds, never thinking twice of it again. The man who had let me burst into a raging fit, throwing daggers and power at a wall of flowers and held me gently as I did it, would also burn the world down if I asked him to.

I felt that more now than ever as he looked back over to the wall I'd been pinned to minutes before, then glared back at Leander. "Just know that if you ever touch a single hair on her head again, I won't hesitate to end you where you stand. I don't give a damn if you're the Mora of Buryon, or if my father liked your company. I'm not him and I *will* kill you."

"Actually"—Leander dusted the front of his jacket with several swipes of his palms, arching a brow at Aeden—"If I could close my eyes and hear those words from you again, I'd almost believe it were Rennick saying that about Savaria. You may not be him, but you are *just like* him." Leander looked to Nya, then to me and lastly Aeden, completely dodging the scorn of Seamus' face. "Even your voice is his. But, your eyes?" He chuckled, glancing up to the ceiling momentarily before his eyes fell back to us. "Stars, your eyes are all her."

The doors swung open, a wide smile on Eoghan and Ikelos' faces. *They'd returned...and came here?* "This looks like fun."

Eoghan walked up to Leander casually, adjusting the cuffs of his jacket while Ikelos dusted the snow from his. They both held out their hands and Leander lifted both brows. "We know you know who we are. Been trying to get a meeting with you for quite some time now." My brother glanced at me knowingly. He couldn't see Aeden or anyone close to him with Vara nearby, but Vara wasn't here. As he glanced over to Aeden, then back to me, I had to wonder exactly how much he'd seen. *Could the Stars be that twisted?* I shuffled uneasily on the bench.

Leander hesitated, rubbing his hands together as he stared back at them. "And who is it that you think I am?"

"You're Leander Earthborne." Eoghan dropped his hand to his side while his other hooked around and slammed into the side of Leander's face, the quick movement making my head spin almost as bad as Leander's had. Aeden chuckled darkly beside me. "Couldn't be bothered to stop a fucking war, could you?"

Ikelos smacked the back of Eoghan's arm like he was scolding a child while Leander rubbed his jaw and chuckled. "Like I told her"—Leander chucked his thumb over his shoulder toward me—"I'm not a hero." *But he could have been. He could have at least tried.* Suddenly, every desire to be nice to Leander so Aeden could get his information was thrust through the swinging doors and long forgotten.

"Doesn't take a hero to show up to negate the passing of a law. To fight. To make a difference," I cut in, with Aeden stopping my ascent from the table this time with a light push on my thigh. Not hard enough to really stop me, but the contact brought me back to my reasons for keeping my cool. *Him.* Even Nya put her hand on my shoulder, pushing me back down as well.

Murrie walked in and immediately drew her ax from her back, frantically darting her eyes between all of us, then cocking her head at Nya. But my eyes went straight to her bag that looked rather empty from here. Shay walked past the swinging doors with nothing in her hands and no satchel and just walked right back out again, throwing her hands up.

Maybe they had been unsuccessful—hadn't found what would bring my memories of him back. I felt my stomach reach into my throat as anxiety clawed its way through. Aeden spread his fingers over my thigh, like he knew. He would always know. And instead of feeling like that was an unfair advantage he had over me—a way to take me down—I now only felt comforted by the idea.

"Nothing I said or did would have changed the law being passed. You're a smart girl, you know that." Leander spit a small amount of blood onto the floor and dragged his fingers over his tight curls. "And you"—Leander pointed at Eoghan, who looked ready to throw another punch, but my brother pressed the back of his hand to his chest, backing him up several steps—"You knew I'd be here, didn't you?"

"I'm a—" my brother started, but Eoghan cut in, slapping the front of my brother's hand with his that still lay flat across his chest.

"We have a collection of intel on you."

Leander lifted his brows again, amused. "Oh, do you? And how is that?"

"Money can buy some crazy things—weapons, armies, information."

"The most expensive guard in all of Sentra," Leander added flatly, moving his eyes to my brother. "I know all about you two."

"He was well worth the cost," Eoghan said, his sneer and fist twisting cruelly.

I made to stand again, but Aeden tightened his hand around my thigh. "Let them figure this out," he whispered, a smile playing on his mouth. He was enjoying the fight and was probably waiting for Eoghan to deck Leander again. Using your fists in this room meant you were rather benevolent—the amount of power alone could rip this entire town apart. But he and Eoghan were clearly acting as a united front—a team. *When had they become so close again?*

Leander turned his head to the side, just over his shoulder. "Love is *cruel* in a lot of ways, is it not, Aeden?" I didn't even have time to stop him before he was up from the table after the first three words Leander spoke. Because those were the very words Aeden said to me. In private. While we were naked in Seamus' home.

Aeden was met with a thick wall of air, his fist stopping mid-air and lighting into one covered in flames as my brother shouted for them all to stop.

And these were the men I had to work with to end my father.

"For the love of the Stars." Ikelos closed the distance between him and Leander and my brows pinched together as I thought, for a brief moment, that I saw Leander flinch when my brother's hand extended out to shake his hand again. *Had he flinched before?* "Ikelos Aerborne. Wonderful to finally become acquainted with you. I'm a—" Eoghan made a sharp noise behind the air shield that held him back just as it did Aeden. "I'm a Seer." He glared at Eoghan over his shoulder as Eoghan crossed his arms over his broad chest, a look of heavy disapproval stamped on every feature of his face. "I know we can trust you because I've seen it. And even though I've told my partner that, he refuses to believe it. I think someone has rubbed off on him lately." Ikelos' eyes slid to Aeden, who was also standing with his arms crossed, looking every bit as displeased as Eoghan was. "I'm just going to come out and say it—we've been trying to reach out to you to make an alliance in the coming war, but have had no luck in actually reaching you to do so. You're a rather hard man to find."

Leander's hand slowly slid into my brother's, but then he jerked it back and pushed both hands into his pockets. "My council knows that I prefer to remain...discreet."

Ikelos nodded. "You've made that abundantly clear."

"Let me also make this clear—I prefer solitude. I am not someone you want as an enemy. The very fact that I have followed you here and finally made it be known is a luxury for you all. What you choose to do with that will be on your conscience, not mine. I don't need my elements to make your bodies bend to my will." My eyes grew wide, taking in every single fragment of light, sending a sharp pain through them. He...Leander could *bend* us? I'd read about a gift like that in a fairy tale—or, what I thought was a fairytale. Even for this world, the story seemed...tragic. About a boy, who could bend and manipulate...no. It couldn't be true.

But my brother's eyes grew wide as well. Perhaps he hadn't seen that part of Leander, though he had clearly seen what he looked like and where he'd be. He darted his eyes to me, then motioned at his side for me to remain still. But I hadn't planned on moving—not when the cost of making a move against Leander was now too great. Yet, Aeden's flames grew in response to his threat having either not heard or cared enough about the consequences, and at some point, Eoghan was right there with a ball of swirling ice in his palm. Perhaps neither of them cared—or maybe, they simply didn't know the extent of that gift.

My stomach shifted from settling in my throat, to somewhere down in my knees.

We were screwed.

"We want an alliance, not a fight." My brother's arms went up as his eyes roamed to Aeden and Eoghan, begging them to stop with sharp looks. Eoghan relented rather quickly, but Aeden didn't. He didn't even look behind him to see how I felt about what he was doing. *Look at me and stop!*

I flicked my wrist under the table, dousing Aeden's flames by taking the oxygen from it. He turned and glared at me, stuck in the trance of ending Leander and most likely trying to protect me, yet again.

"Sit back down. Please, Aeden," I said low, watching his shoulder drop with his name on my lips.

"Listen to your lover. You really don't want the progress we've had so far this morning to turn around. Think of that bed tonight." Leander winked at me and when the faint flicker of flames grew along Aeden's fingers again, I doused it immediately before Leander could see. Then I pushed Aeden with a gentle force of air, trying to guide him back to me.

"Please," I begged again. He gave in, walking backwards to me to keep his eyes on Leander as he worked to slide back into the same spot he'd abruptly left.

He took my hand in his once more, the heat from his flames turning into a warmth that spread through me at the contact. Our eyes locked, and his spoke volumes—*I can't lose you.* My thumb made soothing circles against his rough hand. *I'm not going anywhere.*

Leander began to pace, muttering under his breath and shaking his head with every few words he seemed to disagree with. Ikelos pulled Eoghan back to a table across from ours, both of them whispering to each other quietly between stolen glances at Leander.

"I have a gift, too," I said, breaking the awkwardness in the room. Or, trying to. Instead, it redirected all eyes to me—each set clearly telling me something different than the other, although Aeden's was the only one that sent a too-warm ache through my body.

He didn't want me to admit it, but I knew I had to. We needed an alliance, a way to win the war against my father. If Leander's forces, and he himself, were the key to not only that but also anything Aeden needed to know about his parents, then I would willingly give him a taste of what I could lend besides my name on a battlefield.

"And what, pray tell, is that dear?" Leander's voice was low and full of hesitation I didn't feel. He didn't believe me. Aeden's hand pulled from mine, and a moment later, his entire arm was wrapped around my back. He pulled me closer to him, like Leander would steal me if he knew how valuable I could be. I didn't feel powerful. I didn't have years of knowing what I could do and how to use it—not like a Seer or an Empath would. But Leander didn't have to know how incompetent I was.

"I can travel to places in my dreams, and touch things. Take things. I can—"

"Paige," Aeden growled low, the vibrations felt through the leather of my corset.

I took a deep breath and continued anyway, because Leander had gone stark quiet and still, his green eyes dancing wildly over me. "I can go where I've never been before, see people and hear them speak. I can touch them, too. And—"

"You said *take things*. What *things* have you taken?"

I swallowed thickly. I needed to become an asset to make sure we'd all be safe. And I knew just the thing that would be believable enough.

"This." I reached into my pocket, pulling out the small book Aeden had given me months ago. His lip twitched, only slightly, as I slammed it onto the table.

Leander rushed over, taking the book in his hands. "You took this? While dreaming?" He turned the book over, then flipped through the pages slowly.

I nodded, not daring a single glance away from him. The itch to reach up and take the ends of my hair in my fingers with my other hand was becoming hard to resist. As my hand lifted slowly, so did Aeden's hand along my back. His hand curved over the top of my shoulder, where he began to push my hair away from my neck and—

"This book has little value. Where were you when you took it?"

Aeden's nose and lips brushed over the skin at the base of my neck, just above my collar bone. "I...I uh..." I couldn't think with his mouth on my skin. Leander had yet to look up again from the book, still searching it over, possibly trying to find value. Like I'd have to find a book highly valuable to want to read it in the first place. All books had something of use within them, some *value*, as he put it. Like the fairy tale that told me exactly how fearful of Leander we all should be. But all of those thoughts were being lost the second they tried to pass my lips because *his* were still on me, now with teeth.

Suddenly, the stares in the room shifted from worry to amusement, all except for Leander's because he was nose deep in the worn pages of a book that had nothing to do with my gift. "I was in...the...mountains." The last words left me on a breath that sounded more like a moan, because Aeden's other hand was now inching up my thigh.

Leander finally looked up, making my skin flush even worse than it already was. The book slid back across the table, stopping inches in front of my chest. "Impressive. It has been ages since I've heard of a Dream Walker, much less one powerful enough to touch and take things back." *Dream Walker?* I nodded awkwardly, Aeden's mouth now reaching my jaw, making it hard to react to anything Leander said.

I should have pushed him off, told him to get the hell out if his mind was so far deep in the gutter. But the warmth around my body wasn't the same as it had been when we were together, naked, and wrapped up in each other. It was still gentle—more soft and soothing.

It was all an act.

One Leander was also falling victim to. "Perhaps you should go and come back when the Stars are done toying with you both?" A slight laugh left his mouth which faltered when he looked to Nya, eliciting a growl from Seamus.

Aeden smiled against my temple and chuckled lightly in my ear. His head swiveled to Leander, staying pressed to mine. "Perhaps you're right."

What his idea was, I had no clue. I just hoped it involved at least stopping somewhere to take care of the way he'd just melted my insides without using an ounce of his power. Not any inked on his skin, anyway.

"We can all go back to...Seamus' house...and—"

And the amount of cocky smirks and chuckles with each stop in my suggestion turned the room from one of high tension to one where I pictured Leander would do the thing where he didn't have to move to send glasses around to everyone.

And then part of me was becoming heated for another reason entirely. They were *laughing*, all because they assumed we had no control over our sudden peak in desire for one another. Laughing because it was so relatable to become a pawn to the Stars. Why wouldn't it be with four High Fae who'd gone through the trials, and another one apparently losing his mind to fuck another.

But that's not what this was. It struck me then just how far into an act this was—he was protecting me. Again. Pulling me from the room when I was close to being caught on a lie. Most in the room knew where I'd gotten that book from. And it wasn't a dream.

I'd lied, and Aeden was going to do what he did best—swoop in and be my knight in shining armor. The image always, *always*, sent that grey fog and sharp pain through my skull. He'd done this before. And he'd done it a lot. It was foolish of me to think he could change. That he could stop trying to protect me all the damn time.

The talk around the room picked up, sure enough, around drinks at the table where Eoghan and Ikelos sat. Seamus and Nya had moved there as well, with Murrie and even Shay taking their seats at some point.

When had she come back inside?

I'd been thinking for a while, then. Long enough to look lost in lust, I was sure, even though anger was taking up residence in my thoughts far faster than the reminder of him between my legs was. Although the tension was thick in the air, they had all decided to put that aside with talk of the Stars and previous years of the Winter Solstice, using us as a reference for their banter.

I pushed into Aeden's side when he went to kiss my neck again, his lips trying for a soft, unspoken apology. One he couldn't complete with another shove that forced him to stop.

"Why would you do that?" I whispered, cupping my hand from people who weren't focused on me anymore.

"Paige, I—"

I jerked my knee into his beneath the table. "Don't *Paige* me. You made me look like an idiot just now."

Aeden wrapped his arm around my waist again and pulled me to him before I could shove him away. His fingers curled in along my side like spears, making sure I couldn't move unless I used power—

"Don't you dare, My Queen." His voice of authority sent shivers down my spine, my body reacting without permission as a shudder fell from my lips. *Damn him.* "You use anything other than your words with me right now, and I'll make sure to find a better use of those lips tonight. Are we clear?"

I nodded, biting down on my lip. As enraged as he made me, his touch was even more—no. *Focus, Paige.*

His lips moved to the shell of my ear and I leaned into his warmth. *Stupid, stupid body.* "You're brilliant, you know. But you shouldn't have given yourself up like that."

"He was going to hurt you." The words, the vulnerability in them, came tumbling out before I could stop. "He was going to hurt *you*. Didn't you hear him?"

Aeden glanced over his shoulder to Leander, who lifted his glass to him. "Go on, you two! Can't make the future of your kingdoms without trying!" My fists curled in and in along the table, and if Aeden's body wasn't blocking me, I was sure my hands would be enough reason to set Leander off again. To put us right back to threats and who would be first to test their power against the other.

But we needed him as an ally. He was more powerful than any one of us could have imagined—if what he admitted to was true.

"He won't hurt me," Aeden said too confidently as he turned back to me.

"How can you possibly know that?"

"Because that ring on his finger is an oath ring." He grabbed both of my hands in his, circling his thumbs along the tops of my fingers. He was transfixed in his hold on me—lost in possibly too many thoughts at once. When he looked back up to meet my gaze, his brown eyes sparkled. "It means he swore an oath to my mother, and I have a strong feeling that trying to harm me would break that oath."

Chapter Thirty-Two

PAIGE

Aeden leaned against the outer wall of the bar as I paced in front of him. The sounds of laughter were thick and daunting, like at some point it would all cease and the walls would blast from the use of the power that dwelled inside.

"I really wish you didn't tell him what you're capable of."

I stopped pacing and stood with my legs spread wide, hoping the stance would make him stop looking at me like I was the one at fault here.

"Me?" I laughed. "You're mad that I saved our asses in there?" I raised a finger at him. "You—I don't even know where to start with you."

"Start where ever you want, My Queen." His eyes narrowed. "I've been waiting for you to speak your mind, if I didn't make that clear enough for you."

My voice raised several octaves, blending with another burst of laughter that came from the bar. "You want me to yell?"

Aeden's arms crossed over his chest, making the corded and exposed muscle bulge all-too deliciously against his destroyed tunic. I glared up at the sky, knowing the moon was well hidden but still in full-swing with its Winter Solstice bullshit. My stomach gurgled as my eyes found his again.

"Fuck. I do, Paige. I want you to be open with me." His eyes lingered down the length of me. "But I should have fed you first. I promised I would."

"Why, because you know I get pissed when I don't eat?" I was already mad, and it had nothing to do with food. Well, mostly nothing. "You also promised to not protect me anymore, and that shit you pulled in there?" I flung my arm out toward the bar doors. "So, yeah. Let's start there."

"Let's." He settled into the wall more and smiled softly, like he'd hoped I'd open up with the very words.

I exhaled sharply. "I don't even know where to start." It's not that I didn't know how to stand my ground, but being angry *and* also deeply in love with him made the world shift on a completely new axis.

His brows drew closer together. "Start with how it made you feel, and we can go from there."

We. That golden word that made whatever I felt seem so much greater. Because it no longer meant I was on my own. I had him. "It made me feel...like you don't believe in me. Like you think I'm not capable enough to handle things on my own. Like loving me isn't enough like you said it was. Why can't you trust in me enough to let me make the harder decisions?" Water welled behind my eyelids, and when I went to wipe at them, a faint, very familiar warmth spread over my neck and shoulders. Still, he said nothing. I could see his mind working, trying to find the right words to say, and saw the way that act alone was tearing him apart, too.

"I never wanted you to think that I don't believe in you, or that I don't trust in you. That you aren't capable. It's quite the opposite—I *know* how capable you are. I can see how strong you are, not only when you train and when you absorb every piece of information you can, but it's also when you go through the day's motions without acting as tired as I know you are, or as defeated as I know you feel. I believe in you more than I believe in myself." His eyes turned darker as the clouds above began to blot out the sun. "I just...I can't help myself in trying to be the shield to your dagger. The metal armor to your leather. The body in front of you, ready to fall in order to keep you safe. There's not a thing I wouldn't do, no one I wouldn't kill and no place I wouldn't conquer, all to keep you from harm. You are so much more than just my past and my present, Paige. You are my future, too, in whatever way you'll have me." His thumb flicked over the tip of his nose and his eyes illuminated once more as he said, "I'd die for you because I love you so damn much and I believe your existence holds so much more value than my own. Maybe there really is nothing more between us, like I've thought..." His eyes flicked up to the sky like they always did when Varasyn interrupted his thoughts. He adjusted himself once more against the wall. "My power surges when we're close, Paige. Even my very being has no control once you are near. Maybe it all has no greater meaning than I am so desperately and utterly gone for you and I simply have no control. Like the way I felt that day when I first saw you when I wanted to steal you into my home where there was safety and warmth. I feel like I was meant to love you, meant to believe in you and care for you and trust you. And that's what I'm going to do until every last piece of my existence flickers out in the night sky above."

My hands started to tremble, the earth beneath my feet no longer feeling stable. Certainly, my insides were melting into the ground beneath my feet. But I had to focus. We had to get through this. Or rather *I* had to get through this. "If you believe in me, then why make me feel like that? You can see that it affects me, aren't you worried that it will make me hate you again?" Even saying the word *hate* felt so wrong. I loved him, I knew I did. But I loved my mom, too, and didn't I just act like I hated her?

His tongue pushed into his cheek as he considered me. "I promised I'd try to stop being an overbearing ass, and I am trying whenever I notice it's happening. But if I can't, then I'd rather have you alive and hating me than dead because you loved me."

I flinched. "So you're saying I shouldn't love you, then. That I am too much of a liability to be with because I'm driving you insane. Is that it?" My chest ached at the thought. Maybe he didn't want to want or love me like he did. His entire being seemed consumed with the notion that love could prevail—but I had yet to see that work out for anyone. Maybe this was the last ounce of willpower he had, and he was using it to push me away from him.

He pushed off the wall and closed the distance between us as my heart hammered in my chest. His hands moved slowly down my arms, and when he found my hands, he pulled me into him. I tipped my chin up, fighting back more tears before the rough pad of his thumb grazed beneath my eye, then the other. "You've always driven me insane, Paige. But in the best way possible. I don't want you to think that I don't want you. Or that you aren't enough. Or that you aren't capable. I love you *and* I want to protect you." His arms wrapped around me, pulling me in closer to his ashen scent that I took in and fought more tears as it enveloped me. "Please let me love you and keep you alive. Use it to your advantage—you have a bodyguard without ever needing to step foot in Sentra. And, better yet, I'm free of charge. You won't need to pay me a single coin." I didn't need to look up to see the smile spreading across his face. I could hear it—and it had become my new favorite sound to ever exist.

I laughed against him, burrowing my cheek into him. "What if I don't want a bodyguard?"

"Then take me to bed, and I promise to do anything but protect you."

I reached my hands beneath his tunic, letting my fingers glide over each groove along his stomach. He let out a low groan against my touch. "I'm not here to play the damsel in distress. If you ever try to make me look like I can't handle myself by making me look helpless under your touch again—"

"Who's to say I didn't just want to hear that breathy gasp of yours?"

I flicked his stomach muscles with my fingers. "I know what you were doing. That whole power thing you talked about, it happens to me, too. I can feel when your power is becoming too much, although I thought it was my own at first. Your heat wasn't all-consuming like it was last night. It was soft and gentle and warm."

He leaned down and kissed the crown of my head. I prepared myself for another joke, another way for him to ease the tensions. "I wonder if the others are like that. As much as I don't want to think about what Ikelos and Eoghan are like together, I wonder if their power influxes are shared, too. Or are we just weird together like that."

Weird was a loose way of putting it. I'd kept it in the back of my mind while reading through texts, but was never quite sure what it would be explained as here, and had found nothing so far. Perhaps that meant it was so common that no one thought to write about it—or the opposite. "I could ask, but you seem to be friends with Eoghan now. Maybe I'll just make you ask him, and let whatever embarrassment that pulls from you be the punishment for what you did in there to me."

"Oh, I can think of at least ten other, much more fun ways to punish me, My Queen."

I rolled my eyes, but grinned against him. "Why do you call me that?"

He reached down to my chin and cupped it between his fingers, lifting my chin to meet those gorgeous brown pools of his. "Because one way or another, whether it's by getting the Prydian crown on your head or giving you mine, you will be My Queen."

"You'd give me your crown?" My brows crinkled together. "I don't think that's possible."

His nose brushed the tip of mine. "I told you. There's not a single thing you can't do." His lips moved down to mine, where they brushed and teased but refused to settle. "I'm sure there's another way to give you my crown, or a crown. Like...beside me."

I reared back. "You can't possibly be proposing to me."

"No." He laughed and the rumble of his chest reached low in my stomach. "No, I don't think you'd agree to that right outside of a bar. I told you, I can wait for you. However long that takes."

I rolled my lips in and nodded my head, though now it swirled with so much confusion that it was hard to think straight. "Maybe we should move on to the next thing I wanted to talk about."

His arms lowered down to the base of my spine. "I'm listening."

"What's an oath ring and how did you know what that was?"

He sighed and started playing with the ends of my hair. "I stole a scroll about it from that bookstore."

I giggled. I did that a lot around him now. "Not stolen. It's a free library."

"Huh. That actually makes a lot of sense." He smiled down at me. "Anyway, I don't know why I took it, stolen or not." He smirked down at me and shook his head. "Maybe it was the flame in the center. I couldn't read much of it but there was a small translated section of a few of the words at the bottom and I pieced together that the symbol on the scroll was symbolic of a promise made between a Mora from Vizna and anyone they made an agreement with. Or *oath*, as the translation said."

I studied him, wondering if the way he took to reading was similar to the way I had—used as an escape, a way to fill my mind with other thoughts than those of my mother. I wondered if the way I'd treated him led him to that. My throat turned dry and my nose burned on my next deep inhale.

"Do other kingdoms have the same thing?" I shifted my thoughts back to oaths before he could analyze whatever was written on my face like he always did. "I never saw Gedeon wearing one." Or Eoghan, for that matter.

His finger stopped twirling the ends of my hair. "It seems universal for each kingdom, except for the guards who don't seem to get anything to mark their oath besides payment and a colored tunic. I don't know if they are all made from hedonium like Leander's is, but—"

"Like your bracelet." The last thing we needed to talk about, and possibly the one Aeden would flip his protector switch into full-throttle mode over, was what Leander had called me inside the bar.

"Yes. Like the bracelet I gave you."

Blood rushed to my ears as my hand slid into my pocket. *Dream Walker*. Though when I dreamt, I usually felt anything but the ease the term insinuated.

Aeden eyed my movements, probably wondering why I could no longer look at him. "What's wrong?"

"You know how I said I could touch things in my dreams?"

"Like the shell in Lystos. Yes."

"...And hear things and take things." The tips of my fingers were warming at an alarming rate, like my ears. I finally looked up, finding Aeden's confusion almost adorable. Excitement flooded my system, overtaking that pesky voice in the back that said he would not be as thrilled about what I held in my pocket as I was.

"Yes. That...was a good lie you said in there. About the book. But he was going to see through it and..."

I beamed, matching the intensity of the sun bouncing off the snow beneath our feet through the now cloudless sky. "What if I wasn't really lying?"

"I know where that book came from, Paige. And I love that you take it everywhere with you, but I know, for a fact, that is the same book I gave you."

"Mhm. It is." I grinned wider, making the edge of his mouth quirk up with mine.

"Paige...your smile is infectious. But I have a feeling I won't be smiling once you pull out whatever it is you have from your pocket." His eyes darted to the skies once more, and he growled low. "Is this the part where you stab me?"

I shook my head once to each side, seemingly in tune with the word *no* in my head. Then with all-too eager fingers, I pulled my hand from my pocket, beaming more because of the way he didn't flinch back. Not a single muscle.

My fist rose in the space between us. "I lied about the book."

His eyes moved between my hand and my pocket, then fell to mine. "I think we established that."

I popped my fingers open, one-by-one, until the sun's rays started bouncing off the shiny piece tucked in the safety of my hand.

"Holy shit, Paige." He took my hand in both of his, his eyes wide enough to brighten every single golden fleck as his lips turned up further. "You...you..."

"Took it? From a dream? Yes." I started looping the bracelet around my wrist, and he moved to help clasp it for me. "So, I didn't lie about that. You were wrong."

"You took this from a dream and you think I'm focusing on how you didn't actually lie in the way everyone else, except for Leander, believed you lied?"

"Honestly?"

"Always, honesty, Paige." He glared at me, then back down to where his hands still held onto mine.

"Well, Aeden. I'm *honestly* waiting for that switch of yours to flip and for you to haul me away, so I can't go back in there and live with the not-really-a-lie lie I told."

His hand clasped around mine, concealing the bracelet that marked him a Dragon Heir. The one I couldn't remember getting from him, but when I saw the name as it laid on my father's desk, I knew exactly what it was from what he'd told me before.

"When?" His tone turned dark and firm, wiping the smile from my face.

Here we go.

"On our way to Costa, the first night we stopped." I pulled my hand from his and looped my hands behind my back. "Is this the part where you tell me again—"

"That you shouldn't have said a damn thing about being able to take things?" His hand pushed through his hair. Several times. Then it finally settled along the base of his neck. "I want to say so much. But, most of all, I want to rewind and start with saying how incredible you really are."

"Really? That's what you want to lead with?" I squinted at him and waited.

"It is. You are absolutely incredible. And thanks to Leander, you have a name for what you can do."

"Really shooting for the optimistic approach." I took a deep breath in, fighting the urge to smile again, because it was inevitably going to turn whenever he'd tell me the rest of what he wanted to say. "Aeden the optimist. It has a ring to it."

"I've always been the optimist."

I rolled my eyes. "Yes, all that talk about dying for me and killing people was quite optimistic."

"You're deflecting."

"Maybe."

"Paige, the deflector. Now *that* has a ring to it."

He stepped back up to me in two long strides. "Dream Walker. Taker of *things.*" His hand swept behind my back, and I let him take my hand back into his. It was all so easy, being in love with the man I thought I'd hate for eternity. Trusting him. "How did you get into his office?"

I shook my head, then turned my attention to another burst of laughter from inside.

"You don't know how to direct where you go, do you?" I shook my head again, making concern paint his face. "Does it hurt at all? Moving within those places in your dreams?"

"Hurt?" I snorted on a laugh. "Stars, no. It doesn't hurt. But I do feel like I'm really there. Dream Walker makes it sound easier than it is though."

He tapped on the bracelet, right where his name was etched in. "Evidently," he said, laying on the sarcasm thicker than the blanketing warmth on my neck.

"I didn't even know Gedeon had an office, or where it would have been in that hellhole. Where *I* was. My dream put me there from the beginning, and when I saw the bracelet on his desk, I couldn't resist touching it. And then when I woke up, I was still holding onto it." I followed his gaze to my hand and put my other hand on top of his. "I don't know if I can do it again. I was going to test it out again last night, but—"

"But I asked you to stay with me. And you don't dream the same way when I'm holding you, do you?" His question had less inflection than it should.

Had he held me another time?

"No, I guess not." It was dumb of me to question. I'd woken up several times and seen him close by. Most notably the time I held a knife to his throat, though I was certain I'd drifted into a dream that night. And not a good one, either.

His hand snaked up to cup my cheek. "I don't know how many nights I can go without lying next to you, but I also don't want to be the reason why you can't figure out how to use your gift."

"Well, if we go back in there and you can play nice with Leander, he can tell me more, and we can gain an ally—like we need. And then you might not have to sleep without me next to you."

He kissed me like he was trying to never forget what it would feel like, taking the breath from my lungs. "I fucking love it when you say *we,*" he groaned, the sound moving right to the sweet spot between my legs. The sun broke through a brief bit of clouds again, lighting up the wall of the bar like a spotlight on centerstage—a wall that I had a sudden desire to throw him up against. I could climb him like the sturdy tree he was and shift his pants just far enough down to—

"You know if I take you right here, they will all hear us, right?" Those lips of his turned up like I'd told a joke or threatened him on the mat, but the voice he used was deep and full of desire. "That's not the best way to gain allies, babe."

"Huh?" I'd been hyper aware of his hips pressing into me, and the wall, and then his mouth, but the words were taking awhile to process as he spoke them.

His thumb brushed over my heated cheek. "You got all pink and it looked like you were about to flick that wrist of yours while you stared at my cock." Okay. I had been looking there, too. Which was definitely hard, judging by the strain in his leathers. "Though I am curious, were you going to burn my pants off again or throw me against that wall you were also glancing at?" He smirked down at me, all proud of himself for noticing the way I couldn't resist him. "It was both, wasn't it?"

I shook my head out, trying to clear it. "Sorry." I looked back up at the sky, mentally flipping it off. The moon and all the Stars. I wondered what the Aellethian equivalent to Hell, or underworld—whatever it was here—was, because that's where they all needed to go. Right to Aellethian Hell.

"Don't be. It's fucking hot. But save it for later. You haven't eaten yet, and it appears I have someone to go be more...lenient with."

I nudged into him. "Nice." I adjusted his tunic—what I could adjust of it, anyway—and stood up on my tiptoes to reach his hair, where I pushed my fingers through several times. "Be nice, cordial. You know, like you treat Eoghan now."

He grumbled, "That took time."

"We don't have time. You see what Gedeon did here. How much longer do you think it will be before he goes elsewhere? My bet is not long, if he hasn't already." My hand fell from his hair, and he caught it on the way down, ducking his head down and lifting it to his lips, pressing a kiss there. My heart melted at the contact, making my toes curl in my boots.

"I know." He stood up straight and repositioned his hair like I'd put it before—all swept back and tucked behind his ears like a prince from a fairy tale. Hopefully one that wouldn't scare Leander into bending the blood beneath our skin.

"I'll play nice. Just for you."

Chapter Thirty-Three
Aeden

"Back so soon?" Leander purred his question as he looked both Paige and I over, drawing everyone's attention to us the moment we stepped back into the bar.

It was an odd feeling—being able to hold her hand like *this*. One I'd longed for and dreamt about for entirely too long. The glimmer in her eye hadn't snuffed out when she glanced up at me, but the moment they turned to Leander, they were full of daggers, sharp and vicious.

That's my girl.

"We need answers." There's that *we* again. Fuck, it was taking everything and then some to not drag her back outside and take her against that wall she'd been eyeing. I'd never felt so satisfied yet unsatiated in the same go. My heart exploded every time she looked at me, every time her hand pulsed in mine.

The rest of my body was still tumbling over that ledge.

If Varasyn had any complaints, she was being oddly silent about them.

"You both, huh?" The room went still. Watching, waiting. Taking in the way we stood so united now. I knew exactly what Eoghan would say if he weren't so enthralled in the sight, his cheeks and Ikelos'...damn near all of them, were pinked over from the banter and alcohol, as if that's all it would take to form this alliance we so desperately needed.

"Yes. Whatever you need to say, you can say it to both of us." I kept my eyes to her, watching her small frame take up so much space next to me. She was all I could see and all I wanted next to me.

Screw everyone else in this room.

I knew the moment her eyes caught onto her brother's because that angry, power-filled gaze softened just slightly enough to not alert him. The slight nod he gave to her out of the corner of my still-trapped eyes flashed by quickly—a silent talk between the two of them that warmed my heart all over again.

"That soft heart of yours won't last a minute in a battle," Vara scoffed.

I lifted my head, prying it from the woman who stole every ounce of power within me, and found Leander standing not more than two feet in front of us. I hadn't noticed him moving, let alone heard him approaching.

Vara was right. The very idea sent a giddy sensation through my mind that wasn't coming from me, because Vara was laughing at me.

I scowled.

"We're all going back to the house," Ikelos said as he stood, Eoghan and the rest following him up. Eoghan stretched wide, wrapping an arm around Ikelos' waist and tugging him closer.

"Is there a house left to go back to?" Eoghan, the presumptuous asshole I now considered a friend, questioned as his eyes fixed on our hands and where our fingers were connected. A force of air whipped through the room, sending Eoghan's face to the side with a harsh slapping sound. My lips curved up as I looked down at her.

My girl.

My Queen. My storm.

Leander tossed his head over his shoulder. "Sure is. They cleaned it up last night, save for the single guest room upstairs." My blood boiled at the idea of him knowing that. But the small hand that pulsed in mine urged me to simmer the hell down. "They made quite the mess up there."

Which I tried for all of about two seconds. Before I knew it, I had Leander pinned to the ground with my hands keeping his limp wrists firmly to the sides.

"You saw and heard nothing. I don't know what the fuck happened to you to make you think watching people is okay. But the only reason you are alive is because we need you to be. The second that stops being true"—I lifted his wrists then slammed them against the floor—"I'm going to burn a hole right through your fucking skull and feed whatever is left to my dragon." I heard a woman's gasp, possibly Shay's. "Do I make myself clear?"

Leander grinned widely up at me. "Pristinely."

A tug on my shirt pulled me up and back, not forcefully but I knew it was her. She wrapped her arm around mine and looked up at me, not at all hiding the singular word that was written all over her face. *Idiot.* Yet, she smiled. She loved it when I played rough, though she'd probably never admit it.

Eoghan yawned dramatically, breaking the silence. "We won't touch your room," he said to me, then turned to Seamus. "But we will take a couch. Or a cot. Something. Shay's house was devoid of…everything. Seems it was raided." He eyed Paige. So, they hadn't found what Murrie needed.

The shrug Paige gave was done sloppily. She cared because she wanted to remember me. To have everything back that her father had taken from her.

Leander made his way back to the table as the bar cleared out. Plates of food settled down along the same table in front of two empty seats across from where he sat. "Sit."

And that scowl returned, even as Paige's hand squeezed on mine the entire way to our directed seats.

"Yes. Just like your father. Not fond of taking direction, not very good at making friends, either." His green eyes, so different from the warmth of Paige's, settled on me like venom.

"I don't want to hear about him first. Start with Dream Walkers. What do you know?"

"Aeden," Paige said sternly. "You deserve to know more about your parents than I do about my gift." Her brows furrowed. "I can wait."

"Patience is a beautiful thing, dear. That's very kind of you." He studied us, watching each movement and each shift like we were nothing more than lab rats. Fire blazed beneath my flesh, begging to be released.

"I love him." No waiver in her voice, no crack in those words. She meant it and felt it so truly. Like she was stating a fact—like how many daggers were lining her clothes right now. And all the rage left my body. Every ounce. Every speck that would have burned the walls. Gone.

"*Soft,*" Vara chided in. I reached for that wall, that thread I'd found and pulled on the night before, and gave it a slight tug in warning, eliciting a growl that rumbled through my thoughts.

"Eat up, go on. It's not poisoned, I promise." His hands shooed us along the table. I pushed my plate forward. She sighed through her nose as she took up the fork in her hand. I reached for her hand and held it there on the table and her brows crinkled in aggravation.

"Why would you point that out?"

Leander rolled his eyes. "Because she was poisoned. I wouldn't need poison to kill you, so why would I try hiding it in the food."

I stood, taking both plates and walking them over to the bar. "The only thing she's going to eat will be made by me." Then I walked to the back and got to cooking. I could see Paige's annoyance—the way her eyes turned to fine slits as she watched me prepare food from behind the small cutout just beyond the bartop. The way her beautiful head shook every time I glanced up at her, checking on her to make sure she was still sitting there. After a few minutes of sitting in silence, I watched Leander's lips start to move, and then Paige's.

I'm not sure what was said, but her face went starkly pale. The tapping of her foot stopped, and her arms where they'd been crossed tightly over her chest before, they were now bracing her weight on the bench. Her fingers curled over the edge of the seat and her lips rolled, but she refused to look at me.

No matter how much warmth I sent across her body, no matter how much my power reached for her. She didn't glance once.

I finished in the kitchen as quickly as I could, settling back in with two new plates of vegetables I'd just grown in the back. "Sorry, this is all I could do with what's back there." Which was absolutely nothing. The kitchen had been wiped clean. The salad Leander tried to coax us to eat sat on the edge of the bar, mocking me with whatever meat lay on top of it. "I'll go hunting later." I slid my hand into hers, but her fingers stayed splayed apart.

My chest plummeted into my stomach. "What did you say to her?"

Rage had always been a pesky bitch. Rearing its ugly head at the turn of a hat. And here she was again, morphing Leander into nothing more than what I'd done to Ash, the pile-of-nothing guard.

"She asked about my ring." Leander lifted his hand, letting the hedonium flash in what remained of the sunlight that crept through the holes in the wooden walls. "So, I told her about it."

"The oath ring," I clarified.

"Yes, my oath to your mother." He tapped the flame in the center. "One line for the Stars, one for myself, and one for her."

"Aeden." She turned to me, frail looking and small. So small. So...hurt.

I turned protective, unsure if I wanted to know what oath had made Paige so pale. She looked defeated, and it was eating me alive. "I told you to tell her—"

"Well, I asked!" she snapped at me, just as a loud banging sound erupted in the bar. Each flame and faelight went out and a shout that sounded like our names being called through the walls filled the space between Paige and I.

"Fuck." Leander stood and picked up his cloak, throwing it over himself and running to the door.

"Paige, get back."

"I will do no such thing. You can't...it needs to..." Her brows lowered as she pulled out two daggers, spinning them in her palms as she stood from the table. "Just. Stop. Please." Her eyes rolled up to the ceiling as another crash sounded, taking out a chunk of the back wall. Wood pieces flew in every direction. I pushed her shoulder down, forcing her to the ground with me. Another blast sent pieces against the air shield she put around us.

"Good thinking," I breathed as I reached to my back for the sword sheathed there.

"I told you before I am more than capable."

"Fuck! You two need to get over here!" Leander shouted from the doorway. "I told you the war never ended." He continued muttering to himself as his body swayed in and out of the swinging doors.

"Come on." Her hand jerked back from me when I reached for it. Just like she'd done in Prydia.

"Aeden!" Vara shouted, sending a too-heavy pulse of anger and concern through my mind. I put my rejected hand to my temple.

"What's out there, Vara?"

Paige tugged on my shirtsleeve and then bolted to the door to stand behind Leander. I followed further behind her, the air shield no longer spanning me. A bang and then a thud sent me to the ground, the impact from a wooden shard turning the floorboards into several pieces beneath my unsteady feet.

Leander ran back to help me up with Paige tailing behind him. It was possibly the rattling of my mind that made her look like she was hesitating to help me. That's what I told myself.

She loves you.

I told her I was always the optimist in this relationship, but lately, that was a lie. And the universe was taking those doubts and slamming them in front of us. Reveling in the way it made my body weak and my mind numb.

"Are you okay?"

"Yep. Are you close enough to tell me what you see?"

"It's an army. Small. I see hags, smell the naga. That must be wraiths, and Prydian—"

"Stay the fuck back!" I shouted to Vara as I crouched down on one knee, trying to regain my balance. Paige flinched as she reached my side, and I leaned into her as she tried to steady me.

Her eyes flashed up to the sky. "He's talking to her," she said to Leander, clarifying who my assault was for. "Get up, Aeden. They're everywhere." I stayed down, slipping my hand up to cradle her cheek. She rolled her eyes. "We don't have time for this."

Leander ran back to the door, his wrists unmoved but the sounds and gurgles beyond those doors—he was bending them. Their blood. My eyes flashed beyond those doors briefly, taking in the way the snow was turning red.

"I love you. Whatever he said to you, know that you are everything to me. Without you, I am nothing."

"Aeden—" Leander bound through the doors, sending them into a flurry of back and forth movements just as another chunk of wall came scattering through. Only this time, an air shield made the shards rebound back away from me. From us.

Her eyes narrowed on me, then she hauled me up with her. She started taking her daggers back out from wherever she stashed them before as she supported some of my weight beside her. "I'm"—her eyes darted to the doors, then back to me. "I love you, but"—Paige's brother rushed in beside her, taking her somber face in his hands.

But.

"I'm so happy you're safe." I gave Ikelos a nod, which he returned as the doors swung open forcefully and snapped off the hinges, revealing a massacre in the making. Eoghan stood beyond the threshold, his arm outstretched to the red snow beneath his feet, stepping aside for me to join. The shouting intensified outside beyond the walls, Murrie's grunts and the slicing of metal through skin and scales drowning under the weight of her words.

I love you, but...

But, what?

"You have your blades?" Ikelos asked his sister, and when she nodded, I realized he was asking because he wanted her to join them. Outside. With the bloodshed and the things that would try to capture and kill her.

My jaw ticked as my body moved to support itself fully, but I kept my mouth shut. She was strong, capable. Better than me in most aspects. But my body was warring with the idea. She *could die.* My teeth ground uncomfortably as I bit my tongue.

I gave Paige and her brother one last look, my hand reaching up to cup her cheek as I gave a single nod before bending down and brushing my lips to her forehead. And then I took off through the doorway, joining Eoghan on the battlefield.

Chapter Thirty-Four
PAIGE

"Over here!" The screeching. The curdling screams of terror. And blood. So. Much. Blood.

"Quickly!" I rushed to Shay's side, the blood on her hands thankfully not hers, or the man's beside her who wore a deep purple tunic. Prydian guard. I raised my dagger. "Not him!" she shouted. "Them!" her finger pointed toward a pack of naga, at least five or more, all on their way to Murrie. Her battle-ax slashed through the air, slamming down on the body of a wraith over and over to no avail.

Wraiths are not alive, yet not quite dead. The best way to kill a wraith is to burn their translucent bodies, and—

And then there he was. Aeden's rippling form slid into the dirt, dodging the axe Murrie had slung to kill the wraith closest to her. As he slid, his wrist maneuvered ever so slightly, igniting the wraith into flames. But his focus moved on to the other wraiths that had taken notice as he righted himself up from the ground.

The entire town had come alive with all the wrong things. Including an army of at least fifty guards, all armed and ready. Leander was right. The war...

"Help him!" Shay shouted as she pushed my arm away from her. "I'll gather more men. Don't worry about them. Go help Aeden."

Aeden.

Aeden Fireborne, son of Savaria and Rennick. Dragon Heir. Bonded to...not just Varasyn.

He didn't need my help. He was quite literally born to protect and kill. His entire purpose—wasted on me. Flames roared beside me as I ran right past where he was taking down more wraiths, letting their cries and screams fill the giant space between us that I lengthened by running.

Right into the naga.

Their hissing sounds grew as they flanked, shoulder-to-scaly-shoulder. I readied the two blades in my palms, not wasting a single breath on letting them have the first move. I continued to run, throwing both with precision into the one right in the middle. Right through the heart with both blades crossing through its skin, the hilts bouncing as its body slumped to the ground.

I flicked my wrist to free my blades and return them to my waiting palms, then turned quickly, aiming to run around the entire pack to turn them away from where Aeden was fighting.

I love you. But...

But I probably shouldn't.

He was all that I could think of as more blood and flames filled the battlefield that had once been Costa. I had let myself become consumed with him. And I knew it was a dangerous game to play—the game where my heart could smash into a thousand pieces right as it finally came together.

But that's what happened when Leander said those words. That ring. The flame. His mother.

How could she do that?

I clutched the daggers tightly in my hands, and when I went to throw one again, Varasyn dipped down and took up the two naga I was aiming for between her teeth. Their bodies fell in mangled pieces further down the road where the houses grew thin and less numbered. Where there were already several other bodies, not far from where Seamus' wall of ice was letting hags slowly trickle into his space.

He'd be depleted soon with the size of that wall and the power he was undoubtedly using behind it.

I stopped running and turned, my chest burning with the cold air that filled my lungs. I pushed my daggers back into their sheaths and held my palms up toward the sky. Something brewed deep within me—a storm of wind and hail, a force greater than I thought I'd ever be able to harness.

"Seamus!" I shouted back over my shoulder as the final few naga drew closer to me, their legs bloody and ripped with big holes that resembled what a spear would do.

Or Vara's tail.

"Seamus, you need to run!" Yet his icy wall grew in response, using more and more energy to not shield himself from them, but to shield the ones that were inside from us.

He was going to die.

He was going to die.

I let the storm grow, letting lightning and hail and wind erupt from the swirling clouds that dipped low above the town. My brother was shouting my name from somewhere near the hill, but I had to focus. The nagas started to sway on their injured legs as the wind took hold of them, ripping them up from the snowy ground and throwing their bodies over by where Vara was aiding Aeden with the other side of Seamus' icy shield.

My world stilled—watching him. The cold breath I took was threatening me with dizzy spells as the storm above my head grew and grew and—

It wasn't the ice or the snow that was making me dizzy. It could have been the way I wanted to run to Aeden, to save him, and help him and Seamus with those last few hags that were crawling…all of them crawling and covering the sphere of ice, reaching for them both and…

My palms shook with the wind. Large drops of hail fell onto the empty ground, plunging into the pillowy snow. The divots were coated in red where the hail struck—blood and ice and snow and wind.

My hair whipped violently over my eyes, but through the strands, all I saw was *him*. My legs grew weak, more shouting sounded around me as Shay held onto her men further down the line of houses that were being torn apart, all of them holding her down to…protect her. Shielding her from the things that were being taken up by the storm, and I…

I heard my name.

But my vision landed on him.

Every time.

I shouted for him. Called his name as the rest of my body became numb. My knees grew cold, covered in the bloody snow I'd fallen in. Warm black leather encompassed my body before blackness was all I could see.

"Do you think—"

"No. She's—"

Crackling shot into my head, and my body jerked in response, matching the sound.

"Shhh. I'm here." Warmth replaced the cold I was shaking against. And softness. So soft.

I peaked through hooded eyes, sending more sharp pains through my head. "It...it hurts."

"I bet it does. You officially depleted yourself. Almost fucking died. Congratulations, Princess."

I heard a rustling sound, then was surrounded by a familiar bend and curve of a warm, soft, yet hardened body against me. I inched closer, each one of my limbs and every inch of skin screaming in agony, but settling when his arm wrapped around me.

"Don't listen to him." Aeden's hand slid down, finding my hand that also felt shattered and broken. Another set of hands covered my back and shoulders, sending another familiar sensation through me.

"Nya?" I tried to turn, but my body cried out harder at the movement.

"You might want to stay still, Lass." *Seamus. He lived.*

Another hand landed somewhere around my ankle, but no hands felt anywhere near as comforting as Aeden's.

Because that's exactly what his body was supposed to do.

I tried my luck with shifting away from him, but his grip on me hardened.

"Let me go, Aeden." My voice was hoarse and broken. But it had nothing on the way my heart was battling with itself over the one wrapping his warmth around me.

His nose nuzzled in by my ear. "I've been here every night since you wiped out. I'm not going anywhere."

Every night?

Leander wandered over, his green flashing against the fire blazing in front of us. We were outside, under the scrutiny of the stars. "You almost missed the entire Winter Solstice celebrations there, dear." He slid in like we were friends or something, sitting just behind Aeden.

"Go away," Aeden said before I had a chance. "You're going to make it worse."

I wondered, after days of my absence, if he knew *why* that statement was more true than anything else said so far.

"Paige!" My hand jumped up to cover my ear at the loud sound of my brother's shouts from wherever he was, which was then quickly replaced by Aeden's, curling over my ear like a protective bubble.

Of course, he'd try to protect me there, too.

I squinted again, opening my eyes enough to see white and grey flashing behind Aeden and beside Leander. "You were out for five days. We really thought you wouldn't fully wake up, and I'm—" Ikelos' voice stifled as a single tear slid down his cheek. Eoghan grabbed him from behind, wiping the tear away and cradling him to his chest.

My heart sank to my stomach looking at the way it was so easy for them. It would never be like that for Aeden and I. I thought it finally could be, but maybe I was wrong. Maybe he didn't love me like he thought he did.

But being this close to him, with his arms around me, wasn't helping. It was making me feel selfish—knowing he was practically born to be my protector. He was this way because he had to be.

Not because he wanted to be.

The gold in his eyes sparkled against the crackling flames behind me as he looked down at me. He planted a soft kiss to my forehead and my power surged to the exact spot like it was fiending for him—like he was my drug, and I was the crippling addict that needed just a drop. Anything he'd give. Because soon enough, he'd know.

Leander would tell him, and he'd never be able to really love me again. And before that could happen, I was breaking my own heart in the process.

His hand trailed up to brush my hair behind my ear. "I could die in those green eyes of yours right now. I'm so happy you're awake." *Push him away!*

I darted my eyes from him, aiming them up to the stars to stop the water that welled behind them. "Where are we?" I became overly preoccupied with the trees that danced above us, noting the lack of snow beneath us.

North.

"We wanted to bring you back to Hydrasel, but Gedeon would have gone there. Shay was able to convince the men that had survived to go back and say nothing happened. But that won't last forever."

"So..." I swallowed, and mustering up the little strength I had, I pushed up onto my elbow. The world shifted, but Aeden put his arm up, letting me use him to steady myself. I leaned back away from him, letting the dizziness settle.

There were pieces of stone littering the dirt. Chunks of evenly-cut rock and smaller pieces of rubble dotting the ground. I looked to my brother, possibly with too much worry and confusion written all over my face because his contorted before he shuffled back, giving me a better view of...

Ruins.

Wingbeats sounded above us, and seconds later, the ground rumbled under my hip. Had the ground always rattled that hard when she landed?

She landed?

"Aeden..."

"Home, Paige. We're home."

Chapter Thirty-Five
Aeden

"She knows, doesn't she." I let my eyes flicker up and over the fire, taking in her soft curves, pouty lips, and the way she'd fallen back to sleep shortly after eating and drinking as much as she could. She didn't stay awake long, but it was enough to ease the pounding in my ears that had built to an uncomfortable crescendo.

The fear of losing her while she slept, her will to live battling with her weakened body, caused me to lash out. A lot. Over the past five days I went between yelling and fighting with anyone that tried to get near her or disturb her, to pacing beside her and cradling her against me into the late hours of the morning. The only person I let go near her was Nya, who pushed her healing efforts into her to suppress her body's need for water or food—both of which were hard to give to someone who only woke up for a minute or two at a time.

"Knows what?"

I rolled my eyes over to Leander, who was sitting on an adjacent stone. Eoghan was to my right, fighting the urge to do what Ikelos was doing on the other side of the fire not far from Paige and stiffening his back each time his eyes began to give out.

"You told her whatever oath it is you had with my mother."

"Have." He wagged his fingers from where he sat hunched over his knees. "I *have* an oath with her. Her death doesn't cancel that out."

"What is it then? Spit it out."

He sighed out through his mouth, exhaling louder than necessary. I glared at him, hoping some part of his body would give under the fold he was doing over his knees. A burst of air would surely do the fucking trick.

"Before you were born, while still in the womb, your mother needed help with a deal. With her mother." He jutted his chin to Paige, then reached up to scratch along his jaw. "Sav never asked much of me, so when she came to me needing my help, I couldn't refuse her." He looked off to the distance as his nickname for my mother went on repeat like a broken record in my mind.

"Sav? So you were friends with her, too. Not just my father." He rolled his wide lips in and started playing with the ends of his black cloak. "More than friends."

He dropped the cloak and rolled his neck to me. "No. She never wanted me like that."

"But you wanted her?" Eoghan asked, suddenly more awake than he'd been before. "You thought if you made an oath and did what she asked, she'd love you, didn't you?"

Eoghan chuckled beside me as my gaze hardened on Leander. His fingers picked up the cloak again, toying the ends like Paige would do with her hair when she was nervous or anxious or deep in thought.

"You loved my mother?"

He halfway shook his head, then sighed again. "I thought I did." His eyes skated over to where Nya and Seamus slept up against a tree, their legs spread out on the dirt. "But, no. She was a true friend. And that is *all*."

"A friend you blurred the lines with," Eoghan piped in, pointing his finger at him with a smirk toying on his lips. "You wanted to fuck her, didn't you?"

Leander stilled and dropped the cloak once more as his eyes promised a swift death to Eoghan. "It would be wise not to push the subject further."

Eoghan's hands went up, nudging into me purposefully. I didn't bother shifting my focus. In place of the temporary repetition of *Sav*, the same one that had plagued me for days rang above all else.

Such simple, three letters, coming together to try to end me. To end *us*.

And I thought *can't* was going to be my biggest hurdle of the week.

"Just tell me what the oath was. What did you say to her?" If I thought I sounded wounded before, that sentence just took the cake. Eoghan cleared his throat and glared at Leander, ready to goad him further into submission if he didn't speak.

"I told her the truth."

"Which would be..." Eoghan swirled his hand in the air.

Leander stood up and circled to the back of where he had been sitting, then planted his palms down on it before meeting my eyes. "That you are bonded by blood to protect her."

Vara's head shuffled somewhere in the distance behind me, probably stirring awake from the pounding taking place in my stomach from where my heart had sunken to. *Bonded*. "Bonded by whose blood?"

Leander rolled his eyes again like this was a simple thing to understand. Well, fuck me. I thought I was human months ago. "Your blood, of course. Technically, your mothers blood *and* yours from where you were in the womb. And Celine's as well."

"It would be great if you could tell me the entire story."

"I told you what you asked to know—what I told her. But since you are asking so nicely..." He stood up and cracked his fingers, pushing them out toward the fire as they locked together. I wanted to break each of those fingers slowly, one by one, and let his screams echo through the ruins and beyond.

We need him as an ally. My eyes roamed over her sleeping form once more. We had become a *we*. Instead of breaking his fingers, I pushed my hands between my legs and waited, letting the seconds tick between my ears.

"Story time, gents." He swung his leg back over, straddling the block of stone that at one point supported my home. "You see, twenty some-odd years ago, Savaria was approached by Celine. In secret. They met up because Celine claimed she had vital information for your mother about the battle that was to come. She knew her husband was going mad—he frequently visited a seer in Fireborne territories, and he was told a prophecy that would end him and his reign." He moved to draw his knees to his chest. "That's where the story gets interesting."

"This isn't a fucking bedtime story. These are real people. Act like it." At least I was using my words, not my fists or my power. It would be so much easier to sear the side of his face.

He straightened up, trying to tower over me like this was all child's play. How my mother and father ever tolerated him was beyond me. "I am fully aware that they are people. Were people. But it's better if I tell it like a fairy tale so"—his knuckles turned a few shades paler against his cloak as he started fisting into it—"so I don't react."

Eoghan's brows lowered and mine did the opposite. This man was crazy. It was confirmed now.

"Anyway. As I was saying. The story gets interesting here." His eyes glazed over between the two of us. Eoghan—the much more empathetic of the two of us because he was forced to be by the Stars—returned the look with a muddled one of sympathy.

Poor bastard.

"Her father was told an eerie prophecy that sought to end him, and he kept going back for more information. Each time he went, he would become more crazy about it. I'm not saying he was the best of men before his obsession took him, but he wasn't necessarily bad, either. He was much better than his father ever was, until your father's seed took root and that seemed to shift all of Aellethia on its axis. And what a sturdy tree you turned out to be, may I add."

"So, just so we are clear here, you didn't love his mother, but you loved his father?" Eoghan smirked at him, goading him further. Far enough to draw a snarl out of our earth-wielding ally.

"Rennick was a *friend*. I've bedded countless women *and* men in my thousand years, but never either of them."

I glared at Eoghan before turning back to Leander. "He missed the Solstice, pay no attention to him."

Eoghan scoffed. "At least *someone* in our group took advantage of it."

I glanced back at my sleeping girl, hoping I'd get to see another time with her like we were that night. Hoping I'd have her beautiful thighs wrapped around me as I pushed deep into her, waiting for her to tell me she loved me as I made her see stars over and over again. No buts, or can'ts.

After what Leander had told her, she must've felt like I lied to her. Like I'd known about this through some book I'd read or that scroll I found and it had all been my fault that she didn't know about it before. I could almost hear the questions I'd have thrown my way, but I'd answer them all with complete honesty. I'd do nothing less than that for her.

I cleared my throat. "What...what happened when Celine went to my mother?"

"Celine came and offered her knowledge of the warpath they were to take—his strategies, the way he was building his forces without notifying any other kingdoms. She knew what was coming because of the young seer, who I am now discovering was that boy there."

Eoghan shook his head immediately. "No. No. Ikelos and I tell each other everything. He never said he did that."

Leander cocked his head. "Do you remember what you did when you were, oh...perhaps four at the time? I think that's about how old the original heir to the Prydian throne was then, if I'm not mistaken."

"He would remember doing that." Eoghan looked over at Ikelos, who was now sound asleep like his sister still was.

"Ask him. By all means, do ask the boy. I'd love to include him the next time I tell the tale of the blood bond."

"Blood bond?" Vara questioned, her head lulling again on the ground and her tail curling in further around where her wings had settled.

"Guess I was right about some kind of connection."

Her voice was laced with concern as she filled my thoughts. *"I've never heard of a blood bond."*

"Celine gave that all to Savaria in exchange for one simple thing." He fanned his hands out toward me, flashing a boyish grin. "You."

The tips of my fingers pressed into the space between my brows. "My mother gave me to Celine is what you're saying." The singular time I'd felt consumed by love, starting to move from right under my feet. Just like I'd been waiting for. And whenever Paige was back on her feet again, I'd have that rug fully yanked from me.

I love you, but...

Love had been but a temporary blip for me.

"For lack of a better way to describe it, yes," Leander said.

My vision turned to a thin line as my eyes narrowed on him. "Come up with a better way to describe it," I growled.

"Fine." He picked his cloak back up, studying the frayed edges. "Savaria had nothing else to exchange that Celine wanted—she was a simple woman. Had no need for wealth or riches. Didn't want refuge from her soon-to-be madman of a husband. But the young seer told her, in private, that she was to have his sister and the one thing she wanted, above all else, was for her daughter to be safe. She was a mortal living in this world and saw what growing up in a High Fae household was like more than likely because of Ikelos. So, Savaria traded Celine's knowledge for the protection her son could provide to Celine's unborn child." He tsked, looking over at Paige. "Not even in the belly yet and Paige was already planned for and taken care of. I formed the oath between Savaria and Celine, sealing it with your blood."

We are bound by birth, of fire and blood. That was how Vara described our bond. The one I shared with my dragon. But it seemed more and more like that was also my bond with Paige, our blood fused before birth, filling us both with a fire we couldn't put out.

Paige murmured my name in her sleep, drawing me over to sit beside her. I stroked my hand down the length of her marked arm, feeling that same surge of power flooding to the surface.

Blood bond. "What about our power? Why does it feel so...connected? Is that the blood bond then, too?"

Eoghan had been silent for a while now, but his expressions spoke volumes. He draped his head into his waiting hands as his arms propped up on his knees. He reached around to the back of his neck, then glanced at Leander, waiting for him to continue. To fill me in on what I was still so clueless about.

"Connected...hmm," Eoghan murmured, then glanced up at the Stars.

I probably shouldn't have wanted to know anything further. Any other thing that could potentially make Paige look at me differently than how she was starting to all over again. Anything more that I'd have to think twice about sharing with her, turning me into a dishonest man to the only woman I cared to be honest with.

She used to love me, *but* she couldn't let me in anymore.

She used to love me, *but* she didn't need me like I needed her.

She used to love me, *but* the Stars made her sleep with me.

She used to love me, *but* I was just fun for the night.

It never bothered me to hear that last one before. But, with her? With her, I wanted it all. Love. A home. A family. A future. She wouldn't need to ever question where my loyalty was. That had always been the way I felt around her—like we belonged together.

And it wasn't because of some fucking blood bond.

"Yes. Connected. When we get close, I can *feel* her power, ebbing into mine." Vara sent a ripple of calm through me, making me drop the twisted ends of Paige's hair from my fingers. She'd been quiet ever since I'd sat down beside her. So I went back over to where I was before, needing this conversation to end, so I could lay next to Paige before she'd stop allowing me to. Although judging by the way she told me to get away from her when she woke up, I was thinking we might already be there.

"I sometimes feel that with Ikelos as well, but..."

"But, what?"

"You felt this before you slept with her I take it?" Eoghan asked.

I swiped my hand down the length of my face. "Yeah."

"I only feel that when we...fuck. Usually peaking around the Winter Solstice. Which is part of the reason it is so...intoxicating to partake in it."

Peaking. I glanced back at her. *Peaking* was hardly the word I would use to describe the way our power mixed when I had her moaning so loud, the icy walls shook.

"It's probably because your blood is shared. Bonded blood and all," Leander said as if it were so widely known. My mouth wasn't the only one popping open.

"So this lucky dick gets to feel not only the strength of his own power, but hers as well?" He nudged into my shoulder. "Way to go. Here I was thinking you were so much more because of that dragon over there, but no. Now, I'm envious of that. And her power must be"—he kissed his pinched fingers—"top. You saw what she did in Costa."

Paige rolled to her other side, her arm swinging out from under the blanket and brushing the dirt along the ground, like she was looking for something.

"Her power isn't what makes me want to be near her."

Leander wiped his thumb along his lip. "No, but that blood bond will keep you close-by." *Close-by.* Like how I chose the house right next to her based on a *feeling* and a strong desire to run from my situation at the time. Like how I fought to get back to her when we were separated. The first may have been caused by the blood bond, but the way I needed to get back to her, to *be* with her in the ways I wanted to be?

That was all me.

"How can I break it?" Leander's head went so cocked, it looked like it was set to roll along the stone-ridden dirt. Eoghan let out a low whistle and swept his gaze over to Paige.

"Break it?" Leander asked, his head less than an inch from being parallel with the ground. "Why ever would you break it?"

"Because she wouldn't want to be bonded to me." The answer came out before I had time to process it. But it was true. She'd never let someone else decide her fate for her, and being bonded to me by blood was the definition of a fate sealed. I'd always be there for her, with a blood bond or not, and I'd always love her. But she wouldn't see it the same way.

She'd lose her Starsdamned mind knowing we were tethered together. That yet again another force was at work beyond what she wanted and what she was set to do. She didn't think I was concealing this all from her. She simply didn't want the Stars telling her what to do when she had a strong mind of her own.

And I wouldn't stand in her way. Maybe it was another way this bond worked—that I had to protect her, even if it meant from myself. I could blame the rush of insanity on that alone, at least.

"There is something we commonly turn to here for answers, though it usually just makes you blasted and worn for a week straight until you forget what it was you were so keen on fixing," Leander suggested, his neck straight as an arrow and his eyes wide with the idea rolling on through that murky head of his.

Something was very off with him.

No, screw that. A lot was off with him.

Eoghan chuckled into his fist, then made an exasperated sound as he breathed in through his gaping mouth. "You can't be serious. Pixie dust? We just tried to find that. Shay was tapped, and the pixies hate me, so I don't have any."

"So, go to Forga," Leander said as he shrugged.

"Forga. Where guards from every kingdom are free to roam, seeing as Vizna"—Eoghan spread his arms wide, directing our attention to the ruins of my home—"and its wards fell over two decades ago!" Eoghan laughed again, this time making Paige's head snap up to us from where she had been asleep on the ground. "Yeah, that sounds real fucking safe, seeing as all of Prydia's guards are bound to know that we are all working together by now." Leander opened his mouth, but it snapped shut as Eoghan added, "And we can't send you to Forga, disguised as a simple earth-wielder like you've been doing for fuck-knows how long. You're half here, half "—he swirled his hand by his temple—"elsewhere. I doubt Aeden or anyone else here wants to trust you to gather it for us." Never in my life since I'd been here did I ever envision a day I'd be okay with hearing Eoghan defending me and claiming my issues were an *us* type of thing.

Damn, I think we might actually be friends now.

"Actually, he's the only one I'd be okay to send." Because I didn't give a damn if he returned. He was unstable, and killed maybe ten guards before he fled from the fight, while Seamus and I were drowning in hags. If it hadn't been for Paige and the size of her storm that whipped and threw half the army in one go, we'd be a smaller group.

Seamus would be gone. Murrie, possibly, as well. We came so close to having multiple casualties on our hands, and that was all changed. Because of her.

"What do you need at Forga?" Her sleepy voice cut through me, right down to wherever my heart had found its new home deep in my gut. She sat up, stretching her arms wide, then narrowed her eyes. Right on me.

"Nothing," Eoghan and Leander said at the same time.

I glared at them, then looked back to Paige, who quickly stole every bit of my attention. "Pixie dust." Eoghan nudged into me at my truthful answer, and I could feel the heat of her eyes dance between the two of us, honing in on us both. "It's the ingredient Murrie was looking for. But it could also be helpful in fixing the um…"

"He wants to get rid of the bond." Leander stood and yawned, stretching wide then waltzing over to lay down right where Paige still was. "I assume you no longer need this set up, my dear?" he asked, looking down at her.

She was on her feet faster than he could try to squeeze in and steal her blanket from her. Snoring erupted from his mouth instantaneously and Paige glared down at the Mora who'd just stolen her resting space.

"What do you mean get rid of the bond?" She chewed on the corner of her lip as she moved to sit on the other side of Eoghan, leaving the space next to me cold and empty.

"Get rid of it. End it." My legs started bouncing. "I owe Hyacinth a favor, but what's one more?"

"You *would* owe her a favor. I hope what you got was worth the trade," Eoghan said.

"It was." I paused, trying my best not to overthink every possible thing that could go wrong in seeking out Hyacinth again. But it needed to be done. Unless… "Are there other pixies?"

Eoghan laughed and shook his head as he looked down at the ground. "Nope. Her and her hoard are it. But her domain used to be Vizna, not…where was it that you found her?"

"The Highland Woods."

"Man." His hand clapped on the back of my shoulder and Paige's eyes narrowed on me further from beside him. I wanted to reach over and put her in my lap, where she belonged. "You've got it so bad. Did they warn you about that place?"

"You didn't warn me about the Hollow Woods." I slid my hand into my hair, ending at the nape of my neck. "What difference does it make? Do you know if she stays there, or not?"

"Nope. But you can ask Ikelos to try to find her however he found Paige." He bounced his palm once on my knee. "I'm going to sleep." He leaned back, pressing his palms to his knees, giving him a view of both Paige and I. "Yeah. Not sticking around for this. Goodnight."

"Asshole," Paige murmured under her breath, to which he winked back at her and kept on walking.

I scooted in toward her, not missing the way her entire body tensed up. "Are you okay? How are you feeling?" *Idiot.* I put my hand on her thigh, stilling the way it was bouncing like mine had been minutes before.

She stopped tapping and looked up at me. "I feel better. Wide awake now."

I chuckled. "Sleeping for five days will do that."

"How'd we end up here?" she asked, and when she glanced around at the ruins, it became clear she was talking about our location, not the status of what we were. If we were still a *we* in her eyes.

"Eoghan. We went to the water, took a boat out to wherever his wards began and then portaled right here." Her eyes went wide, and I knew what she was thinking. But I put up a hand. "Ikelos said we would be safe here for at least two weeks before his army would start to spread out again, and Leander is working on getting his people here discreetly. Just like Eoghan is."

"I thought we were safe with the Winter Solstice." Again, I took that as having to do with us. That her and I were safe, that we didn't ruin our hearts in the process of sleeping together. But, again, I was wrong. "But look how that ended up."

"Yeah." The silence stretched on and her teeth started working on the edge of her mouth again.

"Is it weird to not be scared of the war?"

"I don't think it is, but I'm right there with you. If anything, it's giving me a lot of energy, almost like how I used to feel before a big game." My leg started bouncing again, thinking of the bloodshed and the carnage to come. But the outcome when we claimed Prydia for her—that was where most of my focus ended up. Putting that crown where it belonged. Watching her become who she was meant to be, while I remained who I was born to be.

Hers.

"Football, you mean?" I nodded. "Do you miss it?"

"Sometimes. But I think being here is helping me cope with that loss."

"I get that." Her eyes darted down to my leg, and she put her hand on my knee, sending all of my power into a wild frenzy. "Have you tried looking for your people?"

I blinked back at her, my leg relaxing under her touch. "No, actually." I let loose a laugh. "I've been here, with you. Making sure you were okay." In truth, I hadn't thought of leaving her side once. "I thought, we all thought, you might not make it, and I couldn't leave you."

"Doesn't that bother you?"

My brows furrowed. "Bother me?" I took her hand in mine, inching my way closer and closer back into her good graces through her temporary lapse of misguided judgment. I didn't care if what we were had been planned in some backhanded way. This is all I wanted. All I needed. "Does it bother you?"

I knew the answer before she opened her mouth, but she confirmed it nonetheless with a simple *yes*. And then shook her head, seemingly unsure of herself. Fighting a battle I wanted to help her fight. Because there wasn't a single thing we couldn't conquer. Together.

"I just...I don't know. Hearing your purpose has always been to protect me. I get what you were saying now about it feeling like the marks on our skin." Her fingers dragged slowly up my unmarked arm. "You want to break it? Is that for me?"

I watched her fingers inch higher and then lower, making goosebumps form along my skin. "Yes." Her fingers stopped, so I added, "And no."

"Which one is it?"

"Both."

"Both?" Her hand retreated and I picked it up and put it right back on my arm.

"Yes, because your happiness is the most important thing to me, above the desire to protect you." Her eyebrow quirked up. She didn't believe me. "And no, because I love being connected to you." I curled my fingers around hers, feeling that connection come to life. Flooding my senses. "Like this."

I leaned into her neck, brushing my lips over that sweet spot that had her moaning. I needed to be with her like we were that night. I wanted her body as close as physically possible. I needed her everywhere, like she already was under my skin.

"Aeden..." she warned, but didn't pull back. "We should keep talking." She gasped, all breathy and full of desire and it pushed me closer to her. I wrapped my fingers around her neck, pulling her in as my lips trailed up to that perfect jawline. "We can't...we shouldn't be doing this any—" I nipped her sweetly, making her moan instead of sending her to her thoughts.

"No thinking anymore. Remember?" I whispered into her ear, brushing the tip of my nose against her neck as I moved back down. "Stars, I've missed you."

"Aeden—" Her words stopped as I scooped her into my arms and stood. Carrying her brought me back to that night in Jessup, when my fingers hesitated to move as I held her close and carried her to her bed. And then the day we were separated afterward crept into my thoughts.

Her hand reached up to the back of my neck as I continued walking away from the fire, from our allies and friends that were all sleeping and safe. I shuddered as her hand moved to the base of my skull, stopping when she reached the strands of hair by their root. She pulled and I moaned as her lips found my neck and about lost it until I sank to my knees beside another piece of rubble and ruin, where darkness swallowed us, welcoming us to our sweet, endless oblivion of want and need.

Chapter Thirty-Six
PAIGE

My lips sputtered as his knees hit the ground.

"Fuck," he muttered as he shifted me in his hold. I trembled under his hands as they moved up and over my arms, down my shoulders, trailing along my back. I pressed my palms to his face, taking his lips to mine.

This isn't what I wanted us to do, but now that I was here, it was all I could think about.

My hands reached down between us, eliciting a sharp moan from him against my neck. My hand wrapped around the outline of his thickening cock, driving him wild against me. His arms shook as they fell further down, his long fingers wrapping around my hips.

"I need to be inside of you. Please let me feel you wrapped around me, Paige." He groaned as I rubbed his cock through the thick leather of his pants and nodded.

Just like before, I couldn't deny that I wanted him. That I loved him. And then the bond started to throw a wrench into my beliefs, trying to sever the way I loved this man with every piece of my destroyed heart.

He moved his hands from me, leaving me to wrap my legs around him tighter to stay perched on his bent knees. The knees he was going to bruise, as he promised, against all the stone pieces that scattered along the dirt. His pants jostled as he worked them down, one of his arms lifting me just enough for him to push the fabric down beneath his knees, making his cock spring free between us.

I wrapped my fingers around his cock and stroked, rubbing my finger along the tip and spreading the warm precum around with my thumb as he groaned my name into my neck.

"Kiss me," I begged, and he didn't wait. His lips pressed to mine, stealing my breath as his hand found the edge of my waistband beneath my tunic. His hand slid down as his tongue worked in tandem with his fingers, rubbing the edge of my wet slit.

"Get these off. Now." So I did. I stood, lips swollen as I stared down at him and pushed my pants down. I kicked the fabric away and he smirked up at me as I repositioned myself above him.

He braced his weight on one arm, leaning back and watching me as I lowered myself back onto his lap. Slowly, I took in the way his eyes heated under my movements, pushing one knee into the dirt. A burst of air slid beside my leg, and seconds later, my pants were under my knees. Not his.

"Fist my cock. Feel what you do to me." He seethed in through his teeth when my hand wrapped back around him as my other hand tugged on the bottom of his tunic. He smirked again, straightening his back and sliding his hand back and down his neck. His tunic was gone, exposing the hard ridges of his body. It was hard to see in the darkness of the thin moonlight, but I had already ingrained the memory of him into my mind. He was a portrait I'd never surrender, never get rid of.

"You're beautiful," I whispered as I pulled my hand free of his length and trailed all ten fingers down each and every curve and sculpted muscle that flexed under my touch.

"Me?" He chuckled. Then without warning, he removed the rest of my clothing as well, so we were bare to each other. My power went into a maddening spiral, my head turning warm and fuzzy as his hand reached my breast, cupping one entirely in his wanting palm. "If I'm beautiful, what would that make you?"

"Yours." I met his gaze, our eyes locking and burning under the intensity of the darkness and desire that surrounded us. But it was more than that. It had always been so much more than that. I slid my hand down again and took him in my palm. I stroked him several times, watching him come undone with each stroke. Up, and down. Slowly, those golden flecks grew with his hooded eyes. "It makes me yours."

"Fuck. You're mine." His hand moved from my breast and covered mine, where he started to take over the movements, keeping it slow, but guiding my thumb along the thick ridge of his shaft. He moaned more, then tipped his head down to take my nipple in his mouth, where his tongue flicked the hardened tip, pulling a moan from deep within my chest.

His mouth softened around my flesh. "Lift your hips," he ordered and I pushed up, making him take my nipple harder, his teeth scraping just before his cock met my entrance.

A ripple of wind skittered through the leaves of the trees, sending a few pieces of rock and stone rolling. "My storm." Aeden chuckled against me and my brows furrowed for a moment before his cock nudged up and along my clit, sending a jolt of pleasure through me.

"Please," I begged, gripping his hair and pulling him closer to my chest. Every time his tongue flicked the tip of my nipple, another jolt went straight to my core, where he was waiting. Where *I* was waiting for *him*. I wriggled my hips, swirling his tip against me. I went to sink down, but he shifted his cock away, making my slit rub against the ridge he was guiding my thumb against minutes before.

"I need to hear those words, Paige."

"Which...which ones?" *Tell me the words, I'll say anything.* My entire body pulsed in his hands, against his lips that stayed locked on my skin between his panting and talking. And that groan of his. *I might come before he even enters me.* "I'm yours. Use me," I begged again, whimpering against the top of his head.

He shook his head against mine, his hair brushing along my pouting lips. "Not those." His fingers moved back down to strangle my hips, rocking my body against his hard cock. "Fuck, say it. I won't last much longer."

"I..." I looked up at the stars above us, noticing a steady stream of light that filtered in through the trees, landing right above my heart. "I love you." His breathing spiked against my pulse. "I love you, Aeden." I took his face in my hands, needing to kiss him. To have that connection. To have all of him. To feel there was nothing that would come between us.

He pressed into my lips, breathing shakily as he kissed me. His hands lifted me up and edged me just over him. "Please don't ever forget that. No matter what happens, we love each other. I love you endlessly, Paige. To beyond the Stars and the after. You will always have all of me."

He pushed me down, slowly, letting the stretch sink in at a torturous pace. I moaned into his kiss, my body becoming alive and alight with flames and wind in the most maddening of storms.

My knees went to push up, to make this rougher and harder like it had been before. But his grip stayed firmly on my hips as my body wriggled in his massive hands that damn near circled around me.

He broke our kiss, keeping me fully seated on him. The burn was everywhere, the sensations of being full and desperately needing to grind against him becoming overwhelming. But as he stared back at me with eyes as jaded as mine, I knew he wanted to go slower.

He wanted to make love to me.

"Touch me," I whispered. I took his hand from my hip, twining our fingers first before separating them and pulling his thumb to brush along where I needed him.

He knew how to please me, but he let me guide his thumb, letting us both stroke my sensitive bud in circles. His other hand snaked up into my hair, his fingers tightening ever so slightly. "You're tightening around me. It feels…" His voice was like the stone around us—rough and broken. "You." His finger took over as I reached up and around the top of his shoulder. "Feel." His hips started rocking gently, pushing his length in and out only a few inches as I supported my weight on my knees, where my shirt had become another cushion against the jagged stone. "Incredible. Fuck, I'm trying to go slow here. I want to savor this. Savor you."

"Then savor me." His mouth claimed mine again as we rocked together, creating the best kind of friction with his rough thumb as he pushed me further into oblivion.

"Wait." His movements stopped, his thumb replaced by warm air that settled between our warming bodies.

"Turn around."

"What?"

"Trust me." I cocked my brow at him, possibly pouting which made him smirk at me, that dimple slightly popping. "Let me make it feel amazing for you."

"It already is," I whined.

"Paige, spin." So, I did. I stood and turned around, then sat back against him, where he pushed immediately right back in, stealing my breath as he hit some magical spot at the perfect angle.

"Oh, fuck," I whispered as his arm slid around my waist, finding my clit again.

"Ride me, My Queen." His two fingers pressed and circled on my clit, matching my slow motions as I got into a rhythm. My breasts started to bounce, but his other hand wrapped around and grabbed onto one, pinching my nipple with expertly exerted pressure between his fingers. "That's it. You're getting so close. So wet for me. I fucking love it."

Yes. I moaned, tilting my head back against his shoulder as he continued stroking and thrusting. "Aeden." My hand met his jaw. "Harder. Please."

His eyes turned black as night as he looked down the length of my body, flaring wider as he took in the way my hips were swaying in his lap. His hand moved from my breast to my waist, where his fingers dug into my flesh.

"I'm yours to break," I whispered into his neck. "Break me."

"We'll be broken together, then." Instead of picking up the pace, he slowed. But with that slowing came more pressure to my clit, and then all at once, it was lost. I'm not sure if I whined about it, or if I was moaning from the sensations as his fingers slid up my skin, over the swell of my breast, and up my neck. My head stayed tilted up to the night sky in the cradle of his neck and shoulder as his hand slid further until his fingers rested just over my swollen and parted lips.

"Suck," he ordered, that gravelly, husky tone and the scent of ash and earth intensifying between us. He was close, his cock was throbbing, aching inside of me where I tightened around him. My lips parted more, accepting his fingers as he pushed them into my mouth. I let my tongue lapse at the taste of me, licking up and down the length of his fingers as I did what he ordered me to do. "Good girl. Just like that, baby. Nice and slow."

But I needed more friction and his other hand was still on my waist. So, I moved my hand, reaching down and circling two fingers, taking up the wetness between us and swirling it in place. He groaned when I reached down and stroked where we connected, where he was still watching.

I could feel the warm air around us turn to unprecedented levels. His cock swelled in me as his thrusts turned harder, like I'd asked of him. Hard and long pulses that were sending me right to the edge of insanity. His other hand moved to my waist, giving him the edge he needed to tumble me off the cliff I was teetering on. I picked up my pace along my clit just before those stars danced in my vision and my body spasmed at the wave of release. My hand started to go limp, my fingers aching to stop—

"Don't stop. Keep touching yourself." He could tell me to jump and I'd do it. I'd say *how high* and strip my clothes in the process without batting a single eyelash. I was lost to him, to *us*. My cum leaked down to his thigh as he removed his fingers from my mouth and gripped my hips once more, using the leverage to pump harder and deeper, making me moan louder and louder, prolonging my orgasm.

"So damn beautiful." With a few final thrusts, he was spilling into me as my hand worked my clit and stroked down to the base of his cock, where I could feel his pulses surrounded by my delicate flesh. He sighed into my arm where I held his jaw, turning his head to kiss my palm with sweet, delicate kisses.

"I will never tire of this." He wrapped his arms around my waist, keeping himself buried inside of me. "I could go again." Sure enough, his cock was hardening again inside of me, swelling, whereas my insides were clamping around him, still riding out the remainder of the high of my orgasm.

"I'm yours." I smiled, then guided his face back to meet my eyes. "I love you. I'm so sorry I was mean to you."

He kissed the tip of my nose. "We have a lifetime of future fights and apologies. It's nothing we won't be able to work through."

I was, in truth, very sorry about the way I'd treated him. He gave me everything, and fought against his inner urges to protect me as much as he could. But I still felt uncertain about the blood bond. Knowing he might not want me like I wanted him—what would he do if the bond broke? What would happen if—

His fingers squeezed my hips. "Remember, no more thinking. Sex is more fun with less of it."

"Huh. Is that what you did before?" Word vomit. Successfully bringing up his past experiences while I was still wrapped around him. He created such beautiful moments for us both, even when I hated him. And here I was, ready to ruin it all.

"Nothing could ever compare to you, Paige. You were meant for me." He froze as those words came out, because, yeah. He was meant just for me. Acid crept up into my throat. "Fuck. I take that back. You know...just...fuck."

I shook my head. "I know what you meant." I reached my hand back to that sweet spot, sending my thoughts to the fire that blazed between us, keeping it from destroying the moment. I stroked two fingers up his shaft, stopping where we were connected, making him shudder against my back. "Forget it."

"Forgotten." He chuckled again, warm and full of love as he nuzzled into me. "You want me again?" he whispered, moving his hands up to rest on top of my breasts, palming and cupping them.

I buried my face into his neck, swallowing down that lump of nerves and acid from those words he didn't mean to say. But, there they were. At the back of my mind. "Of course I do," I breathed, attempting to sweep it all under that formidable rug or slam it into some steel-coated box I needed to keep closed or throw out for good.

If only it were that easy.

Chapter Thirty-Seven

PAIGE

I stirred awake with the warmth of his arms wrapped around me, his still-closed eyes at odds with the way his lips were quirked into a sleepy, yet very aware, smile. The slightest hint of a dimple dipped in at the edge of his lips where they met with his cheek. I slid my arm from where it was tucked in between us, letting my thumb and each finger after dip into that groove, deepening under my touch.

"Good morning to you too, beautiful." He peeked through one eye at me, then buried his face into my neck, making me giggle. "How'd you sleep?"

I angled my head against the mossy pillow he'd made at some point in the night, or perhaps I did. I'm not sure whose power was doing what. I'm not even sure I'd slept longer than an hour. "Great. And you?"

His brow cocked up when he pulled away from my neck. "No dreams?" I shook my head. "I guess I really do stop it then, huh?" *My dreams. My sanity.* He stopped it all. But where he stopped so many things, he also brought life to so many others. More than I could count.

"It's okay. It means I sleep better." Or just not at all because I'm stuck staring at him throughout most of the night, and whenever I'd finally doze off, I'd wake again to make sure he was still there.

His brows dipped low. "Is everything okay?"

Okay? We were bonded together before either of us had a choice, with the Stars on our heels to keep that oath reflected on Leander's finger. I still had no idea why we were bonded, but I was sure his mother had her reasons. Nothing in any of the books I'd read about her and her reign, short as it was in comparison to most, pointed to her being insane. Much like I believed Leander was.

She had a reason.

"Did Leander tell you anything else about the blood bond between us?" I chewed at the edges of my lips, drawing his now two, very open eyes, to the spot.

"Yeah. He did." He shuffled into me more, tightening his hold around me like I'd run off once he started talking again. "He said your mom made a trade of sorts with my mom."

My mother knew his mother? "What...what kind of trade?"

"Well, you know how he bent our blood and bonded us together already."

I nodded and waited for his eyes to settle back on mine from where they roamed to the darkened sky above us. He pulled me in more than I thought there was room for until his chin tucked just over the crown of my head. He planted a soft kiss before settling there, the beating of his chest changing from rhythmic to thunderous.

"Celine had a line to the future, through your brother, and she found out she'd become pregnant with you. That must have scared her enough to go running to my mother, seeking protection in exchange for information about the battle your...Gedeon was planning."

"So." I swallowed thickly, suddenly needing a lot of water. Gallons of it. *My mother. She never cared that much about me.* "So, you're saying...that..." I still couldn't wrap my head around it. Were my memories lying to me? She holed herself up in her bedroom and drank herself into oblivion.

There were many days I wasn't sure she knew I existed just down the hall from her.

He relaxed his hold on me and pulled back, then tucked his finger beneath my chin, lifting my gaze back to him from where it was fixed to his chest. "She cared about you. Enough to risk her life just to save you. She loved you, Paige." Tears formed behind my eyelids and his thumb brushed just underneath the edge of them, wiping them away before they had a chance to fall. "She wanted you to be protected against him."

It was too much to think about. Too much to take in. So I shifted my thoughts to what else that all might have answers to. "I wonder...I wonder if he knew I existed, then. If Gedeon didn't know about me—"

"What difference does it make?" His voice turned dark and hollow while the space between us heated. That's what Gedeon did to him—made him want to burn shit to the ground. Made him more fiercely protective over me than I thought possible. I shifted in his hold, and then, all at once, everything cooled.

"I'm sorry, Paige. Fuck. I'm so sorry. I didn't mean it like that. I only meant...dammit."

"I know, I shouldn't have brought him up. I was just wondering if...maybe if he'd known about me, everything might be different, somehow. I know he wouldn't be much different." We'd speculated about this before, on that island when our ability to work together had been tested under the guise of *survival skills*. Damn, how the times had changed since then.

"No, he would still be the same man. And you'd still be you."

"But how did he find out about me? If my mom didn't want me to be raised by him, why even...how did they even get to the point..."

His fingers stroked up and down my bare back. We'd made moss pillows and a softened bed of it beneath us, but never once touched our clothing to use it as bedding or to cover ourselves back up. We were still naked, and that was grounding me. Possibly him, as well.

"Love can make people do some crazy things. She must have loved him, but wasn't strong enough to leave him until the threat of you actually being there hit home."

Love, can indeed, make people do some crazy things.

Like sneaking away into the middle of grown-over ruins just to be together. To forget how fucked up everything was. To just be together like our lives would end the next day. None of our days were promised to us, and judging by what had happened in the battle days ago, I wasn't sure how many days we'd have left.

His hand moved up to cup my shoulder, his large hands gentle in a way I wasn't sure people who didn't know him would ever guess him to be. "As for how he knew about you...I'm not entirely sure. Whether he knew about you when he sent you both back, or not." His lips brushed along my forehead. "He missed out on someone truly incredible." He kissed my forehead, sending shivers down like lightning to my toes. "My storm."

All the electricity left me. "What do you mean by that?" I crinkled my nose up at him. "You've called me that before. Why?"

His laugh brought those shivers back through my body. "Really?" His brow quirked up, an amused curve to it. But it wasn't funny.

"Really."

His grin spread to my mouth, though I had no idea why I was smiling. "Don't you remember what happened in Costa before you passed out?"

"I remember seeing you, and then Seamus and all those hags, and then Shay and her army of men she hypnotized to work for her instead of my father, which caught me off-guard because I thought they were hurting her. And Murrie..."

"So, you remember everyone else except for yourself, you mean." He chuckled again. "Typical."

I lightly punched his side, and he let out a pretend groan of anguish. Then just laughed again. "Seriously, tell me." My tone was anything but serious.

"My storm," he whispered against my forehead. His hand stopped stroking the channel of my spine and moved to cup my cheek. "You created a hurricane, Paige. A storm with wind and lightning and hail, and the sky turned green afterwards, like your eyes." His sparkled at the memory.

"That's a supercell."

He looked down at me with furrowed brows, but that grin was still there. "That's what you point out? Really?"

"Hurricanes don't turn the sky green," I replied. "That's a supercell."

He tsked and planted a soft kiss to the edge of my mouth, then brushed over the spot with his thumb. "You would. I tell you how incredible you are, that your air magic has grown so strong that you pushed it a step further like your brother can with his speed and Eoghan with his ice, and you choose to focus on the term I used to describe it."

"Because you were wrong." I reached up to kiss him, a quick peck to the corner of his lips because I just couldn't keep looking at his mouth without kissing him. "And you needed to be corrected."

His grin turned feral, twisting to the sides as his eyes turned heavy. "I can think of other ways you could correct me."

I lightly punched his side again. "I'm hungry."

He groaned, and as his mouth popped open to no doubt give me another quick-witted reply about how he was also hungry but for other things, my stomach grumbled between us. "See?"

He frowned dramatically as he narrowed his eyes on my stomach. "I wish we had pasta here. That's your favorite." His eyes grew wide, and he perched himself up on his elbow as he glanced around the empty, ruinous space only broken further by the trees dotted around us. "Wait."

An hour later, the sun was up and so was the steam above the boiling stone pot of water perched above the campfire. Nya was the first to wake up, followed by Leander. Thankfully, neither questioned where we had been, because I would've turned beet red just thinking about how many times we made love throughout the night.

They both sat around, awkwardly facing away from each other anytime one or the other looked toward them, sniffing the air in confusion to break their glances.

"You made pasta. Without a grinder. Looks a bit chunky." Leander cracked his neck as he looked into what passed as a pot, the steam evading him like he'd done to others for centuries. "Wherever did you find eggs?"

"You don't always need eggs. Water works just fine. Feel free to leave it for the others who don't criticize my food." Aeden moved to sit beside me, letting his power do most of the work for him. A newly-made wooden spoon stirred the noodles in the pot idly while a wooden mortar and pestle, also newly-made with his power, crushed herbs and tomatoes together. He grew everything he needed, right there where we'd slept and said it was the start to his garden he would need when he took back Vizna.

"How many of those books did you work through at Eoghan's?" I asked, sitting back watching everything work around me like he was a male version of Cinderella, if only she used power instead of adorable woodland creatures to help her. My stomach was twisting and my mouth salivating at the idea of homemade pasta, but then my intrusive thoughts kicked in and tried to justify all of what he was doing for me as simply protecting his blood-bound.

"You told me to teach you how to wield earth, so I focused on that first. What kind of teacher would I be if I had no clue what I was doing?" He'd be like me. I frequently felt like I had no clue what I was doing, even though I read through so much. Yet again, most of my focus had been on more practical things of Aellethia—the Triads, rulers, fire-wielders, the beasts we might or might not ever encounter...more fire-wielders, weapons, how to use said weapons and eventually crafting them...and again, more fire-wielders and his lineage. "I spent a few nights reading through the first three or four and then I slowed down a little to practice it all."

"Those days you went off to train elsewhere..."

He nodded. "Some of that was practice, yes. I needed a lot of space for what I wanted to make." *Some.* I still had questions about that.

His hand moved to cup my knee, while his other flicked again at his side. In seconds, a small satchel that rested near a still-sleeping Vara floated in front of us, then fell to my lap. "Open it." I did, searching with my hand but keeping my eyes on him. "You might need to look, Paige. It's not that big."

"What"—I let my hand go to the bottom of the small, leather bag, where my fingertips met with several cold, hard objects. "What is it?"

"Pull it out." He smiled down at my hand where it was still deep in the satchel. I slid my eyes over to Nya, finding her and Leander talking in hushed tones and paying absolutely no attention to us as I pulled my hand free. I turned back to my hand and gazed down at the glass jars, where muted greens and browns and reds and yellows filled the space.

"Potions?" I asked, my eyes now roaming to Murrie where she slept up against a tree close to Seamus and Shay. "Murrie is teaching you how to heal?"

He laughed, then took the glass jars from me in his large hand. He removed his other hand from my knee and lifted one of the jars against the rising sun, shaking it to loosen the leaves. "No, Paige. I have no interest in learning how to heal people, unless that *people* is *you*. And I have no intention of ever letting you reach the point where you need to be healed in the first place ever again."

"Right." I let out a weak laugh, then swallowed as I envisioned other ways his training brought him far from the mountains. We hadn't spoken much about Prydian guards leaking in through Eoghan's wards since that day, but something told me there weren't many guards who were able to leave his wards the same way after Aeden had figured out we were being hunted.

"It's tea." He pushed the jars back into my hand, then stood up and moved to the pot of boiling water that had started to splash over into the flames below. He took up the wooden ladle, and I watched in awe as he crafted prongs at the end of it with such precision. Before he could discover he had nothing to put them in, I went to work on the bowls, flashing him a wide grin as he turned his head over his shoulder at me. "She makes bowls, too." I heard him say to himself as he shook his head and smiled at me again, sending a swell of butterflies through my gut.

I couldn't remember ever feeling like I made my mother proud, and you can forget entirely ever trying to please my father or gifting him an ounce of pride. But making *him* proud? That was filling in all those spaces left by parents who never acted like they wanted me or were ever proud of what I'd done.

And he had grown tea, though I drank mortal coffee as a last resort in Jessup at the hospital, because he knew I preferred the herbal drink if I had the option.

He did it all, for me.

My face was surely going to crack permanently if my grin kept spreading as wide as it was. And then a cup of steaming water and a bowl of freshly cooked pasta and tomato sauce hovered into the space above my empty lap as he said, "If you reach back into that satchel, you'll find one of those tea things you used to use."

"An infuser ball?" I quickly reached down to where I'd dropped the bag beside me and found what he was talking about—a small, metal ball with slits all around it. "When did you get this?"

"He picked it up when I took him out of the house to get what Murrie needed in Amaliro one day. And that was *after* he started that tea garden for you." Shay stretched her arms wide by the tree, then leaned into Seamus' chest, making him shift to take her in his arm as a soft smile spread along his face.

"You..." *Flying*. That one word that aggravated me so much on Eoghan's training deck when I thought he was abandoning me and the training we needed to do was now turning me to goo. "You always said you were flying," I croaked out.

He grinned back at me. "I was. But when I landed, I practiced a lot and one of the things I practiced was...well, gardening." *Yep, definitely goo.*

"You've held onto all this for that long?"

Aeden turned with his bowl in his hand, announcing food for the others before taking a seat next to me. He shuffled in close, his breath warm along my ear as he whispered, "I've held onto more vital things for much longer than that."

I ate mostly in silence, sipping the hot tea and eating the meal he made, feeling full in more ways than one. But the thought that he was doing it all because he had to do them to keep me safe kept creeping in.

So I stood abruptly when I was done and said I had to go to the restroom—a luxurious cluster of trees in the far-off distance. He offered to walk with me, but I told him to continue eating and watch over the rest of them, assuring him I could handle myself.

I watched as that jaw ticked, just as it had when he left my brother and I before joining Eoghan in Costa. Just as it had when he found me in the water that night and told me I'd been so reckless in going out at night all alone. And that slight jaw movement followed by an uneasy and very unconvincing head nod only amplified the whole *he doesn't really love you, he just has to protect you* thought. The one I couldn't shake like my hands were starting to at my sides as I walked to the trees.

The ruins at my feet conflicted with the hooting of an owl and rustling of tree limbs as large squirrels hopped between the saplings. Vizna had been razed to the ground in the battle two decades ago, yet new life had found its way back almost unnaturally. Like an earth-wielder had a hand at recreating heavy brush and thick trees, spreading the occasional mass of flowers here and there that protruded even from stone where they were rooted to.

I didn't dare go to the same spot where Aeden created his garden. Where we slept together and made love throughout the night. I couldn't think with so many reminders of him around. Being in Vizna was enough as it was.

I shuffled my pants down to my ankles and squatted down by a tree, and after relieving myself as quickly as my shaky body allowed me to, I used a technique of water and air that helped clean on more than one occasion. Like it had the day on the island when Aeden begged for a hug.

Fuck, I couldn't stop thinking about him and how much I knew I was done for. I loved him with everything I had. Every tiny, broken and cracked part of me was his. I used to question how I could ever fall for him before, knowing that was our story—two friends who fell head-over-heels for one another.

Now all I questioned was, *how could I not?*

How could I not be so ineffably in love with a man that cared for me like he did? That was consistently there for me. And the way he smiled at me?

Stars, it was hitting me even harder being apart from him. We were only maybe a football field away from each other, and I longed to be back next to him. Ached, for him. As much as I fought the grey splotches that covered my mind each time something reminiscent of him popped up in my mind like it had just as I thought about the distance between us, it never relented. Not fully.

Murrie had wanted to find pixie dust to bring back the memory of him, to make me whole again. But, if we found that, Aeden would use it to break the bond. I didn't know which was worse—never getting my memories of him back, or him breaking something that could mean the end for us.

I swallowed thickly, trying to push the nerves and anxiety that were forcing their way through. My breathing picked up and my chest began to swell and decompress rapidly. I forced air into my lungs, over and over again, but it wasn't working. I fell to my knees in the woods, covered by brush and trees and chunks of stone and tried to remember the ways he said I used to push through the panic.

My fingers swept along my thighs, grazing over cold metal and sturdy, easily-concealable hilts and then my eyes shot forward to a thick tree in the distance.

I *used* to run. Go on walks. Take deep breaths and count. All the things I *used to do* were for a person who wasn't who I'd grown to be today. I stood and pulled out the twin hilts along my thigh, holding two daggers between four fingers before shifting one to my other hand. My chest continued to move like air was being forced in and out, but I knew it was the panic settling in, about to take me for a spin.

Time slowed as I stood and gripped those hilts, then shifted down to hold the blades, taking aim and letting them fly just as fast. One by one, I emptied my pockets of every blade I had on me. And just like before, when the blades ran out, I made my own. I assaulted the tree, narrowing my focus entirely on the way my blades and elements moved through the motions.

Grip, aim, throw. Grip, aim, throw.

Over and over.

By the time my breathing was as still as each of my weapons were in the tree trunk, I heaved down over my knees, letting the shaking subside and my thoughts go freely. Each time a thought tried to creep its way back in, I mentally sat back and let go instead of grabbing hold of each thought and letting them take me. I just let them be as they were—just thoughts.

I would no longer succumb to the oppressions of my mind. I willed it to be, and so it would be.

For now.

Until the next wave of panic hit me.

It was inevitable, but perhaps over time it would get better. With Aeden, I felt like it was possible for it all to go away. Even if he didn't love me by choice or love me like I loved him, I knew deep within me I was changed forever because of him.

I'd never be the same without him.

The rubble beneath my boots crunched as I moved to take the blades from the tree, carefully sorting each back into its place. The woods had been peaceful when my thoughts were ravaging my mind, and for that, it had been the one piece that hadn't further catapulted me into my panic. But now it was darker somehow...and the silence was...it was—

"Don't. Move." *Aeden.* His words were cold and bitter, cutting through the darkness like the small blade that pressed to my neck. I froze with one hand pressed to the tree, my eyes straining at the corners where a stream of light glistened. It was brighter than what was coming through the trees. That fine blade pressed in further as the crunching rubble beneath his boots came closer.

"Don't do it, Hyacinth." *Hyacinth. Wasn't that...the pixie?*

That blade nicked the edge of my neck, feeling like a fine paper cut. Another voice rose, not quite soft, but smaller, yet full of a sound I'd never heard before. Ethereal. Demonic. "One step closer and the rest of us come out to play with her."

Pixies.

I knew pixies clustered in the hundreds, but surely if one was threatened, or felt that way, more would have stormed out. They were known to be nasty, with their sharp teeth and wings, their speed a deadly secondary weapon to none other than their mouth—both by their words and those *teeth*.

It was quite clear how fucked you were when faced with a troll. I felt that during my first trial. Saw the beasts up close and personal and somehow managed to kill one. Like the trolls, pixies were easily set off, but opposite in the fact that because of their size, it would be easy to undermine what they could do.

Unless, of course, that person had read an obscene amount of information on what lived in these parts. Pixies had in fact, primarily resided in Vizna before the war. Which meant I not only read about them because they were vicious beasts in this world, but also because they lived where Aeden should have grown up.

My body was already numbed from the panic attack I'd had moments before—my breathing already settled and unable to rise again so soon. "I'm not going to hurt you," I whispered.

"She won't, but I will." A sharp, shrieking laugh sounded close by my ear. That fine blade nicked my neck again, right before I directed my gaze up to the tree line, where I did spot little pools of light, small orbs in the hundreds, all hovering in place. I could feel their eyes on me, could almost hear their snarls from where they waited...for what must be their leader.

Aeden's steps neared and then stopped once more and I had to assume they were locking eyes. That he was able to see what Hyacinth was holding, enough to make him think twice about using his power, undoubtedly aware of the other pixies above us as well. "What do you want, Hyacinth? Name your price."

"It's funny, isn't it? You already owe me, yet you are ready to offer more. How fitting for the last dragon heir to need something—someone—like the air they breathe." Hyacinth moved a section of my hair, the feeling of her wings beating against my neck burning the nicks she'd given me. *Burning*. The knicks were starting to burn.

"Aeden," I said as my hand itched to move at my side. But then they'd go for him. Or, if their numbers were great enough, both of us. "Aeden. Something is in those blades."

"What blades, Lady Aerborne?" I stilled, my brows furrowing. "These are not *blades*." Her voice lowered and I knew Aeden wouldn't be able to hear her. "But if blades is what you fear, we do have those at the ready above. They may be small, but our numbers are vast. And a thousand cuts along this precious skin of yours will have you begging for death."

"Your price!" Aeden shouted, his boots shuffling another step closer.

Hyacinth laughed, the sound sending shivers down my spine. Those wings stopped fluttering and it took everything in me to not reach up and slap her away from me.

"Don't give her anything," I hollered back, and then lowered my voice, just as she had done. "*I* will pay the price," I told her, knowing pixies relied on their deals to get them what they needed. And the position she was putting us in would give us no other option. Another shrieking laugh and I could feel that familiar heat rising around me.

"You?" Every sound she made was warping and for a moment, my knees buckled.

"What's…what's in…"

"A poison. In case you decided not to play nice." Small feet pressed into my skin as she made her way down from my neck, over the length of my arm until she came into view, her yellow, dulled teeth flashing back up at me. "You are willing to owe me?"

Willing? "I don't have much of a choice, now do I?" I gritted through my teeth, using the tree as leverage as my knees buckled once more.

"What did you do to her?" Aeden shouted, but no movement came any closer. Heat was now making sweat form along my back.

She laughed again, her grin twisting cruelly. "You have to be *willing* to make a deal. We can not force you."

"Here I thought it was my choice to be glared at by hundreds of pixies, poisoned, and threatened." My legs gave way and I fell to the ground, my breathing intensifying as Aeden shouted more behind me. "Tell me what it is you want."

She steadied herself along my arm, having been jostled by my movements. "We need nothing from you as of now, but from *him*"—she crossed her arms over her delicate dress—"from *him,* we will need to call in our favor."

My chest was tightening, my other hand where the twisted pixie wasn't standing falling over my chest. "Fuck you. Make the deal with me, and me alone."

"My dear, he already owes us." Her brows perked up, arching to a fine point in the center.

"I'll take his debt, too," I whispered, unable to use my voice as my throat started to constrict.

Hyacinth rolled her eyes, then studied me. "You would take his debt, owing us not one, but two favors?"

"Anything. Yes. Clear him of what he owes you."

She perused down my arm towards my wrist, stopping right where my bracelet, *his bracelet, lay*. "Interesting..." she said under her faint breath. She lowered her open palms to the base of her wings, and I watched through hazed over vision as sparkling light cascaded down to fill her delicate, small hands. She lifted her palms, winked at me, then blew the specks up into the air as I gasped for breath.

Chapter Thirty-Eight
Aeden

*H*yacinth. After leaving those woods the first time, I should've burned it to the ground.

Every tree, every pixie. It would all be no more.

Paige's back bent in toward where I knew Hyacinth was standing, but I no longer knew what was happening. I couldn't see, and my power was responding by cranking up the heat.

I couldn't wait anymore. I couldn't just stand there and let her get hurt. My ears were pounding along to the same rhythm as my out-of-beat heart. Flames longed to spread through my skin, but if I let them go…I'd hurt her in the process. Either with the fire I'd send to burn every last one of the pixies, or by the pixies I would've missed in the process.

There were more orbs of light than I could count, and the woods were capable of holding more in its depths.

Paige seemed to nod in place, and then she stood, no longer bracing against the tree. Whatever Hyacinth had done to her, it must've started to wear off. Their hushed tones and murmurs, from both above and from the one in charge in front of Paige, filled my ringing ears, but all I could think about, all that consumed me, was that she was there. And she appeared mostly unharmed.

But appearances had a way of being misleading.

I took two steps. Two singular, quiet steps and Paige's head snapped over her shoulder, her eyes moving in a way that told me I should stop.

And then I took two more steps. Her eyes narrowed on me, and then the slight flick by her side stopped me from going further. *Another air wall.*

I scraped my fingers down, my lips curving at the thickness of the wall of air in front of me before I snapped back to reality. I frowned as she turned, then pouted as she walked up to me. I crossed my arms over my chest as she broke the wall between us down and threw her arms around my neck.

That rich peony and rain scent washed over me. I sighed deeply. "What did you do?" I whispered, glancing at the orbs of light that remained hidden in the trees, all except for one. Hyacinth's wings fluttered in the space where shards of ice and wood broke through the thick trunk of the same tree Paige used as leverage.

"I made a deal."

"No," I growled low as I pushed her away from the tight hold I had on her, grabbing her by the shoulders and extending my arms, looking her over. Heat spread from my body to her cheeks, making them pink over. "Why would you do that, Paige?"

She tried to glance back at Hyacinth, but I grabbed her chin and brought her attention back to me. "You shouldn't have done that. I already owed her, I could have easily owed her again."

"You owe her nothing now." *No.* A stone dropped from my chest and rolled deep through my stomach, crushing over vital arteries, cutting the blood off from my brain. Surely, that's what was happening, because in mere seconds after she said that, I was standing in front of Hyacinth, with Paige shouting for me to stop.

Flames danced along my palm, giving Hyacinth that glow she'd been missing. "This was between you and me. Not her. You are on *my* land. You were indebted by *me*. Take it all back. Right now."

"Aeden." Paige's hand rested along my back. "She *helped* me." Help. *Please.* Pixies didn't help anyone without it benefiting them. I'm sure when they told me her name, they knew what I was going to walk into. They knew the trouble I could've caused for both of us. Yet, all they gave me was a name and some pretty words about my bracelet being valuable.

I glared down at her from where she was beside me. "She just threatened you. I saw you. I saw *her*." I cradled her jaw in my unlit palm, then tilted her head. Where there was—"Where did she hurt you?" Hyacinth had cut her with her sharp nails. I had watched that from behind her, feeling helpless, wanting nothing more than to burn Hyacinth down to ash, yet knowing doing so would only make the rest of the pixies swarm Paige. But there was no mark along her neck. When I turned her head back, she smiled softly back up at me.

"I'm okay." Her hand raked up to my forearm, drawing my hand away from her face. "Better than okay, actually."

Confusion took over, but Hyacinth's laugh broke through that. I scowled at the pixie as she continued to laugh. "Nothing about this is funny. What did you do to her?"

"You mean, my boy of flames, what did I *give* to her?" Those same sharp nails tapped along her lips as I raised my hand covered in flames closer to her. "You see, we made an agreement. She took over your debt and relinquished it just as fast. Now she only owes us for—"

"She owes you nothing. No one here will ever owe you a damn thing, because you are all about to be dead." As quickly as her wings beat, I formed a burning orb of fire around her. She shrieked behind the orb as the other orbs above us danced like they, too, were threatened with fire.

I cupped the orb in my hand and shook it, sending Hyacinth's wings to bounce against the flames. She shrieked again, shouting some profanities I didn't care to listen to.

"Stop! Aeden, let her go!" I didn't move my eyes from the burning wings inside the orb. Paige wrapped her arms around my stomach. "Please. Just stop. I'm safe."

"Tell him our agreement, child!" Hyacinth shouted, her wings shriveling under the fire but her teeth unabashedly still there as she snarled at me. "Tell him!"

My eyes narrowed on Paige, on those soulful, stormy eyes that seemed conflicted as she looked back up at me. She bit down on the edge of her lip as Hyacinth shouted again. Paige glanced nervously at the ball of flames, at where Hyacinth would soon be nothing but ash like I so desired her to be.

"I remember you."

That orb dissipated faster than I'd lit it. I was suddenly unaware of anything else around us as I stared down at Paige, a small smile on her face as she repeated her words to me again. I bent and picked her right up, taking her in my arms, where she readily wrapped her legs around my waist.

I grinned as her hands pressed into my cheeks. "You...you remember me?"

She found the crook of my neck and nodded. "Don't cry, Paige. It's okay. I know, it's a lot." Her tears fell onto my shoulder as I hugged her tighter to me.

She shook her head and I could feel her lips spreading into a smile against my skin as she stilled. "It's not that it's a lot. It's just—" She pulled her head back, meeting my gaze. Those emerald eyes never looked so clear. "I loved you so much then, but it doesn't compare to what I feel for you now."

"I love you." I could never say it enough and yet, those words could never mean enough. Could never span the totality of what I felt for her and just how much she meant to me.

She held my face in her hands again and one of mine let go of one of her thighs just to wipe away those tears. *Those happy tears.* I'd never been happier to see her cry in my entire life. Pretty sure I'd never seen her cry from happiness, either. But that's what she was doing as she grinned back at me like a fool in love. Because that's what we were. Two complete fools in love, and very happy about it.

A glimmering light moved between us, where tiny arms crossed over a slightly burned dress. "This doesn't make us even, Hyacinth." I set Paige back down on the ground beside me, all the while keeping my focus on the way her wings had regenerated from where I'd burned them. "You tricked her, and now she owes you, what? What is it that will make this all go away?"

"My boy, she never even told you what deal it was that replaced what you owed us." She tsked, making me scowl deeply at her.

"Out with it."

She rolled her eyes, shaking her wings out in front of me. She made a move toward my shoulder, but I jerked back. "Fine," she said as she moved back to her spot away from my body and in the air. "She agreed to let us stay here, in Vizna, in this patch of what you could consider *woods*, and now she is indebted to us because of the dust we gave to her."

Gentle fingers wrapped around my arm just as my vision was going red. "I only wanted to help you because you've helped me so many times. And now that I remember everything you've done for me, all the times you've been there...I don't regret it one bit."

"This land is just as much hers as it is yours, is it not?" A cold snicker came from those hateful, twisted lips.

"That's not what's upsetting me. Because, yes, this land *is* hers. Will always be. But she shouldn't owe you a damn thing. Giving you the land was one thing, and these woods?" I looked around at the trees, waving my hand to show the extent of them. Not much, but it was *something*. "These woods do not count as my land. She gave you land *and* she gave you the woods." I smirked at her, and pulled Paige in closer to me by her waist. "She owes you nothing."

Hyacinth's snarky face turned sour. "No. We agreed—"

"If you don't accept it, then I'll burn these woods down, granting you that land you speak of. How does that sound?" Paige giggled then turned it into a cough, making me grin more. "I appreciate the dust you gave to her. Where I'm from, we say *thank you* to things like that. So, *thank you*, Hyacinth. But she owes you absolutely nothing."

I'm pretty sure fumes shot out from her ears, or maybe it was bits and pieces of pixie dust that remained fluttering at the tips of her healed-over wings. Either way, it made me quite happy. Elated, actually. Because I won, and she knew it.

Just as I turned with Paige's hand in mine to leave the woods, Hyacinth swept back in front of us.

"Surely, you need more pixie dust for something else." That evil little face was back. "I did hear something about...what was it? A blood bond? My, I haven't seen a bond like that in centuries."

Paige tugged on my arm, trying to move ahead, but those words she'd just said made my entire body freeze as I looked back at Paige. Did I personally want to break the bond between us? No. I'd be happily bound to her for the rest of our lives, knowing it didn't make a difference to how I felt about her. But, is that what she wanted?

"What do you want now?"

Hyacinth beamed. "A simple bed of water will do."

Paige stopped tugging and lifted a brow at her as she repeated, "A bed of water? Like, a lake?" Her nose crinkled as she looked at Hyacinth like she'd just lost her mind.

"It doesn't have to be very big, but pixies do prefer to be close to water, and Lake Viarta is all the way across these ruins you call a home. So, yes. Water. Just over there will do." She pointed to where we were standing before.

"Water. Nothing else, just that?" I sifted through the words, much like Paige was most likely doing right then as well, trying to find the hidden agenda in needing *a bed of water*. But, honestly, what could they do with water? Paige would certainly know, and yet she said nothing.

So I nodded. "Fine. I'll make you a small *bed of water* in that spot you just pointed to, and you will give Paige the dust."

Her lips curved up, pinching her eyes at the corners. "Excellent."

The short walk back was silent, other than the shifting of Paige's hand where she held a small vial of the pixie dust that would end our bond to each other. I thought for sure she'd give it right over, but as she mulled over that vial in her pocket, I could almost hear the gears working in that beautiful mind of hers.

Vara was, somehow, still sleeping when we got back. Something about being back in Vizna settled her. The heavy worry and tension I'd felt almost every day from her was slipping and easing. Maybe that was because she'd been asleep for a majority of the time we'd been back. Or maybe it was the reason why she was able to suddenly sleep so deeply. Like Paige was now able to do, though I wasn't sure I'd allowed her much of that the night before.

"Ikelos and Eoghan should be back soon," Seamus said as he moved to walk beside me. Paige had moved on to sit beside Shay at the base of what must've once been a large column, that hand of hers still deep in her pocket. Her pants were tight enough to see her fingers moving, and I wanted to pull her hand out and just take the powder and be done with it. If not to break the bond she didn't want, then to make her stop being so conflicted over it.

I'd still try to protect her without the bond. Surely, she knew that. But I could understand her not wanting something like the Stars, or anything or anyone else, interfering with her life like that anymore. They'd already put her through enough, as it was.

"Lad, did you hear a word I just said?" I stopped and looked around, noticing we'd walked past camp and were nearing another set of ruins where faint figures that looked like Eoghan and Ikelos were walking toward us.

"No, Seamus." I shook my head. "Sorry. What did you say?"

Seamus put his hand on my shoulder. "I said, well now it doesn't matter what I said. They can tell ye."

I followed where Seamus' hand was pointing, to where Eoghan and Ikelos were walking.

No, running. They were running. Toward us.

"Hey!" Eoghan yelled, and Ikelos started waving his hands in the air as they ran. "Hey!"

My back straightened as I looked around the field. There was nothing on fire, no purple sea of guards or hags or anything that would make them shout for danger. And they were smiling. Widely.

"There you are! We were looking for you. Where'd you go?" Ikelos used his speed to beat Eoghan, and by the time Eoghan caught up, he was keeling over toward the ground, gasping for breath. "Out of shape, babe?"

Eoghan craned his head to glare at Ikelos as he stayed bent over. "You know damn well I'm not out of shape. I can prove that to you later."

I ignored the imagery of that entirely, and shifted back to Ikelos. "Was settling a deal with some pixies your sister thought was a good idea to take part in." He opened his mouth, but I added, "Don't worry, it's done. She's fine." I watched as he peered over my shoulder, possibly checking for flames. "I didn't burn anything down."

"Good. Because that could give us away, you know. Unnecessarily big flames aren't good for staying hidden." I didn't want to think about how much I'd forgotten that. I simply didn't go that route because I didn't want to hurt Paige, and ended up not needing to burn down the woods we'd *gifted* to Hyacinth.

"The pixies are here?" Eoghan asked as he righted himself. "Does that mean you got dust?"

"Yeah, but I haven't taken it yet."

"You don't know what breaking a bond like that can do to either of you. It isn't smart to just jump into it," Ikelos said. *Clearly, someone had filled him in.*

Filled *everyone* in, it seemed. "Did you all talk about us while we were gone?"

"You mean last night when you both left to do Stars knows what, or after you guys left separately again this morning?" Eoghan asked, then pushed his hands in his pockets, possibly sensing my unhumorous emotions. I'm sure he knew exactly what we were doing, as would most people with a brain. "Of course, we talked about you. What else are we supposed to do, talk about a war no one wants to think about?"

Ikelos rolled his eyes from Eoghan over to me. "Which brings us to now, and what we came running over to talk to you about, which was *not* that." I felt that short, brotherly scorn from him as he looked me over. But it didn't bother me. It meant she had not just one protector, but two. A win-win, if you will.

"Maybe ye should've led with that and left the poor lad alone," Seamus suggested.

"Leading with *we found your people* isn't really the smartest thing to shout out across a vast space."

Chapter Thirty-Nine

PAIGE

"How have you been feeling?" Shay asked as I made my way to her. It hadn't shocked me at first, trying to lean on someone else. Someone else that I underestimated. Someone I put into a corner, thinking I could just act friendly with whenever I found it convenient. But now that I was sitting beside her, taking in the comfort of her asking *how I was*, it was making a lodge of guilt well up inside me.

"We found Hyacinth." I kept my hand in my pocket and my eyes on Aeden as he walked away with Seamus, throwing one last longing look my way before he refused to turn back again.

Shay's eyes went wide. "Really? She's out here?" Her eyes scanned the woods we just walked out from as her back stiffened.

"She shouldn't be coming after anyone. I kind of gave her the woods. Technically the land *and* the woods." You know, semantics. "And I got my memories back." It was all just spilling out.

She blinked a few times at me. Then asked, "Of him, too?"

"I guess with five days of being unconscious, everyone talks. So you all know about...us. Right?"

"Kind of."

"Awesome." I let out a shaky breath and pulled the vial from my pocket. "And now I'm just supposed to hand this over to Aeden."

"For the blood bond, you mean?"

I pulled my knees to my chest and rested my head there, turning to look at Shay, the most understanding person in all of Aellethia. "I guess everyone knows about that too, huh."

"I wasn't going to say anything, but you guys were gone for a while and Leander doesn't really keep his mouth closed that well. I guess all those years of keeping his identity hidden really took a toll on him."

My eyes roamed back to the fading figures in the distance, one in particular wearing black riding leathers. "You want to know what else I heard from Leander while you were gone?" Shay's boot shimmied into mine, pulling my wandering eyes back to her.

"Hmm?"

"Well, he said a lot. But mainly, he said this isn't the location of where the castle was. This was some temple dedicated to the connection between dragons and the heirs they were bound to."

"Huh." The column we leaned against did have ridges on it, like scales. Maybe it was a statue? I tried to think back to that imagery along my fathers walls inside his castle, but now that my memories were so flooded with Aeden, it was hard to focus.

Shay nudged her shoulder into me, then lifted her hand to somewhere in the distance, past the trees where Hyacinth now resided. "And beyond there. There used to be a library." My head perked up, lifting from my knees. "Nya and Leander went over there after he said something about it, but they haven't come back yet."

I squinted, searching for any flash of auburn red. "I don't see them. Think they are okay?" I made to stand, and Shay followed up beside me.

"I think they are more than okay. Kind of a weird couple in my opinion, but hey, who am I to judge?" She shrugged and my brows furrowed deeply.

"Couple? Nya and Leander?" The glances between them were odd, but I thought...I don't know what I thought. I wasn't thinking much about anyone else besides the over-consuming feelings I held for the man who might not even feel the same way I did.

Instinctively, I placed a hand on my chest, like I'd be able to still the crushing sensation beneath my ribs. But nothing happened. If anything, I think it got worse when I acknowledged it. Crushing, like how a submarine losing pressure beneath hundreds and hundreds of feet under the sea must feel like. One small hole—that's all it would take to crush the entire submarine. That's what my heart was starting to feel like at just the thought of him only wanting me because he was forced to.

Was I his choice?

Would he still be mine if I gave him the vial I still held in my hand?

"I thought the same thing. Maybe they are just friends, or friendly to some degree. But I've seen that look before in a man's eyes—I know what he wants and I think it's more than her body."

"Like Seamus." I wanted to take it back as soon as it came out. Their relationship was like an unspoken, unacknowledged truth that everyone knew about, but no one ever mentioned that blatantly.

"I suppose, yeah. But I wasn't talking about him." I swallowed past the lump in my throat, feeling that pinprick in my chest that the pressure would soon explode through all over again. How Aeden looked at me bordered on an animalistic possessiveness at most times, sending heat through my body instantaneously. But at other times, when it was just us like the night before, it was deeper than that. Much deeper. My chest tightened again.

"Look. Over there." Shay pointed as we continued walking toward the ruins of the library. I hadn't even noticed that we'd kept walking the whole time, but soon enough, we were there, standing in the midst of what must've been the biggest library in all of Aellethia.

The stone walls were thick, but not thick enough to withstand the destruction that fell upon Vizna during the battle. The destruction the Prydian army reaped on this land spoke volumes about their hatred for a people who were no different from them.

Some walls of the interior were, in fact, still standing. One in particular along the back—where old wooden boards had slanted down into the ground, torn pages and destroyed books littered the stone floor. Where auburn hair blended with brown hands.

"Shit," Leander shuffled back, dropping his hands back to his sides. "Didn't know you'd all be coming here." His darkened green eyes glared back between Shay and I. "Should have figured you'd be making your way here though." He let out a laugh, nervously grabbing the back of his neck.

Nya's cheeks were a deep red, like her hair, when she turned to meet us. "Hey, um." She looked around at the floor, then rushed to a stack of books. "We found these. We were going to bring them back to you."

"But then you fell on Leander?" My brows shot up as my lips curved up. "The last time I saw you in a library, you looked bored. It's nice to see that isn't always the case."

Shay laughed then covered her mouth with her hand. "Anything else here besides those?" she asked, looking at the books.

Nya started moving around the shelves closest to us, shuffling her feet like she was sweeping the floor. I looked down, following what her feet were uncovering. "Yeah," she said. "Look."

Beneath the soot, the ash and papers and torn pieces of book covers and scrolls and most likely the shelves themselves, was a pattern of scales in gold. She bent down, using her water magic to clean the small area she cleared.

"Is that...a dragon?" Shay asked, moving down to the floor to sweep away the debris beside Nya.

I looked around, now aware of the gold dotted here and there along the floors. "Leander, is it a dragon?"

Leander glared back at me. "Of course, it's a dragon. What else would they put on the floor here?"

"I don't fucking know, marble? Like normal rich people would?"

He scoffed, then again without flicking his wrists, he maneuvered pieces of debris from all along the floors and swept them up into the air, flinging them to the far side.

"Dragons, actually," he clarified as my eyes danced wildly over the intricacies of what lay under my boots. I jumped back as a piece of paper wriggled under my heel, fighting to get to the side of the room like the rest of the debris.

Dragons were swirling along the floors in the center of the room, golden scales made of hedonium peeking through varying shades of reds and blues and yellows and greens. More than a dozen dragons arched their bodies, forming a spiral of dragons that flew and breathed fire and smoke. So many dragons, yet I'd only seen Vara.

How incredibly lonely being the only dragon now seemed to be.

"It's beautiful," Nya stood, taking it all in as the rest of us were. Leander gazed around the room like he was fighting back the awe we all felt, possibly holding onto the memories of what this place once was.

"You should have seen it decades ago." He started moving around the room, tracing the lines of each dragon with his boots. "This place, like most of the buildings here—they were all beautiful. I mean, don't get me wrong, you haven't been to Starmere in my territories. Somewhere I'm quite proud of. Buryon is beautiful and lush with vibrant greens, but Starmere is of the greens only found in the heavens above—where the Stars are plenty and the emerald skies reach peaks unseen elsewhere." His head cocked back to me. "Except for your storm you made the other day. That color green—I've never seen that before." Then, he laughed. "I guess we all hide our beauty in the strangest of places."

"I wasn't hiding that. I just didn't know." My focus remained on the dragons. "These dragons"—I moved to the black and gold one, where red bejeweled eyes shined back up at me—"This was her dragon, wasn't it? Ygsavil."

He nodded, that distant, memory-torn gaze of his returning. "It is."

"And this one here, the green one—was her father's dragon."

"Kieryn," he replied. "Lord Urdon's dragon was named Kieryn."

"Yes." I continued around the room, noting the eye color and the way the dragons moved, one on top of the other, like they were placed after the emergence of a new dragon, creating the spiraling form.

"Varasyn would have been placed on top of her father there," he said as he pointed to Ygsavil. Her mother, from what I'd read, remained unbound because Savaria's older brother had died in childbirth. The dragon still hatched, but was free from the bond.

Free like Aeden was going to be if I gave him the powder tucked safely in my pocket.

Leander pointed up to the open sky. "Varasyn's mother was along the ceiling years ago, but the battle seems to have taken out the ceiling as well. They named her Grendwyn, though no one knew her true name. Do you know why?"

"Because only the one bound to them can know their true name first and speak it first. Without a bonded fae, their name isn't ever spoken. The rest of the dragons know it, but won't ever tell it. Not even to their bonded. It's a way they chose to honor the fallen."

Grendwyn.

"How incredibly sad to have no bound to talk to," Shay remarked as she stepped lightly along the floor, avoiding stepping directly on top of the dragons there. "No one to even know your name."

Leander nodded again. "It is doable. Sometimes, preferable." Nya eyed him with concern. He cleared his throat. "That one over there, Janessia." He pointed to the blue and golden one layered behind and slightly under Kieryn, but off to the side of another. "What do you know about her?"

And now I was being quizzed. "Janessia and Waykre were twin dragons. Born and bonded to the twins Kyren and Kal."

"And who ended up on that throne?" Leander pressed.

I swallowed, thinking of Aeden's great-grandfather. The one they called *The Breaker*. Because that's what he was known to do with his power—break people's minds. "Kal." I pointed to the yellow and golden dragon, Waykre, where her neck was lapped-over by the curving tail of Kieryn.

Leander tsked. "Kal," he spat. "Kal was a monster."

I nodded, biting down on the corner of my lip. "Yes. But I believe he was driven to madness." I wondered how often Leander had used that blood bending gift of his to be able to recognize another monster from the one he appeared to be. The one he could so easily be. Perhaps, at one point, he had been. But he had yet to do anything to us. Well, beyond our first encounter, which felt like a lifetime ago and yet had only been not even a week.

"We all have demons, dear girl. It is what we do with those demons that defines us." He eyed my pocket, like he *knew* what I had stashed there. "You'd do well to remember that."

"You talk like you have some experience with that," I replied.

Nya's brows furrowed in confusion just as the ground shuddered beneath our feet. Shay froze in place as Vara's head popped over the top of the building, her golden eyes trained to the floor. Slight rolls of steam moved from her nostrils as those eyes moved slowly over the flooring, and when her gaze turned to where I was standing, I didn't hesitate to step aside.

She craned her head at me, eyelids turning to fine slits before snapping back to the floor. I knew the depth of the devotion, the depth of the bond her and Aeden had, couldn't ever be changed. And I'd never want that. If we were going to be together in this life, I might as well start acting a little nicer before she developed the dragon fire that inevitably came with maturity. How far off she was from it, I couldn't tell. But she was growing. Fast.

And I'd still stand in front of her as if nothing could hurt me. Maybe it was Aeden that had given me that stupid confidence to begin with—that feeling of protection that knew no bounds like a fine shield that coated me. But I wanted him to step behind that shield with me—to stand beside me.

Vara's head jolted upright and jerked back over where her wings were tucked. And then I heard him—*them*.

His hair was damp with sweat, and as he approached me, he lifted the bottom hem of his tunic up to wipe away the sweat beading on his forehead. "Hey," he whispered, pulling the fabric back down, covering the hard muscle my gaze usually lingered to. But I hadn't left his eyes—the same gold in them like Vara's had.

"Hi." He bent down to kiss my forehead, sending that rush of fire throughout my body.

"What's all this?" he asked, taking in the pattern of dragons and stack of books in Shay's arms. "You found a library?" His lips quirked, but it was weak. A half-cocked smile that faded quickly as he continued to look around. "Are those dragons?" I nodded.

"She knows a lot about your history there," Leander added.

He placed his hands on my shoulders, then pulled me to him, wrapping his arms softly around me. "Of course she does." He kissed the top of my head as that warmth covered over that small puncture-hole in my heart, trying to weld it closed. "Is that what you were studying all those months in the mountains?" he whispered against the crown of my head.

"Kind of. Yeah."

He chuckled. "Even when you hated me, you still loved me."

"He's got good news, he's just stalling," Ikelos hollered from behind a pile of debris. "You going to tell her?"

Eoghan muttered something to my brother as I pushed against Aeden's chest, making room for me to look up at him. "Is everything okay?"

He cupped my cheek. "Everything is great." It didn't sound believable.

He didn't sound believable.

He sounded weary.

I peered around at everyone, noticing the absence. "Where's Murrie?"

His hand palmed over my hair as he pulled me back into his chest. "She's with Karla."

Chapter Forty
Aeden

The mountain range around Boste was more than just that.

Much more.

"Come, come." Murrie greeted us the moment we stepped through the blue portal, waving her arms for us to follow.

Paige's hand still rested in mine through and after the portal, and when we locked eyes, the relief poured over me. She remembered that day well, now. But we were still together, as it should have been many months ago.

As it was always meant to be.

She didn't need to speak the words for me to feel them. I kissed the top of her head, and she gave two quick squeezes to my hand with hers.

"Karla's inside, waiting to show you to your rooms," Murrie said. She moved to stand in front of us, making us all stop in our tracks.

"We're going back to Hydrasel. There's a few things we need to take care of." I turned to Eoghan and Ikelos, the blue portal humming behind them. I gave them a nod and watched as Paige released my hand and went to hug her brother. "We'll be back tomorrow for the coronation."

"Coronation?" Seamus asked. "Ye mean he's—"

"Getting crowned?" Murrie crossed her arms over her chest. "As long as everything goes well inside, then yes." Her orange eyes fell to me. "Nothing to worry about. They will love you."

I hadn't been briefed on a plan. Ikelos simply said he had a vision, saw where my people were, and then said that Murrie took off with that speed of hers when she heard there was a dwarf by whatever description Ikelos had given her. But he also added we didn't have time to sit around in ruins anymore, so we didn't really have a choice but to go to where Ikelos had seen.

Red and gold extended in the skies above us as Vara started to gradually descend. "There's a larger entrance around the rocky bend there"—Murrie pointed, and I relayed the information to Vara—"Tell her there's more than enough livestock in the fields in Boste if she'd like."

"Don't go too far. And remember to—"

"Stay hidden." She huffed out a plume of smoke in the air, then banked around the rocks.

Paige was by my side once more, taking my hand in hers. I smiled down at her. "You'll see him again tomorrow. He'll be okay." She nodded, and I knew that wasn't the only thing plaguing her mind. She hadn't yet given me the vial.

"Ready?" Paige asked. I nodded back, thinking only of the vial and not the crown about to be placed on my head until Murrie urged us forward to a flat wall of brown rock covered in thick vines that draped down like a curtain. Murrie stepped up and gathered a fistful of vines and pulled them to the side, exposing...absolutely nothing.

"In there?" I inclined my head to the blank wall while Murrie looked at me like I was the one who couldn't see where we were supposed to go.

"Well, go on then."

I tilted my head. "You want me to walk into the wall?" I glanced down at Paige as she mirrored my confusion. *Glad I'm not the only one fucking confused.*

"Walk in! It's an illusion, you idiot."

I cleared my throat and started walking, noticing the way Paige never faltered at my side. She'd walk into the wall willingly if I led her there, and I didn't know if I really liked that idea or if it terrified me.

But I knew I'd be thanking her later for it.

The wall turned to nothing more than specks of color as we moved through, Paige's fingers going up along the side of the wall that now opened like a doorway into an arched tunnel lit with flames.

"Do you feel that?" she whispered, her gaze trapped on her fingers that lingered on the stone.

"Yes." My power, *our power*, was surging more than it usually did. Just like it had on that first night we slept together. I wondered if the bond made it that intense like Eoghan and Leander had suggested, or if it would still feel like that once I did what needed to be done. I'd always been so good at reading Paige, at knowing how she felt, but with the pixie dust...I wasn't sure what her motives were in keeping it from me anymore. Maybe she was just waiting for the best time. Maybe she was scared it would hurt me.

"Karla is just up ahead," Murrie said as she made her way in front of us once more, where Seamus, Nya, Leander and Shay had also made their way. We were last, because at some point, I'd just started staring off at Paige.

She smiled up at me. "Sure you're ready for this?" I feigned the best smile I could and her brows pulled low. "You don't look okay."

I pulled her to me, tucking the soft waves of her hair behind her ear as the others continued forward. I wasn't worried about getting lost in the tunnel—I was already lost in her. "If you're by my side, I'm ready for anything." No lie there. She made everything feel possible. Gave everything in my life a purpose that no crown ever would.

Her teeth flashed and I bent to kiss the top of her curved cheek. "I'm not going anywhere."

"Don't make that promise, My Queen. I need you in whatever room they put me in because that's your room, too."

She lightly slapped my chest. "How am I supposed to harness this special gift of mine if you won't let me be without you?"

I wrapped my arm around her back, right at that dip in the base of her spine that I liked to caress when she laid next to me. "We'll have to come up with a schedule." I tapped the tip of her nose and gave her a real smile this time. "How about this, I get you twenty-nine days of the month, and the last one or two days you can have to practice your gift." She pouted in the most adorable way possible and I chuckled as she slapped my chest again.

Her nose wrinkled. "Your scheduling skills suck."

I moved to cup her neck, pulling her in deeper to me by the waist. "Like that pretty mouth of yours will do later." I pulled back, just to see the blush I knew I'd painted there with my words.

"Oh for fuck's sake, you two!" Murrie called from deep in the tunnel where she was just barely visible. "Hurry up! You know people are waiting to see you."

I jerked my head up and hollered, "You said rooms." Paige and I moved through the tunnel down the only path there was to catch up to Murrie. "Who is Karla?"

"She was Rennick's—sorry, your dad's second in command."

"How'd she end up here without them?" Paige asked. "That illusion would have been done by his mother."

Leander replied, "This used to serve as a camp to train the Dragon Heirs whenever there was one to train. When your mother trained with Ygsavil, she tested her illusions on the place. It was completely hidden during the battle, but Sav and Ren didn't want to risk everyone's lives so they stayed away."

Stayed away. They should have stayed somewhere safe. Like with a friend. Anger flourished through me, and before I realized it, I'd pinned Leander to the stone wall with my forearm to his neck. "You knew they were out there, and you didn't help. Why."

He raised his hand between us, tapping on that ring of his. His *promise.* "I was told to stay out of it, so I did. I stayed and made sure *my people* were safe from a war I needed no part in. Turns out I was needed for the next one." He swirled his finger in a circle, signifying his importance in *this* war, the one coming any day now. "So I didn't ask any questions. My friends asked me to bind you two and to stay out of it. If you want to be mad at someone, ask the seer what he saw. *He* is the one that said staying *here* would be bad for the future."

Paige pushed my forearm down from his neck, keeping her focus on me. "It's not the time to get riled up about the past. What's done is done."

"Wise Lass, very wise."

I glared over at Seamus as I let Paige's hand push my arm completely down by my side. Then I snapped back to Leander and lifted a finger at him. "You should've helped them. They would still be alive today if you had kept them hidden."

"Or we could all be dead." He shrugged, swiping his hand down the front of his neck. "As I said before, I'm not the hero. Never was. But we all know what you would have done to protect what you love. And we'd all be dead if you were in charge that day for it."

"That's enough." A whip of air pushed Leander firmly back to the wall, where he smirked down at Paige. Nya made a move to step forward, but then stepped back beside her father. "We will all be alive *because* of him. He's already a better leader than you ever have been. What kind of Mora hides himself and blends in with his people so he doesn't have to deal with whatever shit happened to him? I know for a fact Aeden would never do that."

His brow cocked at me. "He would never hide who he is unless it meant keeping you safe, my dear."

Her back went taut as her power pressed in on him, pressing his body deeper into the stone. "The bar at the inn was different."

"Was it? Did he not keep himself concealed so he wouldn't draw attention to you?" He laughed. "See, that's why I was told to stay away. I would have drawn attention. You think Gedeon wouldn't have come to Earthborne territories next if he had even an inkling we were friends?" Paige was silent, but applied even more pressure, making him gasp for air. "Exactly. As I said. All. Dead."

She reined her power back in all at once, sending his ass to the floor. "It doesn't take a hero to do what you should have figured out a way to do. All that shows is that you are a coward."

"Paige..." Nya warned. "You don't know his story. Everyone has a past." She went to help him up from the floor. The second Nya was done helping him up, he smiled at me.

And then I punched him. Right in the jaw. When I turned to walk away, Paige slid her hand into mine. "Nice touch."

I chuckled, shaking out my other hand. "I knew you liked it when I got rough."

"So much like your father." The voice came from a small woman—no, dwarf. Her orange eyes glowed just like Murrie's, but the wrinkles at the corners of them aged her. And where Murrie had an ax strapped on her back, the woman in front of us had nothing—no weapons. That I could see, at least. She was entirely covered in black from her shirt down to her boots, save for the four red stripes on both of her shoulders.

"Aeden, this is Karla. Karla, this"—Murrie stood beside Karla, then bowed deeply—"is Aeden Fireborne and Paige Aerborne."

Karla bowed nowhere near as deeply as Murrie did. It was more like she had intended to tie the laces of her thick black boots without looking at them at all, because those orange eyes never left me. They inspected me, then widened a fraction when she moved on to inspect Paige and the way our hands were tightly woven together. I tightened my fingers and pulled her closer.

"Yes. Just like Ren." She smiled brightly up at me, ending her inspection. "Welcome to your fortress, My Lord." She sighed and glanced up at the low ceiling. "Stars, I've waited so long to see the man you grew to be. You were so small when I sent you to live in the mortal world. Come, let me show you around."

"It was you who sent him through?" Karla had turned to lead us down the tunnel with Murrie at her heels, but turned back just a fraction as Paige spoke.

"Yes, My Lady." Her gaze roamed to our hands again, and I got the feeling she was unsettled by it. "I was ordered to do so by Savaria herself, to preserve his future." She turned back, and just before she started moving again, she added, "*Both* of your futures."

Seamus nudged into my shoulder. "Somethin's not right with how she looked at ye."

"I heard that, *Seamus,*" Karla replied. Murrie had clearly been thorough about who each of us was. Karla cocked her brow up at Leander. "How nice to see you,

Leander. It has been *years*. I take it you are staying here, too?" He nodded back to her without asking whether I liked that idea or not. Unsurprisingly, I didn't.

"Right." Karla turned and waved her hand in the air as she continued on. "You may want to let go of her hand. There are thousands of your people waiting beyond those doors ahead, and some may not be prepared to see—"

"Karla, was it?" I interrupted her, but she turned back around on her heel like I was about to give an order. Because I fucking was. "If the people in that room don't accept that Paige is my queen, and is therefore *their queen*, then they are no people of mine."

"My Lord, you can't—"

"I'll say it again, very slowly in case you are hard of hearing"—Seamus coughed into his fist, covering his laugh—"Paige Aerborne is a queen and will be treated as one. If they don't want to be a part of that, then I suggest they leave."

"My Lord—"

"They. Will. Leave." I glared at her. Glared until she bowed. Deeply. I positioned Paige in front of me, holding on to her by her waist, making it clear who Karla would be kneeling to. "Repeat it."

"They will leave, My Lord," she whispered, tipping her head down again when she saw Paige in front of me.

My thumbs rubbed along Paige's sides, easing the tension I knew she felt. But she needed to know—I would not tolerate anyone not accepting her because of something she had no control over. She had the same right to a title as I did, and if I had to start with my people first, I would.

"I hope you know, it is not me you will need to convince. Remember that when we leave the room." The double door became a dividing line—two twin doors that could lead one way or the other.

"I have no hesitations in believing he will make them see his way is the only way," Leander said. And I believed that was the first sane thing he'd said while in my presence.

"Maybe you shouldn't be threatening them. They need to have the chance to love you, not be scared of you," Paige whispered. "I'll be okay. I grew up hearing the worst about me. Let them judge me."

"No one will judge you without severe repercussions."

Leander leaned into our space, right as we stopped in front of the closed doors. "I can't wait to see how this goes." His attention fell to the doors as he took two wide steps away from me. Another wise choice. "Show time."

Chapter Forty-One

PAIGE

A show, it was.

That's exactly what it felt like we were walking into—an open stage, where a magnificent show with eager faces looking on could admire us.

But admiration was the furthest thing I felt as we stood in that doorway. As we moved through the bodies that stood immediately upon our entry. *His entry*. I knew they weren't standing for me. The slight sneers and murmurs as we passed through weren't directed at the man they'd all been waiting for two entire decades for.

His hand tightened around mine as he kept his head held high. I mimicked his every move, trying not to let my senses be overrun by the sounds and sights of the people who weren't going to accept me. I was the daughter of the most hated man in all of Aellethia. I didn't expect to be—well, honestly, I didn't expect to be on his arm when we got here. I hadn't thought about what they might think of me because I hadn't planned to stay in the picture.

Karla and Murrie walked well ahead of us, giving us the room to not appear like puppets being dragged through the assembly, though the strings were clear to me. I lifted my chin higher, letting my eyes move to each detail I could latch onto as a distraction, keeping them from the sea of men and women with black and red tunics and stripes along their shoulders.

It was a grand room for a grand entry—for being inside of a volcano, I didn't quite know what to think as I took in the curves of the dome-like ceiling, where several small black and golden spherical chandeliers hung with spikes that curved from the base to the top, embers of fire flitting above each point. At one end of the room, a fountain of lava poured from a hole in the wall, and as I followed it down, I saw the lines etching like veins along the flooring, where the lava flowed freely beneath a fine layer of glass, preserving it as it spread through the room.

Now halfway through the space, my attention fell back to the people. One slight glance behind me nearly took my breath away. Most were kneeling, down on one knee with their fist tightly balled over their hearts and their gaze lowered to the floor. But others...others were staring at me as they stood.

"Don't look at them," Aeden said beside me, turning my gaze back to our taut, invisible string. "They will learn to bow to you, too." His voice raised with his last sentiment, and I heard shuffling, possibly of a few of them righting themselves to bow. But it wasn't loud enough to tell me they had all gone down.

I didn't want to be bowed to, I just wanted to be accepted. I could deal with them hating my guts for reasons they were wrong about, but I didn't want it to affect how Aeden would lead them or how others would view him. I didn't know the lengths he went through to protect me, but I could guess. He had the makings of a great leader, but I would be the leech on his heart, taking what animosity he should have for his people and warping it into what could only lead down a path of destruction.

I wouldn't let that happen. I wouldn't let them think he'd go down the same path, make the same mistakes, as his great-grandfather. I wondered if that's what some of them believed as they watched yet another Dragon Heir of theirs proclaim their love for a girl from another kingdom. Mixing and wedding between the two kingdoms wasn't exactly forbidden, but it was highly undesirable. Kal would have been the first to ever do it, but Dacna, the Mora of Hydrasel at the time, died the night of their wedding. Some books recorded she had been poisoned, others said Kal froze her heart when she looked at another fae just before their vows.

I didn't know which to believe, but I did know that Aeden was nothing like his great-grandfather. Yet, the people in this room didn't know that. The ticking in his jaw as we neared the end of the room may have swayed their minds to believe he was another monster, the heavy gait to his walk and the way he fearlessly held my hand in his—a love-stricken monster.

Karla turned to look at us the moment the heavy wooden doors behind us closed. "Well, I think that went rather well." Her brow lifted, waiting for Aeden to reply. He narrowed his eyes on her. "Right. It will take time to process. It isn't you they...don't..." I turned to where Karla's eyes fell as she stammered, seeing Leander draw a line over his neck to silence her. As he looked at me and dropped his finger, he smiled. "But I'm sure they will come around. They know there is no other alternative."

"You have a way with words, don't you?" Aeden said.

"Give her a chance," Murrie said beside her, giving Aeden a stern look.

"Your father used to appreciate my bluntness. Said it was one of the things that made our friendship so great. We were never dishonest with each other, and I don't plan to start that type of relationship with you. So, yes. There will be pushback. People will hate her for what she stands for and the blood that runs in her veins. They know her father is the one who killed your mother and your father, and they are not quick to forget the bleak history of what Prydia has done to their homes. The families he destroyed, the children he continued to murder after when their powers emerged because they had fire along their arms." She lifted her finger, pointing at the weapons strapped along my body. "And they can see you trust her enough to give her weapons, to cover her in them. And when they see those weapons—all they see is the blood her father spilled on our lands."

"She is *not* her father," he seethed as the tunnel's temperature escalated.

Karla nodded, her orange eyes taking in the heat around us like it was a tangible thing she could see and take out of the room—like a cat honing in on a mouse. "As I said, it isn't me you need to convince. But I don't suggest losing your grip on your power. You have people ready to follow you into battle, and far fewer who are wary but will more than likely choose to do so regardless. Think of the *after*, think of the Mora you wish to be and do not let your heart turn against you and your people." She paused, letting out a deep sigh through her nose. "Find a way to lead with your heart, with *both* parts of your heart, and the people, *your people*, will follow you to the Stars and beyond."

She started to turn, but Aeden replied, "Is that why she kept my father a secret, then? Because Paige will not be a secret."

Karla spun slowly on her heels. "No. Your father wasn't supposed to be a secret. But with the war coming, and the growing insanity of the Mora of Prydia, they thought it best to focus on the war instead of their burgeoning love, for the safety of your life."

"She will fight beside me. There will be no question on the battlefield that my loyalty lies with her *and* them."

"Then *show* them," Karla snapped back. She sighed again, seemingly reeling in her emotions and regaining her composure. "There is a meeting in an hour down the hall, not far from where your rooms are." She turned to lead us once more, then added, "Bring her. You can start the convincing with your advisors."

"How can I have advisors when I don't know who to trust here?" Aeden's voice was stern and hollow, like he'd already decided he didn't trust anyone in that room.

"They advised your mother, and—"

"And she is dead, along with a majority of the kingdom. Their advice is not looking too good right about now."

Karla stopped at a door, fumbling in her pocket for what must've been keys. "Meet them first. They will have valuable insights."

"We—"

"Would be happy too," I finished, cutting Aeden off and giving him a look that made him roll his lips in.

And then he sighed before Karla passed him two keys. "Yeah." He put on one of the fakest smiles I'd seen yet from him. "Delighted."

Aeden went to put the two keys in his pocket, but Karla cocked her head to the side. "One of those keys is for her. Her room is down the hall."

"Which key?" Aeden pulled them both back out of his pocket, watching intently as Karla pointed to one. The one she didn't point to, he passed to me, and the other, he tossed back over his shoulder as he hollered for Seamus to catch it. "There. That's settled. It's Seamus' room now."

Karla looked between Seamus and him, then over to me. She gave one, singular nod. "So it is." She reached into her other pocket, giving a key to Leander and another to Nya, then paused when she got to Shay, who shook her head and stepped up next to Seamus. "Well then, I guess having an extra room available isn't a bad thing."

"Sounds like it isn't," Aeden agreed. "You have a room, Murrie?"

Murrie held up her key, but he didn't bother to reply as he turned the knob to our room and pulled me inside, closing the door just as quickly as he pulled me in. In one swift movement, he spun me by my fingers and pressed me against the wall where the heat from the tunnels became thick between us. He looked down at me, curving his finger just under my chin, angling my head up to look at those golden-flecked eyes that burned with an intensity I hadn't realized I'd been longing for.

"Aeden," I breathed. "We only have an hour."

He shook his head and smirked down at me. "Such dirty thoughts." He dipped in and brushed his lips over mine. "I just wanted to thank you."

"For what?"

"For staying by my side, even when those *people*—"

"*Your people,*" I said pointedly.

"*Our people,*" he corrected further, sending a shiver down my spine. "They will accept you. I wasn't just saying that for no reason."

I swallowed the growing lump in my throat. "Aeden, they can't just accept me. You heard what Karla said—my father killed your parents." I waited for his features to shift, for him to flinch back or look at me like instead of hanging the moon, I'd taken it and burst it into dust, shattering the singular source of brightness in a darkened world.

But that look never came.

"I'm the enemy to them. You may want me but I think it's clear they don't."

"They will." He brushed his lips over the top of my cheekbone, the tip of his nose grazing my temple. "They won't have a choice."

"Don't make them think you are your ancestors." He pulled his face back. "Who?"

My brows furrowed. "Kal Fireborne." His look of confusion intensified, so I continued, "*The Breaker?*"

"Like from that book with all the gibberish?" He rolled his eyes. "I don't care about what happened in the past. I'm not like him, just like you aren't like your father."

"*I know that.* But they don't know you."

"They are about to." His fist curled in along the wall above my head, then he released it, flexing them out and easing them back to the wall. His other hand came up, tugging my lip from the hold I had from between my teeth. "Don't overthink it. If I got you to fall in love with me, then I'm sure getting them to do it will be easy enough." He chuckled lightly. "And I know how hard I fell for you. How can they not fall for you, too?"

"I don't really appeal to everyone, Aeden." He pushed back from the wall and crossed his arms over his broad chest. "It's true. Your friends didn't like me at first, and Vara still looks at me like she wants nothing more than to be able to breathe fire so she can burn me where I stand." His jaw flexed as his gaze shot up and over, like he did every time him and Vara were talking. "Scolding her isn't going to help that."

"She says she doesn't hate you," he said. "Just says that two stubborn heads don't collide well at first." His arms wrapped around my waist, tugging me to him. "She's not wrong, you *are* stubborn."

"Says the guy who is all *they won't have a choice.*"

"Because they won't." He started walking backward, pulling me along with him in his embrace. Just past his arm, I could see the makings of a four-post bed. "But that doesn't mean I'm going to act like Kal, or Gedeon, to get the things I want." He paused, cocking a brow as he peered down at me mischievously. "I didn't brutalize you to get you on my side, now did I?"

"I saw the man you were. You proved to me how easy it could be to love you, even if I wanted to throw a hatchet or dagger at your face several times. And now that I remember the *you* from before, I know exactly why I fell in love then, too." I started finishing the path he planned to end on, walking forward while he stepped back toward the bed. His face softened, but he didn't drop my gaze. "I got to fall in love with you not once, but twice." His knees buckled as they hit the bed, sending him back onto the plush top with me above him. "And now those people out there, they will all get to fall in love with you, too."

He groaned as I repositioned my hips above him. "I don't want to think about them right now. Not with you on top of me." His hands splayed around my waist, those calloused, yet gentle fingers fighting to touch skin beneath my corset. "Take this off. I want to touch you."

"No." I pushed him back from where he started to lift up from the bed, sending him back to brace himself with his elbows.

"No?" He smirked, his eyes raking down as he quite possibly was envisioning what I'd look like naked, above him, spread for him. The thought alone sent even more heat to my warmed cheeks and neck. "Did you just tell a king *no*?"

"No, I told my boyfriend no. And he's not a king." His brow arched playfully. "Yet," I added. I shimmied down, settling my knees on either side of his thick, muscular thighs. Thighs meant to hold onto a dragon while riding. I reached for his buttons, loving the shudder I felt come from him as I worked through one, and then another.

"Paige," he moaned. "You said we only have an hour."

I hummed, popping a third button. Honestly, the need for four buttons on these riding leathers was quite ridiculous. I went to work on the last button, but his hand grabbed onto my wrist. "I hope you know that an hour gives me more than enough time to fuck you."

I snatched my hand back, going right back for that button, but glaring at him as I did so. "As much as I would love that, I want to do something for you." I started to work his pants down, watching as that warmth in his eyes turned to molten lava.

"I'm the one who should be thanking you," he growled low, but made no move to stop me. In fact, he lifted his hips just enough to allow his pants to keep going down, letting his cock spring free. My mouth instantly watered at the sight.

"This isn't about thanks, or who owes who what." My lips quirked up to the side as I finished pulling his pants down to his ankles, stopping at his boots. "This is about how much your scheduling sucks"—I parted my mouth, just over the head of his cock and flicked my eyes up to him—"And how my mouth can do *that* so much better." I swiped my tongue out, loving the way he moaned with the simple move. I did it again and he shuddered.

Aeden tilted his head back, that Adam's apple of his bobbing as he swore. I gripped the base of him, dragging my tongue from where my fingers struggled to close over his girth all the way up to the tip again, using the thickened ridge under his shaft as a guide.

"Fuck." He stopped resting on his elbows, his back now firmly against the bed. I did the same move two more times, teasing him until he popped back up on his elbows. Or, that's where I thought he was stopping. His hand was suddenly in my hair, tugging my head back by the roots.

"Open that pretty mouth then, Paige." And I did. As he held my head in his hand, I parted my lips. "Wider," he ordered. "And stick your tongue out." The action felt silly, but there was absolutely no humor between us and that fire was still burning in his eyes. "Good girl."

His hand pushed my head down slowly, his hold relaxing when I gagged not even halfway down. He shifted his hold, then tried again, and again. Pushing my head down just a little further, moaning when my tongue stroked him each time he lifted my head up again.

"You think you can take it deeper?" My eyes narrowed on him at the challenge, and without his hand applying any pressure, I pushed through that reflex, taking as much of him as I could into the back of my throat. I heard him hiss through his teeth as I went back up and repeated the move, going even lower the second time around. He chuckled as he moved his hand to push the hair back from my face.

"Fuck, your mouth—I knew I always loved your mouth. You want me to come down your pretty little throat?"

My hand started to pump him at the base as I nodded, making him curse again. Each pump was sending him closer and closer to the edge, his cock thick and solid and ready to burst. I batted my eyes up at him, watching him lose himself just before his release spilled down my throat. I kept pumping and sliding my tongue along his head as I swallowed everything he gave. I'd never done that before, never wanted to be that close to anyone.

But I wanted him everywhere.

Even if that meant we were walking into a room full of advisors who more than likely didn't want me there, in less than an hour, with his cum on my lips.

I sat up, swiping my tongue out along my bottom lip. His hand raked down his face, his eyes peeking out from behind his spread fingers. "You're going to be the death of me. Have I told you that?"

"Yes. You have." I laughed, moving to lay beside him, resting my cheek to his wavering chest where his heart was trying to level out to a steady rhythm again.

"Damn, I can think of a hundred other things I'd rather do than walk into that room. Into that *meeting*." He sighed, the inhale from his chest rising making me need to readjust myself against him. I had to agree with him. Our training had focused so much on Aellethia as a whole and using our power that we hadn't learned much about what to do in a *position of* power.

"What does Vara think about all this?"

He stared up at the rocky ceiling of our bedroom, then rolled his eyes down to me. "She's shocked you asked what she thinks."

I giggled. "Well, I happen to care what she thinks."

His smile widened to that one that made his dimple puncture his cheek. "She's shocked at that as well." Then he stalled as his gaze fell back to the ceiling. "She says she likes the space they gave her. It's warmer than the mountains and Costa were, and has a lot of room, and she doesn't have to hide in the clouds anymore. She says"—he let loose the sweetest laugh that warmed my heart—"She says she was starting to think she hated flying, but it was the hiding part that she hated."

"Will they let her out at all?"

His head shuffled to face me. "Well, they are under my command, aren't they? And Boste is empty, so they say. So, yes, she can go out." He nodded up at the ceiling, like Vara had that question on her mind, too.

"The whole power surge thing...is that what it feels like between you and Vara?"

He thought for a moment. "No," he finally said. "I can feel her emotions that she puts on the surface, and I can hear her thoughts that she sends my way, but that wall I discovered in Costa...I can shut it all off, just like she can. If we wanted to." He emphasized the last sentence, like he knew where my mind was going.

And he was right. "I want to give you the pixie dust, but I'm not sure what it will do to us. What that would mean for us."

"What...what do you mean?"

"I mean...I don't know what I mean."

He cupped my cheek, bringing me back to him. "Yes, you do. Don't do that to me now." He glanced down, a smirk toying at his lips as he looked back at me. "My cock is still on full display here. You literally have me with my pants down around my ankles, and you still won't speak your mind?"

I laughed, then tried to recompose myself by rolling my lips in. He meant so much to me, but voicing my concerns right before an important meeting we had to go to...it didn't feel right. I tapped on his chest, and made like I was about to sit up, but he pulled me back down to his chest, making me laugh again.

"Not getting away that easily, Miss Aerborne. Speak. Now."

"It's just...what if what you feel for me is more about protecting me than it is about *loving* me?"

He stilled, which I thought meant he was thinking. But when I found the courage to look back into his eyes, I knew he wasn't thinking at all. Not in the ways I thought. He reached down to my hand, and pulled it up to the center of his chest, right beside where my cheek rested. "Do you not feel that?" he asked. "Do you not feel how absolutely out of control I am when you are with me?" His heartbeat quickened, pounding like a heady drum. "I thought we'd moved past questioning how I felt about you long ago. That day in your kitchen"—his hand started stroking over where he placed mine—"When I made you feel my heart then. When I told you to tell me to stop. I know that it isn't a coincidence that we ended up so close together as far as housing went, but needing to protect you doesn't mean that I have to want to breathe you in with every kiss, or want to hold you so close to me that there isn't a single space left untouched between us. I want to be able to protect you, sure, but that doesn't mean I have to love hearing the sound of your laugh, or how just seeing you sets my soul on fire."

Tears bit behind my eyes as I blinked up at him. I wanted to cry because what he said was exactly how I felt about him. I wanted to cry because I'd so wrongly misjudged him, yet again. I wanted to cry because I didn't think to just simply tell him how I felt. I wanted to cry because I wanted to get rid of the doubts I had about our bond, and this was the only way that made me feel like I was shedding a former self and growing. With him.

I should have spoken my mind sooner. Should have trusted him with my doubts without thinking he'd take it the wrong way.

"I'm so sorry," I whispered.

"Don't be. Just know that I do love you, endlessly."

"I love you, too." With every piece I had to give.

"Honesty, always," he breathed against my forehead before gently kissing me there.

"Honesty, always," I repeated.

Chapter Forty-Two

PAIGE

The war room was cold, and we hadn't even stepped foot inside it yet. I could feel it, seeping through the fine crack at the bottom. I was so used to Aeden's familiar warmth covering me that I flinched back when Karla opened the door for us.

Everyone bowed, their fists to their chests as their eyes stayed to the dark floor. A single flame flickered in the corner but there were unlit candles along the walls, which had apparently drawn Aeden's attention as well. He flicked his wrist, bringing the entire room to light.

They bowed lower.

There was a large table in the center of the room, with colored pegs that dotted around a terrain which seemed to mirror Aellethia. The mountains peaked up from the table, and the deeper grooves out further by the arena showed the concave dips of the craters where the Field of Bones was known to be. And close to that, a smaller version of my father's castle, purple pegs clustered throughout the region near his borders.

My throat turned dry.

A man stepped up to us, his shoulders squared back behind his black and red tunic as he placed his hand to his chest. His face was long and oval, and as I followed the trail of a deep burn mark on his left jaw, his eyes snapped to me. His lips parted as his fist began to lower, but Aeden cleared his throat, snapping the man's gaze back to him.

"My Lord, it is a pleasure to finally meet you. We have been waiting for you." His eyes moved to me once more, those cold brown nothing like the warmth I found in Aeden's. They actually looked quite the opposite. He looked at me like I was nothing more than dirt. Like the people in Jessup used to look at me.

"I wasn't aware *we* were late." Aeden cocked his brow up at the man. He knew he was talking about the decades they had all waited for him. He was pushing him. I let go of his hand and moved to study the table closer, ignoring the stares I was receiving.

"No, you are quite on time." The man's voice had been powerful just seconds before. Now, it quavered.

"*Both of us*," Aeden corrected. "We are *both* on time, you mean."

"Y-yes, My Lord."

I reached my hand over the purple pegs, feeling their eyes shift uneasily along with their feet. There had to be at least seven other people in the room besides Karla and the man Aeden was two seconds away from losing his shit on, but I couldn't bring myself to examine them closer.

None of them were the people we brought with us.

"Where is Seamus?" I finally broke my silence. The man in front of Aeden didn't look toward me, and all remained silent. As I went to repeat myself, Aeden did it for me.

"I believe My Queen asked you a question." His warm eyes narrowed on the man, who visibly shrunk into his shoulders.

"I-I don't know who that is, sir."

"Do you not know where your ears are, either?" Aeden asked, angling his head to the side as he perched his fingers beneath his chin. I heard a few snickering laughs covered by false clearing of their throats from around the room. Aeden smirked.

"Yes, sir," the man replied. "I mean no, sir. I mean...I do know where my ears are. Sir."

"What's your name?" Aeden asked.

"Jorgan, My Lord."

Karla stepped up beside Jorgan, where her four stripes conflicted with Jorgan's three. Jorgan tried straightening his back, but under Aeden's glare, he failed miserably.

"Aeden—Jorgan, as well as everyone else in this room were part of your mother's advisory counsel. He has been a valued member for a very long time, and even served under your grandfather, toward the end of his reign."

Aeden nodded his head once, acknowledging Karla but glaring deeper at Jorgan. All that coldness in the room? Gone.

"He has been an advisor of war for *a very long time*, and my group has been here for just over an hour. Yet, he has no idea who Seamus is." Aeden turned to Karla. "Do you know who Seamus is, Karla?"

Karla nodded, her body rigid and firm. It was clear Aeden and his father shared more in their personality than I previously thought, because Karla seemed right at home with the way Aeden spoke to others. How he reacted to them. Testing them. She didn't back down at all. Even though she was a dwarf, she seemed much taller than Jorgan did in that moment.

Aeden pointed to a woman on the other side of the table, her arms crossed over her chest. Half of her head was shaved, leaving the other half in longer golden braids that she flicked over her shoulder, showing her stripes. Two. She slouched, yet still appeared taller than Jorgan, as well. I smiled at her, loving her already. "Who is Seamus?" Aeden questioned her.

"The red-headed ass singing in that room you walked through, you mean?" She paused briefly, then she added, "That woman with black hair was trying to drag him away."

Aeden grinned back at her, then looked back at Jorgan. "She knows who he is."

"So, she does," Karla replied.

The woman glanced at me, her smile growing just a fraction as she watched my fingers hover over the mountains we were tucked in.

"Would anyone in this room care to go get that red-headed ass and the woman with black hair for me?" Aeden looked past Jorgan, ignoring him completely.

"I will," a young man said as he stepped out from behind two others. A dwarf. "It would be an honor, sir."

"Excellent." Aeden crossed the room and stood beside me, his eyes roaming over the map while a hand slid to cup my shoulder. We stayed like that, examining the tabletop while the rest of the people in the room moved to flank the other side across from us. I felt a few glances my way, but chose to ignore them in case they held as much malice as Jorgan's did.

And then Seamus and Shay walked through the door.

"Lad!" Seamus shouted. "And Lass. Look at the two of ye, so fittin'." He wiped his mouth with the back of his hand and then leaned in between us and whispered, "Who're all the sour faces?" Shay moved to stand next to me, and I gave her a quick smile.

"Corvina." The woman with golden braids leaned over the table, extending her hand. Seamus took it immediately, beaming at her. Then she shook Shay's hand with the same friendliness.

A few of the others stepped up, following Corvina's boldness with a mix of their own. Jorgan went last.

"Now the meeting can begin, then?" Karla asked as she took up a position she seemed to take often, the table's stain worn where she stood.

I nodded before Aeden, which made Jorgan glare at me, yet again.

"These pegs, the clusters. They are all groups of how many guards?" Eight. There were eight clusters, two of which lined the northern part of Prydian territories, three others along the western side where the ports were.

The dwarven man, whose name was Luka, stepped up on a stool, raising his torso above the table. "They are estimates, each peg consisting of twenty guards," he answered. *Twenty guards.* There were at least fifty pegs in just the smallest group—at least...at least a thousand men and women, armed and ready. Per group. And those were estimates.

Aeden leaned over the table, pointing to the three clusters grouped along the west. "We knew about these. Well, knew they were stationed here heavily. It didn't make sense at first, but we assume he's searching for something that is somehow more vital than hunting us down. Enough to draw what appears to be over 3,000 guards away from the areas he plans to attack."

"He's had them stationed there for months. Since before Paige's Triad." My brows shot up at Corvina, and I wondered if she was there in that arena on the day Aeden saved me.

Another woman, older with white hair like Karla's but a body young enough to not stand hunched over or have any wrinkles, added, "We have considered relics, or fae with special gifts. Have sent in spies to watch what comes in and out of ships his guards favor, but have found nothing more than loads of fine sands from the Isles of Avicante and boxes of uncut stone."

"Are there any relics that are made of stone?" I asked, feeling Jorgan's icy gaze on me once more. I looked up, confirming his agitation. His jaw worked, but Aeden thankfully hadn't seen it.

Corvina and Karla exchanged a look, then Karla said, "There are several, but none that are confirmed to actually exist. All just fables from thousands of years ago."

"Searching for fables," Jorgan scoffed.

"This entire world was nothing but what fables are made of from where I was born and raised," I shot back, leveling him with equal agitation. "Turns out, there is a lot of truth in those *fables*."

"You sound like you know exactly what he is searching for, *My Lady*." Jorgan's mouth snapped shut the second those words left his mouth.

Aeden didn't wait. Jorgan was against the wall, pressed in with a wall of air, taking the breath from his lungs. He started gasping, his eyes widening as they moved between Aeden and I, then over to Karla, who didn't look the least bit shocked. Aeden released him to the floor, where no one ran to help him. The only one who showed an ounce of acknowledgment was Corvina, who grinned with sheer amusement down at him.

"He's always been a cock," she said low to me, cupping her hand over her mouth. *Yep. She's my new friend.*

"And now he's no longer needed in this room. This room is meant for people who think outside of the box, who choose to be a part of something greater. Not for those who choose to keep their minds trapped in the confines of a bubble smaller than a pixie's asshole." A brief, quiet laughter came from the older woman and Corvina, and a few of the others in the room that I had yet to meet.

Jorgan looked from Aeden to Karla, probably expecting for her to pipe in and override Aeden, but she just shrugged her shoulders at him.

"You all think it's okay that he has her in here?" He looked at me with more hatred than before as he stood. "It's insanity. She is his daughter, she lived in that castle—"

"I was forced to live in that castle, if living is what you can call what I did there."

Aeden squeezed my shoulder. "She doesn't have to explain herself to you," he said more to me than to anyone else in the room.

Seamus moved over to the door, pulling it wide open as he stared at Jorgan. "'ere's the door, ye fuckin' twit. Best move through 'fore I help ye find the threshold meself."

Jorgan grumbled what I imagined were a slew of profanities under his breath, and before Seamus shut the door, Aeden added, "Can you please go get your daughter, Murrie, and Leander as well. I have some rearranging I'd like to do."

Chapter Forty-Three

PAIGE

"I can't believe he did that," Nya said from her seat beside me.

"I can." I smiled, thinking about it. "He's always gone a bit against the grain, I guess you could say." And I could say that confidently now, because I remembered how he was before. He hadn't changed much at all, just grew into the role he was always meant to have.

"Yeah, but...your father never once asked what I would like." She kept her words low, shielding them from anyone who was staring at us in the dining area, which was a culmination of at least a dozen long tables laid out in rows towards the far side of the room we had first walked through. Turns out, that room was much larger than I'd thought before. With a lot of people now retiring to their rooms I found out they were more like shared bunk spaces, it should have left less prying eyes and murmurs.

But that wasn't exactly the case.

"It's a good thing Jorgan wasn't there to hear him ask what position you'd like to have." Through the corner of my vision, I saw the two red lines on Nya's shoulder and smiled again. Seamus left that room with the same three lines Jorgan would have still had, had he not been so closed-minded to there being an heir to the Prydian throne in the same room as him. But he got what he deserved. Probably less, if I was being honest with myself. Maybe

Aeden saw the burn marks and took pity on him. I'm not sure I would have been so kind if the tables had been flipped and I was in his shoes, and him in mine.

"What Gedeon would say now to me if he saw this. Saw *us*," she said. "Beyond being made a tier two healer, being allowed to go out and heal others in battle, he appointed my father and Shay a title, too." She paused, then added, "Oh, and Murrie. But who wouldn't make her weapon's master?"

I grinned at the thought. Murrie was an excellent fit for dealing out weapons and training others on how to use them—something Nya readily declined when Aeden offered a similar role to her. Seamus was now the war advisor that Jorgan had been, with Karla the only one above him. Something must've struck a chord between the two in that room for him to not put Seamus above her. Maybe it was to keep Seamus' head from inflating too much. I'd have to ask him about it another time, whenever he finished up in that room.

Once he made Shay emissary, with a special task aimed to bring together her kind and the Fireborne territories, he started glancing at me. I knew, *knew*, he was going to push the *My Queen* thing. If not in that room, then shortly after, in ours. Officially, I couldn't have a title beyond being the heir to another kingdom, because that was still where I belonged—on the Prydian throne. But his eyes were all sparkly in that newly-lit room, and it was getting hard to breathe.

So, I pulled Nya from the room with me and said I had to go eat. After being in that room for well over three hours discussing ideas—the extent of the armies in all kingdoms, the alliances we'd formed, and going over the fact that trying to get Gedeon off the throne by using our combined voices—the Mora's we were allied with and ours—was futile because he'd attack anyway—my head had started to spin. I was excited for the prospects, the hope that three kingdoms against one gave me, but seeing the sheer numbers of his armies was unsettling, to say the least.

I no longer questioned where all the funds to provide for Gedeon's people went. He had been building an army. And their numbers seemed to level our combined three.

Nya waved a piece of bread in my direction. "Don't think I didn't notice the intense way he was looking at you, too."

I nodded, my teeth finding my lip. "Yeah." Then, avoiding it altogether, I said, "Says the girl who is clearly hooking up with Leander."

She blushed deeply, jerking her head to look elsewhere. Not that it worked to hide the redness that blended in with her hair. "Am not."

"Are too. Can't wait to hear how that all happened. Or *when*, really."

"I can tell you it was long before he found us in Costa. I just didn't know who he was."

My brows shot up. "Oh, now I need to know everything."

"You first. Is he trying to marry you, or what's happening there?" I didn't answer as I picked up my fork and started picking at the vegetables on my plate. "I don't know what that's like in the mortal world, but here, that's a completely normal thing to do at your age, especially for a High Fae. I mean, he's also about to become the Mora of what we now know is not really a fallen kingdom, just a well-hidden one. So..." Her eyes rolled to me. "I'd do it. If I were you, I mean." She paused, then added, "Plus, he's fucking hot."

I choked on the water I'd started drinking, trying to avoid her gaze. "I don't think I've ever heard you cuss before." I set the cup back down. "But I don't think I'd marry someone because they were hot."

"Then do it because you love him, and he loves you, and we could all die tomorrow." *Well, that's blunt.*

Green flashed in front of us as Leander took a seat across from Nya. He smiled at her, which I took to be more genuine than the crazy ones I'd seen before, and then that smile fell when he looked at me. "The meeting is done. Aeden is talking to Karla a bit longer, but he said he would be in your room soon." He winked at me, then removed that mask again when he looked back at Nya.

"I expect that story next time," I said to her, then stood and gathered my plate and cup. Before leaving the dining area, I filled a plate for Aeden and tried to keep my chin high past the few people who lingered around the room that chose to either look my way with hate or disgust, or not look my way at all. I preferred the latter.

By the time I got back to our room and showered, I was sure the plate of food I brought back for him had gotten cold. And he hadn't returned yet. I flicked my wrist, elevating the plate with my air magic above the desk I'd put it on and set a low flame beneath it. Then, I walked to the dark wooden dresser, not sure if anything would be for me inside of it but quite certain an array of clothing in black and red tones would be inside for Aeden.

Imagine the shock on my face when I opened a drawer and found an assortment, fitting for a woman to wear. Perhaps at some point during the meeting, someone had come in and filled the dresser. Or maybe this room had been someone else's before. But looking around at the ornate furniture of what I assumed was high quality, I couldn't help but believe they'd set this room aside for his return.

Each piece of furniture was dark like their tunics, and each detail was red. There were few hints of that element that could only be forged by dragon fire, and I felt like the expense of it only pointed me farther in my belief that the room had always been meant for him.

The entire kingdom waited for him. And he showed up with me on his arm.

I got dressed in one of the fine silken sets meant to sleep in and laid on the bed, drawing the thin covers up high around my neck. I drifted off to sleep with the door unlocked and my body curved toward the empty space beside me.

Before I opened my eyes, before I registered that his arm was draped over me and my leg was tossed over his, I knew he had come back. Because, once again, I hadn't dreamed.

As much as I wanted to use my gift, to be able to harness it no matter the nightmarish things I saw, waking up next to him was more than worth the trade-off.

He was still asleep as I laid there in his arms, not caring about whatever was happening beyond the rocky walls and the volcano as a whole. Those purple pegs grouped on the table? I'd long forgotten the importance of them. Because what mattered most was in front of me.

His lips were parted on an exhale as he breathed deeply in his sleep, the darkened space beneath his eyelids drawing my attention up. His thick, dark brown hair was a little damp and his skin was not only very warm, but also smelled like the bar of soap that was placed in the shower—like honey, better than the lavender I was forced to use before. The honey mixed well with the earthy and ashen scent he naturally had, and the color of the soap alone reminded me of his eyes. Everything reminded me of him when he was gone. I don't know what time he got back, or how long he was awake before he finally came to bed.

Karla must have had a lot of important things to discuss with him in private after that meeting to make him as tired as he seemed to be.

I crawled out from beneath his arm, placing it back down on my pillow in place of my body, then headed for the bathroom. I used my magic to clean my clothes over the large tub that sat in the center of the room, deciding that wearing my old clothes that I'd left on the black stone counter was better than shuffling through the dresser and waking Aeden up. After putting the final dagger back into place, I walked back into our room.

His arm was curled around the faux Paige body, a small sleepy smile on his face as he squeezed it tighter. I tried to refrain from laughing as I slipped out the door. Only to be greeted by Karla.

"Good morning, My Lady. Did you sleep well?"

My face must've reflected how I felt about having her right outside our room, because she took a single step back, giving me room to walk away if I wanted to.

"I did." I looked her over, stopping when I saw she was armed this time. "Do you always wait wherever he is?" If so, I needed to be more prepared.

"No, I mostly came for you, actually." She peeked down the hall. "There is a coronation tonight."

I nodded, waiting for her to continue. I started to think she may have picked up on Aeden's lingering glances at me when he was dishing out titles like he'd been king for years. But then she said, "You have to pick out a dress."

I almost stumbled back into the door. "Excuse me?"

She repeated herself, a little slower the second time like maybe I hadn't heard her. I shook my head. "You want me...to pick out a dress?"

She nodded slowly, matching her words that she repeated...again. And then I laughed, cupping my face with my hand abruptly, so I wouldn't wake Aeden up beyond the door we were in front of. I put my hand over her shoulder, edging us away from the door. She didn't even flinch when I reached for her, just went right along with it.

I liked Karla.

"Why do you want me to pick it? Shouldn't it be purple or red and pre-picked by someone who knows what to wear to these things?"

She looked at me with so much confusion. "Why would it have to be a certain color?"

I paused, thinking back to the ball where a purple gown had been given to me with no option for alternatives. "You're saying...I don't have to wear purple?" I smiled down at her, and her confusion grew so much, her brow and corners of her eyes were crinkling.

"Stars, My Lady. No, you don't have to wear anything you don't want to. We have an assortment of colors. It is customary to wear red or black but we have options and have long foregone those old traditions nearly a hundred years ago, if not more."

I didn't hesitate bending down to her height by dropping down to my knees, and hugging Karla, who I now really liked. She laughed awkwardly as I held the embrace. "Thank the fucking Stars. I hate purple."

When I pulled back, her eyebrows were sky high. "I can have them remove the purple options before you go. It's just down the hall, take a left, pass exactly eleven doors, then take a sharp right, not the bend, and then—"

"Can you walk me there? I'd like the company." I stood, giving her back her space.

She looked up at me and blinked. Several times. "You are...not what a lot of people here expected you to be. I try not to have preconceived notions, but I...I must admit I requested the purple gowns to be added to the collection. I apologize."

I waved a hand at her, starting to move down the hall in the direction she'd pointed to before. I couldn't hear her feet, but I felt her presence somewhere close behind me. "Don't worry about it. It's just"—I waited for her to move until she was standing right beside me before I continued again—"I didn't expect to have choices. Gedeon never gave me a choice of...well, anything."

"I don't mean to be forward, but, I notice you call him Gedeon, and not *father*."

"Right. Really, I prefer Sir Dickhead, but I don't think that people will take me very seriously if I constantly refer to him as that." Karla belted out a laugh, shaking her head as we turned. "He may have been with my mother and made me, through some miracle or act of pure insanity on my mother's part, but he doesn't deserve the title of being a father."

"Gedeon it is, then," Karla replied. "The room is just up here." She moved ahead of me just enough to stop me at the right door, and I absolutely loved that guards were not standing on either side of it. I almost hesitated to reach out for the knob myself, but Karla ended up doing it for me, purely because she was the closest to it.

Peering inside, I smiled even more. Because, just like at the doors, there was no one inside. No one, just at least a hundred dresses, if not more. Karla rushed over to the purple gowns and started taking them down, but I stopped her with my hand. "Wait," I said. "I don't know what Shay or Nya or Murrie would want to wear."

Karla froze, cocking her head to the side after a moment as she stared at me like I had three heads. And then it occurred to me—not everyone had been invited to the ball in Prydia. Just the High Fae. "They are coming, right?"

Karla shook out her head as she put the gowns back into place. "Yes, of course they are coming. Everyone is invited and urged to come. It would be a sign of ill-faith in their future Mora if they didn't."

I bit down on my lip, moving to the red gowns along the right wall. She continued. "It's only...well, My Lady. These are *your* gowns. We had this laid out for you last night after your arrival."

I stilled with my hand mid-stroke down a lacy red dress. The notion that I even had a selection to call my own, in a place that didn't seem all that thrilled to have me, made me think perhaps I'd been wrong about just how many people were against me when I walked in. But I'd felt those lingering glances full of hate and anger. I hadn't imagined it. Had I? "Does that mean I can't share them with anyone else?"

Karla seemed to think about it as she stepped back and away from the dresses. "I suppose there is nothing wrong with sharing them. If I'm being honest with you, I didn't anticipate being asked that. I had to think about what was appropriate. But, now that I think about it, Savaria used to let her handmaids wear her gowns if they wanted to. Said she had far too many and was far too uninterested in attending the events that she had to wear them to."

"Maybe I am more like her than I ever was like my own blood." *Blood.* Karla's eyes widened just a fraction, and I had to wonder if she knew about the bond that was put on us. She'd been very open with me, and as much as I wanted to trust her completely like I used to do with everyone around me, I chose against asking her. I chose against opening myself like that to essentially another stranger, and bit down on my tongue.

After a brief silence, I asked, "How much time do we have to get ready?"

"You have two hours before the guests arrive in the main room, and shortly after that, you and Aeden will be announced side-by-side, as requested by him." *That's at least some of what they were discussing the night before, then.* His intentions were clearly to present us as a united front, but I wasn't sure how well that would sit with the people who were about to put a crown on his head.

"Are you able to ask Nya and Shay and Murrie to come now?" My voice came out weak. I cleared my throat to push through the lump that grew there.

"I can most certainly do that for you, My Lady." She started moving for the door.

"Oh, and Karla?"

Her hand froze on the knob as she turned. "Yes, My Lady?"

"When it's just you and me in the room, if you are comfortable with it, you can just call me Paige. Okay?"

"Yes, My—Yes, Paige." The door shut softly behind her, leaving me with a room full of choices.

Chapter Forty-Four

Aeden

I don't think I'd ever been snuck-out on. Leave it to Paige to be the first girl to ever do that to me.

Several nights in a row of barely any sleep sent me into the deepest one I'd had in a while. I hadn't heard Paige leave, but I knew exactly where she was going whenever Karla got her hands on her.

Which was probably soon after she left through our door.

To say I was excited about what today would bring would be a vast understatement. Being made Mora without going to the arena made me feel like a cheat, but I wasn't focusing on those details. Taking charge of my kingdom—it wasn't the reason my heart rate kicked up twelve notches as if Paige had put each one of her daggers to my throat. Thirteen notches, now that I was thinking of those fingers holding a blade.

A knock at the door had me groaning against the pillow she'd left in her place. At the second knock, I got to my feet.

"They told me to bring this to you. Said you had less than half an hour to get to the main room." Leander looked less than thrilled to be holding my clothes for me. His jaw ticked slightly as I took them from him, noticeably no sign of where I'd punched him before along his face. "Oh, and this." He pulled a fire-bonded blade from his pocket and pushed the hilt into my hand.

"Thanks." I went to close the door, but his boot was wedged in, blocking it. I sighed, pinching the bridge of my nose. "What is it now?"

He pushed the door wide open and stepped in. "You know, I am over a thousand years old. You are nowhere near a single century."

I moved to lean against one of the posts of the bed. "Your point would be?"

"My point is that instead of treating me like someone who has lost their mind, you should value the insights I have. Besides simply calling me an ally, you should look to me for...resolve."

I scoffed. "You do realize everything you have done so far has put this wedge in place, don't you? Does threatening people by forcing them to a wall sound like a productive way to make friends?"

"Much like you did to me *and* Jorgan, I hear. Just yesterday." *Shit.*

"You deserved it, and so did Jorgan." My fist started to clench at my side just thinking about that fucker. How he ever got into his position, I'd never understand. "Paige didn't have a chance to get a word out by the time you put her there. And the way you'd been following us was also not the right way to go about it." My eyes rolled up to the ceiling, then back to him. "And don't get me started on how completely wrong it was for you to let my parents stay out in the open—"

"I tried." His breathing intensified, his green dress jacket rising and falling with each breath. "I tried to get her, and Ren, to stay within my borders. But they were so set in what the future was that the young Seer saw. They tried to find a way around it, but after the battle, all connection to Celine was lost. They couldn't trust anyone else, any other Seer. So they used what time they had left to be together, with you." His eyes narrowed. "And now that I see the type of man you are, I'm willing to bet if you and Paige were to have a child, you'd do the exact same thing. Spend what time you had together, without risking anyone else's life in the process."

My fist curled in tighter. "You don't know what lengths I would go through to keep us alive." And how much I'd rather see the world around us burn before I'd think twice about those flames reaching her *or* our child.

"Oh, I do. I very much do. And with all that unharnessed power, I'm sure you'd try to burn everything down." *Bingo.* His eyes rolled. "As if I haven't heard the whole *burn the world for her* gimmick before. Your great-grandfather would have done it, had he been as strong as you. And they gave him a name for what he did manage to accomplish, as I'm sure you heard."

"What makes you think I am stronger than him?"

"I bent your blood, remember? Melded it to another. And even standing in this room with you, I can sense just how powerful you truly are. How powerful *she* is. Your blood is quite strong. And with the two of you sharing that power—"

"We can't share our power. We can only feel it." Though I didn't know why I felt the need to explain that to him. "For all you know, I already broke it."

Leander tilted his head to the ceiling and laughed, the deep breaks in between each laugh gnawing at my growing agitation. "There's no way you've broken it."

My brow arched. I shrugged and turned, facing the black and red dress clothes and blade as I laid them on the bed. Leander either had a death wish, or had pertinent information he withheld.

"So, she gave you the pixie dust?" he questioned, his voice a little closer than it had been before.

"Yes." She hadn't.

"Hmm. Funny."

My hands started to heat. "I don't see why that's funny."

"It's funny because if she had given it to you, you would have taken it because she doesn't seem so sure about your relationship now, does she?" My hands got hotter, but stayed on the jacket, idly stroking the fine details woven in hedonium. "I guess you could always choose to not take it, to keep the bond and test whether she believes you love her, as you say you do. That it isn't because you were forced to feel a certain way."

"Watch yourself, Leander," I warned.

He didn't. "Perhaps she hasn't given it to you at all, and you truly haven't had the opportunity to test what pixie dust will do to your bond." His voice lowered, seeming to mimic...concern? "Is that it, then? She hasn't given you the choice yet? She must be scared to break it, to lose you. Because she knows exactly what you will do to keep her and if that means severing a bond to prove you love her, you'd do it." His hand fell to my shoulder and I flinched. "I don't believe pixie dust is your answer. I believe what you seek is much harder to come by. That is if severing the bond is what you really want."

"You don't know anything about us."

"I know what it is like to feel love and to not have it returned. I know the pain of it—the torture. Pure agony. But I'm also unsure of just how much binding your blood together truly affected you. It was only meant to be for protection—you'd feel her pain, her suffering, and want to correct it as if it were your own. Prevent it, even. But love can also bind you in ways that blood can not."

Red and brown flashed in the corner of my vision, his fingers tapping along what was mine. He must've found it in the pocket of my clothing Karla gave him. "What do I need if it isn't pixie dust?" The heat had gone straight to my voice, turning it to pure fire, ready to incinerate.

"Logically speaking, your bond was forged with dragon fire." He dropped what he was holding down to the bed in front of where I stood. I stared down at the small red box as he continued. "The oath rings, pure hedonium. Break one of the rings, break the oath. The bond should go with it." His ring fell to the bed next.

"Vara." I tugged on that thread, only hearing whispers of sleep in return.

Leander's voice lowered as he said, "As it was forged, so it shall be broken."

I turned back to face him, finding him leaning against the door, looking all too defeated. "Why tell me this now?"

His face shifted as he started to chew on his cheek. "Having to do anything against your will is no way to live." His eyes glazed over, like he was trapped in a memory. He pushed his hands in his pockets, pushing whatever memory it was aside. "And having your love questioned is not what I intended when I bound you to her. You might think I'm cruel, but I…I simply wasn't taught how to be any other way. Your father and mother were the first true friends I had. Everything I know about love, *real* love, is because of them."

"Will it hurt her if I break it? Will she feel it?" I asked, knowing we were already short on time, and I was nowhere near ready to go to the main room.

"It could weaken your power. Any other man, I'd warn that their true feelings may change, but I don't think that's the case with you."

"You'd be right in thinking that. Nothing will ever change the way I feel about her."

He rubbed along his jaw. "I do know the Stars don't like things being taken from them, and they did bless the bond," he added.

"Fuck the Stars." They didn't need to be involved in it, just like I was about to prove they weren't needed to deem someone worthy of being a Mora or not.

He smiled, one I believed was true. "That's the spirit."

My palms were sweating as I stood behind the set of heavy doors that would lead into the main room. The entire kingdom was filing into it, their voices audible even through the doors. They sounded happy enough, though I wasn't naive enough to think they would all be so thrilled once we stepped through. They would all have to adjust if they planned to stay in the kingdom I hoped to build once the war was over. Anyone with a narrow-minded attitude, like Jorgan, could go work alongside him, demoted to shoveling Vara's shit for all I cared.

I pushed a hand into my pocket, stroking the velvet box. The faint click of heels against stone sent a smile to my lips, but I stayed facing the door. Until the clicking closed in, and a delicate hand draped over my shoulder.

"Can I turn?"

She giggled and tugged on my shoulder until I turned, but I kept my eyes closed. She sighed. "Aeden, you can look. It's not a wedding."

I smiled at that and peeked through one eye, then opened the other.

And then my heart stopped.

"You—" *Speechless.* "You're..." She was wearing red, with hedonium threaded in an intricate swirling pattern that went from the top of those perfect breasts and angled down sharply to her navel. She gave a quick spin as my jaw became as unhinged as my brain, revealing red straps that crossed over her exposed back. That fire mark never looked hotter, that dress hugging each of her curves like it had been made for her. I knew I couldn't actually burn, but I sure felt like I was able to as she continued to turn back around to me, that train of red on the floor now wrapped in a circle by her black heels.

Her eyebrow went up, and she wrinkled her nose up at me as she smiled. "Do you think they will care that I picked this color?"

I grinned. "I love it. It suits you."

"Yeah? But what about them?" Her smile fell as she looked at the door.

"The people should appreciate your choice, because it is that. *Yours*. If they don't like it, they can leave."

"Choice," she murmured. I hadn't noticed the way she kept one hand in a tight fist until she unfurled it in front of me. "Take it."

My brows furrowed as my hand slid under hers. Both of them, cupping her hand in mine. My power went wild as every part of me ached to drag her back to the room, *our room*, and strip her bare.

"I should have given you the choice, and I'm so sorry I didn't. I was afraid that I'd lose you. Lose us. That breaking the bond would make you not love me like I love you. Because everything about me *craves* you, Aeden. And I can't live in a world where you don't feel the same."

I still hadn't touched the vial. "Why...why give this to me if you think I won't love you once the bond is broken?"

Her eyes began to water, and I reached a hand up to brush my thumb just under her glassy green eye. "Because *I* love you. And you deserve to have that choice."

She turned her hand, flipping the vial into my palm. I stared down at it, at the dust that just a few minutes ago had almost no purpose. But now it served one greater than breaking the bond. She gave me the choice because she loved me.

"You don't have to decide now. Just know that it's there, and I'm here. I know we didn't get to choose who we were bound to, but I'm glad it was you." Her lips lifted to the side, just enough to resemble a smile. She didn't want to be forced into a bond, but she was fighting through it. Just like she had done with her trials, no doubt. But she also didn't want to risk being unbound. To risk losing me.

I'd never felt so torn in my entire existence.

Karla made her way up to the door, settling her hand against it as she looked up at us. "Everyone is ready in the main room, along with your brother and Lord Waterborne who arrived a few minutes ago. Just follow the path we have outlined for you, and stop at the altar." She looked at Paige and smiled. "You do look lovely, dear. There is a spot in the front near where Aeden will be standing. Corvina is there already and will stand beside you. When the ceremony ends, she will walk you both to where you will lead the first dance."

Paige snorted, looking at me. "Aeden has to dance?"

Karla blinked at her, then looked at me. "He has to, yes."

I rolled my eyes to Paige. "Why, is that so unbelievable?"

"I don't think I've ever seen you dance before. Beyond the few times I saw you dance in the kitchen at my house." It was nice to know my efforts of trying to get her attention weren't completely wasted.

"I practiced some last night. Karla says I'm quick on my feet."

"Yes," she replied, eyeing my legs. "He said something about a sport called football."

"Football, huh." Paige adjusted the edges of my collar then took my hand in hers, setting the tips of her fingers in the grooves between my knuckles. The perfect fit.

"It's time." Karla pushed the door open slowly, letting fire light trickle into my vision on a sea of flames. Our path was clear, and as we moved, I couldn't help but think of the bravery of the woman at my side. Her hand stayed relaxed in mine, and her chin refused to tip down even under the scrutiny of each set of eyes as they took in the colors she dawned. Forget about my simple black and red. She was a vision cast in flames—a storm more fierce and unrelenting than the Stars themselves.

Corvina guided Paige just out of reach as I turned to face an older man at the altar. Each word spoken and each direction given by the man was obeyed. Every single person in the room remained still as a crown of hedonium was positioned on my head. Every person in the room sent a single knee to the ground and their fists to their chests as their eyes looked down.

I stretched my arm out to Paige, pulling her back to me before the rest of the room could stand. And then Corvina guided us to the circle where we would take our first dance. Our people moved to stand around the circle, their eyes finally back where they should be—on their queen. Yet, I made no move to dance as the elegant music began.

"What are you doing?" Paige looked up at me from where I held onto her waist, my thumbs circling along the curve of her side.

I tipped my forehead to her, my hands squeezing her waist. And then I moved. My hands slid down to grasp along her thighs as I fell to my knees. The crown on my head was unmoved as I pulled out the small red box I'd kept in my pocket.

The music stopped playing, the heat of every pair of eyes in the room setting a blaze along the nape of my neck. Many gasps sounded around the room, but the only one I cared to acknowledge was Paige's, her vibrant green eyes that stole my heart years ago turning to glass as she looked down upon me.

I promised her a crown, whether it be the one from her father's head or the one I'd give her at my side. And that crown wasn't going to come without what I held in my hand.

I flicked my wrist, popping the box open as I looked up at the woman I loved with every fiber of my being. "Marry me, Paige Aerborne. Be mine, in this life and whatever comes after." I took her hand, pushing the family heirloom onto her finger as she nodded. She let out a soft whimper as a tear fell to the floor. "I love you," I whispered up to her.

Paige cupped her hand over her mouth, the tears now streaming down her face as she nodded more. "I am yours," she whispered back.

I stood, taking her hands and twining them in mine as I kissed her deeply. Our bodies swayed well before the music began again, and slowly, others joined us.

But all I saw was her. Paige Aerborne. My Queen.

Bound by far more than blood. She would be my *wife*.

Hours that felt like seconds passed as we danced and ate, and danced more. Each time I took her hand in mine, that connection between us flared. She would be my wife, and I would be her husband. Karla knew what I was going to do—she'd provided the ring, after all. As for everyone else in the room—the shock still lingered. It was clear to see just how many people were unsettled by it, but I wouldn't let that phase me.

Tonight was ours.

Nya stole Paige from me, and I used that time to go out to the balcony. The day had turned to dusk, the sun setting a fire in the sky as it began to fall.

"Brave move, My Lord. Very brave." Jorgan stepped out from the back corner cast in shadows. Even the flaming sun couldn't seem to brighten the space around him as he took two steps closer to me.

"Jorgan. I believe the words you are looking for are *congratulations.*"

He chuckled, pushing his hand through the top of his head. "Not exactly the words I said, are they?"

I sent flames to my palm, finally giving him that light he'd been missing. "It would be wise to think through what you did intend."

He rubbed along the burn mark at his neck, looking at my lit palm, then at the crown on my head. "How do you think the kingdom would feel if they knew their new king was bound by blood to the woman he just tried to declare their new queen?"

"I think that's none of your business, or anyone else's." I tossed the orb to my other waiting hand, keeping the flame controlled when I wanted nothing more than to rip his throat out.

"You see, it is." He moved to the ledge, looking down. Avoiding my heat. "Fables are mostly pointless stories with morals for children. But there is one in particular that is not."

My jaw worked. I should've just gone back to the room, back to my future. But there I was, entertaining the words of a fool. "And which fable would that be?"

"The one about two bound lovers. It's an ancient one, one not well remembered. Not unless you had descended from that line would it have been worthwhile to remember."

"I don't have time for your stories." My skin was growing uncomfortably cold. I turned to leave, shaking my hands from the flames.

"I think you do, cousin."

I stopped and turned back to him. Freezing. My skin was now freezing. My fire rushed to the surface, combating the sensation. "You can't possibly think I would believe you are related to me."

He shrugged, his fingers walking along the surface of the ledge like they served a greater purpose than my presence did. "Believe what you want."

I'd grown tired of him. And annoyed. Frustration ultimately boiled over as a fist made of flames appeared, threatening to tighten around his neck. He smirked over at me, the burn mark along his neck shining under the intensity of the fire.

"You are most definitely my cousin, whether you like it or not."

"Then why didn't I end up here when I was portaled in? There are no wards here. I would have been sent straight to your side." That's what Nya explained in Costa. I'd had a relative out there somewhere, but Jorgan...he couldn't be.

He laughed, the movement of his throat almost grazing my magic. "Seamus had a wife, did he not? The Stars couldn't send you to your other cousin in the castle, that would have been...well, uneventful for them."

"What..." *Nya?* "No, you're lying."

"His wife was your father's sister, though I doubt your friend in there ever knew that part. That girl in there is surely a much closer cousin than I am, but as far as elements go"—he reached his hands slowly up to his jacket and began to undress, being careful to avoid the fire at his neck. I tightened that fist, making him chuckle again. "We are much closer in power, you see."

His jacket was gone, exposing his back and arms. Flames swept up to just under his bicep, where thick vines took over, sweeping down his back and stopping at the middle section between his blades.

Cousin. "My father was Kyren, the twin who *should have* competed in the Triad first. But the Stars made the mistake of letting your great-grandfather go first." He laughed again as he bent to pick up his jacket. My fist followed him as he moved, not burning him, but fully ready to do so. "If they could see how you just took the throne without competing...maybe then my father would have had the drive to kill Kal. Maybe I'd be in your place, if that had happened, and have every mark. Have a dragon bonded to me, as I so deserve. If only I'd been born before my *dear uncle* ascended the throne. I can tell you now though, if it were me in your place, I wouldn't have that *girl* at my side."

"No"—I tightened the flaming hand, burning the edge of his skin, loving the way *my cousin* stiffened—"You most certainly would not have had such a strong woman like Paige at your side." I tightened it again, watching the skin start to burn just before I relaxed the hold again.

And then I turned to leave once more. Yet, the asshole had the gall to raise his voice again. "That fable, cousin. The one of the lovers who were bound, not by blood, but by Starlight, do you know of it? Do you know what happened to them?"

Starlight? "Aeden, don't listen to him. Turn and go back to that room. You are their Mora now." Vara's voice was heavy, like she pulled herself from sleep forcefully just to warn me.

"You are curious, I can see you are."

"Enough." Taking Vara's advice, I made to move for the door again. I could see Paige through the glass, smiling and talking with Nya, the ring on her hand shining brighter than any hedonium I'd ever seen, save for the threads on her dress.

"They died. From the bond."

I froze, feeling a pit sink into my stomach. "Do not lie to me, *cousin.*"

I didn't dare turn to see if the truth of what he said was written on his face or not. "The bond allowed them to feel each other's powers, *her* gift. It became too much. Do you know what turned Kal into *The Breaker?*" *Her* gift? Not from his dragon?

"I don't have time for your continuous questions. You can either say everything you need to say, or this conversation is done." I knew there was a truth to his words. That book I'd taken from Amaliro, the one with the two hands touching. I'd read about Kal before, or tried to read it. Most of it was written in a language I didn't understand, only some passages translated with rough penmanship. I'd lent that book to Paige, and she got just as much as I had from it.

"Spoken like a true king." His breath caught, the flames back to threatening his neck. "Fuck. Okay. The woman he loved from Hydrasel wanted to be bound to him for all of eternity. They were not born with the bond, as you were. But they begged the Stars for one. And one day, the Stars themselves descended upon them, gifting them a bond of starlight. But they did not account for the gift she'd had—bending minds and thoughts. Or maybe they had. But she was never cruel—she never abused her gift."

"But when Kal got a taste of it, he needed more. He couldn't stop. His thirst for power and blood knew no limits. On the day of their wedding, their power surged so much that she collapsed on the floor, blood pooling from her ears. Like what her gift was known to be well capable of doing in his hands. An accident, they said at first. Your great-grandfather rushed to her side, pleading for anyone to help, begging the Stars themselves to use that bond between them to bring her back. He offered his life in exchange for hers, but the Stars never answered. They grew tired of him, saw the way he thirsted for her power as much as his own and turned their backs on him. After he fulfilled his duty and sired your grandfather, he took his own life."

My face contorted in confusion. He had to be lying. That book gave me a name, and had *starlight* scribbled in countless places. But fables had stories behind them. True ones.

"I wasn't lying about not trusting fables. But trust me, cousin, for I was there on the day of their wedding, and that was no fable." My back stiffened once more, feeling the weight of the truth in his words. "I was young, but I remember my uncle begging for his love to return. Had their bond never been created, their power would have never escalated to what it had become. That gift would have remained hers, and hers alone. He went on for years without her, *breaking* the minds of others once she passed. Honing that skill he murdered his love with."

I dropped my shoulders and turned my head just enough to see him. If he was lying, then surely he believed the lie. He rubbed along the new burns on his skin the moment my flaming hand disappeared. "There aren't many bonds like yours or his because they are not meant to be formed. That bond will be the end of you, and when you fall, I will be there." He smirked. "Ready to take your place."

"They will never accept you."

"You speak as if you've been here all along. You mistake yourself, cousin. I've been here for far longer, and now you have proven that you can negate the Stars. That crown on your head will be mine, and once it is, Prydia will also be mine to burn to the ground. Tell me, if I choose to wed your *girl*, will she bleed for me on our wedding night when I fill her with my children?"

Fire burst through the skin on my fingertips as ice cemented Jorgan's hands to the ledge. His eyes widened, but just as Leander was able to use his power without the movement of his hands, so was Jorgan. The ice on his hands melted and a whip of vines lashed across my face.

I rushed into him, tackling him to the ground, burning his wrists as I pinned him there. He seethed through his teeth as he pushed his head forward into mine, making us roll until he was above me. My crown clattered to the side and Jorgan smiled down wickedly at it, like he couldn't wait to snatch it up and place it on his head. I used that minor distraction as a weapon and reached into the carefully placed slip of my jacket, pulling the bonded dagger from its sheath.

His eyes glowed red as he shifted his gaze from the golden crown to the red blade in my hand.

"Cousin," I snarled just before I plunged the dagger up under his ribs, pushing harder when blood began to spill from his mouth. Vara's wings flashed in the corner of my eye, her warmth slipping through my thoughts as she landed on another peak just beyond the balcony.

"*Are you alright?*" she asked as I pushed Jorgan's limp body from me, her tone deeper than I'd remembered it being before.

I yanked the dagger free, watching as his body jolted from the movement, then bent down to pick up the discarded crown. With one more glance at my cousin, I set his entire body on fire and stepped away toward Vara, the crown a cold, forgotten object in my hand.

"*Fine.*"

"*I heard everything, Aeden. You can't lie to me.*" Her head cocked to the side as she took in the smoke coming from Jorgan's still-burning body.

Water cascaded over the blade as I held it out, and I watched as that clear water turned a murky red on the stone at my feet. "*Did you know anything about what he said?*"

"*Of course not. I would have told you.*"

I narrowed my eyes at her as I pushed the blade back into my jacket. "*Would you have? You have kept the knowledge of other dragons from me. Why?*" Steam rolled from Vara's nostrils, her head significantly larger than it was months ago. "*Tell me.*"

"*I didn't keep that knowledge from you because of some bond I didn't know existed, if that's what you are insinuating.*" She'd been listening to my conversation with Leander then, too. She huffed again, adding steam to the trailing smoke beside me.

"*Tell me where I can find another dragon. If there are others, they should be here, anyway. Ready to fight alongside us.*"

"*Ygsavil would love nothing more—*" Her thoughts stopped as she jerked her head away, no longer meeting my eyes.

"*Ygsavil. Your father. Where is he?*" I wrapped my fingers tightly over the spikes on the crown. "*Tell me, Vara!*"

"*I was sworn not to.*"

My hand was soon going to bleed from the pressure. "*Then tell me who does know. Tell me who was not sworn to protect Ygsavil so that I can go find him.*"

"*What I was sworn to do was not done so to protect Ygsavil. It was to protect you, Aeden. You can not go trying to free him—*"

"*Gedeon. He has him, doesn't he?*" No reply. I could feel a gnawing sensation at the back of my throat. She couldn't deny it was him. "*Where is he being kept? Can you show me? Can you take me there?*"

She scoffed and huffed more steam. "*You can not possibly want to risk your life over something a now burning heap of flesh and bones said was true.*"

"*I can't risk it, Vara. If even a fraction of what he claimed was true, then I need to break it.*"

"*I warned you that following your heart wouldn't end well.*"

"*And what happens if what he said was true? You end up without a rider, without a bonded. Is that what you want?*" She was silent for a moment, her wings flexing and resettling along her scaly red body unsuccessfully. "*If you can't tell me, then point me in the direction of someone who can.*"

"*You know who to ask,*" she relented. "*Do not do more than what is needed to end the bond. Do not try to be the hero and free him.*"

Hero. I positioned the crown back on my head and pushed off the ledge. "*I will do what is needed.*"

Chapter Forty-Five
PAIGE

That familiar ash and earth smell filled my space once more.

Stars, I'd missed it.

"Where were you? I missed you." I swept my arms up, connecting my hands behind his neck. The corner of his lips tilted up, right next to a bloodied mark. A slash. "Who did this to you?" Anger filled me as I pulled back and searched the room.

His arms wrapped around me tighter, pulling me as close to him as I could get. "Jorgan," he answered just as I felt his wrist move along my back. Water tickled down the space, cleaning the blood. But the wound—

I started scanning the room again for Nya. She'd been keeping me company the entire time he'd been gone, and with so many people in the main room, I wasn't sure who'd been missing and who'd been there all along.

Clearly, Jorgan had been a part of the former group.

"I'll kill him," I breathed out, reaching up to brush at the wound. Aeden's smile grew slightly. His lips brushed the edge of my cheek before kissing me there gently.

"Already taken care of, My Queen."

I pulled back from him, taking his forearms in my hands. "You...actually killed him?"

He nodded, pulling me closer once more. "Serves him right," I blurted, and he chuckled against me, the vibrations bringing back some of the warmth that was missing from him. But not enough.

"Are you okay?" I asked. He was still for a moment before he nodded. I started to sway our bodies to the soothing music, a slower song that a few others around us were also swaying to.

"I was so jealous that night." His hand slid down my back, resting on the curve he loved to touch. "I wanted to be the one on that ballroom floor. Holding you."

"You know, now that I think about it, I *did* think it was unreasonably warm when I got closer to you." He laughed, his fingers digging into my back like he couldn't get enough of simply holding me there.

"I wanted to be the one whispering in your ear." His palm flattened as it started to trail up. My breath hitched when he reached the straps at the top. "I wanted to steal you away right then and there."

"I'm here now, and you have me," I smiled into his chest, repeating his very words from that night. "All of me." Every tiny piece of myself I could find, that I could give—I'd given it all to him. My days would never begin without him in them, and my nights would never be complete without him beside me. Screw the gift, screw the schedule. I didn't need any of it.

I have him.

"There's one more thing I had planned for tonight," he whispered sweetly against my ear, his nose brushing against the shell of it.

"Just one thing?" I asked, giving him my best *I-don't-believe-you* look.

"Well, one more thing in *this* room." I felt his hand lift from my back, and the music seemed to stop with it. My forehead crinkled as I looked up at him, and then around me as Karla came forward.

"Your hand, dear." The crowd of people stepped back behind the lit candles, leaving the circle hollow, yet with him and I there, it was anything but. Aeden let go of my back fully and moved to put his arm beside me. The back of his hand pressed mine up with his as Karla stepped closer with a red, satin piece of ribbon.

He looked down at me, the crown on top of his head only emphasizing those beautiful golden flecks that lit up, just for me. "What's going on?" I breathed out low as Karla started wrapping our hands.

"Lord Aeden Fireborne, and Lady Paige Aerborne," Karla's voice boomed through the space as she dropped her hands, yet ours stayed lifted, parallel to the floor. "May your love never weaken, may your hearts never sever." The crowd murmured the phrase, repeating it back into the room. My heart lodged into my throat as she repeated it again, and the room followed.

A wedding.

"Let your union be forever, past the Stars and beyond," Karla said, and the crowd repeated.

Aeden smiled down at me, but something was hidden there. Something...darker. Like what had appeared sometime after we'd gotten to Eoghan's. It was distant, his eyes fighting to keep that glow alive. I repositioned my hand, our palms now meeting as I mouthed the words *I love you*—To my husband.

The guests clapped, and I was sure if I looked around, I'd see at least half of those hands belonging to the same bodies where deep glares of uncertainty and hatred also stirred. I knew the ones who did matter—my brother, Eoghan, Nya, Seamus, Shay, and Murrie—they were all somewhere in the room. Watching. But all I saw was him.

Karla undid the ribbon, and when our hands were free, his mouth fell to mine. "Wife," he said against my lips. "My wife."

Heat spread everywhere. "Would it be obscenely obvious if we left the room now?" I asked low as the clapping continued.

He smiled against my mouth. "I don't care if it is or not." He lifted his gaze from mine, searching for someone in the room. Possibly Seamus, getting his approval. "I'll meet you there."

I rushed back to our room, not caring that I had stumbled a bit as I approached the door. The rest of the guests had gone back to dancing and talking, or eating from one of the many trays of food I hoped Aeden was revisiting before he came back.

He'd need the energy for everything I wanted to do to him tonight.

My husband.

I'd never get tired of hearing the phrase. I didn't care that marrying the man came with a crown. I had no idea what that would mean for my future with Prydia, and I simply didn't care.

I shuffled through the dresser, finding what minimal lacy underwear I could and throwing them on. It had grown cold in the room without him, so I waited under the blankets. I thought I'd heard the door opening on a few occasions and fought back the heaviness of my eyelids, but soon, I lost the battle.

The room I woke up in was not ours. It was dark and damp and cold. A few screams echoed from somewhere down the darkened hall. *The hall.*

The walls were covered in artificial blood. Battle wounds exposed, fae dying with their marks swirling and fading on their arms.

No.

I started to run, kicking up my feet harder and harder, my bare feet slapping the wood with each burst forward. I ran until I hit an open space, a familiarly large room with deceiving artistry along the walls. And then black ambled by, swift as night. But it wasn't night that passed me.

"My Lord, he's been spotted."

Purple flashed at my other side. I had to step and look over the banister, my hands wrapping around the ledge. It groaned under the pressure and I stepped back, noticing their voices had stopped.

"What was that, Hector? Did you bring someone back with you?"

I heard Hector grunt. A blow, I realized, given by *him*. The speck of dust not worth calling my father. "No, s-sir. I sw-swear."

"Where is he, then?" Gedeon's voice boomed as a shiver rolled down my spine.

They can't mean—

"Where the fuck is the boy, Hector?" Hector. I raced down the stairs, then started searching for anything heavy. I could kill him now. I could end all of this. They'd never find him. They couldn't have him. He was *mine*.

My best friend. My love. My husband.

I saw Hector's hand reach up as he pointed to a...*fuck*. He was pointing at a map.

But...where he was pointing wasn't right.

"He's here, sir. Just spotted entering the cave."

Cave? What cave?

I searched faster, finally landing on a small statue of a centaur decorating an end table. I reached for it, over and over, watching as my fingers continued to slip through. "Fuck!" I shouted, and both men turned abruptly.

"Certainly one of the maids, sir, throwing their voices," Hector said as he started stomping around the room, close by me. I pushed my hand to my mouth as he leaned in close to where I was standing, my blood pounding in my ears. My other wrist flicked wildly along my side, trying to burn Hector's face, but nothing came.

I should have tried harder. I should have tried to learn. I—

A purple portal formed in the center of the room, and Hector made his way back to Gedeon. "He's going to try to free him, just as we thought. Excellent work, Hector."

Free him? My heart was thrashing under my ribs as I pushed to move after them. Just before the portal closed, I stepped through.

Chapter Forty-Six
Aeden

"Tell me where I can find Ygsavil." Leander's eyes squinted at me as he tried to take in what I needed from him. And then his eyes widened.

"Your dragon told you?" He rubbed the back of his neck. "I thought that went against what Savaria demanded."

I grabbed the fabric of his jacket, pushing him back until we were in the hall leading to the rest of the rooms. "Where is he?"

Leander put his hands up. "I can take you there. You have the ring?" I nodded, shoving him forward as I released him.

He started adjusting his jacket. "Don't you want to see your wife before you go and break it?" he asked, as if it would be the last time I'd ever see her. I wasn't going to let that happen. I'd come right back, but I wouldn't last another minute thinking she was closer to death because of something I could fix. A death I knew how to prevent.

But he was right. I couldn't leave her in the room. She was waiting for me. She'd have questions. And she'd just have to trust me that everything would be alright. *Honesty, always.* "Meet me in five minutes. I'll be at your door."

I took off to our room, smiling when I reached the door because she'd left it unlocked. Again. I turned the knob, taking in the candles that were lit and the dress she'd discarded on the floor. As I stepped inside and closed the door behind me, I found her.

She was asleep, tucked under the blankets of our bed. I moved to sit beside her, tracing the line where her hair had fallen over her cheek. I tucked it back and bent down to kiss her forehead.

She didn't move an inch. Out cold.

"I'll be back before you wake up. I promise." I looked down at her one more time, admiring her soft lips and the way her shoulders were cupping her frame as she slept. It had been a long day, but I would be back.

Before the sun could rise, I'd be back.

As I stood, I flicked my wrist, and then walked out of the room, closing the door quietly behind me.

Leander had a portal ready and waiting just beyond his door as I walked up to it, but his arm barred me from entering.

"What is it now?"

"Protection. You are familiar with it, aren't you?" I almost raised my fist to his face, but fought against that urge as his portal pulsed in front of me.

"What do you mean?"

"Well, since you are now the Mora of Vizna and all, your people need wards." He grabbed my left hand before I could say anything about it. "Press your hand into the floor and put all of your magic, all of the power you can summon, into the space." I cocked my head at him, but sent my knees to the ground and pressed my palm into the floor. I just needed him to hurry the hell up so I could break the bond and get back to her.

So I focused on the power, that feeling I'd had each time I touched Paige, and opened up to it. Letting it free. It was immediate, the pulsing I felt as the earth beneath my palm tried to pull every ounce of my magic from me. As if it had been starved for the wards. "When do I stop?" I tried to push my magic out faster, growing impatient, but noticed the way it was depleting me faster than I was ready for.

"Stop when you can sense the wards around us. Close your eyes and envision every piece of your territories that you have seen. Recall those memories and feed it to your power." I did as he said, pushing everything I could summon into the ground. Soon, my hands started to shake, my body becoming light—weak. But I pushed through.

Leander jerked me up when I started to sway on the floor. "That should do, for now." A smile grew on his face as his portal turned to nothing, disintegrating in the air around us. "It won't be everywhere, but should protect the ones in this place."

"So, that's it then?" I dusted off my hands on my pants, feeling the world move under my feet.

"Now you learn to form a portal. Thankfully, it doesn't take a lot of energy, but it seems your wards are working well." Leander pointed to where his portal had been. As I moved my head to look back at him, the room shifted. He grabbed onto my shoulders, steadying me before my knees buckled.

"Thanks," I grumbled under a shaky breath. "Fuck."

"Ygsavil is tucked away in the eastern edge of the Field of Bones." He pulled a map from his back pocket and unrolled it. "Don't ask. I like traveling with maps."

"Wasn't going to ask." The room shifted again with my vision. He righted me once more as I swayed without turning his attention from the map in his hand.

"Here. Focus on this space here, and then draw only upon your fire to form the portal." A rush of footsteps beyond his door stole my attention, but as they faded, I looked back to the map. "Maybe you should wait—"

"No waiting. I'll be in and out. His armies are nowhere near there." I thought back to the board, having studied that table for hours. There was nothing there, no purple pegs, no encampments.

Leander shrugged. "I'll just go with you."

I snapped my gaze to meet his. "No. I need you to stay here with her, in case anything happens when the bond breaks. If she gets hurt..." I couldn't let myself think about the possibilities. I knew deep in my gut that if the bond stayed, our power could end us. It could end her life, and it would be my doing. "I just need you to stay here and watch her. Can you do that?"

Leander hesitated, probably wondering why I didn't want her brother or Eoghan or Seamus—someone I trusted more—to watch her. Simply put, they'd try to stop me. And I didn't have time for that. He nodded in the end.

I pointed down at his map. "There," I repeated, waiting for him to nod again. And then I let loose on the flames that itched to be released. They'd already been right there at the surface from the wards, but now it seemed to leak into the space like the wards were calling to the fire magic beneath my flesh. A swirling mass started to form slowly in front of us just as the weight of my left leg gave in.

And Leander caught me. "Stay alive. He's been in that cave there for two decades, but the guards were more than likely all pulled for new positions. Ygsavil has been forgotten by most, long thought to be dead." He looked me over before adding, "And before you ask it, I did try once to free him about fifteen years ago." He lifted a sleeve on his right arm, which was completely covered in deep lines and grooves, flesh well scarred over. "This line here"—he pointed to one of the many lines—"Was a parting gift. I don't think he liked me much, but you're her son, he won't hurt you." I could almost hear the *hopefully* he didn't say.

Vara growled in my thoughts. *"Don't you dare get yourself killed."*

"I'll be fine. How hard can it be to get a dragon to breathe fire and melt a ring?"

I could feel the intense worry seeping off of Vara. *"One day, I will be able to do it for you. Would you consider waiting—"*

"No. I can't risk it." Her huff was the only response I got before silence stretched.

I slapped a hand on Leander's back as another wave of dizziness took over my vision. His arm wrapped under mine, his brows raising, then furrowing as I said, "Keep her safe until I get back."

"You have my word," he said. And then I stepped through.

Chapter Forty-Seven
Paige

I stumbled through shards of something white and sharp and...*bones. I fell onto bones.*

Gedeon's voice, though inaudible as my body fought against the pain emanating from my knees, echoed in the vast, cavernous space. I reached down, touching the warmth of my blood as I fought harder to stand. Chunks of bone clung to my skin, yet I swatted it away as I pressed on toward the voices.

I heard Gedeon urge Hector to shift as I rushed into a section, an opening, of what must have been a rather large cave. The shadow that was cast on the stone wall as I walked further...it had wings, an elongated neck and fine spikes that reached toward the ceiling.

I turned slowly, away from where Gedeon stood by a darkened section. It wasn't Vara that was casting that shadow. Wasn't Vara who was lying on the ground, straining against what must've been hundreds of heavy chains. I stepped in closer, wincing back as I walked into...fog?

A thick ring of fog surrounded the dragon that was definitely not Vara. The dragon in front of me was the shade of a night without stars, a darkness I'd only seen in that blip of space between falling asleep and waking up to—to my gift.

Ygsavil.

He was trapped, weighed down by chains and fog and possibly more that I couldn't see around the sheer size of him and where he laid in the middle of the cave that seemed to swallow him whole.

I whispered his name, waiting for the dragon's eyes to snap my way to where I was near his hind legs. But his head was still, unmoving along the ground. He was either sleeping, or staring—fixed—on something. And Gedeon was…silent.

Oddly, all was silent, actually. And then I realized why.

I surged around, using the fog as my guide but steering clear enough away from it to avoid the burn. The *acid*. Gedeon's acid. My breaths became heavy as my gut sank, because I knew exactly who'd be on the other end. Knew who the *he* was when Hector and Gedeon talked about *the boy* before they portaled. I just couldn't picture how he'd gotten here.

And I needed to warn him. To make him leave.

His brown hair was tousled, just as it had been at his coronation—our wedding. But I still didn't want to believe what I was seeing, even as I continued past the angle where several spikes along Ygsavil's body covered the rest of him.

I tried to shout, but felt nothing more than my throat closing the minute my voice reached the tip of my tongue. Like my gift was taking away everything I'd discovered I could do in an instant. I finally reached him and stepped in closer to him, then clawed at his forearms, begging for him to turn around. My arms flailed over and through his body, again and again, failing to strike the solid form of him.

Each time I pushed my arms through him, I could feel his power surge to greet me, even though mine seemed to lay with the rest of my body and had become dormant in my dream-like state. I moved down, testing his clothing, his boots, and even as he bent down and pulled something from his pocket, I couldn't stop trying to touch him over and over again.

I could see my efforts were going nowhere, and it made panic well up within me. A panic that was making it harder to stay within the dream I'd walked into. I could feel my vision start to go black as I watched him uncurl his fingers and place a golden ring down along the rocky floor, the faint clink of it drawing the attention of Ygsavil from Aeden's face, down to the ground.

"Please," I heard him beg in a hushed tone. "Break it."

Aeden's head snapped up and my limbs turned cold and rigid. I didn't have to turn to know who Aeden was snarling at. But I did.

I took a step back into Aeden as Gedeon stepped into view before us.

Everything in me was fighting to stay there, with him in the dream that was anything but. I stretched my arms out and bent them back, attempting to block my father as he moved languidly towards us. I knew it would do nothing, but I had to try. Even though each of my attempts to touch him had continued to fail, I would put my life before his. My body before him. I would be that shield, even if it killed me.

"What a pleasant surprise," Gedeon began. I instinctively lunged toward him with my fist, watching as it continued to move completely through his thick skull. "I knew it was only a matter of time before you came looking for her dragon."

Ygsavil chortled weakly against the floor, sending some bone to scatter in front of us. Gedeon took a step closer to Aeden, and Aeden...

He didn't back down.

I bowed my arms back more and pinched my eyes closed, trying to focus.

Trying to become more solid.

Trying to do everything I could to help him.

"He doesn't belong to you. Let him go and I'll let you live."

"Let me live?" Gedeon cackled in front of us, and just as I opened my eyes, Hector swooped down, changing from a white, feathery owl back into his fae form. I hissed like a feral cat as I stepped back more. "That is rich. So much like your despicable parents."

Aeden stepped in closer, and if I had learned to control my gift better, he would have felt me right there. I was *right there*, and he didn't know it. I would have felt his arms raising as he lifted a finger at the man who killed his parents.

"Fuck. You," he said each word with hate—a tone I'd never heard from him before. Flames lit up in his palm and I finally felt the warmth of him down my spine. Briefly. And then it faded into that cold nothingness all over again.

"You sound just like your parents did—that day I killed them." Gedeon's smile made me feel sick as it spread. "I'm so pleased my daughter had some value in coming here, after all."

"She's not *your* anything," Aeden spat back, his flames growing in his palm. That warmth flickered again at his words, at that flame behind my back as it grew. I reached back in that moment and tried to touch him, *feel* him. Make him feel me. But was met with nothing—no resistance as I slashed through his body again. "She's more valuable than you will ever be."

"She's nothing special. She should have died in the trials."

Aeden looked down to the floor and shook his head. His lips curled up as he lifted his gaze back to Gedeon. "She is *my wife*. And she will still be my wife when I watch her take your crown."

Gedeon sneered, then shrugged his shoulders. "Not if you die." Fog began to spread around my ankles, the slight burn growing with the thickness of it. How cruel the Stars were—allowing me to feel that fog, but not the love of my life. I tried to shove Aeden back, but ended up on the other side of him. The fog spread around Aeden, and as it did, his smile widened.

Gedeon's face faltered, his lips turning down. "You don't burn?" Gedeon voiced aloud, like he had let the surprising thought slip.

"No, I don't. But I bet you do." Aeden spread the flames in his palms to his arms, and didn't stop until they covered his entire body. I moved to stand beside him and away from the burning fog. He looked like the sun standing there next to me—bright and beautiful and glowing, with that smile of his widening as Gedeon took a step back.

I watched as Hector moved to whisper in his ear as those flames roared beside me. Watched in horror as the frown on Gedeon's face turned into a wicked grin—one I knew well. My body shuddered as his strides ate up the space between them, like he felt lighter from whatever Hector had said.

Aeden released the fire from his flesh, hurling it with force toward Gedeon, but he didn't stop. The fire grazed just over the left side of him before a shield of air forced the flames to wrap around him—around his *shield*. I rushed into Gedeon, trying to knock his air shield back, to push him off his feet, but was met with Aeden's flames that wrapped around my father.

I fell to the ground in agony, feeling the burns but not seeing any physically on my skin. I cried out, my voice finally returning, and that's when Aeden's flames stopped.

I felt his eyes land on the space near me, his face contorting as he searched for where he undoubtedly heard me. And in that moment, that short blip of time, everything slowed.

Gedeon's hands raised in the air, the fog at Aeden's feet lifting up to his face where his mouth hung slightly open as he searched for me. That fog—that acidic fog—pressed in past his mouth. I screamed and shuffled toward him, fighting my way across the rocky ground as I watched him fall to his knees. His eyes darted to where I was as I screamed again, but it was as if it was more than my voice that pulled him there.

He could finally see me.

The fog forced its way down further as Aeden reached for his throat. I screamed more and more, unsure if anyone else in the cave could hear or see me as my entire world shattered apart. Aeden fell forward on the ground, gasping as blood fell from his mouth. The fog receded with Aeden down on the ground, still clawing at his throat.

I pushed past the pain, the feeling of being burned knowing none of it mattered, nothing mattered, without him. My nails dug into the stone and I dragged my body to meet his while Gedeon's steps and movements no longer registered to my senses. My body couldn't feel, couldn't comprehend what I was seeing as more blood dripped onto the stone.

Too much blood.

He was bleeding from the inside, and I...I couldn't stop it. I pressed my hands to him, to his mouth as his head lulled to the side, his body finally giving under the pressure. His eyes rolled to the back of his head and I reached up to try to force his eyes open.

"Don't die, please. Don't. Die." I pushed my hand to his heart as I cradled him in my lap, where my body had become the solid structure it needed to be just minutes before. His heart was beating slowly, and my vision started to fade again.

"Please. Hold on. I'll get you out of here. Please, stay alive," I pleaded into his ear, grabbing onto him with everything I could.

His voice was a murmur I couldn't understand as his hand reached up to cup my cheek. I could feel the tears streaming there, but I held him tighter. I held him and begged for my gift to bring us both back.

For him to still be in my arms when everything faded. And then my vision went completely black.

My eyes snapped open in the comforts of our bed, the room still cold and barren. The softness of his hair had slipped between my fingers, the warmth of his body no longer surrounding me.

Because I...I failed him.

My mind raced as his smile filled the void of bleak darkness in my mind, his laughter sending my heart to my throat. The way he held me softly, now turning to faded touches along my skin that ached to have him there. I wanted to throw up. I wanted to scream. I wanted to *fight*.

My hands curled in along the sides of the blanket, meeting something solid and thin.

No.

No, no, no.

Red and white filled the space beside me as I took the flower in my hand. He'd planned to leave me, knowing he might never come back. He had to have known the costs of what he was doing, yet he did it anyway.

I began to sob as I pushed that flower away, my fist turning the petals into nothing more than a crumpled up mess like my heart had become.

He had promised honesty. He had promised he would never leave. I gave him my heart, and he turned it to ash.

Everything about me craves you. Yet he couldn't stay.

That was the night I told you I loved you. And now, I would remember it for the rest of my bleak existence. I'd never get to hear him utter those words to me again. Never get to feel those lips against my skin again.

He told me to stop keeping it all in. And I listened to that, too. My body shook, my legs trembled. The hollowness took over every cavity I could find that I'd given to him—which had been everything.

He was my everything.

I rolled over to cover my face with his pillow, sobbing more as his scent filled my lungs. Every part of me had turned to him, and now he was gone.

My best friend was gone.

My husband was gone.

My entire world, the love of my life.

Gone.

He'd subjected himself to a relentless monster, a monster that would never willingly let him go—if he was still alive.

No. He was alive.

I had to believe it.

He was alive and he needed me now more than ever.

And I'd fight until my very last breath to bring him back to me.

Bonus Chapter: Aeden

Costa Battle, after first break in Chapter 34 (Aeden's POV)

I'd been on the receiving end of being run into, chased, and the body at the bottom of a pit of men before. Football could be brutal.

But battle?

Battle I'd never had the pleasure of indulging in. Had I'd been raised here, battle would be my entire existence. I guess it was about to become my existence, and possibly my end.

With my sword unsheathed and the power that pulsed in my veins, I hurdled into the things that were running right for me.

For her.

For *all of them*.

We were completely surrounded in the most disorganized way. Leander's once black cloak was covered in blood that leaked down to the snow as he ran...and ran.

I didn't have time to think where the fuck he was going because right as I turned, I saw Murrie—battle-ax in her hands as she tried to slice away at a creature that came straight from the worst kind of nightmares. Killing one in an already burning house was relatively easy, though terribly disgusting and frightening, if I was being honest. And watching them start to surround my friend—

Thoughts turned into immediate action before I had time to process. That's what battle was, really—a testament to your ability to act on the tip of your toes, prepared for anything and everything while also believing you were on the precipice of a gruesome death. My death was inevitable. All death was inevitable.

But today, I'd fight to make sure none of it happened to the people I loved.

Murrie's ax was raised in the air as I slid along the ground—a wet, sludgy ground of trampled over snow and dirt. Time seemed to warp as I flicked my wrist on instinct, knowing the bastards made of shadows and bone's only weakness was the flames that came to the surface of my flesh so easily. As I righted myself, more wraiths began to hover closer. Because that's how they moved—as if the tips of their toes dangling beneath their shadow-covered bodies wasn't ominous enough, the damn things floated.

And fast, too.

Time slowed once more. It seemed to be a theme, really. You see the ones you love and hold close to you in danger, and your world stills. Battle had a near-dizzying effect on my brain—possibly, all of our brains.

I glanced over to Paige, her brown waves whipping around her shoulders feverishly as she clutched onto her small blades at her sides. She seemed frozen in place as she took in the sight of her father's men that were more beneficial to us now that Shay had...well, clearly she'd seduced them. Their weapons were still strapped to their backs and their faces mirrored exactly what I'd seen on Seamus' that day in her home.

"Aeden, there!" Murrie shouted as she burst forward with lightning-quick speed at her heels.

My power responded even before my full attention snapped back to the demonic things still coming for us. Without much thought at all, rippling waves of flames devoured each and every wraith that came our way, like my body had taken over what my mind failed to do.

"Again, Aeden!" Murrie's ax came down over and over as their bodies burst into roaring balls of fire, one-by-one. Perhaps she did it as a distraction, or maybe she was pointing out the closest ones for me by doing so. Her blade came down, and I ignited wherever it fell.

Thank the ever-loving Stars Paige could wield flames.

"I'm here!" Vara's red and gold wings lit-up the darkening sky, and my heart rate kicked up. But not at her wings. "Seamus is—"

"Help her! Please!" More wraiths, more flames, more near-death experiences for every single one of us that was fighting with everything we had, but my eyes had fallen elsewhere. To *her*. Paige darted past the slowly growing mass of guards and rushed right toward a swarm of naga that looked starved—they possibly *were* starved. And the way she was raising her blades—

Vara was already banking back around, but I snapped—that broken, defeated tone turning to one of pure molten lava. "*Vara, get them away from her.*"

For once, Varasyn didn't fight me on it. No huffs, no chortles.

Just action.

If the silence wasn't startling enough, a shiver of emotion slid through my thoughts, and if I wasn't mistaken, it was pure pride.

The naga went up in the air, clamped tightly between my dragon's even-hungrier jowls. But where Vara flew to next...I simply wasn't prepared to see—and fully acknowledge like I should have before—the man who'd taken me in on the far side of where most of the bloodshed was happening. Where he'd set himself up as a meat-market for hags, surrounded by a wall of ice. Surely, he realized what he was doing in creating a wall while being inside it.

I searched around again now that the wraiths were dwindling to the last few. Shay was too consumed with getting the few guards she *had* turned to hold down other guards and turn more. Eoghan and Ikelos were working along the other side of a strip of buildings, flanking both sides of the battle. Yet, even though I'd seen the way Paige could handle the same beasts before...I couldn't risk leaving her without backup.

"You keep your eyes on her. Keep her safe. I'll go to Seamus."

"Look up, Aeden. She's handling it well."

My gaze followed where Vara flew to circle closer to Seamus, the darkened sky intensifying in a beautiful, eerie shade of green. *"What—"*

"Run!" Vara shouted, and once again, without much thought, my body reacted.

My boots were slapping up mud and snow and blood as I sprinted to Seamus and tried to ignore the huge storm above the town, his loud battle-cries growing as the bodies continued to fall throughout Costa. More and more blood seeped into the once-peaceful white, yet the hags that were surrounding Seamus seemed hell-bent on needing more than what was already spread all around them. If I wasn't mistaken, I believed I heard Paige's voice projecting from all the way across the bloody battlefield, urging for Seamus to go. Telling him to run, just as Vara had directed me to do.

Yet, he didn't.

Seamus' clear, icy wall was closing in above him, leaving a small hole at the top that hags were desperately clawing their way to get to.

He finally took notice of me, snapping his head in my direction. "Lad! Back away from—"

"Like hell I will!" A hag seemed to notice me right away as I got closer. Several, actually. They unlatched their claws from the wall and scurried back down to the ground, where my sword was already waiting to slice into them.

And that's what I did.

My muscles burned from a mix of the power I'd used on the wraiths, and the weight of my sword lifting and coming back down on the hags, over and over again. The severed bodies of hags began to pile-up around me as thunder and lightning clapped in the low-hanging clouds above. Wind began to thrust a few hags off of their feet, and as I went to raise my sword to slice through another hag that had decided my flesh was the tastiest thing on the battle-field menu, a large gust of wind pushed—no, *sucked*—the hag right up.

My body began to sway under the force and I quickly anchored my legs down with vines to fight against the lifting I felt around my own body. Then more bodies began to succumb to it, too—hags were pulled from the icy-wall, their claws digging in for purchase to stay on solid ground instead of flinging through the air and landing...

Everywhere.

Bodies were flying everywhere. Some in purple tunics, some covered in scales. All covered in blood.

Ice clattered onto the dome as the dozens of hags no longer shielded it from the torment of the skies above. My brows furrowed as I looked at Seamus, pushing my sword back into its sheath with uncertainty, though nothing appeared well and able to hold on through whatever was happening. I watched as the bodies flew in patches, almost targeted, and when my eyes moved from the aw-stricken and confused one of Seamus' and swept over the rest of the town, *that's* when I saw her.

"I'm above the storm, but you need to get to her. Fast."

"Who—" My furrowed brows deepened. *"She's doing this?"*

She's handling it well. That's what Vara said before, and I didn't even process what that could mean. I saw the nagas falling around her, but didn't understand what was happening.

Now, it was clear.

Paige had her arms outstretched on the other side of the battlefield, and before I could ask, Vara had swooped down and yanked me up by her talons. The storm surged, sending Vara teetering as she fought her way through, then dropped me close enough to run up to her.

I caught her just as her body fell to the ground, and all at once, the storm dissipated. I clutched Paige's frail, limp body to mine, searching rabidly for a pulse. The battle had stilled several times, but in that moment, all time completely froze.

Fuck, time didn't *exist*.

There was no movement, my ears were thrumming with the blood coursing through my body like they, too, were on fire. My entire core was shot—my body hollow. A visceral being trapped in a dormant state until her pulse bumped once. One solid, but certain, beat.

And then another.

"Is she..."

I counted a few more pulses, holding my own breath until another came to the surface, surging past my fingertips pressed to her neck. I found the strength to nod and felt a wave of unexpected release from Vara. *"Barely,"* I got out after a few more beats. *"Just..."*

Gentle fingers inched over my hand that held her pulse.

"The girl you showed your marks too...she's a healer, yes?" Vara's voice came in too soft, so unlike her. She was scared, too. The hand on me became two. *"Let her try to heal her."*

Try. I pulled Paige closer to me before Nya could pry Paige from my arms, and whispered into her ear, "I love you, Paige. I love you, and nothing will ever take you from me, do you understand?" I brushed her hair from her ear, her soft lips and delicate face paled over, but the weak pulse was still alive under my touch. Like she was choosing to fight, *to live*, because I was here. If I let her go—

"She needs her help, Aeden."

"Aeden?" Nya's voice came in, but I nuzzled deeper into Paige's neck, breathing her in. I could feel the others around us, the heaviness of their bodies closing in. Their breaths more evident now that Paige's was so faint.

"Oh, Lad," Seamus said low as he crouched beside us. I threaded her fingers with mine while my other hand stayed over her distant pulse. "Let me daughter help. I'm sure she's dealt with depletion." *Depletion.* Fae *died* from depletion. Movement fluttered on the other side of me. "There. She only needs to have her hands on 'er. You can keep 'er to ye."

My voice cracked when I finally replied, "I don't understand what happened. She was using her daggers. And then...she..."

"She can make storms. Fierce ones, at that," Seamus answered.

"Storms, huh." I let out a chuckle that I didn't feel. "She always does smell like rain and, well, storms." Another chuckle, just as faint as her breathing. My hand lifted against her, a slight flick, sending power through her like I did that night by the water. No one tried to still my wrist, and if they did, I'd kill them. Didn't matter who it was, I needed her to breathe more, to take more air in.

I could hear Seamus scratching his beard beside me as Nya's hands settled more firmly around Paige's forearms. "Though, maybe—" Seamus began, but Murrie cut him off.

"I think she's always made them. The storms, I mean. Think of how many times the sky has darkened or become cloudy. I thought maybe the Stars were just having their fun with us but her making them whenever her emotions became too much makes more sense. And you were making her quite emotional, like after we left—"

"The inn," I finished and pulled back from her neck. My wrist stopped moving, and the breath she took on her own stole mine from my lungs.

I swallowed as I looked around. The amount of blood covering my friends, *my family*, was remarkable. I wasn't sure if any of them were injured, but I sure hoped the blood was mostly that of our enemy's. I shook my head, refocusing on Paige.

"I wasn't talking to her, then. I was walking next to Seamus."

"You were talking to Seamus, too, and she was making quite the effort to hear you. I think you were talking about that girl who wouldn't leave you alone. You know, the pretty one," Murrie said, and Seamus nodded. That girl had nothing on Paige. No one would ever compare, but if jealousy played a part in honing her skills, I'd let it slide, this one time.

"But...she didn't have all of her marks, then. She only had two at the time." I looked back down at the woman I loved that I still held in my arms, noticing the way my fingers were wrapping the strands of her hair around each digit like some form of counting. Breaths, maybe? Or pulses?

"And?" Ikelos crouched down in front of us, the color on her face returning with the healing Nya was pressing into her. "She only needed her original nature. Even if she couldn't sense it or use it, that power still forms." Some expression must've crossed my face that told him I was confused, because I was. He shook his head. "You guys really need to start asking questions and stop trying to learn everything on your own. You have the upper hand at having the most skilled wielders at your disposal, yet you never fucking ask questions." He shook his head again and muttered a curse under his breath, his icy hair more pink with blood tingeing the strands. "It's unbelievable, I swear."

I chose to keep my mouth closed because the woman I was holding was his sister, and I knew he was probably just as scared as I was to lose her. His eyes hadn't left her, and when he reached out to brush some of her hair back from her face, I just let him.

I cleared my throat. "Her pulse...it's coming back a little stronger now," I told Ikelos when I noticed the water welling in his grey eyes. "Where is Eoghan?" And then my eyes narrowed and my voice turned cold. "And Leander." He ran early on in the battle, and although I still wasn't in the mood to hunt him down, I sure hoped someone was.

"Eoghan went to get a boat ready for us. Once we pass back into Waterborne territories, he can portal us—"

I snorted. "Where the fuck are we supposed to go?"

Seamus' hand fell to my shoulder. "Your lands, Boyo."

I went to protest, but Ikelos cut in. "Nya can heal Paige, though it might take a few days. And I don't *see* anything happening in Vizna for the time being. So, yeah, we are going there. Unless you'd like to take your chances and go to Hydrasel where Gedeon would *expect* us to go, or we can just give up and go back to Amaliro—"

"We aren't giving up," I snarled, pulling Paige closer once more. "She wouldn't want us to." And when she woke up, because she was going to fucking wake up, I didn't want it to be in chains or somewhere that wasn't safe.

"At least I can land in Vizna, and then we can maybe find whoever is left. Start building that army you need."

"I say we take the leap, Aeden," Shay said. "I'll send these ones"—she chucked her thumb over her shoulder at the brood of guards still under her spell—"back to Gedeon, and they can tell him we didn't make it out alive."

I replied immediately, "That would make him want proof. Better to say nothing happened and they didn't find us. Less evidence of that." To my surprise, everyone nodded in agreement, and another fine shiver of pride rushed through me from Vara. "If he wants to portal here to search, let him." Part of me hoped he'd find the room I made love to his daughter in, and that he'd see the burn marks along the floor and the state of the bed. Which reminded me...

"Here." I shuffled into my back pocket, pulling out one of the portraits from along Seamus' wall, and passed it to Seamus. "I grabbed it before we left. Paige didn't get to make a frame for it, but she did thread it back together." She hadn't finished the frame because that was one of the last pictures she had been working on before she came to find me in that room and I finally got her out of her head. Not that Seamus needed to know the ins-and-outs of exactly what we did. I'm sure he could guess.

"Thank ye." He unfolded it, planted a kiss on the image, then folded it once more before placing it into his pocket. "I really 'ppreciate it."

"No problem." My eyes narrowed past Ikelos, making him turn his head. "Seems like that boat is ready."

"Think Leander is holding that down, at least?" Seamus joked, making Shay and Murrie snicker.

Ikelos looked down at Paige once more, and when he looked back up at me, his lips rolled in. "Are we sure we need Leander?"

Nya's hands stilled. I could tell she wanted to defend him for Stars knew why, but she stayed silent.

I finally answered. "Yeah, unfortunately, I think we do. Paige would say we were the biggest idiots if we let an entire kingdom slip through our fingers—one with an army—actually, are we even sure he has an army?"

Ikelos nodded. "Our intel said he does. Well trained, too. He doesn't have the numbers, but it seems he's been purchasing the higher-priced guards at Sentra for a long time now."

I laughed. "Are you saying that jackass...that's why he mentioned how much you cost?"

Ikelos scratched the back of his head as he replied, "Probably." His hand fell, now stained with red in his lap.

"Everyone ready?" Eoghan came up from behind Ikelos, crouching down beside him, then glanced at Paige. "Will she be okay until we get to Vizna?"

Nya answered, "She will be fine. I just have to stay close to her and keep my hands on her—"

"Won't that make you deplete yourself, too?" Everyone's eyes fell to Leander, who, not-too-surprisingly-at-all, was *not* guarding the boat.

Eoghan made an incredulous face at him and went to speak, but Nya cut-in. "I'll be fine, Leander. Really."

For once, Leander actually looked like he cared. A lot. He turned his attention to Eoghan. "The boat is fine, by the way. I anchored it down."

"Bet your power is nowhere near depletion," Eoghan quipped back. "In fact, how many exactly *did* you take out before you ditched us?"

As much as I wanted to hear his response, we didn't have the time. "Talk about it when we get to Vizna. Or some other damn time. We have to leave. What if there's another wave of those things coming?" I took Paige up with me as I stood, and Nya followed, her hands staying glued to Paige—wherever she could reach as I walked to the boat in the distance.

"Now you're thinking. I like this side of you."

I smiled. *"You like all sides of me. Don't start lying to yourself now, Vara."*

The good thing about Vizna? Eoghan could portal in.

The bad thing? *Any* Mora could portal in.

"You sure we're safe here?" I knew I'd ask Ikelos that a hundred more times for however long we stayed. I also knew he was becoming agitated with me, but was fighting against saying anything. I knew exactly why, too.

"Pretty sure," he replied all too quickly, his eyes turning to fine slits as he looked me over.

"You wanna go ahead and talk to me about something?" I sat down beside Paige, her body curving in toward me from where she slept on the furs and blankets that made up her bed on the cleared, dirt ground.

Ikelos kicked at a chunk of the rubble as he set up another bed. "Don't know what you're talking about."

"Bullshit," I said back. "You do know I know all the faces Paige makes and when she has something that's eating away at her, she makes that face"—I pointed at him—"that one. Yep. Same face."

He huffed and Eoghan chuckled as he came up beside him. "It's true, babe. You do make this cute little face when you're all upset about something. Though, I think it's cuter on you than it is on her. On her, it looks evil."

"Does not." I glared at Eoghan. "But that's besides the point." I raked my fingers through my hair, deciding against sliding in next to his sister right in front of him. "It didn't seem to bother you before. Pushing us together. So, what? Now that we are together, it's an issue?"

"No." Ikelos' tone completely disagreed with what he said. "That's not it."

Eoghan chuckled again. "Totally is."

"Eoghan!" Ikelos' wrist flicked, sending Eoghan to the ground where he laughed more. "It isn't funny."

"Sorry. Have to side with Aeden on this one. You and I *did* push them together."

Ikelos rolled his eyes. "Did not."

I looked back at him, then shrugged my shoulders and moved to slide in right behind Paige. When I wrapped my arm around her and her unconscious body relaxed against mine, Ikelos averted his eyes.

"It bothers you. Just admit it so we can get past it."

"Oh, babe." Eoghan tugged Ikelos down to his lap. Ikelos seemed to stiffen. "Relax. I think everyone here knows you and I are together, too," Eoghan teased. It was never a question if they were or not, but Ikelos apparently had reservations about intimacy. I thought back to all the catcalls Eoghan made around him and the way Ikelos always diverted his next words and moved him along.

"Is that it?" I asked. "Are you against PDA?"

"What in the Stars is—"

I raised my hand, moving it from Paige briefly. Her pulse was stronger now, and with the warmth of where we relocated, her color had fully returned. But she was still knocked out. Nya said it could be a few days, so that meant I had nowhere else to be than right here. "PDA—stands for public displays of affection."

"That's interesting." Eoghan's face brightened as they settled in on their bed. The rest of our group had left to either hunt or use the restroom, both of which I doubted Leander and Nya were actually doing with where they went off together. "Is that what this is, babe? You—"

"No! It isn't that. It's—"

"So it is something, then." I took a moment to look him over, to look at the way he was still focused on my arm around her. And then it hit me. He's a brother. He's just as protective. "We were...um...safe. You know. During"—I looked down at her— "sex. She took someth—"

"I'm fully aware. Who do you think gave her that?"

My brows furrowed. *Okay...so if it isn't the way I completely ravished his sister, then...*

Maybe it was the part I had been concerned with when she all but admitted it would be hard for her to deny the Stars too because I was attractive. But I wanted something deeper than attraction when it came to her. I wanted love. "It's not like I plan on ever leaving her—"

"But what if you do?" He answered back, aggression thick in his voice. "What if you leave and she gets hurt?"

Ah. "I'm not ever leaving her, Ikelos. She's it for me. Always has been, always will be. I love her more than anything or anyone. If anything, you should be concerned with *her* leaving *me* if our relationship is so unsettling to you. I mean, I get it. I clearly don't deserve her. And it's not like I have anything solid to offer her other than my hopes and dreams and maybe one day a bright future if we can even make it that far without dying."

Ikelos and Eoghan turned silent at my admission. I heard them whispering to each other and took that time to just look at Paige. Knowing that whenever she woke up, I'd have to find out why there was a *but* at the end of her *I love you*.

Maybe she'd forget all about it and we could get past it. But something told me it wouldn't be that simple.

Nothing was simple when it came to us, and honestly, I wouldn't have it any other way. I liked having a love that I had to fight for everyday, whether that was physically or verbally. It meant I had something worth fighting for—gave me a deeper purpose than any I'd felt before.

Loving her was the best possible purpose I'd ever have.

Ikelos' words snapped my focus back to him. "Sorry, I didn't mean to make you think...I know it can't be easy being so uncertain about everything. I guess I didn't put myself in your shoes"—Eoghan nudged him—"okay, I *didn't* put myself in your shoes at all. I apologize." Another nudge from Eoghan, and he added, "I can't picture anyone better for my sister than you. Really."

I couldn't fight the grin on my face. "Thanks for that. I'm happy she has you, too."

"You're welcome." Ikelos smiled back, Eoghan's arm draped over him just as I was with Paige across the small campfire that burned between us. "You know, I'll probably still look at you funny because, well—"

"He *is* mad about the sex, Aeden." I chuckled as Ikelos nudged his shoulder back into Eoghan.

"I'm not *mad*."

"Would it be better if I told you that she said she loved me?" I asked and Ikelos froze. I believe Eoghan did, too, though half of his body was covered by Ikelos now.

"It makes it a little better. Somewhat."

They were silent for a moment, until Eoghan asked, "How was it?" Which elicited another nudge from Ikelos, followed by grumbles of him probably saying he didn't want to hear whatever I had to say about it.

I smirked back at them, but when I looked down at Paige, my smirk faded. Even unconscious with blood still covering her clothes from a battle well-fought, she was the most beautiful thing I'd ever seen. I bent down and pressed my lips to her warm forehead, and for a second, I believed I saw a smile form on her lips before fading away.

I smiled again. "Like I said, I don't deserve her."

Acknowledgements

Thank you so much to everyone who has been along for this ride! It's crazy to think about how normal being a writer has become for not only myself, but also my family. So thank you so much to my family, friends, editor, beta readers, arc readers, and all of you who support me with even just a simple shout out on any social platforms! It means the world to me and more.

I will never say it enough—THANK YOU ALL SO MUCH! You are all the fuel that keeps me going, pushing me past those harder days. Your kind words and thoughts are always appreciated and so cherished.

THANK YOU, THANK YOU, THANK YOU! I can't wait to share more stories with you all!

About The Author

Elsa lives with her family in Florida, where it's usually too hot to do anything other than stay inside and read or write. Originally born in Iceland—the land of fire and ice and way too many tall descendants of Vikings—Elsa loves the idea of strong lead characters who fight (sometimes in more ways than one) for who they are or who they want to be (or be with).

Though never an avid reader until she hit her motherhood era, Elsa took to writing just as quickly as she did to reading, with genres heavily favored in romance/fantasy and contemporary romance.

Leave a review if you can! Reviews help indie author's like me so much!
https://www.goodreads.com/esportmanauthor

You can find more by E.S. Portman here:
Amazon:
https://www.amazon.com/stores/author/B0CWDKJ38L/allbooks?ingress=0&visitId=31737aed-7225-4c73-b017-534d474adc99&ref_=ap_rdr

Author's Website:

https://www.authoresportman.com/

Instagram:

https://www.instagram.com/esportman.author/

Made in the USA
Columbia, SC
17 September 2024

9765bc4a-0726-49ef-a2a1-5eacae012d98R02